Untouchable Spring

Kalyana Rao is a writer, one who believes in the revolutionary ideology, an important functionary of Virasam, Viplava Rachayitala Sangham (Revolutionary Writers' Association) and a Dalit. He began his career as a playwright and wrote around fifteen plays, significant among them being *Tolipoddu* (a work on which university research was carried out), *Satire* and *Lockup*. His work, *Antarani Vasantam* (2000) is a contribution to the growing body of Dalit writing. He is presently writing a sequel to *Antarani Vasantam*.

Alladi Uma and M. Sridhar teach English at the University of Hyderabad. Their translated works include *Ayoni and Other Stories* (a collection of short stories), Rachakonda Viswanatha Sastry's *Beware, the Cows are Coming!* (a novel), K. Siva Reddy's *Mohana! Oh, Mohana!* (a volume of poems) and Allam Rajaiah's *Bhoomi* (a collection of short stories).

Untouchable Spring

G. KALYANA RAO

Translated from the Telugu *Antarani Vasantam*
by Alladi Uma and M. Sridhar

Orient BlackSwan

ORIENT BLACKSWAN PRIVATE LIMITED

Registered Office
3-6-752 Himayatnagar, Hyderabad 500 029 (A.P.), India
E-mail: centraloffice@orientblackswan.com

Other Offices
Bangalore, Bhopal, Bhubaneshwar, Chandigarh, Chennai,
Ernakulam, Guwahati, Hyderabad, Jaipur, Kolkata,
Lucknow, Mumbai, New Delhi, Noida, Patna

ISBN 978 81 250 3945 7

Originally published in Telugu as 'Antarani Vasantam'
Viplava Rachayitala Sangham, Andhra Pradesh, 2000

Typeset in Adobe Garamond Pro 11/13 by
OSDATA, Hyderabad 500 029

Printed at
B.B. Press, Noida

Published by
Orient Blackswan Private Limited
1/24 Asaf Ali Road, New Delhi 110 002
E-mail: delhi@orientblackswan.com

Dedication

Mother
Father
Shyam
Mahesh
Murali
Lakshmirajam

—To you all, this Spring with love.

When I started writing 'Untouchable Spring', I thought of dedicating it to my mother and father. But by the time the novel was to be completed as a serial, Shyam, Mahesh, Murali and Lakshmirajam become martyrs along with them. That's why I dedicated it to the four of them along with my parents.

Mother was born in Sambasivapura agraharam. That is close to Kavali. Father was born in Alakurapadu. It is close to Ongole. Alakurapadu is to the north of the agraharam. According to our people's reckoning, mother is a northern daughter-in-law. Father is a southern son-in-law.

Father's name is Gangolu Ramaiah. An elementary school teacher. Mother's name is Balanagamma. Mother would perform a number of *vratas* (Hindu rituals). In our community's words, '*vokka poddulu*' (eating only once). Father would offer *prarthanas* (Christian prayers). Her 'vokka poddulu' did not come in his way. His 'Christ' did not come in her way. Different religions. Same caste. Mother, Balanagamma, died in my eleventh month. My grandfather did not even take her photo thinking it will cut down her life span. After mother died, the mother who brought me up is Kamalamma.

Shyam, Mahesh and Murali were revolutionary leaders who led a people's war movement. The three of them came from different backgrounds. Shyam (Adireddy) was extremely poor. He came from a large joint family. He grew from an ordinary status to an extraordinary one. Mahesh (Santoshreddy) came from an educated family. Was highly educated. Theorist. Philosopher. Murali (Naresh) came from an educated middle-class family. It was the revolutionary movement that brought the three of them together. Andhra police arrested the three of them on the night of 1 December 1999 in Bangalore. Shot them. Keeping the corpses in Koyyuru forests, faked an 'encounter' to show they were killed in it. Lakshmirajam was a dalit. To fake the Koyyuru encounter, they shot Lakshmirajam, dressed him in olive green and declared him as Arun along with the three top leaders.

Preface

This Spring was forbidden then.
Now, too, forbidden.

The caste of birth forbidden.
The chosen struggle forbidden.

It may have been yesterday. Maybe today.
Maybe any time.

This Spring was forbidden then.
Now, too, forbidden.

1

First, I will introduce Ruth to you. Then I will tell you the story.

Those who know her as a writer may ask me not to dare introduce their favourite writer to them anew. True. She has written innumerable stories. Innumerable poems. But I am not going to introduce you now to Ruth, the writer, or to her writings. Just to Ruth. The Ruth I know.

Ruth sits all by herself all day. Since Reuben's death, she has been sitting alone for many years.

She sits alone and stares at the sky. In the sky a lone star is visible. The rest of the stars disappear as if they have nothing to do with her. Then in front of her eyes, on the half-broken high wall, appears the painting of Jesus on the Cross.

The region used to be beautiful then. More than medicines, it was the environment that would heal the sick. She used to be a nurse there. Her Reuben was the hospital's pastor.

The past recedes. The present is before her. If we build a nest and perch in the past that has gone by, the present too will become the past. But Ruth says her memory does not relate to the past. She says Reuben is always her present.

As silently as Reuben came into her life, he left just as silently. He who went away did not go just like that. He showered innumerable springs on her all through her life and left. He narrated how a memory blossomed at every turn and withered away. Told stories. Wove poems. Causing an upsurge he left, asking her to keep this memory in her heart. In truth, it is not a memory. A surge. How to contain that flow!

He started to tell his story on a moonlit night. He told it over many nights. He said the same thing over and over again. He laughed as he narrated. Cried as he narrated. His eyes sparkled then. His eyes got wet then. She hid that sparkle in her eyes. She smeared that 'wetness' on her eyelids. In truth they are not just the memories he shared. Wet eyes wrench the heart. Touch the spinal chord. They haunt.

He and his ancestors swam in the savage flow of flood waters. Some were washed away. Some sought shores like untiring boatswains. What kind of a man was her Reuben! What a wonderful person—that beautiful untouchable! These words may sound strange. But Ruth uses those words simply, naturally. She used to speak those words to Reuben himself. 'Oh, my beautiful untouchable man!' She would call him like that innumerable times. Then Reuben would look at her like a child. His eyes would be filled with innocence.

Something that happened many years ago. It seems as if it had happened only yesterday. Not yesterday, it seems to be happening right now in front of her eyes. She had set out with him when he told her he would show her his ancestors' place. On foot. Soon after their marriage. It was the first time they had walked together, just the two of them, after marriage. A journey along the stream bund, the sky spreading the moonlight. The flutter of tiny little fish jumping about in the stream. As she walked along with him, alone together. An amazing solitary experience.

Then he began narrating.

About the downpour of moonshine.

About the movement of the rapid stream.

About the untouchable spring.

'We've walked a long distance. We've got to walk this much more. It may take the whole night. How do you feel? Are you tired?'

'No. It's new. It's strange.'

'Shall I tell you a story?'

'Tell me.'

Reuben had not yet begun the story. For a moment they didn't know what happened. A night bird darted in from the side making a horrendous noise. In the moonlight, they kept looking at it as long as it was visible. Its cry kept ringing in their ears.

'*Yennela pitta*.* Always like that. It shrieks as if something catastrophic has happened. Speeds past as if someone is chasing it. Is not seen again. Is not heard again.'

---

* *Yennela pitta* is an imaginary bird the writer conjures up using the words *yennela* (moonlight) and *pitta* (bird). The expression also draws on *Yennela Dinni*, the place Yellanna and others come from.

If Reuben were to tell her those things now, she would not believe him. She remembers the bird vividly. Hears it, always. Whenever she remembers the story Reuben narrated, she remembers the yennela pitta.

It was a story told to Reuben's grandfather by his grandfather. There is Siva in it, Parvati, too. They have a cow, Kamadhenu[1]. It gives honeyed milk. Normally, a cow's milk does not ooze honey. But Kamadhenu's milk is suffused with honey. With that milk Parvati makes a feast for the gods and goddesses. Only the gods have a right to that feast. *Rishis* are the only special invitees.

There is a young man who takes care of this Kamadhenu which has special powers. His name is Chennaiah. One day he is tempted to drink the honeyed milk. He reveals his desire to Parvati. Parvati says no. But the young man cannot overcome his desire. He repeats it to Parvati many a time. Parvati tells Chennaiah, 'Go, ask Kamadhenu, yourself, Chenna.' He does just that. He reveals his desire to Kamadhenu. A wonder! As soon as Kamadhenu hears the request, she collapses on the ground—dead.

Siva and Parvati come to know of Kamadhenu's death. The news travels to the gods and goddesses. Siva and Parvati think of cooking Kamadhenu's meat and offering it as a feast for the gods and goddesses. Kamadhenu's milk used to ooze honey. Anticipating how delicious her meat would be, all the gods, goddesses and rishis swarm around the dead Kamadhenu, smacking their lips.

But there is a problem. Kamadhenu has to be moved from the spot where it died. 'That's the custom,' say the gods and goddesses. 'If that's not done, the *sastras* will not accept it,' say the rishis. Everyone agrees. But even all the gods and goddesses do not possess the strength to move the dead Kamadhenu. Finally, the rishis suggest that Jambavanta alone has the power to move it. Siva calls Chennaiah. He orders him to go and get Jambavanta.

'*Thatha . . . Maha . . . digira.*' ('*Thatha . . .* great . . . come down.')

Chennaiah shouts so loudly that he can be heard in all the corners of the world. Whether Jambavanta climbed down from the sky or rose from the earth, we do not know. He appears from somewhere in the three worlds. He looks at Kamadhenu. He sees the gods and goddesses. He speaks to the rishis. They tell him what to do. That's it. Jambavanta lifts Kamadhenu with his left hand. The gods and goddesses bless Jambavanta. The rishis shout cries of victory. On such occasions, gods, goddesses and rishis do just that. That may be a convention. They tell him how far and where he should take Kamadhenu. As the gods, goddesses and rishis follow him, Jambavanta takes Kamadhenu to the place where they ask him to.

The gods cut up the cow. Skin it. Then they ask Jambavanta to divide the meat of the cow into two parts. They ask him to cook only one part. They say that they will recite a *mantra* and bring Kamadhenu back to life. They depart. They are immersed in a discussion about the cow's meat they are about to eat.

Jambavanta does not divide the meat into two parts as told. He starts to cook the entire meat. As he is stirring the meat, a piece falls to the ground. It gets smeared with mud. That piece becomes defiled. Chennaiah cleans the piece and puts it back in the meat that is being cooked.

Siva and Parvati come to know of this. The gods and goddesses are furious with Jambavanta for not dividing the meat into two parts. They are angry with Chennaiah for putting the defiled piece of meat into the meat being cooked. Neither Siva nor the gods can do anything but curse when they are angry. Siva curses. He curses Jambavanta and Chennaiah to live in *Kaliyuga* eating the meat of dead cows and sweeping the bazaars. All the gods, goddesses and rishis sing a chorus that this curse would last till eternity.

Jambavanta and Chennaiah eat the cooked meat. In Kaliyuga, Jambavanta's children become *madigas*. Chennaiah's children become *malas*.

Reuben had looked at her as if to say that the story was over. She did not speak a word. She is silent.

'How's the concocted story?' he asked smiling.

'My grandfather told it so convincingly. His grandfather narrated it as if it were really true. The story of my birth and your birth. Where did we come from? From a curse. From the wrath of the gods. From the piece of meat that fell out. Why is it so?' Though he spoke forcefully, he did not speak in anger. He was smiling as he spoke. But she did not say anything even then. She searched for the yennela pitta. She felt it would be nice if it went by making a deafening noise. She said this to Reuben. He replied that he would call out to the yennela pitta. He cried out almost like the yennela pitta. His shout would have reached a great distance, tearing through the silence. It would have echoed till a great distance.

At that time it had just seemed like a strange tale. It would not appear simply strange now. It would appear grotesque. Would seem as if there were no other story more cruel than that. She feels that in Reuben's laugh that day there was rejection of and ridicule for that story. It comes back to her. If she sifts through every detail carefully, she feels that when she unthinkingly talked of the yennela pitta, Reuben imitated its call. Now she feels it was not an imitation. She was not able to hear a man's agony in the imitation that day. Truly, it was the agony of an untouchable. It was a condemnation of his birth that was so cruelly painted, of the crime committed on him in history. A true remonstrance. A rejection, indeed.

That's why Ruth says that her memory is not past. She says it is an untouchable spring. Beginning like waves upon waves and touching the sky, it breaks out and booms like the thunderous sound of the oceanic wave, she says. There is no twist in the tale for that spring. All that there is a continuation, like a song . . . like a poem, plumbing the depths, scraping the conscience.

2

Ruth's memories are many years old. Some of these are those she had shared with Reuben. Some are from the time before Reuben met her. Others are about the ancestors Reuben had introduced her to. Of Ruth's sweet thoughts of the yennela pitta. Of *Yennela Dinni* that the yennela pitta tapped awake at night.

Reuben said that to think of Yennela Dinni was to remember the flute tunes that are born between the lips of the untouchable. That was where Reuben's grandfather Yellanna was born. He grew up there. Sang songs. Danced.

Yellanna did not write songs. He knew no alphabet to write them in. All he had was a feeling heart, a shareable experience, tear-shedding eyes, swelling nerves, a turbulent blood-stream . . . that was it, the song would weave itself. He wove the song like that. Not just weaving the song, he danced, too. They called him singing Yelladu. Dancing Yelladu. But his father's sister, Boodevi, called him 'Yellanna'.

Recalling Yellanna's song and dance, Reuben would sing their praise. In his last days he would speak about them again and again. He would then turn into a child. It seems that when Yellanna donned the role of Hiranyakasipu they would beat the drums asking pregnant women not to come. True—they say this in that village even today. They sang Yellana's songs for us. Village life peeped out through those songs. The moving tune that combined untouchability and hunger was heard. That Yellanna could bring to mind Narasimhaswami in *Chenchulakshmi* as if he was right there was narrated by the elders who in turn had been told so by *their* elders. Those words brought to Ruth's eyes the happiness that was hidden and held somewhere in some corner. Yellanna was a great artist. Reuben was born in a great artist's family. Now Ruth is an heir to that family.

How wonderful it would be to ask her to hide only Yennela Dinni Yellanna's song and dance in her heart! How securely she would have hidden it! How many times she had recollected it and remained a *pallavi** to that song! She would be the *talam*+ to that dance. But the background to the song comes to the fore. The rhythmic steps of ghastly time that had merged with that performance danced in front of her eyes.

Yennela Dinni was not such a great place. That does not mean you can think of it as insignificant. There could be thirty houses of Reddys. Only one brahmin house. That was the karanam's house. Washerman, barber, *balija*, cowherd, potter—together all would probably make the same number of houses. Two on the Reddys' mound, two on the brahmins' lake bund—*yanadi* houses. At a distance, twenty mala houses. Further off the same number of madiga houses. The place where those who belonged to the four castes lived was *ooru*. The place

---

* *Pallavi* is the initiation or the main motif of a song. *Charanam* is the conclusion or base of the song.
+ *Talam* is the rhythmic beat of a dance or song.

where malas lived—*malapalli*, where the madigas lived—*madigapalli*. Amazingly, all those parts put together formed Yennela Dinni.

There is a proverb: 'If there is an *ooru* won't there be a *palle*?' Ruth would keep the proverb in mind and reflect on it now and again. As she reflects she will see a cruel horizontal line across the lives of the people of this country. On that side of the horizontal line, the touchable people, on this side, the untouchable people. That side is definitely the upper portion. This side is undoubtedly the lower portion. Yennela Dinni was not an exception to this dividing line. We cannot sketch it without drawing this line.

Yellanna's life was on this side of the horizontal line. One did not know when his ancestors were pushed on to this side of the line. Several hundreds may be born every second on this earth, maybe thousands; or maybe much more. Yellanna, too, was born like that. Born like everyone else. He, too, cut his umbilical cord with his mother and was born with a sudden shriek. In that shriek, there was not that strange warning, 'Oh, you upper caste people! I, an untouchable, am walking on your pure, regal paths. Move aside. Move aside.' He shrieked like everyone else. He announced his birth like anyone else.

Like each one's birth touching one's father's heart, his, too, touched his father's heart. 'A male,' he shouted out to the caste elder. He filled the caste elder's stomach with toddy and felt elated. Like all other mothers, his mother, too, might or might not have heard his shriek in her tired state. But Boodevi looked repeatedly at the face of the tired Lingalu and at the tiny body of the child that shrieked. The midwife said the shriek was very loud. She did not stop there. She said, looking at Boodevi, that the child was born with his father's sister's nose. Then Boodevi noticed. She searched for her image in the child. She stopped at the nose. She wanted to hear the midwife's words again.

The day they bathed the mother and the child, they named him. Yerrenkadu said he would name him after his grandfather. Boodevi wanted to name him after her father. Yerrenkadu did not oppose her. Not just now, Yerrenkadu had never opposed his sister. It was not as if there was no reason. There were two children before Yerrenkadu. There were two after Boodevi. The four siblings had died. Only the two of them remained. They grew up in Yennela Dinni as if each had only the other. His father wanted to give Boodevi away to someone in Kolla Dinni. Yerrenkadu did not agree. He said that they must give his sister only to someone in Yennela Dinni. They performed Boodevi's marriage joining their half *kunta*♦ of low, swampy field to the *kapu's* field. Though he disposed of the entire swampy piece of land to meet his sister's marriage expenses, Yerrenkadu did not feel bad. His sister got married to a man in Yennela Dinni. She was living next to his house. That was enough, he felt.

Yerrenkadu's brother-in-law, Yenkatanarsu, was not to be taken lightly. Actually, Yennela Dinni was not his ancestors' native place. They were from the Chirala and Perala region. Yenkatanarsu's grandfather had come to Yennela Dinni, bringing the loom along. When his grandfather sat near the loom and wove, they would look at him in amazement at Yennela Dinni. After the old man passed away, Yenkatanarsu's father worked on it for a while. When he died, the loom remained more as a symbol and was shelved. Though Yenkatanarsu did not weave on it, he did not stop going to Chirala and Perala, bundling the bed-sheets and coarse dhotis woven there and going around villages to sell them. He would spend two or three months a year like that, roaming.

There was no dearth of grain at home. Though they found it difficult between the old and the new crops, they were able to somehow pull along on the whole. There were *ana* and *beda* coins on him but no rupee notes. Boodevi gave betel nut and betel leaves to others but never knew the taste of those bitten by someone else. 'What's there for her? Her husband goes around villages and brings her things. She places the cot right in the middle of the house and squats on it.' Those who did not like her would say this scornfully and those who liked her would say it affectionately.

Whatever anyone might have thought, Yerrenkadu would act only according to his sister's wishes. Even when he was to marry Lingalu, he sent Boodevi to meet her. When Yenkatanarsu said, 'What's this, are you marrying her or is she?', he replied, 'If my sister likes her, then I'll like her, too.'

♦ *Kunta* refers to one fortieth of an acre of land.

Boodevi went and saw Lingalu, and spoke about it the whole day. She said, 'The girl is good, *anna.*' She said, 'She can carry hay for five bullocks at one go.' 'A home without a male child, you'll survive,' she said. 'The girl is like the branch of a tree,' she said. Boodevi did not lie. Lingalu was no ordinary person. If she stood up, she seemed to tower above the thatched roof. 'You must increase the height of the entrance, anna,' Boodevi said.

Yerrenkadu asked whether the eyes of the kapus and *karanams* would redden if he raised the height of the entrance. It was not as if Boodevi did not know this. If the mala's entrance was high enough for one to get in without bending down, this information would reach the ooru somehow. That debate would end in the *sastras*. Among the elders of the Rama temple, there should be no talk of the malas. If such a thing happened, they would have to put up with it for ten generations. They did not raise the height of the entrance though Lingalu became the daughter-in-law of Yennela Dinni. But whenever Lingalu bent down to go in, Boodevi would say, 'It would be nice to raise the height of the entrance, anna'.

Yerrenkadu was not able to do just that one thing Boodevi wanted. For the rest, he had to do what his sister wanted. He wanted to give his grandfather's name to his son. When Boodevi said they should keep their father's name for the child, he did not object.

The caste elder looked at the child and said, 'Sinasubba.' Yerrenkadu said, 'Not Sinasubba, but Yelladu.' 'Not Yelladu, but Yellanna,' said Boodevi. The caste elder said, 'She has great love for her father, Yerrenka.'

Boodevi lifted her nephew up. '*Ayya,*' she said. 'Yellaiah,' she said. 'Yellanna,' she said. With that call, she somehow created her own world. She appeared as if she was in a hurry to carry on her work in that world. Her nephew was born with a nose that measured up to hers. With the fingers of the little hand, she measured her nose.

In the ooru, the elder karanam gave fifty acres of wet land to the younger karanam when he died, two mango groves, five acres of groundnut mound, twenty arm-lengths of palm groves, and vast uncultivable land. It did not stop there. He handed over the karanam's duty in five villages and then died. In the palle, Boodevi's father could only bequeath his nose when he died. That, too, he did not give his son. He gave it to his daughter. Now the grandson snatched it away. Saying, 'The property of my household is mine, *attha*' he measured the nose in the womb itself and was born with it. He was not his father's pet. Nor his mother's. But his aunt's. Paternal aunt Boodevi's, pet. As *Malachi* tree is witness. As *Yellamma* goddess is witness. As *Mungamooramma* in the outskirts is witness. Paternal aunt's pet. Thinking like that, Boodevi erected her entire future only around a single principle.

The caste elder asked them to tie the uncle's *pancha*. Yenkatanarsu, came forward. But Uncle's pancha did not mean yellow silk. Only a black loin cloth. Yenkatanarsu tied a loin cloth around the child. The child kicked out with both legs and struck Boodevi's nose. A few urine drops from the loin cloth fell on Yenkatanarsu. 'Pour it into her mouth, wretched . . .', he uttered an obscenity as usual. Boodevi said, 'Don't say that. We have given him father's name.'

Boodevi brought up her nephew with dance. Brought him up with songs. Laying him down on her legs, she sang Kamamma's story, bathing him. While patting him to sleep, she sang Lakshmamma's story. Listening to the song, he danced. Listening to the song, he ate. Listening to the song, he slept. Lingalu, the mother, left him with Boodevi. Boodevi did not conceive. She thought her nephew was her own son.

Those days, when there was little to do, women would eat whatever was available very early in the evening, clear up everything, and in the moonlight they would gather in front of Boodevi's house. Boodevi would begin Nallathanga's story. She would begin with, 'Daivaraya— Daivaraya.' The song that went, 'In the town of Kashyapoori,', would extend till the midnight moon waned. The refrain of the song was '*thontaddindakka*', which the rest of the women would sing. Yellanna would sit on his aunt's lap in the midst of the women. Curbing his sleep, yawning, he would say, 'thontaddindakka'. When he said that, Boodevi would find it endearing. She would cuddle her nephew and make him lie down on her lap. In the middle of his sleep, he would mutter, 'thontaddindakka'.

Yellanna, while growing up, picked up whatever tune his aunt sang. Sang whatever song she sang. Carried by his aunt, he would watch puppet shows. In the morning he would jump like *Ketigadu*. He would say, '*Attha*, you're *Bangarakka*.'* Boodevi would feel elated.

When *yerra gollalu* came to the ooru, there was excitement all over. They would put up street plays for ten to fifteen days in a row. Among all of them, Boodevi was crazy about the *Chenchu Natakam*.† She would go to the play, taking her nephew along.

The yerra gollalu would perform in the outskirts of the ooru. They used to erect a palm post on either side tying a palm frond connecting the two and place a large table in the middle. The musicians playing the tabla and harmonium would sit on it. People singing in the chorus would stand around the table with cymbals. Those who performed would do so in the space in front of the table. Till the performance lasted, castor oil torches and lamps with *dindiga* seed oil would glow.

Karanams and kapus would sit close to the performers. Behind them, people from the washermen, barber and potter castes would sit. The malas would sit on the mala mound. The madigas would sit on the madiga mound. Those two groups would be far away from the arena. Sitting like that, they would not be visible to the village elders and elders of other castes. They would not come to the mound till the performance began. Generally, the play would not begin till the karanam and the higher kapus arrived. After the higher kapus came, the karanam would stride in leisurely. As soon as he came, they would praise him to the skies. Then the *sutradhara* (narrator) would begin the performance. Once they knew the karanam had come, the malas and madigas would get to the top of their mounds. By mistake, if they arrived early, the elders would find fault with them.

Yellanna would tell his aunt, 'I can't see.' If she stood up and lifted him, she might be seen by the kapus. Might be seen by the karanam. Normally, they would not turn around. But if by chance they saw them, it was like asking for trouble. But she would dare stand up for the sake of her nephew. The performance would last

---

*	See note 14.
†	See note 15.

till the morning. Yellanna would give up his sleep to watch the performance.

'*Chettulekkagalane—O Chenchita puttalekkagalane.*'* Saying this in the morning, he would pat his aunt's back. Boodevi would feel as thrilled as if she had conquered a mountain peak. He would not stop at that. In the same vein, he would weave his own song. 'Can you cook rice, Boodevi, can you cook curries, can you cook curries and give some for Yelladu's belly?' He would sing like that. Boodevi would look at him amazed. He would change the lines when his aunt looked at him. He would weave a new one now. 'Why do you look like that—oh, *attha*, how's my song?' he would sing. Boodevi would laugh. She would roll in laughter. Laughing, she would drag him to Lingalu. She would tell her how Yellanna danced, how Yellanna sang. Lingalu would stare at her sister-in-law.

One day, Yellanna had a new experience. It was not new for Boodevi. Not new for her brother. Not new for her sister-in-law. It was not new for the older people who were born and brought up in Yennela Dinni. It was new for Yellanna who was seeing the world just then.

That morning, after seeing the play at night, Yellanna felt like going towards the tents in which the yerra gollalu lived outside the ooru. When he said this to his aunt, she said no. He did not understand why his aunt was saying no. Actually, he wanted to see the play from close quarters. If he were to tell his aunt that they go near and see, she would say, 'No, let's remain here.'

Taking the *saddi*♦ box and basket, the aunt went looking for dindiga oil seeds. The child thought of going to the yerra gollalu and coming back by the time his aunt returned. He did just that.

Near the yerra gollalu's tents there were many like him. They were looking, fascinated, at the crowns that were being repaired. He, too, made his way into the crowd that was looking with interest. Really, those crowns appeared strange. In the meanwhile, he noticed someone looking in his direction. That person did not simply look at him. He struck up a conversation.

---

* I can climb trees —O Chenchita, I can climb hills.
♦ *Saddi* refers to the left-over food from the previous night.

'Aren't you a mala?'

'I'm Yerrenkadu's son.'

All those around him stared at Yellanna. The one who asked did not stop at that. He started lashing him on his back with a palm frond. Before Yellanna could understand what was happening, he felt as if all those at that place were about to pounce on him. He ran involuntarily. Felt they were chasing him. It seemed to him as though they were pelting stones. They were falling next to him. One hit him hard. He did not stop. He kept running. He did not know in which direction he ran. But he did not stop. He ran a great distance. So far away that the ooru was not visible . . . he was still running. He jumped over bushes. He jumped over mounds of thorny brambles. He stumbled over logs. As he struck some boulders in his path, he fell flat on his face. Broke his nose. Blood flowed. He scraped his knees. His feet did not feel like feet. They looked like pieces of broken red sandalwood. Even then, he did not stop running.

The stream came in the way.

There was no way he could stop. As he ran, he jumped into the water. The water came up to the waist. He was simply surging ahead. Water rose above his chest. It was strange. Around him, the water was red. Red streaks on black shoulders looked grotesque in the sun. He was going deeper still. He lifted his hands. A circle of blood around his neck. A gradual change. As if getting on to the shore all of a sudden . . . water below his chest, then below the waist . . . he reached the shore. When he did, he realised he did not have a cloth around his waist. Did not know when it had been washed away. He looked puzzled. He was walking on the shore of the stream with nothing around his waist.

On this side of the stream, Yennela Dinni. Did not know what was on the other side. There was just a path. And he did not know whether he could walk on that path or not.

3

They say. Many elders. Among them are prophets. *Sanyasis*. Philosphers. They all say tirelessly. That at birth itself what a man's life will be like is written on his face, that things will happen only according to what is written, that nothing will change even if he thinks otherwise.

Philosophies have gone a step further. There is a 'nest,' there. A parrot comes into that nest. After a while, the parrot abandons the nest and goes away. Don't know where it goes. They say to the Infinite.

But in fact, the nest that the parrot stayed in and left is on a spacious stage. On that stage innumerable entrances. Innumerable exits. One after another. As per the instructions of the director behind the stage. Like puppets on a string.

The puppets cry. The puppets laugh. A parrot-puppet is mercilessly chopped up and dies. A baby parrot, just born, announces itself to the world in its feeble voice. All parrots. All people. Spreading across the world. Occupying the entire stage.

All this is philosophy. Theory of the fate-line. Has no beginning. Has no end. Infinite. Incomprehensible. Except for a few. Something they alone can explain.

Let them die. Let those few cry themselves hoarse on the stage and die, their throats parched.

No need. Ruth does not need all these.

These philosophies, these deceits, these parrots, these puppets, these stages—not necessary. What she wants are lives. What she wants are realities. Yellannas in her memories who run with their lives in their hands.

When she thinks of it, Ruth feels uneasy.

When she thinks of Yellanna, Reuben's ancestor, when she thinks of him running as a child many years ago, she feels as if that deceit was born on the earth, had pierced through the sky and was at an unattainable height.

Yellanna's looking for a second at the path in front and walking on without turning back appear strange to her. She cannot understand how that young boy could walk like that. Fear would have given him that strength. Actually, he did walk a great distance. Did not know when the sun came right above his head, when it slid down the horizon and vanished. The twilight began as a thin streak and gradually became dense. Then Yellanna merged with the darkness and walked. He was sure that now he would not be seen by anyone. Once he gained that confidence fear left him. Felt like sitting down. Felt he had enough freedom to sit down. He sat down. He lay down on the sand mound. Up above, the sky. A star here, a star there.

Yes!

On which stage did this scene take place? That forbidden stage came alive in Ruth's memory—whose creation is it?

Who is the creator? Half man. Half animal. Not god. Not devil. Not man. Not monkey.* A terribly distorted shape that no other living being had.

Who is that terribly distorted one that prepared the scene and its stage for Yellanna? If it is the yerra gollalu, they would not practise untouchability with Yellanna. When he went to see them, when he pushed his way into the crowd that was watching, when that crowd was of upper castes—that Yellanna should not be in that crowd, that if he were there, his back would be lashed with palm fronds, that he would be chased till blood flowed, that he would have to cover his naked waist with the blanket of darkness . . . Who is that half man who drew the line on Yellanna's forehead and on his life? Who is that half animal? What must be the name of the awesome, distorted one ? The answer is clear. It is in the shape of papers. The term *smriti* is also appended to his name.

That half animal is Manu. That terribly distorted Manu. He expounded the *dharmas,* special dharmas, expounded the principles of the caste system. They say he is only one. The *puranas* say that he is not one but many. They say the ones born of him are human beings. Why then could he not see Yellanna as a human being?

He said. The one called Manu said. His dharma said. That one would be born a *chandala* if one killed a brahmin. If that were true, how many brahmins must have been killed for so many malas and madigas to be born in Yennela Dinni? Manu must identify the brahmin whom Yellanna killed. Will have to identify. If he does not, the castes that protect his dharma must. The upper castes must.

---

* The Telugu text plays on the '*narudu*' (man) and '*vanarudu*' (monkey) here and a little later on Manuvu (Manu) and *manavudu* (human being).

Revenge, anger, tears. Filling Ruth's heart, filling Ruth's thoughts . . . after all these years . . . after generations . . . when so much of sadness turning into a stream is encircling her.

Ruth turns into a volcano when she thinks of Yellanna, of Boodevi, of Yennela Dinni and the cast-away lives, and when she is reminded of such instances. Her tent of memories is filled with perspiration. She feels suffocated. All the memories seem to melt and flow like lava. Enraged, the sequence of memory is lost. A search begins again for the order. She would need to make a great deal of effort to recollect Yellanna's shape that lay alone on the sand mound in the dense darkness staring into the sky.

At first, Yellanna looked at the stars, confident that there was no fear of death. Then he remembered hunger. Along with hunger he remembered his aunt. She had kept fried dry fish in the pot in the sling hung from the roof. She had asked him to eat it with rice. She had shut the thatched door and asked him to lie down under the *pandal*. Had asked him not to go anywhere till she came back. But he had not listened to his aunt's words. Actually, it would have been better had he gone along with his aunt for dindiga seeds. He did not think it would turn out like this. He did not think going there would turn out to be such a crime. He was now beginning to understand why his aunt had asked him not to go. But why should he not go? That was the question, the sense of turmoil raised in his tender heart.

Now his aunt would search for him. Foolish one. She would weep searching for him. He thought of going back. Going back for aunt's sake. Before sleep, aunt would not just sing for him but tell stories, too. Last night when she was telling him a story, he said, 'I'm sleepy, *attha*,' and slept. 'Remember, Yellanna, . . . the prince came to *Pedarasi Peddamma's** house. If you ask me to start the story from the beginning tomorrow, I can't do it,' said his aunt. It would have been nice if he had got her to tell him who Pedarasi Pedamma was.

---

* Pedarasi Peddamma is the figure in Telugu oral tales who guides explorers. It is believed that she lives on the moon spinning the wheel, surrounded by children. She represents the lower class rural woman's practical wisdom, as the witness of the times and incidents.

She must have been good. She must have been good like his aunt. She sang songs. Told stories. How many stories she must have told the prince. . . !

He was overcome with sadness. Hunger . . . aunt . . . once more, he thought of going back. But where was he now? How far was he from Yennela Dinni? Complete darkness . . . . He was unable to decide which way to go.

Exhausted, he tried to see what was ahead.. He kept peering into the darkness. His eyes hurt. No use. He thought of spending the night there and going back in the morning. He thought of telling his aunt he would never do such a thing again.

He could not tell if darkness was blowing or the wind was blowing. It felt as if cold was being brought from far away. The touch of the wind was cold. Not just the cold, the wind brought along a rhythmic sound. He turned in the direction of the sound.

He could see a light far away. It was a feeble light that peeped through the palm trees on the high sand mounds. There seemed to be a village there. He did not know what it was. Yellanna did not know that it was Pakkela Dinni and that Ganga *Jatara* festival was taking place there.

Except for lamplight in a house, the brightness of the starlit sky and the voyage of the moon above, he never knew loneliness that was like a vast sand desert. It was strange.

He got up.

He started walking.

He did not stop. It appeared as if the light was getting submerged. The thought that in the midst of trees drenched in darkness there was a high mound did not occur to him. When he walked a little further, there was in fact no light visible at all.

Yellanna was naked. He was truly a child of nature now. Nude Yellanna. Playful light. Enveloping darkness. Stars like holes in a torn bed-sheet. Sand mounds. Nothing was by itself. All together— nature. All together—movement. There was no untouchability to this movement. There was no state of untouchability in this union. There was no caste in this movement. There were no four parts within it, no fifth outside of it. There were not hundreds of sub-castes. There was no caste-centred respect, position, disrespect or lowliness. This movement was not mean. This movement was not unjust.

Darkness. Darkness of a thatched screen like a protective circle shielding him. He felt free. It felt as if his hunger and his aunt were moving away from him, as if the stirrings that were proclaiming his freedom from the depths of his heart were finding release.. That stirring might be a song. The song might be fear. Might be hunger. Might be his aunt. Above all, it might be a proclamation of the freedom he had achieved. Now Yellanna was walking, accompanied not only by darkness but also by the song.

Wind has a naturalness about it. Whatever it touches, it speaks out its feeling clearly like the feelings of the one there. Yellanna's song too would emerge just like that. It would go ahead weaving like that. Difficult to say. It might not be possible to be definite and say whether the song was making Yellanna walk or whether Yellanna was walking along with the song. He stopped singing and listened. A rhythmic sound was approaching.

The light that had vanished was spreading and moving forward. Now it was not between the palm trees. It looked like a fire outside the ooru. People around the fire. Without his knowledge, Yellanna's footsteps were quickening their pace. The sounds and light were mingling and coming closer.

The light in the midst of sounds was like speeding lightning amidst breaking clouds. Anguish was making Yellanna walk. It was not a walk. It was a run. A driving force that had been pushing him for generations. The stirring of an artist's heart.

The scene was very close. Was wonderful. There, around that fire, a deluge was dancing. Charged-up emotion, thunder, lightning, cloud. Breaking out somewhere, crashing down like thunderbolt somewhere. A grotesque scene . . . a turbulence in Yellanna's tender heart.

A crowd encircled the fire. He pushed his way in. There was a tremor near the fire amidst the crowd. The deluge emanated from there.

Yellanna's eyes were full of rage. He looked at those who were creating the deluge-like roar above the thunder in front of him. Their attire was impressive. Better than God Narasimha. Better than Chenchulakshmi. Colourful towels tied around the heads. Necklaces of coins around their necks. Shawls covering them. Some red, some green, long *jubbas*. On the membranes of the thunder that had tensed up the moving *kaduru* sticks. On the other side, friction caused by a cane. An immense roar forming. A circular movement. A horrendous sound. An awesome dance.

The *Urumula Nrityam*[2] of the malas

Yellanna's feet were moving. His legs were shaking. The feet refused to remain on the ground. Some rage. A turmoil somewhere else. The sound ceased. Yellanna's heart seemed to stop suddenly.

The song began.

The musicians of the Urumula Nrityam began their song. In the song, Ganga was overflowing. All along the way, the land was dry and parched. It was groaning for water. Ganga must be born in the dried-up bed. The cracked earth must drink greedily. Ganga must fill up. Ganga must swell. Ganga must touch all the worlds. Till then the thunder will not stop. The dance will not stop. The song will not stop.

The song was going on.

The era was still unborn. The world was not born. Ganga was born. The cunning Ganga. The jealous and mean Ganga. The devil that fed on corpses. Abuses. Curses. Getting upset with Ganga. For a mouthful of water. For a small crop getting wet. But the Ganga that was born before man or god, the Donakonda Ganga, the Ganga that filled the earth . . . had given her word. Gave her word to man. Said she would not in the case of children go back on the word she had given to the elders. She would not in the case of little children go back on the word she had given to the children. She would not in the case of little children go back on the word she had given to the infants . . . The song was continuing. On Ganga, on Ganga's word, on Ganga's life.

A little respite in between.

A sound again breaking that pause. In the finale, a crashing sound. A rhythmic dance making the sound its own. Like heroes in the shape of rings, with entwined legs, the entire body swaying, and jumping—like labourers bringing down Ganga to the earth. . . . A jump for every sound. A shout for every jump. All force. All deluge. The end. The beginning.

Yellanna could not contain himself.

Did not remember Yennela Dinni. Did not remember Boodevi. Did not remember the lashings with the palm fronds . . . Fear of life, the running, crossing the stream with rings of blood . . . walking to unknown regions . . . darkness . . . hunger . . . aunt . . . stars—did not remember anything.

Right in front of him something he could relate to was happening. On his head a coloured kerchief. Round his neck a shawl hanging . . . a jubba over his entire body . . . in the neck thunder.

A feeling.

On one side the rhythmic dance of the kaduru sticks. On the other side, the grating noise of the cane sticks . . . he in the ring. He in the song . . . he in the dance. His entirety was being born and brought up here.

The vermilion dance began.

Those who had poured well water over their heads. Those who with both their hands had held a bunch of peacock feathers on their heads. Those listening to the roar of thunder closing their eyes. Those swaying with turmeric on their chests and vermillion smeared on their foreheads . . . those who had until then controlled with difficulty the rage that the sound of thunder produced. . . . A crowd all around. The masses. An untouchable crowd. A mala and madiga crowd. As *bandaru*♣ vermilion was being sprinkled, the crowd muttered, 'Harom, Harom, Hara . . . Hara, Hara Hara,' swaying with frenzy, and dancing like Siva. . .

Vermilion dance. . .

A ferocious earth. Blood soaked. Dance. As if a war was taking place. As if it was the world's battlefield and nothing else. Swords hitting the chest, for Ganga, for a mouthful of water, postures, many furious Sivas seeming to dance the *tandavam* of deluge . . . illusion, reality, dance, war, the grotesque, life-like dance, like song . . . Urumula dance.

♣ *Bandaru* vermilion is a mixture of vermilion, neem leaves, turmeric and other ingredients.

The grand thunder-spring of the untouchables. Just as everything was stolen. Just as life on earth was stolen. Urumula dance having been stolen and hidden in temples by the upper castes as Perini dance.

The tempo of the dance was proceeding with great fury. Those who could not stand it, those who were weak, were moving back. Yellanna did not withdraw. Came forward instead. Came very much ahead. He said, '*Harom, Hara, Hara, Hara.*' A voice that burst out of the heart. '*Harom, Hara, Hara.*'

The sound stopped. Urumula Naganna turned towards that voice, towards Yellanna who had shouted. Silence was more fierce than sound. Yellanna, the nude Siva. Was looking piercingly. On his head neem twigs. On his body the blood-like vermilion that people had sprinkled.

Urumula Naganna kept staring.

He looked at the child Siva in front of him.

He saw Siva's third eye in the two eyes of the child Siva. He looked at the feet of child Siva. Well formed, wonderful, beautiful, as if born to dance. . . . Gazing like that, he signalled to the Urumula people. The sound was rhythmic. Dance was in the shape of child Siva. Touching the earth, jumping—beautiful feet, swaying waist. Eyes that were spreading inspiration. A sharp pointed nose. . . Siva was a boy. Siva's colour was black. . . Siva was Yellanna.

Urumula Naganna kept staring.

'Who are you, my child?' Naganna asked.

'I'm a mala from Yennela Dinni,' the child Siva replied.

'What's your name?'

'Yellanna.'

The sound became a roar once more.

Till the child Siva collapsed tired . . . the thunder was being heard. After the concluding song was sung, after they prayed to goddess Ganga, the sound stopped completely. Deluge. Peace afterwards. Now Yellana lay down on Urumula Naganna's chest and placed his head on his shoulders.

Urumula Naganna's coarse hands were caressing Yellanna's back affectionately. Without opening his eyes, Yellanna asked, 'What's this place?' 'Pakkela Dinni malapalli.' Saying this, Naganna kept walking.

In Yennela Dinni, Boodevi was not aware of this incident.

4

Yellanna was sleeping soundly. Urumula Naganna was not able to sleep. Yellanna's arrival seemed to have caused some turmoil in him. Something forgotten seemed to have pushed itself forward. He came beyond the house front.

The morning star had just come out. The early morning cock was crowing its heart out. Near the wooden peg, the young calf was tugging at the rope for its mother's milk.

It was three days since Naganna came to 'Pakkela Dinni.' Gangamma Jatara had ended the previous night. If the *pedda* mala♦ were to give him the fee for the dance, he would return to Anantapuram that day itself. The Urumala dancers who had come with him had already left the previous night. He had stayed behind to collect the fee for the dance. He did not know what to do with Yellanna when he returned with the money.

When Yellanna, who was tired from dancing, continued to sleep, he woke him up and poured water all over his body. He gave him clothes to wear. When Naganna served him food, Yellana ate eagerly, famished. When he asked, 'Why did Yennela Dinni chase you away?', the child's eyes were clouded. When he drew him close, he burst into tears. Then he told him. The same old story. The usual story. The terrifying story. The sorrowful story. But there was no way out. Was such a story Yellanna's alone? Didn't he have one? A crueller story. From that same Yennela Dinni.

Dharamaram Urumula Naganna was famous not only in the Anantapuram region but also in the coastal areas. Gangamma would not want to have a jatara without Naganna's troupe, without that troupe roaring thunder. Pointing towards Srisailam Mallanna, Urumula Chandrappa put the *urumulu*♣ on Naganna's shoulder for the first time.

♦ *Pedda* mala is the head of a particular mala group.
♣ *Urumulu* are a sort of drums.

Who was Urumula Chandrappa? What was he to Naganna? He had taught Naganna the nuances of playing the urumulu. *He* taught him how to make his throat voice the depths, the breaks and the ferocity in the song of Ganga. He taught him how not to miss a beat in his steps. Not just that. Saying, 'Come, I'll tell you the secrets of the *puranas,* Naga,' he told him many secrets. 'The brahmins didn't say all this like that. They said it like this. They said everything wrong.' He said this as if he was speaking to himself. He gave life to Naganna. He introduced him to the world as Urumula Naganna and went away.

Naganna has a special place in Ruth's memories. The same intensity of rage Reuben experienced when he spoke about Yellanna, he experienced when he spoke about Naganna. It really feels so. That that untouchable body housed a wonderful living art. When such a thought occurs, it is not the eyes that shed tears. Her heart. Her entire life.

In reality what was Chandrappa to Naganna? Naganna's mother, Latchimi, said, 'He's your *sinnabba*, like your father's younger brother, Naga.' He called him that. He called him sinnabba. When Chandrappa was alive, he called him only *sinnabba*. But on the day he died, he said, 'Call me *appa,* Naga.' He tried to call out loud like that. The old man passed away, smiling. '*Appa, appa,*' he kept calling. There was no Chandrappa to hear him.

Naganna did everything for Chandrappa according to convention. His brother's children disputed over the half a kunta of land given for performing Urumula dance. The dispute was decided in their favour. When the pot was broken in the corner of the house, there were fifty *beda*, thirty *ana* and three hundred *dammiddee* coins. He was asked to take the money. He took the money. But he did not keep it. He divided it among the troupe that danced with Chandrappa. He formed a new troupe. He earned a name for himself in Rayalaseema and the coastal region.

Urumula Naganna's eyes were remarkable. His voice was remarkable. His dance was remarkable. Not just that. He knew numerous secrets of the puranas. He could outsmart any learned person. That was how people talked about Naganna. That was how life went on. But Yellanna had begun a turmoil in Naganna that day.

When he said, 'I'm a mala from Yennela Dinni,' the present raced back at one go and stopped there. He remembered the hurt the past had inflicted.

Naganna had been born in Yennela Dinni. His father, Narigadu, had been born there. Mother, Latchimi, too had been born there.

Father did not have even a tiny parcel of land. All that he had was an axe to fell trees. He could fell a palm tree with ten blows. Striking a blow here and a blow there, he would chop the tree into bits right in front of their eyes. It was not possible to say when he climbed up the tree, chopped the fronds and got down. His life was tied to the palm tree. Naganna would go with his father to fell the palm tree. Mother, too, would come. His father would bring down the kernels for him. Mother would bet with him about eating the kernel before she could cut another. He would eat it like that. Before mother cut up a fruit, he would scoop out the kernel with his thumb and eat it. He would eat all the three kernels even before she broke the fruit. Naganna would feel like laughing, thinking of it.

After eating the kernels, he would go towards the ridges in the fields. He would string thin snail shells with palm withes into a necklace. If he shook the necklace rhythmically, it would sound just like water rolling down. He would keep the necklace near crab holes and make a sound. The crabs would think water was entering the holes and come up. He would hold the crabs that came out. He would break their large claws and would put them into a palm frond. Sometimes he could not catch them easily. They would run along the bank. They would lift their claws and frighten him. Even then he would catch them. Like that, he would catch about ten to fifteen crabs by the afternoon. He would light a fire with palm leaves in the field and roast them. As soon as father washed his feet and came to the canal bank, mother would bring the food basket. Father would eat the roasted crabs with rice, and praise Naganna to his mother saying, 'That's what a son means!' Father would say he was just like *his* mother. Naganna did not know what his grandmother had looked like.

Father would chop the palm trees till afternoon. Then he would cut them to pieces. By the time the work was over it would be evening. In the meanwhile he would, along with mother, pick and place the snails, beat the shell on the shore and put the meat in the pot. For firewood, they would collect palm sticks and make them into bundles. They would not stop with just that. In the eastern wasteland there used to be a *tumma* grove. Along with his mother he would collect tumma stalks. They would dry the tumma stalks and give them to Pattapu Subbulu. The latter would bring *karavadi* fish and *sora* fish. Mother would make *sora pittu*. If he said he would not go to the tumma grove, she would ask if he did not want karavadi fish and sora pittu. As soon as he heard those words, he would go with mother to the tumma grove.

Mother would keep the bundle of palm stalks on his head. She would keep the tumma stalk on her head and carry the snail meat pot in her hand. By the time the cattle that had gone to feed in the wasteland came back to the village, mother, father and he would be heading home. After they reached the lake bund, they would bring down the load from their heads and sit down. Father would climb the palm trees and bring down the toddy pots. Like that he would climb five trees. Among the five trees, he would smear lime on the rims of only three of the pots. He would not smear lime on the rims of two of them. Into the pots smeared with lime, 'juice' would ooze. Into the pots not smeared with lime, 'toddy' would ooze. He would hide three palm fronds at the foot of the trees. Father would drink toddy in his frond. Mother and he would drink palm juice. The juice would be sweet. Father would bring the juice home everyday. Not adulterated toddy. Not adulterated juice. Father would bring home the leftover toddy after he drank some. He would sell the toddy he brought home for food grains. Sometimes he would sell a potful of toddy for a dammiddee. If he got five dammiddees in his hand, father's face would glow. If there were grains for that day's meal, mother would jump with joy.

Boiling the juice, one would get palm syrup. On letting the palm syrup stand, palm sugar crystals would settle at the bottom. Naganna would cut raw mango, dip it in the palm syrup and eat it. When this syrup filled two or three cauldrons, they would boil it again. They would get thick jaggery-like syrup. They would dig holes and pour the syrup into them. The jaggery would solidify. Father would go out occasionally to sell those jaggery blocks.

In the summer season the palm fruits would ripen. Some would become overripe. They would roast and eat the ripened fruits. These would be broken up and the skin peeled. They would boil the skin. The skin that was boiled would taste very sweet.

The palm seeds that remained after peeling would be buried. They would sprout. Digging the ground in a row, they would pull out the sprouts. When the boiled sprouts were put on the pandal at night and got soaked in the early morning dew, they would be wonderful to eat in the morning. He was fond of eating them like that. The inside of the hardened seed would taste really good.

In this way the palm tree had been entwined with the lives of mother and father. Naganna's childhood was spent among the palm trees, on the fields and in the shade of the tumma groves of Yennela Dinni. He did not know how many among them had died by now in front of people's eyes, or got stuck to their beds counting their days, and continued singing and dancing like him. In fact, how was Yennela Dinni now? It came back to memory after many years.

Yellanna said he was Yerrenkadu's son. Said he was Boodevi's nephew. At that time Yerrenkadu was a very small boy. Who clung to his mother. Boodevi had not been born then. Yerrenkadu's father had been the watchman at the elder karanam's mango grove. Not just a watchman, it looked as if he practically lived there. It was a kind of bonded labour. Horrid even to think of it. Naganna was happy his father was not like that. But father too had to fell palm trees free for the karanam and cut palm fronds.

In fact, a mala or a madiga could not live in Yennela Dinni without doing bonded labour. The life of Yennela Dinni was all under the elder karanam's surveillance. It revolved around the lines he drew. Most of the vast area of Yennela Dinni was in his hands. Very little was in the hands of other castes. Though the Reddys had some land, they were just under-tenants. The other castes had a cent or a kunta, but they too were dictated by him. Malas and madigas had no land at all. People would say that Yerrenkadu's father had a piece of land on the eastern side. Perhaps so. Yerrenkadu's father would carry manure from the dump in baskets there. That's all. No other mala or madiga had any land.

The elder karanam was an extremely cruel fellow. Had no pity. No compassion. Did not have a generous nature. He had one son. And a daughter before him. He gave his daughter away to someone in Nellore region. The son-in-law had a number of *agraharams*.* In the very second year after the marriage, the son-in-law died. Collecting the money she got by selling some of the lands in the agraharams, the daughter came back to Yennela Dinni. She leased out the remaining lands.

The brahmin from Kolla Dinni would look after the monetary dealings of the karanam's daughter. There were rumours that he did not stop there. He went to the extent of making the karanam's daughter pregnant. Nobody knew what happened. One day, the Kolla Dinni brahmin died vomiting blood. After that, not even a month passed by. The karanam's daughter hanged herself. The barber Ramulu told everyone in the ooru that her body was full of wounds. Everyone knew everything. Knew that it was the elder karanam who had killed the Kolla Dinni brahmin, his own daughter and the foetus in her womb. But no one spoke out. The barber, Ramulu, who told everyone in the ooru about the wounds on the daughter's body, left the ooru and nobody knew his whereabouts. Among the barber families in Yennela Dinni, one ceased to remain there. The elder karanam did not feel bad about his daughter's husband's death. He praised the younger karanam's luck. The younger karanam did not get angry over the fact that his father had cruelly killed his sister. He counted the silver coins his sister had hidden in the chest of her poster bed. The elder karanam was elated that a precious jewel was born to him when he saw the younger karanam counting in that manner.

Father would tell the entire story, as if he were whispering into mother's ear. When he thought of the karanam, the karanam's lands and those guarding them appeared in front of his eyes.

When the first rains came, the higher-ups among the karanam's servants would come to malapalli and madigapalli. 'We have to harness the karanam's plough, one per family, come,' one of them

---

* Landed property gifted to brahmins.

would say. Karanam's fields had no boundaries. He would get the ploughs not only from Yennela Dinni but from surrounding villages, too. Ploughing would be done for a week. Ploughing and levelling would be done all at once. The entire mala and madiga families would be on the karanam's land. In the afternoon, lunch baskets would arrive. When the malas and madigas sat down in a line, trusted workers would serve them on palm leaf plates. That was their wage. Nothing more than that. The same during planting the saplings, too. For plucking the saplings, for carrying them in loads, for planting them again, only the mala and madiga families were used. They would say a man and a woman per family, but actually entire families would be there. For that too only the afternoon meal was the wage.

In some cases, it was only for the afternoon meal that families after families would go. In fact, that meal was like a *mantra*. What was surprising was that one woman would start a commotion, saying the pickle 'was served more for that one' and another would say, 'it was served more for this one.' Their bickerings would not stop at this point. The people of that house would be called all kinds of horrible names. The quarrels would sometimes lead to a fight. Sitting on the ridge, the karanam and other elders would look at all this with amusement. They would seat the malas and madigas in different rows. Each one to his caste, the karanam would say. The two castes should not come together on any issue. That was what he wanted.

No sooner was the sowing over than the watch would begin. Other castes would not come to guard the karanam's fields. A person from each home from these two castes would take turns to guard. It was the same when it came to harvesting. Even the threshing was done in that way. The wage was only an afternoon meal. But in the threshing floors alone they would be given three small baskets of grain per house as 'karanam's largesse'. After this they would let go of the grain on the threshing floor. They would fight over it. For the empty ears of grain that remained on the floor, for the hard grains hidden in the cracks of the earth, these people would vie with each other. They would go to the extent of drawing lines with their family names on the threshing floor. Even then, fights would not cease. They would not remember the bonded labour they had done during the whole year. The fight for the leftover grains on the floor would not stop in a day. The women's fight at the threshing floor would turn into something like the bazaar fights in the palles. Sometimes, the elder karanam himself would give the verdict. He would abuse and sometimes get them beaten up, saying, 'Feeling sorry, I left the grain on the threshing floor for you and you want to kill yourself fighting, you riff-raff donkeys.' It was strange. It was atrocious.

If the fight for the grain on the threshing floor had taken place independently in the mala and madiga streets, it would not have mattered. Sometimes it would take place between the two palles. Under such circumstances, the karanam himself would distribute the grain. None would even think that each one of them had a right not just on these grains but also on the grains filled up in the karanam's granary. They were asking the very same karanam who had turned their labour into bonded labour and exploited them to apportion things to them. The karanam, who was waiting for just this opportunity, would try his best to drive a permanent wedge between them. He would postpone the solution. He would wait to learn whether anyone's head had been broken. As a child in Yennela Dinni then, Naganna did not understand a thing. Now, as Urumula Naganna, he was able to understand the reality he saw.

Using the malas to beat up the madigas and the madigas to beat up the malas, the karanam would bolster their pride, saying each of their castes was great. They would fight hard.

Naganna was able to see his shape in Yennela Dinni right in front of his eyes. With the loin cloth covering his waist, too. Sometimes with just a loin cloth. Such long hair. Hair tied in a tight knot. The *bottu* prepared by mother in the coconut shell. The hair now was just like it was then. Only it had become tangled now.

The malapalli and madigapalli were on the threshold of danger in Yennela Dinni. They were near the stream. If there was flood, water would come first into those palles. The flood would break down the bank of the stream. If the harvesting began in a succession of such floods, both the palles would certainly be washed away.

Many times they thought of raising the level of the two palles. There was a mound on the vacant top of the ooru. If the palles were built there, there would be no danger. But building them there was no small matter. The upper castes would not tolerate the untouchables living on a higher plane. They would say that the malas and madigas ought always to live in the lower regions. If they lived on a higher plane, the arrogance of the upper castes would not tolerate it. That was why the desire of the malas and madigas remained just that—a desire.

In Yennela Dinni, these wretched people's lives remained mere desires. They were distraught with desires. They were ruined due to their desires.

It happened just like that with father, Narigadu. His life was ruined with desires. Only that it remained as the mala's mound. How did it come about?

At midnight it started to drizzle. It did not stop even in the morning. The day passed. It did not stop raining. The next day passed. The rain did not stop. It kept raining on the third day. The third day's rain was accompanied by wind. The wind blew on and off. Now and then it would change direction and blow. Once in a while a warm steamy wind gushed out.

An atmosphere difficult to comprehend. In fact, the rain was pouring down on the hearts of the poor in Yennela Dinni. The wind was blowing over their huts. The poles of the houses were swaying due to the wind. The mud walls were collapsing. The roofs were blowing off, twirling in the wind and falling somewhere.

There was no sign of the rain stopping soon. The wind had increased and had not come down. But in fact, it was stopping, and then blowing hard. When it stopped, it appeared as if nature stood still and as if some unimaginable fear was haunting the people. When it blew, huts and palm trees were becoming one with the earth.

In the meanwhile came thunderbolt-like news. There was fresh water flowing in the stream. The elders were running towards the stream. The fresh water was spewing foam and flowing. The water was crossing the bank. Only a month ago, there were floods that breached the bank and came up to the *Maluchchamma* tree. Once you crossed the Maluchchamma tree, there was *Yellamma's** temple.

* Yellamma, Maluchhamma and Mungamooramma are local goddesses.

Once the floods crossed Yellamma's temple, they would cross *Mungamooramma*. Then there would be no malapalli. No madigapalli. If the land between the Maluchchamma tree and Yellamma temple was flooded, the danger would be enormous.

Even at four, darkness was overpowering. A new sound was heard amidst the floods. As if it had conspired secretly with darkness, the water from the stream touched the Maluchchamma tree. As if there was a pact, the bank of the stream went on a rampage.

'No use. If it crosses Yellamma temple, both the palles will be submerged completely, Mutta,' said the mala elder.

'We should see to it that it doesn't breach, Subba,' the madiga elder joined in.

They did all they could to ensure that the flood did not cross Yellamma temple. In the roaring wind, in the heavy downpour, holding their lives in their fists, to live, to save the lives of their people, without reference to age, they chopped palm logs and placed them across as barrages, stuffed hay stacks and did all they could. Father took part in all the work. Madiga Mataiah was there with father. Those two were working, daring their lives to prevent the floods and the breach.

The breach of the bank could not be stopped. The force of the water did not diminish. It kept breaching. It kept swelling. It was ready to pounce on the palle.

In the meanwhile, the roar of the wind surprisingly stopped. It felt as if noting had happened and as if an awesome silence had encompassed the entire world. The experience caused fear. The deluge that would come after such peace stood right in front of the eyes.

Water was flowing around Yellamma temple. Mungamooramma had been submerged. There was heat in the atmosphere. Like turmoil in the ocean, the force that had been struggling to find a way out would burst in no time.

The people of both palles gathered together at one place. Children huddled close to their mothers. Cries. Shrieks.

'Let's go to the mound on the other side of the ooru.'

'The elders in the ooru will kill us.'

'The flood will drown us.'

'If the belly of the ocean bursts, there is no escaping the floods.'
Talk amidst chaos. A mad rush. Cries. Fears.

In that confusion, hurry, cries and fears, father was heard saying
aloud, 'I'm going over to the mound. Those who want may come
along.'

Everyone looked at him surprised, confused. Father carried
Naganna on his hip. Mother placed the basket on her head. Mataiah
went along with father.

'If you want to live, come along. Whoever comes in the way will
be the target of this axe . . . those who want to live, come along . .
. we'll die any way . . . Yellamma too has been submerged. Come,
come, you coward bastards . . . come on, you . . . '

When Naganna recounted the *Parasurama* story now, he
remembered father. Father who wielded the axe was in fact
Parasurama.

'Till now we had no piece of land here. Now we won't have even
our lives. I don't want to die. I want to live.'

No sooner had father taken a step, than the people got up like a
flood. As the floods chased them, they were running ahead of the
floods. If they had to go to the mound, they had to go through the
ooru. Water all around. Those who had walked till there, stopped
as if a spell was cast on them. Father turned back to look. Everyone
looked confused.

'Walk. If you want to live, walk. . . Must live. We must live . . .
walk!'

The belly of the ocean must have burst. The roaring wind had
brought along the deluge. Endless rain. Cyclonic storm. . . . For
the first time, the untouchable storm fell on the ooru. For the first
time in the life of Yennela Dinni, so many malas and madigas were
walking amidst houses of upper castes, on their paths, in the middle
of the ooru, crossing the lanes of the temples . . . walking towards
the mound.

It was indeed a cyclonic storm.

The sound of the central pillar of the temple crashing down with
a horrifying noise . . . the sound of the tiled shed of the karanam
crumbling . . . the scene of the cattle tied to wooden pegs breaking free
of their ropes and rushing about grotesquely in the raging tempest.

The real stamp of Naganna's childhood.

Ordinary masses. They have stepped on to the mound the upper castes had till then prohibited. Floods around the mound.

Even so no fear. A very high mound. In such a roaring wind, in such rain, in the awesome stormy night, getting wet, shivering, straining on hungry stomachs—on the mound, at a higher level than the upper castes. Some obstinate courage. Confidence that they would not die.

That night passed by.

When they looked from the mound in the morning, it appeared as if malapalli and madigapalli had been washed away. Water everywhere . . .

Nothing is more of a cheat than nature. The sun was shining as if nothing had happened.

They poured the rice they had carried in baskets, pots and boxes in one place.

Father spread out his pancha.

Madiga Matiah collected and poured the rice there.

Subbaiah thatha took out the flint stone. No matter how much he struck it, there was no fire. Muthaiah took over. As he kept striking, it lit up. There was fire. With that fire even wet wood would burn. If only there was fire, there was no question of not burning.

What they cooked, what they ate, they did not know. They ate. They ate together. The two ate together. When Subbaiah thatha coughed, Muthaiah thatha patted him on his head. When Muthaiah thatha had hiccups, Subbaiah thatha gave him water. It might have been flood water. He gave him water. Sometimes tragedy could be wonderful.

It looked as if the rain had stopped completely. In the ooru, people gathered around the central pillar that had collapsed. Those who had climbed on to the wall of the temple seemed to have looked towards the mound. Did not know what they said. One after the other they climbed the temple wall and looked round.

The day went by.

The water had retreated as hurriedly as it had rushed in forcefully—having wiped out the malapalli and madigapalli, it had left a pole standing here and a pole standing there, as if to say that people lived here till yesterday.

It seemed strange at night on the mound. They lit a fire for the sake of light. Women, old people, and children, around the fire. As for the younger people, they sat away from it. The rice they brought along was enough for the morning. As they had eaten late, they did not feel hungry yet. But as the night went along, they started feeling hungry. With what was left, they fed the children. Unable to resist sleep, they slept on the wet ground.

When he looked for father, he was not there in the crowd.

'Ayya!' he cried out.

'But yes. Where is Narigadu? . . . ' someone else asked.

'Mataiah and he went that side. Must be to relieve themselves,' someone said.

Subbaiah thatha looked around.

Muthaiah thatha rose up to his full height and looked.

Both searched the entire mound. Not just father and Mataiah, two more of that age group were also missing.

'Where could they have gone?'

All around, wherever they looked, water . . .

If they got down from the mound, water up to the waist. Pits in between. The entire Dinni was full of ups and downs. In the floods one could not make out which high portion had been washed away and which low-lying area had gained height.

'Wretched rascals. Where the hell have they gone without informing?'

The night was receding. Everyone came to know about the four of them. Anxiety in everyone. Mother was looking perplexed.

When there was commotion in the water, all of them looked in that direction. As the noise neared they looked out eagerly. It appeared as if far away four shapes were coming along, pushing through the water. As the four shapes approached, it was clear how heavily they were trudging along. On the shoulders of the four, gunny sacks. They climbed the mound, threw the gunny sacks on the ground and sat down tired. Everyone was looking surprised.

'What's this, Nariga?'

'Rice.'

'From where?'

'From the sahukar's shop.'

'That means. . . ?'

'Light the fire. Have to live. That's all. We've to live. Our children have to live. Light the fire.'

No one spoke. The fire was lit. After cooking, they woke up those who were sleeping. At midnight everyone ate greedily.

The sky was peaceful. The water had receded by an elbow length from the stick planted at the foot of the mound. The stream was drawing it in quickly.

After everyone slept, when the pedda mala, the pedda madiga and a few others were still there, Mataiah said, 'The elders in the ooru had a meeting.'

'The sahukar too was at the meeting.'

'Even when we broke open the lock of the shop, his wife and children did not wake up.'

'If they had got up?'

'. . .'

'The meeting must be about us.'

'Anything may happen.'

'Let's die, let's die here.'

'If any one moves from here. . . . , we'll bury whoever moves right here.'

Both the elders looked in fear. The karanam was a cruel man. Experience was making them all the more scared.

'We aren't born only to die . . . '

'They tell us not to live on heights. The stream tells us not to live on low-lying areas. If we come to the top, they'll kill us. If we are in the lower areas, the stream will kill us. No matter what, death is inescapable. But . . . listen . . . listen to our words. We aren't born only to die.'

'That means. . . ?'

'We are also born to kill.'

Father and Mataiah said the last words in one voice. Though children of his age were sleeping, Naganna could not sleep. He sat near father. He sat yawning. He was on this side of father. Mataiah on the other side. Between the two of them, an axe. A knife that can butcher cattle.

'If rain hadn't come, if floods hadn't come, if the stream hadn't breached and Mungamooramma hadn't been submerged, not one would have come here if we had asked them. Floods chased us. Floods united us. All of us moved together. We can live here . . . '

'It felt strange when so many of us walked through the ooru. They had remained in the houses due to the storm. Otherwise, wonder what it would have been like!'

'How would it be? If there had been no storm, would we have walked amidst their houses to know how it would be!'

Laughter.

It was morning.

The water had receded. The banks were visible here and there. Because it was sandy soil, though there was so much water, it was not slushy. White sand mounds as if nothing had happened.

The real story began now. The karanam did not come atop the mound. The sahukar did not come. They did not know what was decided at the meeting . . .

But . . .

Everything was over on the second day. No idea how it happened. Father who had gone in search of sticks for the huts did not return. Came back a corpse. Mataiah brought him on his shoulders.

'"I'll look for the sticks. You look for the leaves, Mata", he said. After collecting the leaves, I looked out for him for a long time, he didn't come . . . When I went towards the forest, at the turning to the forest, he was lying in a pool of blood . . . '

The crowd that had gathered around the corpse wailed. They beat their chests.

'Narigadu didn't die . . . my brother . . . didn't die . . . he didn't die! . . . ' Mataiah was crying out loud.

Mother had collapsed on the ground quite some time ago.

On the third day, the crowd on the mound had scattered. Everyone knew how father had died. Everyone knew who had killed him. But no one spoke out. Had no strength to speak. Narigadu who had the strength had died. Mataiah who had the strength was roaming around muttering, 'He's not dead. He's not dead.'

The huts sprung up in the old place itself. Mother remained in a state of shock. She remained looking at the ones building the huts. They also built a hut in the name of father.

Together, all of them performed father's last rites. But Mataiah continued to say, 'He's not dead . . . he's not dead . . .'

But he was not seen from that night on. No one knew where he went. No matter how much they searched, father's axe, too, could not be found.

As Mataiah said, father did not die, Narigadu did not die. Even now, 'Mala's mound' stood just like that in Yennela Dinni.

For a long time it was rumoured that a mala was roaming around there like a ghost. No idea how the mound was like now. Could be dense with palm trees. No idea whether they would pluck those fruits or not. No idea whether they would cut the fronds. No idea whether they would draw out the toddy. The mala's mound existed without malas being there.

You tear up your guts, they would only fall at your feet.

True. All tearing up. Guts being torn up.

A month after father's death, it became necessary to bid farewell to Yennela Dinni. When the southern people were going north for harvesting, mother, too, joined them. The elders of Yennela Dinni asked her to stay back. Mother said she would go for a little while and come back.

When he was leaving Yennela Dinni, he cried a lot. He felt uneasy leaving father, palm trees, ridges of the rice field, crabs running, tumma grove and everything else. Felt as if his childhood came to an end in Yennela Dinni.

'We'll come back, Naga.' Mother said. As she said it, she stuffed the end of her saree in her mouth.

They went around Yelamma temple. They bowed to Maluchchamma tree. When they were crossing the field ridges, a crab was running. He held it carefully. Equally carefully, he left it down the ridge. It started to run. He could not stop laughing. That was the last memory. The last emotional bond with Yennela Dinni was the running crab.

Did not think the journey north would distance him from Yennela Dinni permanently. Came to know Urumula Chandrappa there. Better to say he entered mother's life than to say he came to know

him. He came for Ganga Jatara. Even after the jatara was over, he did
not go.

One night when he got up from sleep, he saw Chandrappa sitting
in front of the lamp and telling mother something. Next morning a
bullock cart stopped in front of the shed they lived in.

'Get in, Naganna.'

Did not ask where to. Got on to the cart. Mother, too, sat down.
Chandrappa sat near the bullocks. The cart crossed the village. After
crossing two or three such villages, they got down from the cart. The
cart went back. Did not know which village it was. Mother cooked
next to the Rama temple. They slept there itself that night. Walking,
getting on to the cart, sleeping at night at some place or the other,
they reached Dharmaram. That was Chandrappa's birth place. That
was the place where Urumula Chandrappa grew up.

Naganna grew up there. Grew up to a marriageable age. Got
married. After Ramulu came to live with him, mother passed away
happily. As if she had completed her work, as if she had nothing
more to do, she bade goodbye to Dharmaram, as she had done to
Yennela Dinni. But this was a permanent farewell.

When mother passed away, Chandrappa remained with her. He
sat right next to her. Mother died in Chandrappa's lap.

Ramulu became pregnant. Chandrappa said they would call the
child Latchimi if it was a girl. 'What if it is a boy?' said Naganna. He
said he would name him Naraiah.

Life had decided to make him a lonely man. Chandrappa died.
Unable to deliver, Ramulu died. The child in the womb, too, died
along with the mother.

All this while, he spent his time amidst the sound of thunder. His
life was filled with Gangamma's song. Was filled with the excitement
of the vermilion dance. When he had nothing to do, inexplicable
pain and fear would haunt him. Mother, father, Chandrappa,
Ramulu and the stillborn child would haunt him. That was why he
did not give respite to the moving feet, the roaring thunder and the
singing mouth.

Now when he saw Yellanna, he did not know why, but he felt
tired. He felt like talking to him at leisure.

He felt like telling Yellanna the *puranic* secrets Chandrappa had told him. He felt like sharing with Yellanna the steps and movements Chandrappa had taught him. Yennela Dinni had chased away this child only for him. Naganna thought that he had come searching for him alone.

When Yellanna talked at night, Boodevi's name was heard repeatedly in his words. He did not mention his father's name that many times. Did not mention mother's name that many times. He would not come with him to Dharmaram leaving Boodevi behind. Not sure if he would come. Did not know why. Felt as if the Naganna of yesterday was not there this morning. Felt as if he could no longer tolerate the loneliness of being without any relationships, for those bonds had been severed. Yellanna reminded him again of his childhood.

The dusky darkness had not yet passed. Naganna felt like walking towards the fields of 'Pakkela Dinni'. He felt as if this tiredness would not go unless he sat under a tree and drank half a pot of the toddy just tapped. No sooner had he taken a step, than he felt as if Yellanna had got off the cot. When he turned back, Yellanna had not just got up from sleep but had come near him.

They walked towards the fields in the dusky darkness.

'You've walked a long way, my child.'

'I don't know. Don't know if I walked or ran. Don't know anything.'

'Will you learn to dance?'

'I know.'

Naganna burst into peals of laughter. It appeared as if the dusky darkness was running away due to that laughter.

'Can you also sing?'

'Attha taught me.'

'Okay, will you learn Urumu?'

'I'll learn . . . but, aunt doesn't know.'

Naganna laughed again. Birds that were tasting dew on the blade of grass flew away in a flutter.

'I'll teach you. Will you come to Dharmaram?'

Yellanna did not speak. Naganna stopped near the toddy tree. He saw the toddy tapper bringing down the toddy pot.

Having the tapped toddy poured into the frond, Naganna looked at Yellanna as he was about to drink.

'Will you drink?'

'I drink only the "juice".'

Immediately, he remembered his childhood. Father who had brought down the toddy pot. He who looked forward to the 'juice.' His mother. Tears filled his eyes. Naganna put his fingers through Yellanna's hair and caressed it affectionately.

The tapper brought the 'juice' pot that was kept under another tree. He poured it into the frond and gave it to Yellanna.

'How's it?'

'Sweet.'

'Drink . . . not just once . . . as much as you want.'

Now there was not even dusky darkness. Mild sunlight was spreading across the fields.

Naganna, walking on the bank, stopped near the crab holes.

'Let's make a conch necklace.'

He kept looking at Yellanna who said those words. He drew him close affectionately.

'When I was young I caught a lot of them with conch necklaces. Now I gave it up . . . Leaving Yennela Dinni, I left the crab I had caught . . .'

'Do you know Yennela Dinni?'

'I was born there.'

Yellanna looked at him in surprise. Naganna began his story. The story did not end even when they reached home.

The elder from Pakkela Dinni's malapalli said they had to stay that day to collect the fee for the dance. They killed the hen that afternoon. Brought toddy. Fell asleep. By the time he got up, Yellanna was sleeping with his legs on his tummy. He caressed his feet. How wonderful his feet, he thought! As if made to a measure. These were not feet, they were the sound of steps that did not miss a beat.

Yellanna when he got up talked about his aunt. He said aunt would be crying for him. He wept wanting to see his aunt.

The moon was seen in the sky. Looking towards it, Naganna shut his eyes tight and asked Yellanna to come forward. When Yellanna came in front of him he opened his eyes and looked at Yellanna's face.

'Attha too is like this.'

In the pale moonlight, they walked towards the field ridges. They sat in front of each other on the ridge. As if he had made some decisions in his mind, Naganna looked into Yellanna's eyes.

'We'll go to Yennela Dinni when it's dark.'

Yellanna looked on happily.

Suddenly the yennela pitta shot through making a noise.

'Wretched bird. Doesn't let us sit in peace. When the moon comes up, that's it . . . how proud it is! Proud bird.'

But Yellanna kept looking at the yennela pitta that was flying away, raising a din.

Felt as if it was going towards Yennela Dinni.

How would Yennela Dinni be now, thought Naganna.

Poor aunt would be crying in Yennela Dinni, thought Yellanna.

Did not know how far the yennela pitta went. But its call was still being heard.

Many years later, this happened.

As Ruth heard it, as Reuben imitated it . . .

5

Ruth feels as if Naganna and Yellanna who were walking in the hazy morning light, stamping on the dew-filled grass on the road to Yennela Dinni, are walking right in front of her eyes.

In Ruth's words, that is a beautiful scene. A wonderful journey. One of them is known. The other needs to be introduced. That recognition has not come so easily. That introduction is not all that easy. Unless they have a lot of worth, people of those castes do not get recognised. They are not lucky enough to be well known. Many artists were buried in the depths of the past. There are no records that history has made a note of them in its pages. In this country caste is more important than art. Art is also weighed in the scale of caste. As for those of certain castes, not just being not weighed, they have not even been allowed near the scale.

Ruth thinks. Thinks over and over again. So many songs have taken birth on this earth. Who poured life into those songs? Who gave the tune to those songs? Why don't researchers and historians think a bit carefully?

They ploughed the fields. Made beds. Watered them. Plucked weeds. Protected the cobs. Harvested the crop. Prepared the threshing floor. Threshed the grain. Heaped them. Separated the chaff from the grain. They did everything. Half hungry, under the stars in the sky, on sand mounds, folding their knees into their bellies, they slept. They did not get hold of the fields. They did not get hold of the field beds. The grains did not belong to them. Without anything belonging to them, they rained sweat on the earth. Like that, they were kept cruelly away from the fruit of their toil.

The song was born from every work done on the earth. Planting saplings, plucking weeds, harvesting the crop and labouring, the coolie mother sang. To forget hunger, to forget the child crying out for milk, to forget the pain of the bent back, the pallavi was heard from the silent voice. Distributed charanams through toil. A coolie mother, a mala mother, a madiga mother. Hundreds repeated after that pallavi. Hundred voices sounded like one voice. What did they call that song? Called it a village song. Said it was a duet. Said that the folk song was immortal.

Ruth speaks. Says it does not matter what people think about her saying this. She asks us to mark the words in those village songs. Analyse them. She says only those words that come out of that life roll out vibrantly.

Planting the saplings, they sang the sowing songs. Plucking the weeds, they sang the plucking songs. Reaping the harvest, they sang the harvest songs. They hid life in those songs. They made them voice love, sexuality, humour, compassion, not artificially like great poets wrote, but very naturally like air, water, sun, moon and stars.

Just as the land they toiled on did not belong to them, why has this wide knowledge become so narrow as not to acknowledge that it is they who wove those songs that have survived? What is surprising is that there is no shame for being narrow-minded. This attitude rules the literary world proudly.

Ruth remembers. That in those days Yenki-Nayudu *bava*[3] enjoyed great popularity. It is there till today. If she were alive, in the last days of her completing a centenary too, Yenki and Naidu bava will remain a symbol of Teluguness. Perhaps so. There is nothing sinful or wrong about it. But which stars in the sky have swallowed Subbi, Koti, Lachchi, Maremma etc., who sweated out on the vast universe to weave words and songs? Which vicious snakes bit them?

Ruth says these are not questions. Ruth says there is no need to look for answers to these questions. But she only feels bad that recognition and awareness have all turned one-sided. She detests it only for its remaining such a hatred. In truth her memories are only representations of that pain and hatred.

'All of it happened like that. It really happened like that. Nagannas and Yellannas did not go after recognition. Didn't dance to be known. Didn't sing. Art was in their veins. In their blood. In the depths of their hearts. In their very sweat.'

Reuben used to repeatedly tell those words to Ruth.

'Naganna used to think his dance was only to worship Ganga. Only to please Siva, he thought. He was under the illusion that the roar of thunder that touched the heart and reverberated in nature was to bring down Ganga. His rhythmic beats and expressions of emotion, all stopped there in the jataras. But every bit of the 'puranic secrets' that Chandrappa told him, the words that Naganna spoke whenever necessary, were only to say that he and his people were not any less. What was visible in him then was revolt. He may not even be aware that it was revolt. But it was definitely a revolt.'

Reuben analysed Naganna thus. Ruth thinks that that is true. If we proceed a little further, we will feel Ruth's belief is true. In front of the eyes, Naganna.

When they reached the outskirts of Yennela Dinni, Naganna stopped and looked. The village of his childhood. After many years, he was stepping there. When he left, he had gone with mother. When he came back, he came as companion to Yellana. That day he tied his childhood in a bundle and left. Today he was coming back carrying pain and loneliness. They crossed the stream.

'Let's sit down there, my child.'

Yellanna sat down. This bank. The bank of Yennela Dinni's stream. Naganna sat against the tree. He shut his eyes tight. Yellanna did not know what emotions were overpowering his heart. All that Yellanna knew was the eagerness to hide in aunt's lap.

'Let's go.'

Naganna opened his eyes and saw. Yellanna was anxious to see his aunt.

'We'll go, my child.' Saying this he broke a tumma twig. He asked Yellanna to brush his teeth. He asked him to go behind a tree if he needed to relieve himself. He hid behind the mound as he brushed his teeth.

As he was dipping into the Yennela Dinni stream, Naganna remembered father. He used to ask his father to hold his nose saying he would slide into the water with nose closed like a fish. Father would search for him here and there. As if he could not find him, he would say, 'Where are you?' Saying 'Here!' Naganna would jump up and climb on to his father's shoulders. Father would carry him like that to the shore. He would sit in the mild sun till his body dried. As he sat like that, in the sand under his feet crabs would move about. If he kept his feet like that and caught them, they would bite him. If he moved his feet, they would run away. If he chased them, the tiny little crabs that hid themselves in sand would run; not one, but hundreds of them. As if a mat had been woven, the tiny little crabs' running would look strange. They would in a line become one with the water. That was a game. . . . The childhood that belonged to the earth hid such wonders. In truth, that was something wonderful!

'I will stop for the sun.'

Saying that, Yellanna got on to the bank. Naganna, too, came on to the bank. He took the sacred ash from the cloth bag. Put it on the forehead. Smeared it on the throat. Yellanna looked on.

6

From the day Yellanna had left, Boodevi had not eaten. Those who were searching were continuing to search. Yenkatanarsu who had gone with a bundle of clothes had come back that day. Throwing the bundle down, he had been searching for Yellanna from that day on. Boodevi had asked him not to come home until he brought Yellanna back. That was what she told Yerrenkadu too. Taking her sister-in-law along, she looked around in all places she could.

What happened near the yerra gollalu's tents spread to malapalli by word of mouth. Those who had chased Yellanna talked enthusiastically about their chasing him. That, too, came to be known. Coming to know of it, Boodevi was not able to tolerate it. She set out saying she would see the end of them. Elders dissuaded her. People of her age group restrained her. Then she shouted and commanded them, 'Bring my child back.' She berated the elders, wondering how they could be called elders. But nothing happened. There was no sign of pride in the elders. There was no movement in people of her age group. She said that if she did not find Yellanna, she would put an end to those who had chased him away. She said she would turn their lives to ashes. Yerrenkadu stood listening to those words. Yenkatanarsu was afraid of the lengths to which Boodevi wanted to go. That night the two of them did not sleep. They stood guard in front of the house.

If Boodevi was bent on doing something, she would go to any lengths. She would not care what would happen later. Yerrenkadu knew that quite well. The pedda mala told Yenkatanarsu, 'Restrain her mouth.' The pedda mala knew how dangerous it would be if her words reached the meeting place. Yenkatanarsu panicked at the pedda mala's warning. But there was no stopping Boodevi's mouth. Mothers and sisters said she had gone mad. Coming to know that the pedda mala wanted her to control her mouth, she went towards his house. The pedda mala snarled at her. He said, 'If you keep abusing like that, the entire malapalli will turn to ashes.' Boodevi answered him word for word. She said, the palle would turn to ashes if it had elders like him. She did not stop at that. She abused the ones who beat up Yellanna by name. When she abused the pedda mala, his pride was hurt. If she abused the people in the ooru, he would tremble with fear. This problem reached its height right in the middle of the palle. Yenkatanarsu felt there was no point now. He pulled Boodevi by her hair. He fell on her like one enraged and kept beating her. Actually, Yenkatanarsu was not angry with Boodevi. He was scared as to what would happen if the elders of the ooru heard these words. That fear made him crazy. Yerrenkadu remained watching. Till now, Boodevi had never been beaten. But now she received a beating. What did she do to get that beating? His eyes filled with tears. He was a coward. Actually *he* should have uttered the words she did. If he could, he should have done something to those who had chased away his child. If someone from his caste had done this, how angrily he would have responded to that family! What indignation he would have demonstrated! He felt disgusted with himself. Bent his head down.

Yenkatanarsu's crazy rage had not abated yet. Did not know what he would have done if Lingalu had not prevented him. Lingalu stood between them. She felt bad at seeing her sister-in-law beaten. She cried her heart out for Yellanna. More than that, she could not tolerate the lashing on her sister-in-law's back. Boodevi was not just her sister-in-law. Like her unborn child. Or like a mother. She was fighting for her child. Did not know what it would have been like if one man from malapalli had talked like Boodevi but Boodevi was greater than all of them.

'What did she say, my sister-in-law . . . when all the men are cowardly, my child spoke. Not just my child, I, too, am speaking . . . kill me too. She's Yelladu's daughter. Subbadu's granddaughter. Not cowardly . . . '

Yenkatanarsu looked at her stunned. He now realised how he had behaved. Yerrenkadu had beaten Lingalu many times. But was unable to beat her now. He was not just a coward. He was a thoroughly useless fellow. Lingalu lifted her sister-in-law up. She sat in front of her sister-in-law inside the house.

That night there was a meeting in the middle of the palle. In the meeting, there was more discussion about Boodevi abusing the pedda mala than of Yellanna. More than that Boodevi had abused the ooru elders. The discussion was about what to say if word reached the ooru. Yerrenkadu was not there at the discussion. Yenkatanarsu was not there. When they were asked to come to the meeting, they refused. Yenkatanarsu lay on the cot in front of the house. Yerrenkadu sat on the mound. A man came from the meeting and said, 'They are asking you to come.' When they were called a second time, they could not refuse to go. That would be considered wrong in their caste. They looked into the house. Boodevi sat, resting her back against the pole. Neither one of them had the courage to say they were going to the meeting. They got up with the intention of going. No sooner had they taken a couple of steps than they heard Boodevi crying. They met Lingalu who was coming to her sister-in-law's house after cooking food in her place. She did not speak to the men. She heard her sister-in-law crying. She went straight into the house.

As if they were waiting only for these two, the elders at the meeting said, 'Come, sit down.' They said, 'Why did Yellanna go like that? If he hadn't, would all this have happened?' Yenkatanarsu did not speak. Yerrenkadu did not speak. For a while each said something about this. Some said, 'He is a small boy. What does he know?' Some said, 'When they beat him, it would have been good if he had come home.'

'What would we have done had he come home?'

Yerrenkadu did not say those words. Yenkatanarsu did not say them either.

The pedda mala looked around as if to ask who said those words. The other caste elders also looked on.

"Why did you go, you wretched rascal!'—saying this Yerrenkadu *mama* would have given him a few kicks. The elders would have shouted, 'Never go like that and invite trouble'.'

It was the same voice heard again.

'Who's that fellow? Come forward and speak.'

Pittodu who was sitting in a corner in the dark came forward. Yenkatanarsu looked at Pittodu in surprise. Yerrenkadu thought that if there was a real man in Yennela Dinni, it was Pittodu alone.

Pittodu, who had come forward, looked directly at the pedda mala. He looked at others as if to greet them. He reminded them how Boodevi had beaten her own chest and mouth and cried the child was nowhere to be seen. All had asked why he had gone near the tents but why had no one tried to find out what happened, he questioned. They had come to know how he went, and why he ran. He asked whether any of these elders had the courage to question those responsible for the boy's act once they knew what had happened. He berated them and asked them how it was wrong of the woman who had lost her nephew to abuse them.

Pittodu spoke sharply. The elders could not swallow his words. Youngsters sat down more comfortably. They felt as if they themselves were asking these questions. Yenkatanarsu thought he was not saying anything wrong.

Pittodu was thought of as a firebrand. He did not have a good name among the elders. He would speak without mincing words. Actually, they would not have called him to the meeting. Even if he was not called, he would come and sit there. He would not keep quiet when the elders were speaking. He would get up hurling obscenities at them. The crowd would pull him away in the middle of it all. He would leave saying, 'Die, you bastards. Die your deaths.' This would happen at every meeting. But this time he did not go away like that. He did not speak obscenities. He spoke something that stayed in each one's heart: 'If Narayi mama were alive, he would have hacked those bastards to death.'

The elders were startled by those words. They remembered Narigadu. The mala's mound was just like that. The youngsters had heard of Narigadu. Now Yellanna was not a part of the meeting. Boodevi was not there. Narigadu remained. The ghost of the mala's mound hovered over the meeting. It made the pedda mala who was conducting the meeting lose his sleep.

Though the pedda mala went home, he kept remembering Pittodu's words. He had told the truth. There are Naraiahs among malas and madigas. There are Mataiahs. Everyone was not, as Boodevi called them, cowards. Not all were those who went around with bent heads. Actually, the pedda mala did not like going with a bent head. He would have wanted to walk with his head held high. But when he saw people from the ooru, his head would bend down of its own accord. The feet which till then had walked freely would step aside. The walk would turn into that of a sick person. He did not like his walk changing like that. His father was the pedda mala before him. Thick moustaches. They used to call him Moustachioed Subbadu. Definitely, he bent down a bit on the day Narigadu died. As he grew older he grew thin like a stick. He was then middle-aged. He was as old as Narigadu. He always thought of Narigadu. Was a courageous man. Was stubborn. As for Mataiah, the same determination, the same verve.

It was about ten years since Narigadu died. There were rumours that a ghost was wandering about on the mala's mound. It was abandoned. So many years after the death, they wondered what the rumours were in malapalli and madigapalli. As it was a village, the rumours took a different shape each day. At midnight some tall man would roam around with an axe. He would merge with the darkness. He would walk till the karanam's mound. At the turn of the stream, there were whirlpools. He would drown in those whirlpools. He would not be seen again. It would happen like that sometimes. Sometimes, it would happen twice a week. Another time once a month. For a while such a thing would not happen at all. Lots of stories were circulated. There were those who thought that Narigadu had turned into a ghost and was roaming around. There were those who would say that they heard the sound of him holding an axe and felling a tree. Once in a while, they would say that it felt as if he was rushing towards the karanam's cattle shed. They would say he jumped over a thick bush in front of the karanam's house and ran away. The stories took a different shape each day.

They would crowd together in hordes and say that when the sahukar was coming with the things from the fair, he felt someone was hiding in the middle of the tumma grove, turned around, spotted a dark shape coming from the grove, jumped out of the cart and ran, and when he went back for the cart, it was there just like that; he felt if it were a thief, the things would not have been there, and so it must most definitely be the ghost of the mala's mound. Did not know what happened there but the sahukar was laid up in bed with fever due to shock. Those who cast spells, cast a spell around the house. For a couple of days, there was a lot of hue and cry in the sahukar's house.

Another story that went around caused more excitement than this. As that happened to the karanam, it caused a lot of commotion. When the elder karanam was coming from the cattle shed of the eastern fields at midnight someone chased him. The elder karanam fled. He was terrified. But he repeatedly said at the meeting that nothing like that happened. Not that there was no reason to say that. He felt that his amorous dealings at that hour would be exposed.

But because the karanam said no, everyone had to nod their heads in front of him. Later they laughed and talked about it in his absence.

But the elder karanam's son, the younger karanam, did not take it lightly. He attacked the elder karanam. Not even caring that he was his father, he threatened to kill and bury him if he had amorous affairs at his age. He had kept a watch over the elder karanam so that he could not go out at nights. He called the elders of the ooru. He said that this was not like a ghost story to him. The elders said that for whatever it was worth, it was better to call the big sorcerer. The younger karanam did not ignore the elders' words. He did follow their advice. But he did not refrain from carrying out his plan. He gathered the youngsters of the ooru. After a certain hour, ten people would patrol each direction. The strange news that young men of Yennela Dinni were patrolling at night spread to the neighbouring places. When someone from Yennela Dinni went to the neighbouring place, people would surround him. The same news—about the patrol. Even at the fields, more than one would keep watch. At each place two or three malas and madigas would be on guard. Once the watch began, real fear overtook everyone.

No one knew what happened but there was no sign of the ghost for a long time. The elders said that this was due to the greatness of the big sorcerer. The youngsters said it was because of the watch. Five years went by. The pedda mala's father passed away. The younger karanam got married. There were no other significant incidents to report in Yennela Dinni. Except that there were a few changes on the land. The younger karanam sold some of the lands in Yennela Dinni to the tenant farmers. After a few farmers bought the lands from the karanam in Yennela Dinni, they became small-time landlords. Except for those few, the rest of the people's lives were as before. There was a difference in their behaviour. During the jataras they began to stand a little in front. If that was the change in the ooru, there was a different kind of change in malapalli and madigapalli. They did not know why it happened like that. Apart from doing bonded labour for the karanam, the two palles were being referred to by the names of the small-time landlords. Not only were they called such and such a Reddy's mala or such and such a Reddy's madiga, they were also being divided on those lines. That was to say the two palles had to work according to the old norms on the karanam's fields. As for the others, a particular Reddy's mala or a Reddy's madiga had to work in each of their Reddy's fields.

It was then that some unforeseen incident occurred. The younger karanam had not thought that would happen. The elder karanam did not think so. The small-time Reddys who were just being counted in the list of important people did not think so. Among the farmers, Subbireddy and Atchireddy did not think of it at all. It happened. The entire region . . . it happened as quickly as one stopping to take a deep breath.

This was how the incident took place. It was more than a week since the younger karanam had gone to his in-laws' place. The news had also reached that it would not be possible for him to return for another week. The elder karanam sat in the meeting till late in the evening. Then he came up to the house in the company of Subbireddy and Atchireddy. These days, Atchireddy was going about like that. It felt like a status symbol to him. He was taking care of the tenancy and handing it back to the farmers. In other words, after the younger karanam it was Atchireddy's name that was spoken first in the ooru. This would appear strange to Atchireddy sometimes. At times, he would feel proud. The farmers, who would stand up when the elder karanam and the younger karanam passed by, would also stand when Atchireddy passed by.

'Now, you may go, Reddy,' said the elder karanam as he did everyday. Atchireddy left, bidding goodbye. The elder karanam did not go inside the house. He walked as a matter of routine towards the eastern field near the cattle shed. It had become a habit to go there when the younger karanam was not in the ooru. They say the amorous nature that comes with birth will not leave till death.

The cattle-sheds in the eastern field were on the stream bank. Though they were supposed to be cattle sheds, cattle were never kept there except during summer. In front of the sheds, the banyan tree with hanging branches occupied about a kunta of land. They would tie the cattle under its shade during day time. The karanam's shore was under the shade of the banyan tree. If you crossed the karanam's shore and went on to the other side, there was a mile-long palm grove. The palm trees too were dense. A buffalo with horns would get caught somewhere in there.

They said that the brahmin from Kolla Dinni who was close to the elder karanam's daughter was killed there. Not just him, but many lives stopped seeing the light of day there. Better to say that the karanam saw to it that they never saw the light of day rather than say they never saw the light of day. The cattle shed of the eastern field, the karanam's shore and the palm grove in front of the shore present a sort of fearsome scenes. At such a late hour, only the elder karanam could go there all by himself. At such a late hour, only Atchireddy's mother could wait for the karanam under the banyan tree.

For many years now, Atchireddy's mother had been sitting under the banyan tree at an unearthly hour. She would sit there for the karanam. She sat when Atchireddy was a small child. She sat there when he worked as a young boy in the elder karanam's fields. She sat there like that, after his marriage, when he took the karanam's lands on lease and was an under-tenant. She had to squat there even when the younger karanam sold the land and he became the owner of two acres. Sitting like a little ghost, under the banyan tree, on the edge of the karanam's shore, at an unearthly hour when no man dared to come, she sat waiting for the elder karanam.

Her husband, Peddireddy Subbireddy, was not a man to be taken lightly. He was a bull-like man. He would slog like oxen. He used to graze cattle in the Nallamala Hills. Had land to live on. Rugged land. The yield, nominal. Of little use. Found it difficult to survive. He went out into the world driving his cattle. Atchireddy was a tiny tot. Selling the cattle,[4] he tried to find a living. On the way, sweet potato carts[5] joined him. Those carts came to Yennela Dinni. They came with those carts to Yennela Dinni. The karanam bought the good ones among the cattle. He sold the useless ones to the madigas. The karanam looked Subbireddy up and down. Asked his name. Subbireddy told him. Said his wife's name was Rangayi. The karanam looked on benignly. He asked him to work for him. He gave wood to build his hut. He asked him to take the leaves from his trees. He appeared like God. Subbireddy kept the money he got from selling the cattle with the karanam.

Peddireddy Subbireddy was reduced to a servant. His cattle became the karanam's cattle. He used to graze them along with the karanam's cattle in the karanam's wastelands. Rangayi looked after all the work at the cattle shed. Whenever Subbireddy took his salary he would keep it with the karanam. He never asked him how much there was. The karanam too never said how much there was. Time was proceeding on its own.

One day, Rangayi asked Subbireddy to settle the accounts. She said they should go back to their village. Subbireddy was unable to say no to his wife. He asked the karanam for the accounts. The karanam looked surprised. For the first time he came across a servant who asked for the accounts. Subbireddy appeared strange. This strange feeling had never been a part of the karanam's experience. Was unable to stomach it. He had never known a strange person like Subbireddi before. He should not have known such a person. Not just now. Should never happen.

'The woman is adamant.'

The karanam did not speak.

Subbireddy was staring at the ground and the karanam looked towards Subbireddy. He kept looking like that for a long time. After this, he said they could see the accounts the next day.

The karanam looked into the accounts the next day. There was no Subbireddy to take the money. He slept at night in the cattle shed. The next morning he was found dead due to snakebite.

His co-workers were not surprised that there were no marks of snakebite. Rangayi did not say that the throat was dark as if someone had strangled him to death. She saw in the karanam's accounts the additions and subtractions for Atchireddy. That was it. In front of her eyes, Subbireddy was burning in the flames. Their shared life too was burnt in those flames. What remained were the ashes of the crematorium. That was the life under the dark banyan tree. When she sat under the tree, she wished that the reptiles would bite the karanam on the way. But no reptile would bite the karanam. During the recent ghost incident, she hoped that the ghost may strangle him. But she thought the ghost was a lie. Even when she sat here at midnight, nothing happened. No terrible ghost was seen in the palm grove either. There could be no greater ghost than the karanam.

The karanam himself was a big ghost. She thought so many times. Thinking like that, she lifted her head and saw.

The man in front was not the karanam. The karanam did not have a beard. He would not appear so dark even in darkness. In fact, there would be no axe in the karanam's hand.

Before she could figure out who it was, the karanam came.

It was then that the incident took place. The incident that shook up all villages. The incident that spread the name of Yennela Dinni to each and every village.

It happened then . . .

The incident of the elder karanam's head being chopped off by madiga Mataiah's axe.

As Rangayi was witness.

As the dark banyan tree was witness.

As the karanam's shore and palmgrove were witnesses . . .

Rangayi became dumbstruck. Became as dumb as the banyan tree. As dumb as the shore. As dumb as the palmgrove. That dumbness frightened Mataiah.

'He killed Narigadu. He died in my hands now.' He felt like saying this. He looked straight at Rangayi. Rangayi was looking silently. Looking like a dumb person. He decided not to. He decided not to say anything. Both the palles appeared before his eyes. That was why he decided not to say anything. But Mataiah did not know that in Rangayi's silence, in Rangayi's dumbness, Mataiah's figure seemed like the figure of God. Mataiah was not a ghost. Mataiah was God.

Mataiah went away just as quickly as he had completed his job. He went straight to malapalli. He stopped next to the pedda mala's cot. He patted and woke him up. The pedda mala got up irritably. He did not at first recognise the man standing in front of him. Then he recognised Mataiah. After many years. He had gone away saying, 'He didn't die. He didn't die.' He had come back now. Had changed a lot. The pedda mala asked him to sit down. Mataiah did not sit down. He said they should go to a secluded place. Both came out. Sat on the stream bank.

The night stars were twinkling. Fireflies were rushing past like bright diamonds. Fish that were swimming against the current were jumping very high. A little distance away, on the edge of the bank where the two were sitting, the thin stream that was flowing over the pebbles was making a strange sound that appeared to be close by. In truth, nature that night was not silent. Not dark. It was its usual self, like stars, like fireflies, like fish swimming and jumping up against the current, and like the water-music nature had created for itself. Otherwise, it was like the echo born out of the depths of the heart of a courageous man.

Then Mataiah narrated all that had happened. The pedda mala listened. Mataiah's words produced fear in him. Mataiah's words infuriated him. Mataiah's words appeared as if they had tugged at his nerves and let them go. Did not know why but they made him cry out aloud. He hugged Mataiah and wept.

The sound of fish swimming against the current jumping at one go. The endless noise of the water flowing in the midst of the hearts of the pebbles.

The pedda mala felt like suddenly getting up and shouting out loud so that the people of malapalli and madigapalli could hear him. 'Our Mataiah killed the elder karanam. The brave man is next to me. Get up and come.' But he could not shout out. He remembered the houses in the palles he wanted to shout out to. Remembered the people. Immediately fear overcame him. He controlled his rage. Actually, Mataiah himself had wanted to tell Rangayi why he killed the elder karanam. But he held back. The pedda mala, too, stopped for the same reason Mataiah had stopped.

'Rangayi!...'

'Did she recognise you?'

'Don't know.'

That night, the two of them came to a decision. They decided to keep the information between the two of them. If it came to be known that Mataiah had committed that act, both palles would be reduced to dust. That was why they came to that decision.

After coming to that decision Mataiah got up. The pedda mala felt uneasy as Mataiah was leaving. He felt like spending hours with Mataiah. But the morning's scene stood before his eyes. It was not safe for Mataiah to remain there. There was danger if Rangayi recognised him. That was why he could not say no to Mataiah when he said, 'I'll make a move.'

Along with Mataiah, he got down from the stream bank and walked towards the lake. Wading through the waters of the lake, Mataiah went, turning back and looking often. The pedda mala stood staring after him. It appeared as if the entire light was walking on the other side of Yennela Dinni's stream. A brave man always walked like that. Like the lightning flash across the sky, like the sunbeam spreading over the earth, like the typhoon completing its job in seconds.

It was then that Rangayi came. He looked surprised. He looked frightened. She did not appear to have run. She appeared as if she had come searching, calmly.

'Mataiah is God,' she said. It sounded strange to the pedda mala. He did not speak. He did not feel as if he was at the stream bank of Yennela Dinni.

'I will hide the fact in my stomach . . . Even if the entire ooru is upon me I won't say . . . '

She kept saying like that. She said she was born in the Nallamala hills. She said she had come searching for a living to Yennela Dinni. She said she had sacrificed Subbireddy to Yennela Dinni. She said that it was the karanam who took away his life. She said he then seduced her. She said she yielded to him for her child's sake. Saying these words, she cried. It felt as if his sister was crying. She said she looked forward to the karanam's death. She said Mataiah was God. She said those words many times. When Mataiah came away in a hurry after killing the karanam she said she followed him. She said she waited for him outside, when Mataiah sneaked into malapalli. She said that she had wanted to come to the stream bank when they sat down there. She said she restrained herself because she did not want Mataiah to think she had recognised him. She very much desired Mataiah's safety. She said he should live forever. She said he should add her years to him and live. Saying all this, she went back. She started walking back as calmly as she had come and as calmly as she had spoken. He remained looking at her till she was visible.

Mataiah who was walking on the other side of the stream.

On this side, the pedda mala.

Rangayi who was on her way to the ooru.

That dark night hid within itself the reality of the lives of untouchable people and the lives of women hidden in the life of Yennela Dinni.

There was a lot of hue and cry in Yennela Dinni the next morning. What happened within, the pedda mala did not know. But the two palles did not become targets of danger. He thought that was enough. Thinking so, he had spent all these years. He had hidden that bitter truth in his heart all these years.

Did not know why, but he felt it was difficult to hide any longer the Mataiah and the Rangayi he had hidden all these years. He thought that the truth he had hidden should not die with him. He might not live much longer. If he died, Mataiah was not there to tell the truth. Did not know what happened to him. Rangayi was not there. After the son was old enough to take care of things, she had left Yennela Dinni. She said she would come back after selling her fields in her village. She said she would stay there till the sale of the fields was over. The fields were sold. Yet she did not come. The pedda mala knew she would not come. On the day she left, it was he who drove the cart for the journey. She spoke to him during the entire journey. Said she would not come back. Mataiah was the only man she would remember in Yennela Dinni, she said. She said it would be good if they met accidentally on the way as they had met the other day.

They came to know after many days that she joined Brahmamgaru's *mutt*. In those days malas and madigas would join that religious group in great numbers. If not this, they would become a part of Nasaraiah's religious group. Ramanujam's religion had entrenched itself among the malas and madigas. Brahmamgaru's religion might not have had such an impact on Yennela Dinni but it had a lot on regions like Kanigiri, Kandukuru, Kambham, Kurnool and Podili. Nasaraiah's religion had spread to regions like Vinukonda, Narsaraopet, Bapatla, Darsi, Markapuram and Palanadu. That was an effort man made to retain his identity. There was no caste discrimination in the preachings of Sri Virat Potuloori Veerabrahmam. Nasaraiah began a serious attack on caste. Ramanujam's religion said there was no caste discrimination. That was why the malas and the madigas were attracted to those teachings. *Bhajan* societies were formed.

Once a troupe came to Yennela Dinni singing Brahmamgaru's *tatvas*. They sang tatvas in malapalli and madigapalli. The songs were pleasing to the ear. The songs would speak about Kakkadu. The malas and madigas felt he was like their own son. After that the troupe went to the ooru. The people in the ooru did not allow them to enter. Rangayi left for her village the third day after this happened.

Some said she was still alive. Though she came twice to Podili, she did not show any interest in visiting Atchireddy. People did not know what happened. But she did not come to Yennela Dinni.

Mataiah's courage, karanam's death and Rangayi's greatness should not be entombed without anyone in Yennela Dinni knowing about them. The pedda mala thought about it quite keenly. Not just that he wanted to tell the truth to Pittodu.

Told him. He woke him up at night and told him right there, where Mataiah had said good-bye. He talked of Mataiah. Talked of Rangayi.

After listening to everything, Pittodu looked at both the palles in Yennela Dinni. He looked at the pedda mala. There were unheard sounds in the heart of Yennela Dinni. There were quite a few.

That night Pittodu did not sleep. In the darkness, he went towards madigapalli. When Poladu was in front of the heaps of meat, he asked him to pick up one. Usually, Poladu's wife would come to malapalli with heaps of meat in the daily basket of chopped meat. Poladu said, 'Pittoda, you're so greedy, aren't you?' 'As she said it was calf meat, I wondered if it would last till it reached my place,' he said. That was not the truth. He did not know why. He felt like coming to madigapalli and he came. That was it. 'You've come any way. Why don't you eat a bit of *nalla*⁶ before you go?' said Poladu's wife. On hearing the word, 'nalla' Pittodu came alive. He said, 'Bring it, attha.' 'You rascal, why don't you take it for your wife?' said Poladu. 'Let him eat. Why for her?' said Poladu's wife. When Pittodu said, 'Whatever you say mama, attha is special,' Poladu's wife tied the cooked nalla into a bundle and placed it in Pittodu's hand. When Poladu said, 'Don't you eat all the pieces in the nalla, keep some for your wife,' Pittodu walked back home smiling.

At home, Chinnammi said Yellanna had come back. He kept both the bundles in the hands of Chinnammi and went towards Boodevi's house.

The entire malapalli in Yennela Dinni was in front of Boodevi's house. Boodevi hugged Yellanna and was crying. He saw a man sitting a little distance away on a cot. There was a crowd around him. Pittodu wanted to keep looking at the man. After a while, he came to know that the man was Urumula Naganna and he had brought Yellanna home.

7

The malapalli of Yennela Dinni at first looked strangely at Naganna. Those who had seen the Urumula dance here and there recognised him as Naganna. Some kept looking at his grey hair and the sacred ash on his face and said, 'A guru.'

But for Boodevi, Naganna did not look like a human being. It appeared as if goddess Yellamma had sent him. That was what she was saying aloud too. The people were talking openly about him. He was listening to all of it quietly. He was searching for his childhood friends. He was not able to see the resemblance between the figures of those days with the people now. But he recognised the ones who were his father's age then. The pedda mala of that time might not be alive now. But he saw the elder who came shouting at the crowd. He was of his father's age. The pedda mala's son who had now become the pedda mala was bent with age. He was looking at Naganna in admiration. He felt like saying, 'I'm Narigadu's son.' Yellanna had not yet got off his aunt's lap. He did not know how to say he was so and so. After leaving Yennela Dinni, he had come back only now.

He kept staring at Yellana's father, Yerrenkadu. No use. Was difficult to recognise younger people. In fact, he was not able to figure out Yerrenkadu in his imagination.

When he was looking around like that, his eyes fell on a dark boy who was staring with wide open eyes. He was short. He was like the *nallanchi* bird that slips away from the hand even as it seems to be caught. Looking at the youngster reminded him not of Mataiah but Nallenka mama, one of the other two, who had carried bundles and crossed the floods along with his father. Nallenka mama was the youngest of the four of them. The same scared looks. The same dark skin. His hair was reddish like the colour of a *jamudu* crow. But a strange attraction peeping out of those disturbed looks. Yes, the figure of Nallenka mama. Just then the boy was saying something. As he spoke, eyes that looked around in all four directions at one go. Eyes of a nallanchi bird.

'Come here!'

He came. He looked as if he would slip away if he was held. He was not only like a nallanchi. If one looked at his swiftness, he looked slippery like a *buradamatta* fish.

'Name?'

'Pittodu.'

Could not stop laughing. Was really Pittodu. Nallenka mama's son.

'Father's name?'

'Nallenkadu.'

Nallenkadu in the flood waters. The youngest among those four. Fast heart beats. Flood waters behind the eyelids.

'Do you know my father?'

Nodded his head—everyone was looking with gaping eyes as if they came to know something new.

Pedda mala joined in. He said that Nallenkadu had died recently.

'Chinarangadu?'

Chinarangadu was one of those four. He was not found no matter how much they searched. Could not help asking. Someone said, 'Sinarangayi thatha is calling.' He looked eagerly.

Chinarangadu was sitting on his haunches. Resting due to the heat of the sun. A stick in his hand. Was not looking in this direction. Turning his back this way, he was looking in the other direction. They said he could not see. A loin cloth wrapped around the waist and tucked into the thread around the waist.

A small child placed a hollow vessel in front of Chinarangadu. They said she was his son's daughter. That child would also mix sour gruel with rice in the hollow vessel and bring it wherever Chinarangadu sat in the sun for warmth. She would give a roasted chilli to her grandfather. She ate along with her grandfather from that plate. After eating like that, when she poured water into the vessel after rinsing it, Chinarangadu would drink that water. That day too, the girl did the same and looked at the crowd in front of Boodevi's house. She looked straight into Naganna's face. Small eyes, mischievous eyes. A running nose. A parting in the unkempt hair that started in the middle and went awry. The girl was quite cute. She stood making faces. Her name, Simpiri.

'How do you know Sinarangadu?'

'How's Mataiah?'

On hearing those words, there was a change in the pedda mala's face. He looked keenly at Naganna. Searched. Searched a long time. Of which tree was this seed? What happened to that tree on this mound? What kind of a tree was that! The pedda mala searched wide-eyed for the tree that had dropped this seed. Did not stop. The flood behind Naganna's eyelids could not be contained. Yellamma could not stop it. Mungamooramma did not stop it. Malutchamma tree had been swept away in those floods a long time ago. He could not contain it any longer . . . Did not have the strength to contain it.

'I'm Narigadu's son.'

Those words were in fact pushed out by the flood of tears. Amidst well-wishers, on the mound where he was born, on the mound that poured life into him. Tears did not stop. That day he had cried for father. Why was he crying today?

'Narayi mama's son!' Pittodu repeated these words many times. Shouted aloud. Boodevi stopped caressing her nephew and looked in that direction. Chinarangadu who was basking in the sun said, 'Simpiri, go get the stick.' There was an unusual agility in Chinarangadu. Simpiri had not seen that agility in her grandfather before. Everything was strange. Chinarangadu groped his way forward and stood in front of Naganna. 'Where's Narigadu's son?' He kept saying.

Though we may think otherwise, nothing is of greater value on earth than sacrifice. However small that may be. No matter how small the man who does it. Its strength is its own. It builds a nest in people's hearts and lives immortal in their words. Those who see only dark spots in life may be suspicious of its value. It may not be that valuable. But Yennela Dinni's malas were very ordinary people. They were people groping for light. That sacrifice would not appear small for them. It would not appear as something to be brushed aside.

Naganna held Chinarangadu's hands. Chinarangadu asked about his mother. Did not tell the entire story. Only said that she was dead. Tears rolled down the sightless eyes. Chinarangadu would scare him in childhood saying, 'I'll carry your mother away.' Naganna would be scared that he would really carry her off. Once in a while he would say, 'Come along, my girl,' and pull mother's hand. Naganna would get angry. He would pull, asking him to let her go. Father would keep smiling. Chinarangadu would not let go of her at all. He would bite his hand. He would let go saying, 'He's bitten me.' He would place the thatch of the house carefully at night. He would latch the stick tied in the middle with the rope securely to the front wall. To prevent the thatch on the other side of the front wall being removed, the stick tied to it would be stuck to the wall on this side. Even then a suspicion. He would pull at the stick and test. The thatch would not move. When his mother would ask why he did that, he would remind her about Chinarangadu's words. Mother would laugh. Would roar with laughter. Only his mother would laugh like that. No other mother could do that. If he heard a sound through the slits of the thatch in the middle of the night, he would get up. Mother would say, 'Chinarangadu mama has come. Chase him away.' When he looked, it would only be a spotted dog. He would pull the stick, remove the thatch and shoo the dog away. He could not stop laughing.

Meetings and partings are sweet. Are painful. But meeting Yellana, meeting Pittodu was something special. They were the final stopovers in Naganna's long journey.

He did not think Pittodu was such a close person. When he was told that Pittodu had in fact married his father's elder brother's son's daughter, and when Chinammi said, 'Stay back,' he thought of staying back. He did stay back. The child in Chinnammi's arms climbed on to Naganna's shoulders.

Naganna was not alone now. Yellanna, Boodevi, Pittodu, Chinnammi—all of them were his people. . . He became all the more close to their child. That child would scratch his nose. Pull his hair. Chinnammi's colour, Pittodu's hair, the child was wonderful. Naganna named the child himself.

Subhadra.

Pittodu could not pronounce it. Chinnammi could not pronounce it. Even then it was Subhadra. The new name was becoming familiar in Yennela Dinni.

Time was speeding by. During its passage, Yennela Dinni became a target for many changes. Now Yellanna was not the nude boy who had run away to Pakkela Dinni. A young dancer and musician who had grown a beard and moustache. Dancer Yelladu. Singer Yelladu.

8

Ruth remembers Reuben's words.

Some have snatched wonderful opportunities and infinite resources from this country. Number of years have gone by.

So many crimes, such hypocrisy as if knowledge is their property. They ruled, covering themselves with the blanket of caste, holding the sword of caste. Took lives.

They are the lords of the universe. Equal to Gods. We must pray to them, must look after them, must revere them. Must mortgage our entire selves to them. There is purity in their feet. All the holy shrines are hidden in their left foot. Must wash them. Their feet. Then infinite holy shrines will be visible.

Some more years passed by on this expansive earth. Kings died. Their kingdoms collapsed. The white man crossed the oceans and began to ride over this terrain. Some more years went by.

Wonder. Nothing was destroyed. Caste, untouchability, criminal acts, looting—nothing ended. In fact, those who said everything was in the Vedas began seeing everything in the white men's feet. Do not know what happened to the holy shrines in the left feet of the locals. They started to accept holy water from the white men's feet. All higher positions only for them. At one instance *Bhagavadgita*, at another a colonial mindset. That's the only difference.

Strange. Saw everything only in English. Completely abandoning Vedic chants, the speeches began on European lines. When a line was drawn there, the brush here also drew the same line. When an actor removed half his moustache there, here too the actor cut it according to the same measurement.

Literature was born like this. Painting was born like this. Drama meant this. It would not be otherwise. Resolutions were made. Judgements were given out. If one were to count the names, except for one or two that could be set aside, all the others were *Bhagavadgitas*. All were of colonial mindset.

Some were praised to the skies. Some were stamped into the nether world. Ravi Varma[7] was one of those praised to the skies. They wrote about the beauties he alone could capture. True. There are many beauties that he could not capture. Except that they are untouchable springs. The cast-away movements that showered and shone on this earth.

Rajamannar[8] does not like to see the roots of Telugu drama in those outcaste movements. These 'blessed jurists' who search for Telugu drama behind European curtains cannot find drama in the rhythmic feet of Yellanna's acting and dance. It is not visible, that's all. As Viswanatha[9] asked, why is it not visible? It is not visible because it is not visible. What is more, a certain Krishnamurthi can only see crooked shapes in Yellanna's faces.

Ruth is stupid. Must cut off Reuben's tongue. In the past, they poured lead. A developed age. Now it must definitely be cut off. Do you mean to say there is dance in the mere jumping of the malas, the madigas and the yanadis? Do you want us to search for the roots of drama? What right do they have to say this? Whatever has to be said must be said by those who have a right to say. Only when it is said like that will it become a theory. The words of several good-for-nothing people like the malas, madigas, yanadis, yerukalas, washermen are mere good-for-nothing words. The word 'intellectual' applies to only to a few. Perhaps the others will come under 'good-for-nothing' category*. This term 'good-for-nothing' seems to be a new term. It would be good to turn the pages of the dictionary. If it is not there, it would be better to add it.

---

* Playing on the sound of the word, *medhavi* (intellectual), the author coins the word *alagavi* (good-for-nothing)

How should expression be? It should be in a particular way. Should jump up for reason. The other person must not know why you have jumped. You should not jump like human beings. From somewhere, somehow, if you float in air, you must be like gods or demons. Take a step, place a foot there, pull it very daintily, and turn around with ease, if you combine 'Om' with 'thom' that is grace. That is dance. That is the crowning moment of acting. In the creation of the great sage, Bharata, there, there lies the entire secret.

In the houses of the malas and madigas of Yennela Dinni, no cream of milk was kept, no balls of butter. If there was anything at all, it would be dried fish. If not that, it would be *Yendorikalu*?[10] No child Krishna would come for them. There were no Yasodammas who are told, 'Have you heard, Yasodamma?'[+] while beating Krishna daintily in dance and scolding him in the musical tones, *sa re ga ma*. The Yasodattha of Yennela Dinni would not sit at that time outside the threshold awaiting a beautiful, extremely dainty and tuneful complaint to be made. She would be cutting *isukadoosaraku* greens into the curry vessel. Otherwise she would be pulling out weeds in a field not her own. She would search the entire earth for a morsel of food for the moment. All, only a search. All, only a struggle. To that Yasoda when child Krishna would open his mouth the entire world would be visible. That Yasoda would be awe-struck. On her face, wonder and amazement. But to this Yasodattha when the child opens his mouth, she would see hunger. She would not be awe-struck. She would cry. On her face the wonder and amazement would not be visible. She would abuse the night that had not kept the leftovers of food for the following morning. She would curse her birth. But her anger would not be satiated. She would beat her child. After beating him she would draw him close. She would hide him in her hungry stomach. Asking him to search for grains of food if only he could find them. Thus Reuben narrated for hours and days together history

---

+ Perhaps a reference to either a line from the Kuchipudi repertoire, '*Vintalu vintiva Yasoda?*' (Have you heard of the wonderful deeds, Yasoda?) or a line from the popular film song, '*Nee chinni Krishnudu cheyu allari panulu, vinnava Yasodamma?*' (Have you heard of the mischievous pranks your little Krishna has played?).

and literature. Those were not mere words. They were heartaches, the nails through the cross.

Reuben! How much this literature has done injustice to the child's role! How unnaturally, how artificially has it shaped it! Can one do such injustice to a mother's role . . . ?

What is all this, as if the scene has been frozen at a spot after death, as if it danced after stopping. A crooked physical shape. A wonderful crooked shape. A beautiful crooked sculpture. How even the beautiful is so ugly! It really seems that the meaning of beautiful must be re-written.

Ruth remembers time and again the sparkle in Reuben's eyes and the mischievous smile that showed on his face when she told him on hearing his words that the meaning of beauty must be re-written. When she thinks of it now, Ruth feels like laughing.

What else did Ruth say? Those words must be recollected exactly. Reuben had in fact recited poetry that day. Ruth had seen the beauty of poetry only on that day.

What did she really say?

'When you talk of beauty, I remember something, Reuben. How was your Yellanna's Subhadra? Was she beautiful? More beautiful than me? . . .'

'Pick up the stars, arrange them and draw a line of *muggu*. How would that be? She was like that,' said Reuben. Actually, what a poet Reuben was! How did he get the skill of picking the music from the pigeon that flew through the slits in the rocks,[11] of chiselling and arranging it?

Ruth has etched this imaginative picture in her heart. She is not able to get the right strokes. But, she keeps thinking of the word, *chukkala muggukarra.*♦

'Yellanna himself wove a song that she was like that. He brought down the stars into his weave. Combining one star with another, he kept Subhadra there,' said Reuben again.

♦ *Chukkala muggukarra* refers to the beautiful patterns drawn in the courtyard or inside the house resembling the patterns of stars in the sky. Here, the author compares the beauty of Subhadra to it by referring to her as *chukkala muggu karra.*

The Reuben who said that remained looking into Ruth. Then Ruth felt that the final words ought not to have been said. But she had spoken them. 'More beautiful than me . . . ' Did not know why but those words felt uncomfortable at that time. Reuben did not turn his eyes away.

'Your grandson will sing of your beauty.'

Though they very much wanted to, they could not stop laughing at those words. She can still hear that laughter. That was a laughter they shared along with Subhadra and Yellanna. Ruth wants to stop there and wants to recollect that laughter over and over again. When she remembers it, she remembers Subhadra. She was a daughter-in-law who had stepped into the house just like her. She did not go away just like that. She departed remaining behind like a song.

Chukkala muggukarra stands in front. How did she grow? In Naganna's heart, on Pittodu's affection. How did she learn to take steps as she tricked Chinnammi? If Boodevi was asked, she would say she grew up bundling up affection. As for Lingalu, she would look at the girl without blinking an eye. When the girl played hopscotch, she would think what could be lost if she jumped over this threshold. Yerrenkadu would tell Lingalu not to be greedy. Yerrenkadu had no confidence that Pittodu would give his daughter to Yellanna who danced and went from place to place.

But what did Yerrenkadu know? If anyone knew anything, only Boodevi did. Yellanna wove a song. She thought he was weaving an ordinary song. He interspersed stars in his song. Drew muggus. Sang it for them. He did not sing it at all times. After the village slept he sang it over and over again. One day the truth came out. Boodevi did not think that the girl in the song would stealthily come to his cot. 'Oh! You, Chukkala muggukarra!' She said in Subhadra's hearing. The girl was startled. She ran, stepping on the thatched gate. The songster was scared. But the girl turned to look back as she ran. A strange look. A look like that of Pittodu. A look of the fishing line. The fish cannot but be caught. But Boodevi felt sorry for her. She appeared to be frightened. It was surprising that it appeared like that to her.

It was the peak of summer. On purpose she went and stood under the *gangiregu* tree in front of Pittodu's house. Subhadra would place a cot and lie down on it in the shade of that tree. Boodevi went there. As soon as Subhadra saw Boodevi, she got up with a start and was about to go into the house. A scared bird. She took after Pittodu's looks, not his courage. Boodevi held her hand and made her sit down.

While Subhadra sat on the cot she sat on the floor. She gave Subhadra a wooden comb. Subhadra was perplexed. She placed the wooden comb on Boodevi's hair and tried to find lice. 'Not lice, *muggukarra*. My back, my back is swollen. Prickly heat.' Saying this, she pulled up the blouse on her back. 'Sit on a wooden plank, appa,' said Chinnammi bringing a wooden plank. Boodevi sat on the plank. Subhadra started scratching the spots of prickly heat one by one with the wooden comb. She would not have done that had her mother asked her to. Under different circumstances she would not have done that for Boodevi either. She remembered the previous night's incident and agreed. Even otherwise, Subhadra was of the view that aunt Boodevi was a good person.

Chinnammi began to speak about this and that. There would be no head or tail to Chinnammi's conversation. Subhadra felt that it would be better if mother did not speak. But Chinnammi could not but speak. After some random talk, the topic of Subhadra's marriage came up. Subhadra heard unexpected words from Boodevi's mouth. Boodevi said, 'Why don't you give her to Yellanna? Lingalu's wish would be satisfied.' 'What is there for me? My husband's wish. The girl's wish.' Saying this, she hurled sharp words to indicate that her words had no value in this house. Subhadra scratched hard on Boodevi's back. 'That's enough, my dear. Why are you showing your anger towards her on my back?' said Boodevi. Subhadra was hurt. 'That's enough, come, sit here.' Saying this, Boodevi made her sit on the wooden plank, and she sat on the cot. She said, 'Sinni, give the *iribbani**.' Chinnammi gave the iribbani. Subhadra untied her hair, Boodevi put the iribbani in her hair and started parting it and pulling it down. However much she tried, she could not find any lice. 'What kind of hair is this without lice?' Saying this, she placed the iribbani aside, and started stroking with her fingers. Though copper coloured, how well groomed her hair is, she thought. She said the same words

---

* *Iribbani* is a long wooden comb used for taking out lice from the hair.

aloud. 'For some, copper coloured hair is fine. If she had black hair, it wouldn't have been so good,' she said. Chinnammi felt at that time that if the girl moved into their house, she would be happy. But she did not know Pittodu's views.

If anyone had enough to eat in Yennela Dinni, it was Pittodu. Pittodu had a good reputation for carpentry. He went around villages and built houses. By the evening, he would bring something or the other for Subhadra. In Pittodu's eyes, Subhadra was always a young girl. He was not bringing Subhadra up like all the other girls in malapalli. He bought anklets for her feet. Bought studs for her ears. When she wanted to wear a nose ring, he got Lakshmi of the *yerukulas* and was next to her when she pierced her nose. He had a nose ring made that fitted the nose well. It was only Subhadra in the entire mala and madiga palles who wore a saree below her knees. They would talk about it as a strange act in the ooru. He heard the Reddys comment about tying the saree like that. No one said it to his face. They knew that if they said it, Pittodu could use his foul mouth. When he said, 'Polayi mama, the child wants slippers,' Poladu got soft leather and stitched nice ones. He also did some art work here and there. Though it was soft leather, Pittodu rubbed castor oil on it for three days.

When she went to Bitragunta *tirunala*,[12] wearing her saree below the knees, slippers, hanging earrings and a nose ring, Madireddy Subbayamma's daughter-in-law Sulochannamma asked, 'Who's this girl?' When people next to her said she was Pittodu's daughter, she said, 'She looks like the karanam's daughter,' and praised the girl's colour, hair and dress. She asked her to come to her. She looked at the girl's dress and bottu again and again. Coming to know of it, Pittodu took her *dishti* to ward off evil all through the night. Chinnammi took all the dishtis that were needed. Not knowing what other disthi had to be taken, they sent for Boodevi. They told her in detail all the dishtis they had taken. After listening to everything, Boodevi broke the betel leaf, applied spit on it and put it on Subhadra's cheek. She said, 'That's enough, Pittoda.' What was funny was that her body was hot that night. Pittodu abused Sulochanamma's eyes with all the abuses he knew. In the morning, he came to know that it was not Sulochanamma's eyes that caused the body to be hot. However soft the slipper, would it not bite if it were new? The big toe was sore. That was all. 'Why does my daughter have sores on her big toe, Polayi?' Pittodu pounced all over Poladu. Poladu laughed and said, 'That's the hard surface of the slipper, rascal. Everything will be all right by tomorrow.' It subsided just as he said. Pittodu said, 'It's Polayi mama's blessings.' That was how he brought up Subhadra. That was why Yerrenkadu suspected that he would not give the girl in marriage to his son who danced. But Boodevi felt that Pittodu would not say no to his daughter and go somewhere else. Not that there was no reason to believe that. She knew how much Subhadra liked Yellanna. She also knew better how Pittodu's hard heart would melt if he saw tears in the girl's eyes.

It happened just as Boodevi imagined. Pittodu looked for a match from Kolla Dinni. He said they would come for a feast the next day. Then Subhadra spoke in a cut and dried manner. That if at all she married, she would marry Yellanna. Then Pittodu thought of Yellanna in a composed frame of mind. He was the only child of Yerrenkadu's family on the one hand and Boodevi's on the other. He himself had only one daughter. Yellanna would go around villages to dance. Let him go around so long as he returned home. There was no need for him to toil to take care of Subhadra. After thinking like that, he conveyed his view to Chinnammi. Chinnammi whispered it to Boodevi. Boodevi, Yenkatanarsu and Lingalu went along with the pedda mala to Pittodu's house for the feast. They decided on giving the girl three rupees and six anas as bride price, anklets and ear studs. Fixing the auspicious time and performing the marriage took place in the next few days. Boodevi said that Yellanna and Subhadra would live with her. Yerrenkadu said okay to this.

9

Subhadra did not come in the way of his dancing and singing. As for Boodevi, she felt satisfied if he returned at night even if he roamed around during the day. Did not know what it was, but Yenkatanarusu went around villages saying it was for business. Yellanna was going around villages saying it was for dancing. Only the two women were left in the house. Somehow Boodevi did not like that mode of behaviour. But she was looking after Subhadra better than Chinnammi did. She felt as if more than Yellanna, Subhadra was close to her, as if born to her. She would feel that the sooner she got pregnant the better it would be. Subhadra fulfilled Boodevi's desire and became pregnant. Had a male child. It was Naganna who named him Sivaiah. Sivaiah was the whole world for Boodevi and Subhadra.

The impression made on Yellanna in childhood was not erased. As a young person he developed a knack for singing. He perfected the rhythm of the dance steps. When he was older he was determined to learn the *Chenchulakshmi*[13] play. He urged Naganna. Naganna not only had knowledge of Urumula dance but also Bayalata of Rayalaseema. Chandrappa who had made him such an artist was no less an artist. He knew *Veedhi Bagotam*.[14] To sum up, Chandrappa had a good command of the folk. It is that knowledge which he instilled, along with that of Urumula dance, in Naganna. Chandrappa had a natural anger towards the pundits. In that anger, he narrated many stories. Rather than say narrated, it would be better to say wove. All that Chandrappa told him, Naganna told Yellanna. He combined it with dance and song.

'A Maharashtrian, our man. He narrated the puranas with puppets. Let these pundits try and create the Ketugadu and Bangarakka[15] he made. Where will their Krishna and Radha stand in front of our Bangarakka and Ketugadu?' He used to say such things. After saying everything he would ask, 'Haven't you understood? Must understand. This is a small matter. If you dig, there's a lot. If you want to bury, it's quite deep. Must dig. Must scoop out basketfuls of mud. Must fill huge pits.' He would go on like this. Yellanna would fix his eyes solely on Naganna and listen.

One day, he narrated a story saying, 'Brahma is a great crook.' Brahmadeva wrote a play and gave it to the gods. *Surasura Puranam*. The play began. Among the audience there are gods and there are demons. In his natural style, Naganna said, '*Suras* means gods and *asuras* means demons.' When he said that, he had confidence that not only they but we too knew the meaning.

The play began. It was half way through.

There was commotion in the audience. The *rakshasas* (demons) were impatient. In the play, injustice was being done to them. As a writer, Brahma plotted. As a director he took the side of the gods. The rakshasa characters were losing. The rakshasa spectators could not tolerate it. They revolted. They kicked soundly the ones among the gods they could lay their hands on. The gods ran in all four directions. '*Ore*, Yellanna! He. Who? That Bemma, the crook of the world . . . when his loin cloth was coming off and he was running. He was going to defecate on the banks of Ganga . . . Will Ganga keep quiet . . . Who is she? Whose mother is she? Our mother. The mother of the Urumula people. "Bemma, don't do such dirty things," she said. Not just that. "Your *rishis* are polluting me. Take them away too," she said. Brahma cut a sorry figure. Ganga called her thousand and one sons and thousand and one daughters. The thousand and one sons were just then draining honey from the hives. The thousand and one daughters were just then working on the fields. Hearing their mother's voice, Ganga's children left their work behind and assembled at their mother's bank. They saluted their mother ten thousand times. They asked her to tell them why she had called them. It was then that Ganga saw the children. Her eyes were filled with tears. The children were shaken. They said their mother's pain was theirs. "Come, *amma*, Gangamma, primeval Gangamma! Oh golden doll! We are your children, amma. We are your babies, amma. Tell us what to do, our mother. Tell us, amma." They thus prayed to their mother. The mother's heart melted. She was overwhelmed. She touched the children's bodies. She moistened her children's throats. She said, "Chase away the stinking pundits." Ganga's children made Brahma and his rishis run around the three worlds. Chasing them, they came near the mother. Seeing her children, the mother swelled and rolled. A swelled up stream merged with the ocean. The swelled up stream irrigated all the fields. Ganga calmed down. But, Yellanna! The pundits who were chased by Ganga's children conspired. They put on curtains for the play. They built tents around the curtains. Closing the temple doors they performed Surasura Puranam. Have you understood? They don't have the courage to perform in front of the people. We are not like that. Our jumping is only in front of crowds. Whether Bangarakka dances on the screen, whether

Alisigadu tells jokes, whether Narasimhaswami is on the way out, it is all in front of the people.'

Thus Naganna would tell Yellanna all the secrets of the puranas that Chandrappa had told him. He would ask, 'Have you understood?' just the way Chandrappa had. He would say that the matter was a small one but that it was as deep as you dug. He would say it was a pit as far as you could fill. Must dig, must fill, he would say. Yellanna would listen. Would listen intently. He did not think there was so much difficulty in digging. Did not think burying was such a big task.

One day when the full moon cast her full glow, he made the Bagotam troupe sit on the sand mounds of Yennela Dinni.

They would toil all day long. They would assemble on the sand mounds at night. They would learn as Naganna taught them. They would not keep the written play of Chenchulakshmi in front of them. Whatever Naganna said were Chenchulakshmi's words and song. The same for other roles too. It took them two months to learn the text. Everyone ought to know the entire play. Each one would have to be in a position to take on any role. Another month was taken up to learn the steps. On the whole, the play was ready to be performed in three months.

At first Naganna asked Yellanna to perform Chenchulakshmi's role. But they could not find anyone for Narasimhaswami's role. So Yellanna learnt that role. From then on that role was talked about in the neighbourhood as Yellanna's.

It was known in the neighbouring places that the Bagotam troupe had got together in the palle of Yennela Dinni. It became a kind of wonder to the ooru of Yennela Dinni. It became a joke. They would make fun of it with those who came to work. It became a topic of amusement at the meeting place.

The first performance was at the malapalli of Yennela Dinni. Yellana played the role of Narasimhaswami. Subhadra sat between Boodevi and Chinnammi and watched Yellanna's song and dance without blinking an eye. When they quarrelled saying, 'Adilatchmi, I'm going hunting and will be back,' she thought, 'Did he ever tell me anything like that when he went somewhere?' When he told Chenchulakshmi, 'I can climb trees, I can climb hills,' she thought to herself, 'Just boasting, ask him to climb a tamarind tree and pluck the fruit, and then see his greatness!'

She said aloud to Boodevi, 'He can't climb a tamarind tree.' Boodevi pulled Subhadra close. Subhadra moved very close. It was not Yellanna or the actors along with Yellanna who performed the play. It was Naganna who performed. He played every role that was needed, from the sutradhara to anything else. The play that began after the night meal lasted till the morning.

Performing here or at what level it was performed was not significant. People from the neighbouring mala and madiga palles came. They knew that people from such castes did perform in Rayalaseema in that manner. They knew that in the northern regions too they performed this here and there. They had at least heard of Sindu Bagotam of the madigas in Telangana, and Veedi Bagotam in coastal Rayalaseema of the malas. It was in fact new in the Yennela Dinni region. That was why people came from Kolla Dinni, Pakkela Dinni, Chintalagunta and other neighbouring villages. The malapalli and madigapalli of Yennela Dinni were packed with kinsfolk. The local people killed chickens to satisfy their relatives. It looked as if the entire moonlight of a moonlit night shone on the palle of Yennela Dinni. Women dressed in the best they had. They removed the knots in their hair. They decorated their hair with flowers. As for Boodevi, she was ecstatic. Looking at her nephew with make-up smeared on his face, with shoulder blades glistening, jewellery in the ears, a necklace, a sword and other such ornaments, she remembered the Yellanna who had got on to her arms and said, 'Attha, I can't see.' She felt like laughing. She wanted to take his dishti to ward off evil. She thought of doing it after the performance. As for Naganna, he put some camphor on a coconut, lit it, rotated it four times around Yellanna and threw it on the ground. Boodevi thought Naganna had a large heart.

Those who in the past had sat unseen at a great distance, now sat on wooden planks and sheets they brought along next to 'the circular space reserved for the performance.' That was an amazing experience. It was also new to watch it from so near. If the one who was sitting got up for some reason, he found someone sitting there when he got back. When the one who came back asked the person who sat in his place to get up, fights, shouts, abuses, all happened quite openly. When Pittodu sat down with a stick and swung it around saying, 'Hey, sit down,' the people said, '*Abba*, that's Atchireddy!' When any jatara took place, when *pandaram* happened finally or when *saddi** took place in the ooru, Atchireddy would swing his stick like that and threaten. That was a kind of power. That was a kind of authority. But Naganna was very happy with that commotion. He could pinpoint the reason.

Something strange happened before the performance began. In the surrounding areas, that was discussed more than the performance. The prayer to Gananadha was over. The song on Potulooraiah too was over. Then Naganna, the narrator said, '*Arey*, servant.' Then the one playing the cymbals came forward and said, 'Ayya.' 'Are you guarding the gateway?' he said. 'I am. Come soon, ayya. Got to releieve myself urgently,' he said. Everyone burst out laughing. Naganna waited till that laughter subsided. People were laughing freely watching the performance. They were not afraid that the karanam would see. They were not inhibited that the rich kapus would listen. The performance was theirs. Those who performed, those who were watching were they themselves. When the laughter ceased, Naganna said words that lifted their self-respect to the sky. Words that gave a different turn to tradition.

'Arey, servant!'

'Ayya.'

'Have the great pedda mala and the pedda madiga who is as great come and adorned the seats?'

The same expression.

That single word. . .

Silence. The people wondered whether they had really heard the words they had. What did he say? Ah! Did he say that! The crowd was wonder-struck. The sky was a picture where the moonlit clouds were scurrying hurriedly for some odd reason. A severe turmoil in Pittodu's blood, did not know why, or even if he did, he did not quite understand.

---

* *Pandaram* and *saddi* are offerings of food made during rituals.

'Why don't you speak, servant . . . Have the great pedda mala and the pedda madiga who is as great come or not? . . . '

He said it again. Now the people heard it very clearly.

'They're coming, my lord.'

The people turned to look behind. Naganna had told the two of them not to come till they heard those words. The two of them were sitting on a mound far away from the performance. They felt as if they were sitting, as was the practice in the past, till they were called. After their names were called out, they thought it was not like that. They felt difficulty in walking that short distance. They did not know how to take those steps. It was new. It was strange as the crowd looked towards them.

'We have two karanams, Pittodu,' said someone. Loud peals of laughter. In the midst of that laughter, the two elders continued to walk and sat down in front as if they had made that final journey. The performance began.

Narasimhaswami told Adilakshmi that he was going hunting. Adilakshmi did not agree at first. She finally agreed. Narasimhaswami saw Chenchulakshmi in the forest. He liked her. If he were to be her companion, Chenchulakshmi needed to find out certain facts starting from whether he could climb trees to whether he could squeeze honey from the hive, all that an ordinary forest boy could do. Narasimhaswami said he would do everything. In the play you could witness only real people. Not gods, goddesses, mantras and *maya*. You could only see the every-day life in those characters. When Chenchulakshmi asked her questions, old Subbaratnam in the crowd said, 'Oh girl! Find out whether he'll reap the harvest?'

Someone said, 'Yerrenka, does your son know how to reap the harvest?' Yellanna, in the role of Narisimhaswami, said without flinching, 'I know that, too.' 'What boasting, *peddamma*!' said Subhadra to Boodevi. 'Naughty girl!' Boodevi said, pinching Subhadra's cheeks. Subhadra was looking, with her head almost in Boodevi's lap.

Chenchulakshmi told Narasimhaswami to ask her father. The talks between Chenchulakshmi's father and Narasimhaswami began. Chenchulakshmi's father would say how much the 'bride price' was. He would say a *seer* of betelnuts. He would say five bundles of leaves.

When he said that, 'Not a seer of betelnuts but a seer and a half, Kotiga,' someone from the crowd piped in. Kotigadu played the role of Chenchulakshmi's father. Someone else said, 'Not a seer and a half, two seers.' That was someone from Pakkela Dinni. Someone else said, 'It's only a seer and a half in Kolla Dinni.' Another said, 'For Chintalagunta, betelnuts don't count . . . leaves, leaves not five bundles, but seven.' 'What counts is Yennela Dinni's practice!' 'What counts is Pakkela Dinni's practice.' . . . A big debate began about bride price in the crowd.

Yellanna was surprised.

Naganna was happy.

Kotigadu was looking on, unable to understand what practice to support.

The real play was going on like that. In the midst of the crowd, along with the crowd. . .

'And now which bride price do you want, oh, King of the mountains!' Yellanna, as Narasimhaswami, asked.

'Add everything and say, Kotiga,' the pedda mala gave his verdict as if he was opening the *patanam moota*.[*]

Sutradhara Naganna took the role of the elder on Narasimhaswami's side and started speaking. He said, 'Okay, King, according to the convention of Yennela Dinni, according to the convention of Pakkela Dinni, according to the convention of Kolla Dinni and according to the convention of Chintalagunta—we'll add everything and give as many seers of betelnut and as many bundles of leaves as the total. Do you agree to give your daughter to our Narasimhaswami?'

The crowd said that was good.

As for the fights of co-wives, that between Chenchulakshmi and Adilakshmi, there was no need to talk about it. It was such fun!

The performance continued till morning. They watched it with contentment. More than that, they watched it freely.

---

[*]   A few days before the wedding, a bundle containing the bride price — betel leaves, betel nuts, etc. — is carried by elders from the bridegroom's place to the bride's place. This is known as patanam moota. The pedda mala opens and distributes it.

Kalyana Rao

After the performance was over, Pakkela Dinni malapalli people said, 'You should perform in our palle.' Kolla Dinni said, 'Afterwards, in ours.' Chintalagunta people said, 'What about our palle?'

Yellanna said it was up to Naganna. Naganna said yes to all the three villages. All the three villages said the performance was great. By the time they came to Chintalagunta, Narasimhaswami's awesome godly figure was clearly visible in Yellanna. Naganna thought that the differences between the Narasimhaswami with Adilakshmi, the ferocious Narasimhaswami, and the Narasimhaswami with Chenchulakshmi were clearly visible in his acting and song. Yellanna was a natural actor. Not just an ordinary person. In fact, Veedhi Bagotam is a great representation of the combination of song, music, dance and expression. A society. A culture. A living art of turning gods and goddesses into true village folk, of conversing and of performing amidst people without the obstructing curtains.

Everywhere around, the only thing you heard was that if you had to see anything, you had to see Yennela Dinni Atelladu perform. After the Chenchu *natakam* they learnt *Prahlada*. Yellanna left a mark on the crowd as Hiranyakasipu. He grew to such proportions that they beat the drum to advise pregnant women not to come to the performance. Naganna in his last days began Potuluri Veerabrahmam's play.

While on the one hand Atelladu's name and fame were growing, on the other there was the beginning of a strange atmosphere among the upper castes. That was not just among the elders of the upper castes of Yennela Dinni. That atmosphere which was hard to swallow even for them was beginning to be seen in Pakkela Dinni, Kolla Dinni, Chintalagunta and every village in other neighbouring areas. As for the elders of the ooru of Yennela Dinni, it appeared as if it was something that was shameful.

As Chandrappa had said, the matter was small. But there would be a great depth. If you buried it would take a lot of mud.

The performance of Atelladu was on only in the mala and madiga palles. That was not a problem. They would not any way call them and organise a performance in the ooru. Atelladu's name was known not only among the malas and madigas but also among other castes. After coming to know that the performance in Yennela Dinni was good, the washermen, barbers and potters went at first to the neighbouring village on some pretext and saw it. Later they went saying it was to see the performance. It did not stop there. They started going to the Yennela Dinni palle itself . . . Even then, this was not a big issue. But the Reddys did not budge. That was enough for Atchireddy.

But as to where the problem began, it was customary for the narrator to ask before the performance, 'Has the karanamgaru come, have the kapus come?' and to begin the performance only after their arrival. Once in a while, if the Reddy came late and asked for the performance to start all over again, it would begin again. But in Atelladu's performance, the sutradhara Naganna was not asking, 'Has the great karanamagaru come?' He was saying, 'Have the great 'pedda mala' and the 'pedda madiga' who is as great come? The two of them were coming and sitting down like karanams. That became the major issue. For the young karanam, for Atchireddy and for some other elders of Yennela Dinni it was as if they had been put to shame. The upper caste arrogance could not digest that change. In their eyes, Naganna and Yellanna appeared like big criminals. They thought they ought not to swallow the heinous act of raising the mala and madiga to the level of a karanam or a kapu. They thought of teaching them both a lesson.

They made Dibbalamitta the scene of the battlefield. Dibbalamitta was a mile away from Chintalagunta. That was Atchireddy's in-laws' village. It was well known that there was no one around those neighbourhoods who was as much of an obstinate fool as Atchireddy's father-in-law. When there was an argument, he hit his wife with a three-legged plank and she died. Without even informing her people, he performed her last rites. As washerman Mangaiah's land was next to his, he pushed the life out of him till he made it a part of his. When the elder karanam was still alive he would visit him often. It was then that he saw Atchireddy. He gave away his daughter and along with her gave five acres of wet land and two acres of dry land. Once when he came to visit his daughter at Yennela Dinni he heard the younger karanam and Atchireddy discussing Atelladu. He said after listening to everything, 'If it were me, I would kill those two bastards.' When he knew that there was a performance in Dibbalamitta he sent word about it through a man to his son-in-law and asked him to let him know through the man what he should do. Atchireddy sent word through the man, 'What is there for me to say? Let him do what he thinks fit.'

Bukkireddy sent word to the mala and madiga elders the day before the performance. He told them that if Atelladu's performance took place in Dibbalamitta both the palles would be reduced to ashes. He thought that it was unnecessary to say anything more to them. And if they still wanted the performance to take place, he said they should not call out to the pedda mala and the pedda madiga the way the karanams and kapus were called. He said they could have the performance if they did not call in that manner and then told them they could go home. That very night a man went from Dibbalamitta to Yennela Dinni. After telling them what Bukkireddy said, he told them, 'We'll have it later, Yellanna.' Yellanna looked at Naganna. Naganna began to think. He felt that the battle was turning another way.

Till now, neither Naganna nor Yellanna had suspected that inviting the pedda mala and the pedda madiga before the performance would turn so vicious. When Naganna came to know of Bukkireddy's threat, he remembered Chandrappa's words once again. He thought there was a lot to be dug, a lot to be filled. He thought that his life was being pushed in another direction without his knowledge. He looked at Yellanna. He thought that Yellanna was not a fish in the net. He thought he was a fish swimming against the net. He felt that the fish was unaware it was swimming like that. He felt that he ought to tell Yellanna all that was happening now. He sent word for Pittodu. He asked him to go to madigapalli and bring Polayi, and Mataiah's nephew Musalaiah. He asked the man who had come to stay overnight and then go back. They walked towards the stream bank.

The four of them sat down on the bank. Naganna told them all that had happened. After listening to everything, Polayi said it would not be right not to have the performance. Pittodu said that the performance must take place. Musalaiah remained silent. As far as possible he remained quiet. He spoke rarely. Mataiah's father's sister's son, Musaliah, reminded him of Mataiah. The situation of the palle, if the performance took place, was quite evident. They thought it would be better to go to that palle that very night and talk. They felt they could take a decision right there. After the meal, they walked towards Dibbalamitta along with the man who came. A strange mist combined with moonlight dew was running over the sand dunes. The barks of watch dogs of the fields were heard. Dibbalamitta was not that far away. Could reach before the moving star appeared.

That very night, at the very hour the four of them sat at the stream bank, the elders of the ooru sat at the meeting place. Atchireddy was proud to hear one or two say in the conversation, 'If there's any one who is a man, it's Bukkireddy.' A couple of others praised Atchireddy too. The young karanam did not find those words palatable. He felt that Bukkireddy was usurping his father's place and Atchireddy his place unobtrusively. He wanted to divert the conversation.

'Isn't Naganna Narigadu's son?'

As soon as the young karanam said it, Atchireddy looked at him. It was not because the young karanam did not know that Naganna was Narigadu's son that he was asking the question. He said it purposely. Atchireddy knew that the young karanam would not say anything just like that. For that moment he said yes and kept quiet. Even when everyone else left, the two of them sat on at the meeting place. As if they had decided together, 'Farming on the mala's mound' occurred to them both.

'That day itself we should have prevented,' the young karanam said.

'Which day?' Though Atchireddy knew which day, he wanted to hear it from the young karanam's mouth.

'The day the malas and madigas started farming on the mala's mound,' the karanam said calmly.

The farming on mala's mound appeared in front of Atchireddy's eyes.

10

Not just the farming on the mala's mound but the younger karanam's words, 'Let the devil's mound eat the devils, Atchireddy,' struck Atchireddy as significant.

That day the younger karanam had said just that. But in fact there were many fields other than the mala's mound that did not count in the surroundings of Yennela Dinni.

Even now people knew of those only as karanam's fields. Not that
the people of Yennela Dinni did not also understand the true story of
the gifted lands. No one had the courage to talk about the extent of
land the elder karanam had encroached upon, not only in Yennela
Dinni but in the surrounding villages, in the guise of land gifted to
him.

The people belonging to the categories of washermen, barbers,
potters, blacksmiths and the carpenter castes did not know how
much of the lands given to them in exchange for their bonded labour
was encroached upon by the karanam. Everyone knew of the two
acres of land that was given as gift for the potters' clay. Only the
elder karanam knew it was approximately five acres. The washermen
knew only of the lake and the six acres adjacent to it for washing and
drying clothes. The rest only the elder karanam could tell. There were
no devadasis in that village. But twenty-five acres were accounted for
in the name of the devadasis. The karanam would say it was part of
god's land. It was the karanam who enjoyed all of that, whether it was
in the name of god or in the name of the devadasis. The gift of land in
exchange of the bonded labour would be cancelled out with the grain
measured out during harvest time. The bonded labourers did not ask
if they had lands, and if they did, how much they had. The karanam
did not say. It was no wonder that the people of Yennela Dinni did
not know that there was 'land gifted in exchange of work'. But those
gifts were there in the karanam's accounts.

When Naganna had just arrived in Yennela Dinni from
Rayalaseema, when in some context the words '*muddala inam*'
were mentioned, Yerrenkadu and Yenkatanarsu had their mouths
wide open. But only Pittodu insisted on his telling them what it
meant. When there was a border dispute between Yennela Dinni
and Chintalagunta to the east of it, Naganna jokingly said he would
resolve the fight if he were given 'muddala inam'. It was then that they
heard that expression. There would be a person appointed to resolve
the border dispute; he would determine the borders and would place
balls of rice (*muddalu*) along the borders. That was called 'muddala
inam'. Such things that surprised people like Pittodu brought
luck to the karanam. What is surprising is that when the British
government started paying the village servants in terms of money, the

major part of these paymernts remained with the karanams and the
landlords as their own property. This is an amazing drama performed
concerning land.

The younger karanam was indeed very farsighted. He sold lands
to the peasants with foresight. He was observing quite keenly the
contours of the village which were changing day by day. He would
sometimes think of leaving Yennela Dinni and going to Nellore.
The elder son was studying. The son-in-law had a good say under
the landlord's patronage. Even in the ooru, farmers like Atchireddy
were gaining importance in the governing of the village. Bukkireddy
of Dibbalamitta gave some lands to Atchireddy when he gave his
daughter in marriage to him. The previous year he had bought ten
acres of land. As there was wasteland next to it, he encroached on
it and added it to his fields without even a word to the younger
karanam. When he turned a blind eye to Atchireddy, a couple of
other farmers too did the same. Ordinary people calling themselves
as belonging to such-and-such a reddy did not for some reason please
him. Some things that happened without his knowledge were not in
his favour. There, under those circumstances, he said, 'Let the devils
eat the mala's mound, Atchireddy.'

But the younger karanam did not call them and say, 'Mala's
mound—you cultivate it.' On the day of the border dispute between
Yennela Dinni and Chintalagunta, Pittodu and Naganna talked
about a number of things in a light vein. Pittodu felt a bit agitated.
He tried to egg on people of his age group. He felt a little hopeful.
They said, 'It would be good if you egg on the madiga youth.' The
madiga youth in madigapalli got ready. Musalaiah and Poladu came
forward.

Naganna drew up the strategy. They thought of chopping down
the trees on the mala's mound first. They thought that if the karanam
asked or if farmers like Atchireddy asked, they would say it was for
firewood. They set out rather scared the first day. They stopped after
chopping down two or three trees. Those who went that day were
all young. Only Naganna was with them. Though he did not cut
the trees, Yellanna stayed on with Naganna. Because Yellanna went
there, Yerrenkadu almost had fever from fright. The second day, the
number increased. They chopped trees until afternoon. It appeared

as if no farmer paid any attention to it. The third day the number increased further. They chopped down about half the trees and the thorny bushes of the mound.

It was then that the ooru started to think. The elders of the ooru had a meeting. They asked the malas and madigas to assemble under the *geviti* tree in the morning. Outside the village, on the road separating the two palles, is a huge neem tree. Some say it was there even before the village was born, and some others say that the elder karanam's father planted it. *Gemudu* tree slowly became the geviti tree. There was also a platform under it. If they had to call the malas and madigas they would do so under that very tree. To give verdicts to the malas and the madigas in the ooru was not considered proper. That was why they did not call them to the usual meeting place but to the meeting place under the geviti tree. Some came from malapalli and some from madigapalli. The younger karanam sat on the platform. Atchireddy too sat next to him. The other Reddys sat in the back row. The barber, Veeraswami, and the washerman, Singanna, whom they had brought along, stood on either side. Far away from them stood the bonded labourer, Yellamanda, and the paid servant.

'Mala's mound has remained unused. We thought of cleaning it up.'

Naganna spoke those words. The younger karanam kept staring at Naganna. Naganna was Narigadu's son. It was not as if the younger karanam did not know how Narigadu had died. The younger karanam had his own suspicions about his father's death. But for 'Rangayi' in between, he too would have gone a long way. Atchireddy had fallen at his feet appealing to him not to drag his mother on to the streets. In any case, the father who was dead would not come back. That was why though there were all kinds of talk outside about his father's death, he kept his thoughts to himself. Not just that, the changes that were taking place in Yennela Dinni too were making him think in a different vein. Whether Atchireddy or the other reddys noticed, the younger karanam did not know, but he noticed something. The meeting at the geviti tree happened very rarely. When such a thing happens, however much the malas and madigas were asked to come, so many people would never come. Sometimes they had to be threatened and brought to the meeting. But now a great many had come. In the past, when something happened, each one would blame the other. But now Naganna himself began to speak. The younger karanam thought that there was another thing to be noticed. When they used to work in the elder karanam's fields, even the meal baskets for the malas and madigas were kept separately. Even at the meeting place they would sit in separate groups. Now it was not like that. All of them sat together. The looks of Pittodu among the malas and of Poladu among the madigas seemed slightly different. They seemed suspicious. The looks of the pedda mala and the pedda madiga did not seem agitated. They were not scared. The younger karanam looked at Atchireddy. Though it was not new for Atchireddy to take part in the meeting, it was new to sit next to the karanam. The karanam thought it would be good if Atchireddy did not sit next to him like that but sat in the row behind him.

'We thought of telling you after chopping down the trees.' It was not as if the younger karanam did not know that Naganna was not telling the truth.

'When we wanted to tell you earlier, we came to know you had gone to Nellore.'

The younger karanam thought that those words were in fact appropriate to his status. He felt that for someone desiring change it was good to guard his status to that extent. Whether Naganna had told the truth or not, he felt he had placed him on a higher plane.

But as for Atchireddy, he did not like those words. In the words of Naganna where he said, 'We wanted to inform you after chopping,' he felt the 'you' included himself. But the second remark revealed that he was not included. Even if the karanam was not there, could they not have told him? He did not like their considering him so low.

'What if he wasn't there? Aren't we there? You could've told us,' he said unable to contain the words. Atchireddy's words made the karanam angry. But thinking it was better not to say anything aloud, he said, 'If I weren't there, you could've told Atchireddy.' Though he said that, he was worried Naganna might say he was wrong not to tell Atchireddy. He felt it would be good if he did not say so. Naganna did not say anything. The younger karanam was happy that he did not say anything.

Naganna had his own reasons. Not that the karanam was unaware of it. After all, intelligence is no one person's property. From the rat in the hole to the snake next to the hole—each to its own intelligence. Except that 'hole' alone is the problem. This institution has only dug pits for the Nagannas. It asked them to live in the darkness of the pit. Nagannas would not but learn to dig *elikalugu*. If they kept quiet, it would not be history. There would be no progress in it. It would be like history written and cast away by some rishi with matted hair. For every hole dug by the rat in the fields, there would be a second secret outlet elsewhere. That's known as the elikalugu. That passage might have been made a little late. That's the only difference.

The younger karanam was looking at Naganna. As for Atchireddy, he was unable to tolerate the fact that not a word was coming out of Naganna's mouth. He came to the conclusion that it was not right to speak in such a calm manner with the riff-raff. He was mouthing curse words. The younger karanam kept watching. It was not Atchireddy that he was watching. Not his words. He was observing Pittodu's eyes when Atchireddy was mouthing curse words. He was studying Musalaiah's looks. He was thinking of Polaiah who was moving uneasily. He was measuring the impatience in the looks and the agitation in the movement with a karanam's sense of accounting. His father's death came to be on the debit side. Atchireddy's behaviour came to be on the credit side. He thought it would be good if the land belonged to them. It was not the intelligence of a single day. The white man was not doing anything new on this land when he divided and ruled. He only used what was already there.

The elder karanam used to keep dividing the malas and the madigas. He drew lines scientifically so they could not unite. Then, there were no Atchireddys in his circle, at his level. When he drew the line and said, 'Do this much, Atchireddy,' he did just that, gave him his share and kept the rest. During the younger karanam's time there appeared a huge change in status. The Atchireddys were not in a state where a line could be drawn and they would accept what was given. At one time Bukkireddy would come asking, 'What shall we do, *pantulu?*' But now, he was saying, 'If I were to. . . ' In dividing, the younger karanam was moving the pawns in another direction.

'It would have been good to have told Atchireddy.' He said this easily, two or three times.

'But Atchireddy, let the devil's mound eat the devils, Atchireddy.' Saying this, he got up. Whatever might be, he felt the meeting ought to end with his words.

'Let's go now.'

Saying these words, he got up. Atchireddy got up unwillingly. On the way, he told Atchireddy, 'Families shouldn't sit on our heads. But they aren't clearing up the mala's mound for families to live, right?' He kept talking. No matter what he said, Atchireddy found the words empty.

Pittodu did not think that the problem would be solved like that. Pittodu also did not like Naganna saying, 'We thought of telling you after we chopped down the trees.' When he told this to Poladu, he said, 'What else could he say other than that, *alludu*?' As for Musalaiah, he said, 'I too didn't like it.' That night, he asked Naganna outright. Naganna did not laugh it off. He explained his thinking in great detail. 'They did not storm the field. They called for a meeting. I felt a slight rift was developing between the younger karanam and Atchireddy at the meeting. That's why I spoke like that. As it's the devil's mound and as the karanam thinks that the elder karanam's death too is tied up with it, we've been able to get the land. Otherwise it wouldn't have been so easy,' said Naganna.

Whatever be the reasons, the malas and madigas made the mala's mound cultivable. They shared a piece of land each. They ought to remember Narigadu and Mataiah. Their sacrifice. Their courage. The blood they shed. The debt of blood they repaid. History continued like that. Not just the head of Sambuka or the thumb of Ekalavya. The examples of dalit history did not stop with them. The revolts, the struggles, the sacrifices and the courage of the untouchables—that history had not taken into account or even if it had, had not given it due importance—were not lucky to see the light and became one with darkness. Those who speak with little knowledge would say something or the other but struggle is not an ideal for the malas and madigas. It is a necessity. As it is a necessity, the Narigas and Mataiahs dared so much. There is no page in the history of the struggle of this country that has not been soaked in their blood. There is no instance which is not connected with their courage. They have fought for the land. They have fought for their livelihood. They have fought for their self-respect. The present too is the same. The present life struggle too is the same. That is not an ideal. A necessity.

In fact the mala's mound was cultivated. It became a thing of the past. But Atchireddy and the younger karanam were reminded of it in the self-respect hidden in Yellanna's performance. The younger karanam took the giving up of the mala's mound lightly. But he was unable to tolerate placing the mala and madiga elders on the same plane as the karanam at Yellanna's performance. He took it as a grave insult. But he only thought that he should not soil his hand. That was why he told Atchireddy, 'We should have confronted them that day itself.' That which happened that day was not going to be repeated again. But if he were to suggest, 'I didn't pay heed to your words, Reddy,' Atchireddy would lift him on to his shoulders. In fact, that was what actually happened. The younger karanam instigated Atchireddy and went to his daughter's place. The enraged Atchireddy charged directly towards Dibbalamitta.

Yellanna and Naganna came across a strange atmosphere at Dibbalamitta. The people from both palles were finding it difficult to speak to them. That atmosphere put Pittodu, Musalaiah and Poladu in an awkward situation. As if the pedda mala and the pedda madiga had concurred, as if there was nothing more they could do, they said, 'Perform without addressing us.' They said, 'If not, we can't live confronting Bukkireddy.' They also came to know the news that Atchireddy too was in Dibbalamitta. There were strong rumours that the reddys of the neighbouring villages were coming in bullock carts to Dibblamitta and that they would attack the palles any time. Naganna thought that the price of self-respect was too high.

'Why are Atchireddy and his father-in-law more concerned about their status than the karanam?'

'Who said the karanam isn't concerned? He instigated them and slinked away.'

'The people of the ooru will come. Why should you address the elders like that? Stop it. And perform.'

'Women and elders are so keen about seeing Yellanna's performance.'

'Perform without addressing like that,' said Bukkireddy.

'To perform as he wants, are we cattle confined to his shed?'

'What a man!'

Words. Around Yellanna. Around Naganna. They kept listening. Did not understand what to say. Had to say something. Had to decide on something. That something was whether to perform without addressing the elders with respect? Or not to perform? Yellanna thought they had to decide on one of the two. The entire problem was not in performing. It was with the elders. The palles did not dare have a performance addressing the elders with respect. Doing such a thing needed a lot of courage. Therefore, Yellanna thought not to perform would be the best way to save self-respect. He felt he should at least retain that. He said that to Naganna. Naganna too was waiting for that decision. Actually, he himself thought of saying that. His life was now in the dusky twilight. Yellanna was the newly blazing dawn. He thought that it was good that the decision came from there.

Not only that, this atmosphere had an impact on his life. He felt that some unknown turmoil and anxiety were squeezing his heart. He felt as if he was not in a state to accept defeat. An unknown uneasiness was swirling in his heart. Yellanna looked at Naganna. He felt as if darkness was visible on his face. So he took the opportunity and said, 'Let's not perform now. Let's do it another time.' Everyone felt unhappy. The elders asked them to perform. Yellanna thought self-respect was more important than performance. He repeated it. Said they could perform another time. Said they would definitely do it. Naganna looked at Yellanna. He felt that Yellanna's eye was never that red before. Naganna now knew what was foremost in Yellanna's heart. Land to till, house to live in, clothes to wear and performance to enact. None . . . none . . . not easy to get any of them. A lot to dig and fill up. He looked into Yellanna's eyes once again. They remained red. He thought, let them remain like that. He felt they should remain like that.

The walk to Yennela Dinni was very heavy. Pittodu, Musalaiah and Poladu were saying something. Yellanna was walking silently. But Naganna was unable to bear even the silence. He was unable to understand in which direction this incident would turn Yellanna's life. Yellanna was an artist. Response was the special characteristic

of an artist's heart. The nature of his response would depend on his
understanding of the people of Dibbalamitta. If he could understand
the fear of these people and if a response came out from him that
would root out this fear, there would be a new meaning to the redness
in the eyes. It would remain like the rising flood that took a turn
and like the love that was shared. Instead, if in a different manner,
this response arose out of trusting these people and from a feeling
that nothing should be done, that would pave the way for danger.
Responding is a very sensitive aspect of an artist.

Naganna was finding it difficult even to walk. That which happened
then seemed like a scene where an enemy kicked him on his chest
and went away. A bullock cart was kicking the dust on the Yennela
Dinni dust track and was racing towards Yennela Dinni. That was
Atchireddy's cart. Pittodu said that the din of the bells was that of
Atchireddy's bulls. Naganna too looked in that direction. That cart
was going towards the road leading to the ooru. Naganna was feeling
breathless. He kept hearing the din of the bells tied to the bulls. The
din was proclaiming his defeat and Atchireddy's victory.

The walk was not easy. Dusky darkness was enveloping them.
He said they ought to go towards the mala's mound. They turned
towards the mala's mound. As they approached it, Naganna's heart
was beating very rapidly. They came to the mala's mound.

'Let's stop here, my *bidda*.'

Yellanna looked at Naganna. He used to call him bidda (child) at
first. He had not called him that in the recent past. That too he said
it now like one who is tired.

'Let's sit down for a while.'

Darkness completely enveloped them. They had grown *taida* crop
all over mala's mound. The cobs had come up. In a few days it would
be up for harvesting. All were tender cobs. Naganna looked leisurely
at the milky cobs. He thought it would have been good if it were
moonlight. Even then he thought darkness would not come in the
way of his viewing. Pittodu shouted to the man near the guarding
platform to get some drinking water.

'The crop is good . . . no problem for food.'

Everyone said yes to Naganna's words . . . Even in that darkness
Naganna seemed to be searching for something. Everyone looked in

the direction he was looking. In the middle of Atchireddy's fields, near the guarding platform, a torch light was visible.

'That's not Atchireddy's father's property. It is not in the karanam's accounts.'

They looked in the direction in which Naganna was pointing his finger. In the barren land between Atchireddy's fields and the mala's mound, black tumma trees appeared like devils with their hair flowing.

'This field boundary should be there.'

Yellanna looked piercingly at Naganna. He patted Yellanna, who was looking at Naganna like that, on his back. He got up and drank the water that the man at the guarding platform brought. He was speaking all along the way. It appeared as if he was straining to speak. His voice sounded feeble. He spoke the entire night. He said the performance must change. He said the song must change. He sang a few songs. Those songs appeared new. Hunger, land, tears, malas, madigas—the songs were full of them.

Yellanna stayed back with Naganna that night. As Naganna was singing new songs, he sat confining those songs in his heart. He said, 'Listen to the song of Ganga, bidda.' He sang it. It was not Bagiratha who brought Ganga to the earth. It was the Urumula people. Bagiratha was a lie. The Urumula people were the truth. Deluge was born out of the sound of the thunderous Urumulu. Those who made the first farm sectors were the madigas, malas, yerukulas, yanadis and the girijans who slept in the hearts of the mountains. They made fire. Brought water. Ploughed the land. Cooked food. Whoever came, came only later. Whoever came to snatch the food away from the mouth came only later. He kept singing like that. He sang till the early hours. The first cock crowed. 'Am sleepy. Come, bidda,' he said. Everyday he would get up in the early hours. That day he said he felt sleepy. Closed his eyes. Did not open them again. Did not know which way Ganga ran breaching the banks. Did not know which far away shores the sound of thunder was touching and creating a deluge.

Naganna went without revealing the secret of death in the secrets of Chandrappa's puranas. But Naganna sang quite some time ago. The song of the *visurrai pata*.[16] The sticks alone, the relatives. The wood alone, the kith and kin. The logs of the pyre, brother-in-law and sister-in-law. Fistfuls of mud, the heartbeats. Relatives and close people sit around. Shed tears. Then each to himself. Goes away. But though no one went along with Naganna, Naganna remained in Yennela Dinni.

Yellanna did everything for Naganna. Till he performed everything, he remained with a strong heart. After everything was over, he felt as if nothing was left for him and everything in front of him had come to nought. He remained all alone staring in all directions. He was searching for Naganna in every direction. He brought to mind every word Naganna spoke before his death. He felt as if the new songs he sang, the words he spoke and the song of Ganga, all told him something new. He was unable to make out what was new.

All the people from the villages from whom he took advance for the performance were coming and going back. He was returning the advance and sending them back. Did not feel like performing without Naganna. Could not tolerate Naganna's defeat. Otherwise he would not have died. Self-respect. That was no small thing. Whatever it was, should have performed in Dibbalamitta. The people of that ooru ought to have come forward to settle it one way or the other. He abused them for not coming forward like that. Immediately he remembered Naganna's words. Naganna had taught him to love. Naganna had taught him to hate too. Naganna had hated the younger karanam and Atchireddy. Though the malas and madigas of Dibbalamitta did not support him, he spoke affectionately with them. All the way long he kept showering love on them. Near the mala's mound, how he had pointed his index finger at the barren land even in darkness! He had said it was not Atchireddy's father's. He had said that this boundary should fall on the other side. Strangest of all were the new songs he had sung that night. Why did he sing them? Songs of hunger, songs of the piece of land, songs of the huts around. Why did he sing them? In the song of Ganga, fire, water and food. What were they the occasions for? Could not come to a conclusion. There was something. There was something he had not done so far, something he had to do now. That was what Yellanna was unable to understand.

Life was full of inexplicable agony, dryness, a loss that could not be filled, a thirst that could not be quenched. What happened to the happiness he experienced while performing? Where did the artist who had journeyed along with him till then go? The one within him. The one who sang. The one who wove songs. Why was he becoming just sage-like, and dumb?

That did not mean Yellanna became completely sage-like and dumb. Only shadows were lurking about his creativity. The relationship between the society and himself was weakening. If he remained here any longer, there would be danger of its not only weakening but also being severed.

He sang. Till now happiness and contentment alone were the reasons for his singing. Where was the impetus for it? It was somewhere. All this was the search for it. Trees, hill, crow, *koel*, tears, perfumed water, hunger, field, fallow land . . . if he thought again . . . hunger, field, fallow land . . . and again . . . again field, fallow land, hunger, self-respect . . . it stopped there. Everything stopped there. The ridge here should fall on the other side . . . should fall there . . . near Atchireddy's fields, right there, actually there. There, it should fall there . . . Should address the elders, the pedda mala, the pedda madiga better than the karanam so as to make Atchireddy die of jealousy. Should definitely address. When not addressed, when unable to address like that, dance, word, song . . . self-respect, would all remain vague, mere words.

How he came and how he went away! What did he do and what did he leave undone before he went away! The Urumula mala. Yennela Dinni's Naganna. Narigadu's son, a great artist. What in fact did he search for? When what he searched for seemed to be found only to slip away, he stopped, a pathetic sight—like one who did not know how to walk. Lying down like that, as if tired out, not opening the eyes he had closed. Yellanna's tears would not stop. All the struggle would stop there. Would not proceed further. Heart filled with turmoil. Life full of anxiety. Felt like revolting against something, and yet was unable to understand that revolt.

Let's think like this for a moment. Let us search whether the relationship between the society and the artist had weakened anywhere, in unrest, in agitation, in revolt, in great revolutions. No.

Did not happen like that. An excellent artistic creation occurred. Every change on earth kept changing the art. Let's go to the corners of the world. Everywhere it happened like that. At every corner it was confrontation that remained as history. If you pour all the words born from *Manishadam*[17] to *Mahaprastanam*[18] in a heap, what you find in that heap are just three words. Turmoil, agitation, revolt. That turmoil is art. That agitation is song. That revolt is dance.

In fact, what was happening within Yellanna without his knowledge, without his understanding, was just that turmoil, that agitation, that revolt. But they were not clearly visible to him. Narigadu, Mataiah, Naganna standing in front, touching his heart, water gushing out of the eyes, they were floating every second. But how many such Narigadus, how many such Mataiahs, how many such Nagannas? That question was troubling him. He wanted an answer. He felt he ought not to stay there for the answer. Felt like going somewhere. Did not know where. That was where he made a mistake. But he still went. We cannot even say he made a mistake. If he stayed there, his protest would end with Naganna. It would become an utter chaos and confusion in that lack. That was why he went. He crossed Yennela Dinni and went beyond. Once when the upper caste arrogance had chased him he had run naked beyond Yennela Dinni. Now he went of his own accord. He went in search. He left chukkala muggukarra Subhadra behind. He forgot Sivaiah's smiles. He left Boodevi to Yennela Dinni itself. His ties with his father and mother were in fact weak. He did not remember them when he left.

For a week before he left, he played with Sivaiah. Sang with Boodevi. Boodevi was thrilled to see a spark in her nephew's face after many days. Spent time with friends. He played *kolatam* with his troupe. Chinnammi sent for Boodevi and asked her to make *sajjaboorelu* for her son-in-law. All of them ate along with Boodevi there that day. Subhadra did not think that life would be such a powerful swell of the stream. During that week one night Yellanna sat amidst his friends and wove a new song. A very long song. He took the cue from a folk song his aunt used to sing the whole night and sang it.

In that song figured Narigadu, the flood, the journey of the malas and madigas to the top of the mound. Narigadu's death. Mala's mound. It proceeded like history. When the brave Naraiah fell to the ground, the heart ache of Mataiah. The hearts of friends broke. After the song began, the people in the palle came there one by one. Saw the scene in front of their eyes. Yellanna did not imagine that his song would have such an impact. The song continued for two hours. It was not a *burrakatha*. Not a *harikatha*. It was the sequence women would sing in a leisurely manner after finishing their meal. Yellanna made a number of changes in that very sequence. The elders asked him to narrate it as a story the following night. The story began the next day. It went on not for two hours but for three hours. The women in fact cried out loud. The men wiped their eyes. Pittodu who heard the story could not contain himself. That night he called his son-in-law to come near him and told him about Mataiah. He said it, even as he thought he ought not to.

Yellanna listened to everything. After listening, he felt that life was not tears alone. He felt his story would not end in tears. In fact, he felt no story should end in tears. Mataiah occupied all of untouchable life. Life was greatly courageous. How courageous—as courageous as Mataiah. The song was weaving itself. The story took a different turn. The shape of Yennela Dinni village, the status and situation of the malas and madigas, the elder karanam, land—the story began like that. It took a turn with the floods and Narigadu's death. It ended with Mataiah killing the elder karanam. Thus he wove the story.

Yellanna did not know he was pouring life into a heroic tale. In fact what Yellanna wove was a circle of a heroic tale. But perhaps there might not have been more than thirty stories as in Katamraju's heroic tale circle. But there are two heroes. One brave man died a heroic death. Another brave man repaid the debt of blood of that brave man. There was land behind both these people. There was self-respect. Yellanna perhaps was not aware of such a reading that day. But he wove. Yellanna might not be the Srinatha who wrote 'Palanati Yuddham.' But he was a great artist's responsive heart. Words were his property. Words that he knew. Words that people around him knew. Life was his experience. The reality that was born and grew up around him. He did not run along with the tune. He dragged the tune along with him. That was naturalness. Every folklorist did just that. He was not imprisoned anywhere. Did not imprison meaning in any prison.

Pundits call it a wind-swept song. The synonym of a spontaneous outburst is a wind-swept song. Like every natural action, change, turn, slowly wafting breeze happening very freely in nature . . . like the flute played by the cowherd in any which way that pleased him.

He said, 'I have a little work. I'll be back.' Subhadra did not imagine that a little work would cause so many years of separation. Boodevi did not think that going and coming back would mean such a distance. They looked out for him on the day he said he would go and come back. They looked out for him the next day. On the third day, Pittodu placed a towel on his shoulder and set out. Yenkatanarsu said he too would go along. They went around all the villages they thought Yellanna would go to. No trace of him.

11

In fact, Yellanna did not go with the intention of not coming back. He intended to come back. But even he did not know when. He was swept away like that. Like the leaf being blown off by the whirlwind in a direction it does not know, he did not stay put at any place for even ten days. Only in Guntur district did he stay in one place for a few months.

He wove songs on growing fields. He sang, sharing the toil of the labourers bending down to plant the seeds. He spoke out verses about carrying saplings at the field ridges. He spoke of every happening like the harvesting of crops, of threshing heaps of grain and of every act on the field. That was all he did. To weave on and on as and when things took place.

Whichever village he reached, he would go to the malapalli and madigapalli. He would spend the few days he stayed there with them. Those few days, songs all night long. Lot of excitement all night long. He did not name himself *mala bairagi**. The people called him that. He kept quiet, allowing them to call him so.

He had Subhadra in every song he wove. He sang as if he was talking to Subhadra. Subhadra was the pallavi of his song. She

---

* *Bairagi* means an ascetic.

was the real thread of his weave. He wove garlands of songs round that thread.

In the falling rain, in the glistening cloud, in the flowing irrigation canals, in the tender cool breeze wafting across the field, in the tender leaf-cups, in the tumbling desires, in the heart that is stirred, in the cry of the yennela pitta, in the silence, in the dance, in the life-line—like that, at every edge of his life, his pallavi was Subhadra. Like that he roamed about taking Subhadra's memory along. If he was asked, who was this Subhadra, he would not say a thing. He would laugh and keep quiet. It was that laugh that made him a bairagi, made him a mala bairagi.

Those were the days when the white man Brown[19] who had excavated Vemana[20] was toiling hard for the Telugu language. There are a lot of amazing things in Telugu literature and culture. We cannot ignore them as accidents. In the days when Brown searched for Vemana, in the research done on palm-leaf manuscripts, there was very little invasion of brahmin writers. It was only because of this that Vemana could surface.

Brahmin pundits[21] swarmed around Brown. Brown did not have the opportunity to see people like Yellanna. Those brahmin pundits and copy writers went around villages and collected works. All *satakas*, all ancient puranas and histories, *Kasi Puranas*, *Vishnu Puranas*, *Suryatanaya Parinayam*—you know how far they went, so far that they passed off even the magician's magic and spells as Telugu literature. Leaving aside Vemana, Kavi Chowdappa,[22] *Sumati Satakam*,[23] and Potana's *Bhagavatam*,[24] they passed off even those that were not Telugu as Telugu. The Velagapudis, the Mulagapakas, the Ravipatis, the Chilakamarris, the Samudralas, the Tippabhatlus, the Puranams, the Puvvadas—all of them together saw to it that there was no opportunity for the real Telugu word to be unearthed and to be preserved.

As if justice was ever done to the lives of Yellanas! Their emotions were betrayed. The injustice done to their word and speech is not insignificant. They took the life out of people's culture. Being opportunistic, they gave authority to the culture which is not of the people and crowned it. Wanting to retain the power of their postion, these scholars did not hesitate to curry any kind of favour. They forced down the art and literature that only five or six people appreciated on ninety per cent of the people.

The art, the literature and the culture outside the temple became those of the ordinary people. All the lifeless struggles inside the temple became art and came to the fore. Shankuntala of Kalidasa and Varudhini of Allasani of the past, the recent Yenki of Nanduri and the present Kinnera of Viswanatha are all imagined beauties. But Yellanna's Subhadra is no figment of his imagination. The caste she was born into and was raised in is not a figment of the imagination. The steps she took, her looks, and Yennela Dinni are no figments of anybody's imagination. A real-life picture that combines blood, flesh and breath.

Even so, it is not Kshetrayya's song. Not Annamayya's song. Not Tyagayya's song. Not the golden tamarind leaf pendant for Sita. A mala's life. A madiga's life . . . An untouchable's song. That's why Yellanna's songs never got written as a book. No matter how much people obstruct they cannot stem the outpourings of the human heart.

Wind carried Yellannna's songs. When labour migrated from that village to this or from this village to that, it carried those songs. In Nellore district there was no malapalli or madigapalli that did not utter Yellanna's songs. There were no fields that did not sing the group song.

It was then that an incident took place. It was an incident that happened when scholars were searching each and every village enthusiastically for palm-leaf manuscripts, for correcting them and displaying their skill in establishing the authentic texts.

The potter, Pedakoteswarudu, started writing *dvipada*[25] poems alongside making pots. Wrote a lot. Also had the reputation of writing well. But a great one among scholars born to the Samudrala family flung a witticism that Pedakoteswarudu's pots were better than his dvipadas. The world of pundits applauded. Like that, they lightened their hearts' burden. That which is poured into a conch alone is sacred water. Even if it is utterly obscene, what the brahmin speaks alone is the Veda. Whatever is spoken must be spoken by them alone. Only when *they* utter, Sanskrit becomes Sanskrit. Telugu becomes Telugu. Finally, even if English has to become English, it has to be spoken by them. If need be they can make a Brown of a Brahma and a Brahma of a Brown. That's exactly what they did. They called Brown, for having collected and brought to the open the works of Vemana who abused brahmins, the enemy of Hinduism. The same brahmins who criticised the dvipadas as '*mudivitulu, vidhavalanjalu, padakavitalu*' worked as coolies at so many dvipadas a rupee when Brown showed interest in the dvipadas. Strange beings! Saying, "*Chi*, this is a donkey," they have the ability to hear the *omkara* note in its braying if the need arises.

Potter Pedakoteswarudu did not write dvipadas on Siva. He saw greatness in Janga's dvipadas. He wrote of Potuluri Veerabrahmam[26] in his dvipadas. He condemned hierarchies in the name of caste. He gave up his caste. He moulded the wheel of life on the potter's wheel. Everything was mud. Brahmin, reddy, potter, washerman, mala, barber, madiga—everyone was mud. As the wheel turns, as it is moulded, that which comes out is the shape of man. He is just one. Like that, in the manner that struck him, he wrote his *Vedanta*. Pundits made fun of it as mud pot Vedanta. But he did not withdraw. He made Vinayaka with mud. He sold that for a beda. When that was being bought for the *poojas* he laughed louder than the scholars. He went to malapalli. He sat near the well of their loom and talked. When he was hungry he drank sour gruel from their hands. Except that he asked them to add a little dried ginger. He would go to madigapalli. He would eat there if he was hungry. He would not ask what was served to him. Now and then, he would say he was searching for 'Basavadu'.[27] The potters would not allow him into their houses. He would go to the houses of those who allowed him to come in. He searched for Basavadu in the people around him. He spent his life searching.

He would say that the real form of his dvipada was a combination of Veeerabrahmam and Basavadu. Such a potter, Pedakoteswarudu, heard of mala bairagi. He heard his song that wind and toil brought along. He wanted to see him. Coming to know he was in the neighbouring village, he set out with a bundle of roasted *chenna dal* and jaggery.

He searched for his way to the destination he wanted to reach. He reached the village by dusk. He asked around for mala bairagi.

The pundit of that village recognised him. He asked him loudly, 'For whom?' He said in a very calm voice that it was for mala bairagi. The pundit looked at him strangely. He asked again. He questioned that pundit, 'Why did your God make you deaf?' The pundit got angry. 'You don't have the right to walk on the royal path, that too in the brahmin bazaar to meet the mala bairagi. Tradition doesn't mean making pots. Get out of here at once.' Saying this, he took the copper pot on the platform to sprinkle water from the pot. Some people surrounded him. 'This potter was walking through the brahmin bazaar to meet the mala,' he started screaming, 'Chase away this outcast.' The potter Koteswarudu looked sharply at that scholar. He lifted his foot. He took out the mud on his foot into his hand. Saying, 'My foot has become impure with this mud,' he shook off the mud right there. He cleared his throat and spat. Saying, 'If this spit is untouchable, pick it up with your sacred hands and throw it away,' he walked towards malapalli without turning back. Everyone stood staring. Even though he left, the pundit kept ranting. He said, 'The potter caste has excommunicated him.' He said, 'Don't keep quiet about such a man who has insulted us so much.' He screamed aloud saying, 'Come forward to save *dharma*.' The spirit of dharma possessed some. They swayed. They thought they ought to teach a lesson to the traitor, potter Koteswarudu. They got ready to lay siege.

Mala bairagi was not in malapalli. He came to know that he was on the yanadi's mound. He walked towards that mound. The yanadi's mound was nearing. A wonderful, light tune was heard. The sound was that of a *dappu* (drum), but it did not sound like the sound of a dappu of the madigas. That was a strange sound. Accompanied by the tune of a flute, the voice was not that of a man. As he went closer, the song became clear. Now a male voice was heard.

Bhamaro, my name they say is Abhimanyudu.

As for my father, he's Arjuna, my mother Subhadra

Bhamaro . . .

The *ragada* composition began at the place 'Bhamaro, my name.' At 'they say my name's Abhimanyudu', the chorus joined.

Potter Koteswarudu stopped at a distance. A wonderful scene in front. His eyes searched for mala bairagi. He assumed that where he cast a look, the bearded person sitting on a sand mound and looking intently must be the mala bairagi. He was about to take a step ahead. In the meanwhile, a sonorous light voice.

What does it matter who it is, go away.

Why are you joking with me?

Keep away, don't come near. Keep away.

At 'keep away,' ragada again . . . Mala bairagi looked on, lost to the world. The potter went up to the mala bairagi. Suddenly the song, dance and beat stopped.

He told him who he was. Told him why he came. Mala bairagi looked at Pedakoteswarudu. White hair combed in front. A twisted beard that was three-fourths grey. Must be an old wound, a bandage tied round his foot. His looks were direct. If he looked sharply, his looks seemed capable of burning the other person to ashes. Did not know why but Koteswarudu felt like according him a guru's status. Though he did not say it aloud, mala bairagi looked with as much reverence at him. Pedakoteswarudu sat next to mala bairagi.

Stars in the sky. So much commotion, theirs. How they ran from this end to that! Why did so much of starry light spread on its own volition on the sand mounds? Why did nature love those who merge with it so well?

'It's many years since I left home. I saw the dance of the yerra gollalu. I saw the dances of *kotha indlu* and *kota konda* people. I also saw the dances of the chindu people, the china madiga and the chilakala people. I also saw the dances of the jangam people and the people of Jangalipalli. I saw the dances of the dasari and the pitchikaguntala people. Okay, I danced the mala people's dance. But I couldn't find the control of the yanadi's dances anywhere else. The greatness lies in their waists. No other caste possesses such a beautiful waist. That waist was born for dance. One might have that curve but everyone can't have its exact stamp.'

Mala bairagi kept talking. The potter Pedakoteswarudu was looking at him in amazement. He felt there was no jealousy like that among pundits and the treacheries involved in attaining the highest position. In fact, it is only in folk art that there is purity and integrity. There is frankness and naturalness. That's why it is still alive even though it has been thrown and cast away.

'How are the stars . . . ?' Pedakoteswarudu began.

At these words, mala bairagi looked at the sky. Constellations of stars. The running of lone stars from one constellation to another. No matter how long you look, your thirst is not quenched.

'Sing a song on the stars. I came all the way just to listen to you. Sing all night long. I'll write down every song you sing. In Cuddapah, there's plenty of paper. It is also sold in Nellore. The white man is putting on paper all the verses which were on palm-leaf. All the pundits are searching every village. I'm roaming about for Basavadu. I want his words. I've written most of it. Let's light a fire. I'll write in that glow. I've brought along good leaves.'

Pedakoteswarudu stopped speaking and looked towards mala bairagi.

The fire place was glowing. The fire, the twinkle of the stars. Nothing would be defeated. Everything would unite. How would they merge? Ought to see with the heart. That's it.

At night, a strange sound was heard. Yanadi Ramanaiah was hitting the dappu with a stick. The stick of the dappu merged with the strange sound of the night. At one go nature stretched its body and opened its eyes really wide. It made the strange excitement its own, every moment. Hiding would be like that.

Mala bairagi began to sing. Pedakoteswarudu was writing.

How far away was Yennela Dinni? Not so far away. It was being hidden in Pedakoteswarudu's writing.

The night was passing by, saying 'Friends, I'm unable to wait, don't think otherwise.'

The voice of mala bairagi. The rhythmic beat of the stick on yanadi Ramanaiah's dappu. The writing of potter Pedakoteswarudu. The showering moonlight. Nature that is getting wet. The gentle breeze that unites.

What was happening here! What literature —as the glow of the fire place was witness! What music! Why this wonderful creation! They say it is *satyam*, the truth. They say it is *sivam*, prosperity. They say it is *sundaram*, beauty. Why has this trinity become untouchable?

There were a thousand thoughts in Pedakoteswarudu's mind. What heart-wrenching pain to the mud pot that was gaining a beautiful shape on the wheel and whetstone! What anxiety to get away from that heat! When it was mud, when it was just mud, what life in its every atom! How much friendship it had with flowers, trees and reeds! Isn't it so, isn't that very mud these songs? Isn't that very being this song? Why don't you allow such naturalness, such full-blooded life to live? Spewing sastras, why have these pundits ruthlessly killed the word and the song? These burnt pots. These breakable pots. Lifeless images. How wonderfully has this weave of the mud united with nature? 'Tell me your name, mala bairagi. I'm writing down. I've written down Subhadra. I've written down Yennela Dinni. I've written down Naganna and Mataiah. I've written down Narigadu. Tell me your name. Do tell me, tell me.' Pedakoteswarudu asked even as he wrote.

After two *jamus,* mala bairagi said stirring the embers of the fire, 'You've asked me, I'll tell you. Yellanna. Atalelladu. Patalelladu.'

Pedakoteswarudu kept looking like that. Next to him, the yennela pitta darted away, making a horrendously shrill call. Yellanna felt like laughing.

'Listen to its cry.'

Its cry was heard a long way off.

'What do you hear in its cry?'

'The heart-rending voice of an untouchable.'

'Heart-rending voice. How did you weave that phrase?'

'Not I. Life. Life wove it. Isn't it so? Isn't it the weave of life? When young Yelladu ran like that and stopped . . . isn't it the sound of the Urumula dance that saved him? That's life. It's the one that wove. Dance and word. Song was born in my house. Word was born in my house. Dance learnt its beat from my life. That's why, no matter how far they flung me, they only ran towards my house. They were born with me and will become dust with me.'

'You're a Vedantist.'

'That's the crown of pundits. I don't want that term. Mine is life. A man's life. The life of the dust.'

'Sound is at your feet.'

'No. In my heart.'

That's how it went between them till two jamus went by.

Afterwards, the two of them went into deep slumber. Yanadi Ramanaiah's stick kept beating the dappu, even as the man had slipped into sleep a long while ago.

Dawn broke. Pedakoteswarudu tied up all that he wrote into a bundle and placed it in mala bairagi's hand. He said no. Mala bairagi said, 'Keep it with you.'

'I'll see you later, Yellanna.'

'Many years since I heard that name.'

Laughter. They bade goodbye to each other, laughing. They walked a long distance even as they said goodbye. Yanadi Ramanaiah was smiling, with his eyes. Speaking, with his eyes. His waist would display dance and his eyes his emotions. He had no need for the word except rarely.

They stopped at the boundary that divided the mala and madiga palles from the ooru.

'I won't go this way.'

'Why?'

'When I came, I wiped the dust off my feet and flung it. I came only after I cleared my throat and spat.'

'The side road isn't good.'

'The path is never good. It'll improve as you walk along. All that needs to be done is to walk. This isn't Vedanta. Life's lesson.' Saying so, he laughed. Yellanna laughed. Ramanaiah's eyes smiled.

He hugged Yellanna close to his chest. He hugged Ramanaiah to his chest. Farewell ought not to be so painful. Even so, there was no other way. He gave up the path taken by everyone and introducing the walk to the path not trodden by anyone, he went ahead. Mala bairagi Yellanna and Yanadi Ramanaih stood gazing at him.

Did not feel like turning back. Ramanaiah looked towards the top of the only palm tree that had grown tall. He tied a string to his leg. He tucked a knife in his waist. He sat near the top of the palm tree. He cut two palm fruit bunches that were hanging down. They remained there cutting the palm fruits and eating them.

Only because they were like that did they hear the cry of pain. No sooner had they raised their heads than they saw Pedakoteswarudu running for his life. They saw the upper castes chasing him. They saw sticks, crowbars, spades and axes in their hands. They saw the brahmin running ahead of everyone. They saw their friend fall to the ground right in front of their eyes. They saw the crowbar that had pierced his back and the stick that had attacked his head. They saw the written pages flung by the brahmin burning in a corner. Though they were at a distance, they saw all this in a second. They ran screaming loudly. Their shrieks reached malapalli. Reached madigapalli. The anthill burst in yanadi's mound. Screaming, everyone was running towards that gruesome scene.

Seeing people coming, the upper castes having done all they wanted to ran away. The ordinary people reached there.

Potter Pedakoteswarudu in a pool of blood. The last written record of mala bairagi Yellana being burnt away.

Yellanna placed his friend's head on his lap. Pedakoteswarudu looked towards Yellanna. Looked towards Ramanaiah. Looked towards people surrounding him. Laughed with contentment. Called out, 'I'm going, Basavadu!' He spoke the last words to Yellanna.

Yellanna himself lit the funeral pyre.

Who was this Basavadu?

How could one meet him? Yellanna thought looking into the flames of the pyre. He knew Potuluri's verses. He had never heard of this Basavadu. But he had heard of this Basavadu from Pedakoteswarudu two or three times. Those were the last words, too. Naganna had not included this in the secrets of the puranas. Perhaps Chandrappa had not said it. But of what period was this Basavadu?

He remained there till the pyre burnt completely. He gathered the ashes and built a tomb. Ramanaiah planted a *sampenga* sapling there. He planted a fence of *gangiregu* trees around it. Even after Yellanna left that village, Ramanaiah continued to sprinkle water on the trees.

Yellanna returned to that place after two years. Ramanaiah was moving about in the shade of those trees. Now it looked like a tranquil forest. Ramanaiah appeared like an ascetic devoid of sham and hypocrisy. The smile had not vanished from those eyes.

That night in the moonlight, the aroma of sampenga flowers. Mala bairagi Yellanna's song stirring that silence. The sound of the dappu sticks of Ramanaiah. One more time a strange experience for nature. In the moonlit shade of the gangiregu trees, the fireflies moving about as if on some business. As for the stars, were they quiet? How much of excitement in them!

Mala bairagi Yellanna would come there like that once in a year or two after roaming about the villages. Ramanaiah remained like that in the shades of those trees. Wonder! Once a year malas, madigas and yanadis assembled there. The tomb of potter Pedakoteswarudu became a meeting place for the ordinary people. In every corner of this country an occasion like this is truly a wonderful scene. The year mala bairagi Yellana came, it would be an arena of art. The dance, songs and plays of yanadis . . . the roaring sound of dappus . . . a meeting arranged on their own by those below the line. What name would tradition give to this meeting? Something or the other. All the more surprising was that the potter's community would fast on that day. If such a meeting of upper castes took place, it would turn into a holy shrine. Saying that some God passing by stepped there, a *sthala puranam*. There was no place here for such unbelievable fantastic imagination. No artificial tradition imposed this. There is a beautiful scene combining dance, word and song here. That's all.

12

Yellanna was moving from village to village.

Sivaiah was growing up in Yennela Dinni.

There was nothing more that Subhadra could do than wait for the wandering Yellanna and to work her heart out in the fields for the sake of the growing Sivaiah. Everything, a hope. A hope that Yellanna would return some day. A hope that even though the father was not with him, Sivaiah should grow up well. Hope knows no distance. Knows no proximity. It has no place for gain or loss. That's why it is called hope. For man to live, the dependable medicine that was born before man is hope. It only knows to make man live. It does not at all know how to kill. If in fact without that hope, that small hope that Yellanna would some day come back, that great hope to bring up Sivaiah happily in Yennela Dinni, Subhadra would have caused great heartache to Pittodu. He would not have been able to bear that ache.

Yerrenkadu died on the cot yearning to see his son. Telling Sivaiah, 'How can I say no to my husband and live?' Lingalu looked out for her own path. Did time stop, did the wind take a vow and sit tight that it would not cross the outskirts of Yennela Dinni? Did summer stop just right there? Did the branches keep quiet when the trees shed leaves? Did new shoots not sprout? Nothing stopped. Along with time, along with its tread, along with its racing, tears of joy and sorrow had been sprinkled in equal measure in the mala and madiga households and frontyards of Yennela Dinni. The muggukarralu were continuing to draw patterns.

Pittodu said it was not possible to build houses roaming around villages. He sat in front of the house making ploughs. The big adze that is to be carried on the shoulder, the small one that is to be held in the hand and the chisel were all lying idle. Except that Chinnammi was holding the rope to catch hold of the drill. Looking at the two of them like that was like seeing them observe penance. All that penance was only for Sivaiah. Sivaiah was not a God. If he were a God, they would have been satisfied with a coconut. They would have applied this much of sacred ash on their faces. Sivaiah was a grandson. This was a penance forgetting their age for his sake. Toil. All that was left for malas and madigas. That was all that they gained. Toil.

There was some change somewhere on the globe. The white man aimed straight and shot at the weaver's livelihood. In the north the looms had stopped moving and the thread started moving only on the wheel. Someone would come and give the cotton. Then he would come and pick up the thread bundles. The rate was so many dammiddees per bundle. The spun thread would go to a mill somewhere. What would happen to the cloth? Everything was the white man's trick. The trick of the black middlemen who had joined hands with the whites. Not just the regions of Chirala or Perala. It was just like that in every place that depended on the loom. The salis dependent on weaving, the malas dependent on weaving, no matter who—that was it.

Till this point Yenkatanarsu would keep the advance paid near the well of the loom. He would tie up the cut bedsheets, and the panchas he bought at the well of the loom into a bundle and roam about. But it was not so now. The houses that spun the loom now stopped with making the thread. They stopped with making the bundles of thread. What could he do with spindles and bundles of thread? To go to the mill was something new to him. The language of business there was different. The mode was different. Had changed a great deal. He could not digest the change. He thought there was no point in going around. On his final return he brought stacks of *gogu* skein. He began weaving the string for the cot. He stayed back home. He began to make different patterns with the gogu skein. It transformed itself thus into the cot string, the belt for the bullocks with bells, the loop around their mouths to prevent them from eating and the nose-string and reins for them. Yenkatanarsu felt that the life that was tied to the cotton cloth would end with the gogu skein. They planted gogu plants on the fields of the mala's mound. When it was ready for use, they would pull it out and dry it. They would soak it in the water in the stream. They would take out the gogu after it had soaked. Boodevi would find it strange when she saw Yenkatanarsu keep the soaked gogu in front of him and remove it from the water. It would appear quite nice. The man was staying in and around the house. At that moment she would remember Yellanna. The happiness of the man staying at home would be swept away by some wind. Even so, it was wonderful to see the gogu skein turn into so many kinds of art.

We call them the arts. We say there are sixty four arts. How did those arts come to be? If we think about it, it feels somewhat strange. It is both surprising and wonderful. How have those live arts that have given life support to so many come to be! To skin the animal's hide very skilfully, making it soft, to make pots with mud, stick and wood, to milk if there was enough milk, to churn butter, to melt it and make ghee, to extract oil from sesame, coconut, castor seeds, and wild dindiga plants, to spin cotton, to weave cloth, to hold the plough and to dig it straight into the earth and plough, to sow, to thresh grain, to scout for the place where there is water, to plant a stick to indicate the place and to find either drinking or salt water, to weave coir baskets and different things, with palm, with gogu skein, with palm leaf, with bamboo, with cane, with date palm, finally even with the water reeds growing along canal banks, to turn iron into knives and axes in the furnace of a blacksmith, to build houses, to hang on to the village and to hang on to life—how many arts!

How wonderfully the folklorist has said that art is only for the masses. To think of it, what is hidden in people's lives is not small, insignificant art.

What wonderful artists are Poladu who skins the hide of a buffalo skilfully with ease, Pittodu who carves wood, and Yenkatanarsu who makes the thread dance in myriad ways!

Sivaiah would put his fingers into the greyed beards of those three people, then stroke them, and watch them performing their tasks. He would ask Poladu, 'Thatha, how can you skin the hide so well?' Poladu would say, 'Tell that wretched Pittodu to skin like this.' Sivaiah would laugh aloud. 'Can you wield the plough like him?' Poladu's wife would berate him. He would skin the hide saying, 'She won't tolerate anyone saying a word against him.' On either side of the hide, as Sivaiah and Poladu's wife would hold it, Poladu would hold it on one side, stretch it, spread it on the ground, stretch it further and nail it on four sides so it would not curl up. So that dogs would not touch it, he would overturn the string cot and place four stones in the four corners. Sivaiah would remain watching all that. He would also be close by and watch the hide being soaked in water after it was dry. Making the soaked hide soft would appear amazing. Sivaiah would share this feeling of amazement.

Pittodu shaping the top would appear amazing. Chinnammi's hand moving as she pulled the rope while the top was being made, too, would appear very appealing. When the top was given to him after driving a nail and saying, 'Go, play, Siva,' he would take the top and run towards Yenkatanarsu. Yenkatanarsu would put the thread around the top. When Yenkatanarsu was spinning the thread so finely and so adeptly, Sivaiah would look with wide open eyes. When he tied a little single bell at the knot of the thread and asked, 'How's that, Siva?', the child would jump on to his shoulders. He would roam around the entire bazaar like that and then would slide down at one go. Running from there, he would reach madigapalli. He would spin the top in front of Poladu's house, stroke Poladu's grey beard and tap his cheek with the little bell on the string. The bell would ring sweetly. Looking at the spinning top and listening to the ringing bell, Poladu would pick up two small pieces of hide. He would make anklets. He would put them round Sivaiah's feet. Only

Sivaiah knew how ecstatic he was. Looking at him, Boodevi would feel, 'I brought up Yellanna as someone even more special.' In the meanwhile, inexplicable sorrow would touch her heart.

Pittodu, Yenkatanarsu and Poladu were crushed completely. But they were doing something or the other as if their patience was not lost. They did not feel like getting up from around the winter fire. Boodevi was crushing betel leaves and betelnuts and giving them to Yenkatanarsu. Pittodu would say his teeth and jaw hurt when a meat piece touched them. Poladu was a bit better than the two of them. When asked what it was, he would say, 'This is a body that has eaten seven heads at a time, Pittodu, wretched fellow.'

When the three of them sat together at one place now, it was only to talk about the past. Their conversation would be about how Atchireddy became prosperous. It would be about how the younger karanam took to living in the city. As he left, the younger karanam did something. It was not known whether he did it for good or bad. He gave the entire fallow land between Atchireddy's field and the mala's mound to the malas and madigas. No one doubted whom it belonged to. They were not yet far away from the belief that government meant only the karanam. Atchireddy said it was not possible to give it away like that. The younger karanam said, 'I felt like giving and I gave it away.' Atchireddy did not get the opportunity to say no to the younger karanam. But he spewed out all his anger in the presence of the karanam when the malas and madigas distributed it among themselves. The karanam, too, wanted just that. He felt there ought to be some problem between Atchireddy and the malas and the madigas. That was why he acted like such a charitable person. The mala and madiga elders said that the younger karanam was not 'one like that' compared to the elder karanam. No one knew the meaning of 'one like that'. It could be anything.

The fallow land that the younger karanam donated created the situation he wanted. In Yennala Dinni, the water collected for the fields was distributed in a particular manner. That method was determined by the elder karanam. First, the karanam's fields must be watered. After that, the prosperous reddys, then the poorer reddys, followed by the other castes. Till the mala's mound began to be cultivated, the malas and madigas had no problem about water. By the time the sequence was up, the water flow in the culvert would stop. The mala's mound would not be watered. It was about the days when Naganna was alive. In the fallow land that the karanam donated, when they watered the fields of the karanam and the reddys, the canals in the fields would overflow. Such an overflow would turn the stony path in the fallow land into a water canal. If there were pits here and there on the way, they, too, would be filled. Along with that, the ground water in the fields, too, would reach there. Naganna had diverted that water towards the mala's mound. They turned the water on the bullock cart track and the ground water into the pits. They made the pit large. They placed a water lift on that pit. From the water lift to the mala's mound they made a waist-high sand mound. They turned that into a canal. The water from the water lift would reach the mala's mound through that high sandy canal. They would operate in turns.

After the fallow land was donated, Atchireddy was seething with anger. He had had an idea of adding all of it to his own. He was not able to digest the fact that the malas and madigas had got hold of so much land. He incited his fellow reddys. He diverted the water that flowed through the field canal. Even if the ground water flowed into the fallow field, it would only come to ten or fifteen tubs of water that would not be enough to wet the fields.

The culvert water irrigated the karanam's fields. It was irrigating Atchireddy's fields. After that it would have to moisten the poor reddys' plots. If something remained, it would wet a cent or a small piece of land of the people of other castes. That year it did not seem as if it would go that far. If the culvert water did not wet it, there was nothing else that would happen to the mala's mound but dry up. The malas and madigas did not know what to do. The overflowing water had been diverted and was reaching outside Atchireddy's western field. There was no possibility of utilising it from there. Atchireddy's lame excuse was that as the pathway was meant for everyone and as the fallow land belonged to the malas and madigas, if the joint pathway was filled with water like that, there would be no path for the reddy carts to travel. The malas and madigas said, 'Anyway, what has never been there, how can you get it now?' Atchireddy jumped all over them saying, 'Hasn't the fallow land that never was yours become yours now?'

The malas and madigas were unable to find a way out. They understood Atchireddy's jealousy. They gathered at one place. They keenly felt Naganna's absence. In their conversation, the karanam's scheming was not exposed. It was not possible to understand it too. It was Atchireddy who appeared as a big traitor to them. They gathered like that for two days. Placing the burden on Pittodu and Poladu's heads saying, 'You do something,' on the third day, they began to slide into Vedanta. 'Did we depend on land all these days?' On the third day, Poladu, Pittodu, Musalaiah and five others of the same age sat at the meeting place.

It was midnight. Nothing was clear. Mallaiah came out with the water cauldron from the house in front of the meeting place. He said, 'Won't you come for water, Pittayyamama?' 'Is the middle of the night already?', asked Pittodu. 'You think it'll wait for you?' Saying this, he went away.

'How will it be if we do like this?' said Poladu.

'How?'

'Aren't we collecting drinking water in the middle of the night . . . like that?'

Pittodu did not brush aside Poladu's words. He felt a way out had been found.

There was no drinking water well for the malas and madigas. The entire village had only one drinking water well. They called it the central well. Except there, everywhere else there was only tasteless water. That well was to the east of the geviti tree. Except for the malas and madigas every one else in that village drank only that water. As for the malas and madigas, they would stand a distance from the well carrying pots. If kind-hearted upper castes who came to draw water felt sorry and poured water into their pots, they would get water to drink. Otherwise not. As long as they poured the water these untouchables would praise those kind-hearted people, and those kind-hearted ones would keep abusing these untouchables. For a potful of water, there would be a big fight. Every morning that was a strange scene near the well. Pleadings, insults, abuses, rejections—all for a mouthful of water, for quenching thirst.

On some occasions, no 'kind-hearted person' would be sympathetic. On days of work, they would never be kind. Sometimes, one had to keep waiting till noon, as scalding sand burnt the feet, for the kind-hearted one, for the kind-hearted one who would pour water. Look, it is at such times that men would become water thieves. They would wait till midnight. They would go stealthily to the well. They would draw water stealthily. Knowing that they would lose their lives if they were found, they would run with the water pot. It was normal to tumble and the pots to break while they ran. The theft of water would happen only during days of work. On those days, it was not possible to sit at the well with eager eyes. For the lives of labourers, only those few days were festive days.

'Do you think we should divert the flow of the water channel stealthily?'

'There's no other choice.'

Pittodu felt like laughing. Theft for the throat getting wet. Theft for wetting the throat. The man was an untouchable. His piece of land, too, was untouchable. Theft, to be able to 'touch'. Would the sastras give this another name? Would the society think of this act as something else? Did not know. Pittodu's laugh did not know any of this. All he knew was the struggle for life.

Dark night. Nothing other than the water of the flowing canal could be heard. The beating of the heart could be heard only by Pittodu, Poladu, Musalaiah and Mallaiah. Mallaiah was well known as a water thief. Among the malas and madigas there are such well-known thieves. That is the strange thing in the great culture of this country. Mallaiah himself went near the water channel at Atchireddy's field.

The senior paid-servant at the water channel had gone home. He would return only after the first star rose. Whatever was to happen had to happen before that. Near the channel, the stopping of whirlpools of water for irrigating the fields was visible. The water from the culvert came up to that point, from there, it would go whichever way it was diverted. They would then build a bund on the other side. For the bund to hold, they would even stuff it with palm trunks. Mallaiah stood there and looked towards the fields. There was no problem of breaking it till here. In which direction was the water to be diverted? What direction should it to be diverted for it to go towards the sand mound canal at the mala's mound? If it was diverted towards the poorer peasants, it could be reached from a shorter distance. But Atchireddy's fields had not yet become wet. If the water were to flow towards the poor farmers that night, there would be a lot of suspicion. He placed the shovel on his shoulder and came towards Pittodu. Pittodu and Poladu were near the culvert. They were awaiting Mallaiah's clearance. If Mallaiah were to tell them to lift the sluices they were ready to lift them. Just in front of the mala's mound, they had placed four others. They had to divert the water towards fields there. Mallaiah brought the real problem to the fore.

All sat under the palm tree. They were unable to decide which side to divert the water. Poladu got up. He went towards the row of the newly grown palm trees. He cut the palm fronds and made a ring to climb up the trees. Very silently he got on to the tree they sat under. He brought down the toddy pot. Pittodu said laughing, 'Toddy thief.' They drank toddy. They walked towards the mala's mound. They walked all around the mound. All of them together came near the water channel. Pittodu took the spade that was in Mallaiah's hand. He diverted it towards the fields of the poor reddys. They made it appear as if it was not diverted by a spade but as if the bund had broken. All the stored up water in the canal flowed only that way. They thought that that was enough for that day. They felt that if they broke it the next day it would not appear as if it was freshly broken. It happened just like that. Atchireddy abused the senior paid-servant. As the bund looked just as it was at the poor reddys' fields, it did not appear as if the canal was broken on purpose. But as for the water, it filled the entire route of the canal.

The next day they did according to plan. They let the water flow as much as it would till the star appeared at midnight. Dark night. Thieves' hour. Water too changed direction like a thief. Like a thief it wet the throat of the mala's mound.

The day broke. A strange experience in malapalli and madigapalli. Inexplicable fear. Incomprehensible anxiety. Happiness at seeing the wet mound. But happiness too had lurking fear. That experience too was anxiety. But courage had no fear. No anxiety. If it did, it would be no courage. As it was not so, Pittodu, Poladu, Musalaiah and Mallaiah sat on the mala's mound itself. Their thought was how to wet the two corners that needed to become wet. It was then that an unforeseen incident took place.

We cannot believe that it happened in this manner then. No one for the life of him agrees that ordinary people are so courageous. But some things happen in that manner.

No one would have imagined. That Subhadra would have so much courage. Yennela Dinni did not imagine. Even her own father did not think that his daughter had so much guts. He only thought she was adamant.

This incident occurred on the third day after the mala's mound got wet. Then the poor peasants' fields were getting wet. While the poor peasants' fields were getting wet one midnight, the mala's mound was getting wet the second time. They thought that much of water was enough for that year. There was a discussion in Atchireddy's meeting as to how the mala's mound had got wet without using the water lift. They caught hold of Chandrayi, the most timid person in malapalli, tied him in the cattleshed and lashed him soundly. He revealed everything. Atchireddy was enraged. He sent people to attack the mala's mound. They caught hold of Pittodu, Poladu and whoever they could lay their hands on, threw them down and beat them with sticks. Though it was not an unexpected incident, they did not think it would happen so suddenly. Everyone was confused. Atchireddy's people assaulted them as per their plan and went away. Pittodu's arm was broken. There was a big blow on Poladu's waist. Mallaiah escaped but Musalaiah was hurt.

The malas and madigas watched, stunned. In the time it took them to get over it, the damage that was to be done was done. None of them was able to look at Pittodu and Poladu who were hurt. Pittodu's arm was bleeding. Poladu's back was bleeding. The malas and madigas were shedding tears.

Subhadra was amidst that blood. Subhadra was amidst those tears. She picked up the spade next to her. All were watching. She tucked her saree tight between her legs. Everyone was looking at her with wide-open eyes. She swirled the fringe of her saree and tucked it in. She was like the yellow golden wire glowing in the sun. Eyes were like a burning furnace. She moved forward with the spade.

'Where to, Subhadra?'

That was not only Pittodu's voice. Not'just of Boodevi. Not of Poladu alone. It was the voice of a number of untouchable people. 'Where to, Subhadra?' were the words uttered by all the malas and madigas of Yennela Dinni in one voice.

Subhadra did not stop.

She did not wait for anyone's words. They were not steps but a run. A run filled with vengeance. Did not know why she moved. Did not know where she was running to. Poladu's wife shrieked crazily. 'Stop, Subhadra . . . Come, my co-wives . . . Stop, my bidda . . .' Crazy running. Mother running for the child. That was Boodevi running. After that the mothers and daughters of Yennela Dinni . . .

'Stop, Subhadra . . . Stop, Subhadra.'

Subhadra stopped. Near Atchireddy's water channel. She stepped on the edge of Atchireddy's water channel. Subhadra was a weak turmeric stick. Subhadra was the delicate golden wire that would burn in flames immediately if the workman were to lose his concentration . . . bent her waist. Stubborn strength. She sent down the spade powerfully into the channel. She dug the mud and threw it to one side. Water gushed out. Lifting the spade she stood like that. She looked like Kali at Atchireddy's men who were looking wonderstruck at the sunshine over the flowing water dancing on her golden body. At that moment, Atchireddy arrived.

On that side the malas and the madigas. On this side, the reddys. In between people of other castes working in Atchireddy's fields. Among them washermen, barbers and potters were watching. They kept looking on.

'Subbappa, a goodess has sprung up.'

The washerwoman, Venkayi looking stunned.

'Is she Subhadra . . . '?'

The potter's daughter-in-law who had recently come to live with her in-laws asked Venkayi.

'Yes, it's that girl. Real gold . . . Has never crossed the threshold. A mala. Pittodu brought her up like a maharaja's daughter. Her husband's Atalelladu. He went away to places to perform.'

'Wretched fellow. How could he go?'

'Her life has become wretched like that. It's for the child that she stepped into the fields like a daughter-in-law of the Bayyarapu household.'

The sun was not right on top. He hid in Subhadra's eyes that were looking on, sharply.

The scene was chaotic.

The scene was lashing the heart. It was an unimaginably strange experience as if something was going to be burnt to ashes. The reddys were unable to fathom how to comprehend it. The malas and madigas did not care how it was going to end.

All that they were seeing was just one thing.

A woman. And a mala at that. She had diverted the water in the canal and stood holding the spade. She was throwing a challenge to move her if they had the courage.

'A spirit has possessed the girl!'

Chukkireddy of the reddys said this. Atchireddy was next to him. Chukkireddy did not stop at that. Chukkireddy was of the firm view that only those possessed by the spirit could do this.

'It's so even in the jataras. That girl's body swells. The eyeballs won't move. The mouth won't utter a word.'

Atchireddy kept listening. As he listened, he looked towards Subhadra. It was true—the eyeballs were not moving. Was not shifting her gaze. Did not bring down the spade she had lifted up. Was not withdrawing the foot she had placed. The water was flowing round her feet. Atchireddy stared. Did not know why, but a small shiver went down his body. Chukkireddy kept talking. In fact Subhadra did not appear like Subhadra to Chukkireddy. That girl was possessed by mother goddess. Only mother goddess could do that.

The beliefs of the palle are strange. One cannot find reasons for them. They recognise every wonderful act in gods, goddesses and ghosts. That is why so many village deities reside in the life of the palle. They believe that human beings do not act in that manner. There are hundreds of mother goddesses like Poleramma, Ankalamma and Mungamooramma. Parvati is a perfect untouchable goddess. Malas call her 'Paratamma' endearingly. Mungamooramma was Pittodu's household deity. She is the sister of Parvatamma. In this manner, there was a goddess in each house in the malapalli of Yennela Dinni.

There was a god. All of them were siblings of Parvatamma. In fact, if Subhadra collapsed on to the ground here and now, she would indeed become a goddess. She would become Parvatamma's sister or niece. There a stone would sprout. Yenkatalakshmi who read the future that would be possessed by a spirit. In that possessed state, Subhadra would say, 'I've no temple, Atchiga.' Atchireddy would say he would build a temple. She would spit on the ground and ask him to build it before it dried up. Mungamooramma asked that of Pittodu's great grandfather when he was alive. Since then, to this day there had been no temple for Mungamooramma in Yennela Dinni. Subhadra would take on Parvatamma's form. Would become a part of Mungamooramma. That was why she would place that condition. But that would not happen. There would be no temple built there. But a jatara would take place. Subhadra could have become a water goddess. Could have become a goddess of the water channel. Could have become a field goddess. Could have become a goddess of plots. Or could have become even goddess Subhadra. What was strange was that Atchireddy could have himself performed the jatara every year so that his family would not be a target of Subhadra's ire. If turmeric and vermilion came from Pittodu's house to Yellanna's house every year, Yellana's progeny could have brought that on the day of the jatara. It could have happened like that.

Subhadra had broken the bund of the water canal. She stood holding up the spade. Subhadra was the daughter of the mala household. She was born in the untouchable caste. If she was just a mala or an untouchable she would not have dared do such a thing. She would have stolen at night like Pittodu or Poladu. She would have, like Mallaiah, stolen well water at midnight. She would not have dared to do such things in front of all reddys, not caring for the repercussions. Therefore, it must be a goddess that possessed Subhadra. In the jatara Subhadra would be possessed by a spirit. Therefore, in truth, it was a goddess who had entered her. Chukkireddy would believe that. Chukkireddy would not believe even if Subhadra shouted loud and clear that it was she, Subhadra, who did this work.

Washerwoman Venkayi was extremely fond of Subhadra. She very much liked her form. When Subhadra was young, Chinnammi took her in her arms and went to the washerman's shore. She put the child down on the sand and put the wet clothes to dry on the banks. Venkayi saw the child as it was crawling. She felt as if gold was glistening. She could not keep quiet, just watching her. She looked this way and that. There was nobody else on the shore. She lifted the child. Again she looked around. She would have to put up with abuses if she lifted a mala child. She felt no one was watching her. She kissed the child. Chinnammi was looking as she was washing the clothes in the water. Venkayi lifted the child and hid behind a tree. As Chinnammi did not know why she went there, she went near the tree, peeped and was surprised. Venkayi had given her breast to the child and was suckling her.

'I'm feeding her.'

Chinnammi stood looking around. If someone saw a mala child in Venkayi's lap and saw her feeding it, they would not keep quiet. The child drank as much as it wanted, pushed the breast aside, placed its tongue against the palate and said 'Ta'. How happy Venkayi was! Looking into the child's eyes, she said many times, 'Sinni, how did she get those eyes?' Wasn't that child this Subhadra! How crazily she laughed when she said, 'Ta'. How she kicked her on her stomach with her anklet on her tiny legs! In that manner the one born in a mala home and who stood with her foot on Atchireddy's water channel was no human being. No way. A goddess. Was definitely Mungamooramma. Was Parvatamma for sure.

'She's a goddess's child, you fellow . . . How long can she remain like that . . . bring the spade down . . . '

Venkayi ran towards Subhadra. As for the potters' new daughter-in-law, she was only looking at Subhadra's nose ring.

Atchireddy heard Venkayi's words. He retreated. He felt he should not remain there any longer. Chukkireddy did not stop speaking. He kept talking. He said Venkayi's words were true. As she recognised this like he did, she said, 'She's the goddess's child.' Not just then, he kept speaking even after he came back to the ooru. Venkayi went around each house and kept saying that Chukkireddy said so. Atchireddy's wife dragged Venkayi to the backyard and asked her to tell her all that had happened. Chukkireddy settled the issue. It was the goddess that had entered Subhadra. Though Subhadra was born in a mala's house, she was brought up in a different manner. The way she went around was entirely different. If Subhadra who had never mingled with a crowd before did such a thing it was all the handiwork of the goddess. Most certainly the work of the goddess. Venkayi believed Chukkireddy all the more. She added more to the story. Atchireddy's wife involuntarily lifted her hands and paid obeisance.

What is surprising is that on the third day, Atchireddy offered food near the Malutchamma tree. The malas and madigas ate that food. After they ate, they were chased away with neem twigs up to the outskirts. Now the water that was flowing in the fallow land began to flow through the cart track. There began the use of the water lift, and the mala's mound started getting wet once again. Years passed by. No matter what people thought, no matter how many stories took birth, Subhadra was only an ordinary person. A very ordinary person indeed. A mother who toiled for Sivaiah. A housewife who awaited Yellanna.

That was all in the past. Pittodu, Yenkatanarsu and Poladu would sit keeping all that in front of them. Their past kept returning to them and stopping with Subhadra. It would stop with the worry as to how Yellanna was, till Sivaiah came and scolded them a bit. During sankranti days, they would never get up from near the fire, lit for the cold. While in summer, they would keep talking and would sleep at the meeting place. At some hour Poladu would get up, dusting off the sand, saying, 'Rascals, if we fall asleep why don't you wake us up?' Their lives would go by in Yennela Dinni in that manner. Yennela Dinni would appear strange to them once in a while. Sometimes they would love it so much so as to say, 'If we die, we'll do so here.' Sometimes they would be irritated enough to say, 'Wretched place, it'd have been nice to have been born somewhere else.' Yesterday went by somehow. Today would go by like this. Tomorrow, there would be nothing they could call their own.

Subhadra had no such disappointment. All she had was hope. She would get up in the morning. She would go towards the mala's mound. She would spend the entire day digging, weeding, or doing something or the other. Next to her piece of land were Pittodu's and Boodevi's. They were cultivating crops in all the three together. Whether paddy was planted and harvested, or whether gogulu grew, it was all in that land. Even when the three pieces of land were put together, they would be two cents less than an acre. Subhadra would not listen even if Pittodu asked her not to work. She would not pay attention even when he said, 'We can't see you toil so hard, my little one.' She was no longer a little one. Sivaiah was right in front of her eyes. Yellanna who was not present there was in her heart. She had drawn a circle for herself. She was moving about within that circle. She did not care what meaning the palle ascribed to that circle.

She moved within that circle for many years. Her hair was greying here and there.

Pittodu said it was early greying. Chinnammi felt like laughing. For Pittodu, Subhadra was still a little one. If she went to the mala's mound forgetting her slippers, he would run carrying them and would not return till he had made her wear them. He would not eat till then. Where one has no property, affection is indeed the property, love alone is life. In truth, what wonderful lovers are the poor! Why do they love a person like that? What greater value is there in the world than doing such a thing? Preachers teach values. The poor live them.

Once she came to know the news about Yellanna through coolies when they migrated for the harvest season. Finding this out also happened in a curious manner. The coolies sang as they were harvesting,

Listen Subhadra.[28]

The mouse drank the water under the roof. || Listen ||
Listen Subhadra.

How will it rain at a cloudless place? || Listen ||
Listen Subhadra.

How will the stream fill up without rain? || Listen ||
Listen Subhadra.

How will the field become wet without the stream filling?
                                                         || Listen ||
Listen Subhadra.

How will we plant saplings without the field getting wet?
                                                         || Listen ||

Listen Subhadra.

How will the corn flower without planting the saplings?

|| Listen ||

Listen Subhadra.

How will the grains fall without threshing the yield? || Listen ||
Listen Subhadra.

How will the granary fill without the grain falling? || Listen ||
Listen Subhadra.

How to pay back the *namu** without the granary filling?

|| Listen ||

Listen Subhadra.

The *namu* is paid back, hunger remains. || Listen ||
Listen Subhadra.

The year-long crops are measured out to the landlords.

|| Listen ||

Listen Subhadra.

The mouse drank the water under the roof. || Listen ||

She listened to the entire song the coolies sang. The song began
with her name. Her name was in the refrain. The voice of the girl
who sang was also sweet. The way the girl changed the tune at the
end of each stanza was just like the way Yellanna did.

It was Yellanna who wove that song.

It was Yellanna who had constructed the song in the village the girl
lived in and sang it. He must have sung it many times. Otherwise,
that change of tune could not have been reproduced. She only knew
that the coolies came from the north. For the Nellore region, all of
Guntur and Krishna came under the northern region. To which place
in the north did they belong? She shared her doubts with Boodevi.
Boodevi, too, listened to that song. Poladu's wife who was working
next to her also listened. Both of them, too, could not but think so

---

* *Namu*: During non-harvest times, poor people borrow a sack of grain. They
pay back an extra sack or half during harvest time. This is known as *namu*.

as Subhadra's name was in the song. When Subhadra told Boodevi this, her hunch was strengthened. She wanted to meet them at night. Subhadra, too, said she would go along to meet them.

The northern coolies were staying on the reddenadi mound. The reddenadi mound was in the middle of the field. There was only one family of yanadis there. Reddenadi came from Chakicharla. There his father and grandfather took care of the reddy and lived where the cattle feed was stacked. Did not know how many years ago they had set up their family. They forgot their family name. The older son of the reddenadis came to Yennela Dinni. He guarded the reddy's fields and remained on the mound. The male reddenadi, the woman and their two children. The mound was very big. The coolies who migrated there during harvest time would stay there. They left for that place. When they went past madigapalli, Poladu and his wife went along with them to keep them company.

Subhadra looked up as she walked.

Shining stars. Tender moonlight. You could call it a crescent moon. The tender moonlight wondering whether it ought to shine on the paddy heaps spread out on the ground. In the paddy fields which were empty as paddy was not spread out there sounded the quacking of a flock of ducks driven there by their owners. They sounded very strange. Like the singing of a chorus of experienced singers. They would stop all of a sudden. A strange silence. Would commence again. Once again in unison.

At such times, Yellanna would stop and listen. One could not understand why he was fond of listening to those sounds. Thinking of how much Yellanna would be elated at the coming of the flock of ducks at the close of the harvesting season was indeed amazing. That, too, in tender moonlight. Yellanna would refer to such an instance as bright moonlight. Once in a while he would refer to it as cool moonlight. Subhadra did not know the difference between bright moonlight and cool moonlight. It was just that her man would say such a thing. She did not search for their distinctive features when he was next to her.

But now she was searching for them. When the moon rose, when the shining stars were twinkling, when the flocks of ducks were flapping their wings and quacking, the bright moonlight on the muddy ground among the fields and at the edge of the field canals that were almost dry. How would it be? The wonderful moonlight. Why would it be that? However much she searched, her search would come to nought. He made it so. He gathered all the moonlight from Yennela Dinni and left just the Dinni behind. The mean one.

How many names he gave to the moonlight! Was it just one or two! Tender moonlight, full moonlight, ripe moonlight, flour moonlight—how many such names! Felt like laughing. Sometimes, he would give such a mischievous name and burst out laughing. Now he would not have found any moonlight here. Everything was pitch dark. Black smoke. All that remained before her, however, were the songs and words he had woven. How he wove songs about her! Thinking of this, her heart swelled with pride. She would forget she was the mother of a grown-up child. Everything was stealthy moonlight. Felt like singing. Though the women walking behind her could hear her, though Polayi mama walking in front could hear her, her lips were moving. A silent tune came out from the depths of her heart. But she alone could hear the tune. She was not the one singing, it was he. Yellanna. Yelladu. The one who held her heart in his grip. The one who had sketched her picture in the moonlight the way he desired. How he said it!

On the mattress of the sky
On the cotton sheet
Subhadra, the starry flower bunch
Subhadra, you're truly a real coral.

Mattress of the sky, cotton sheet, starry flower bunch. How would each one be? As if he would say what each one was for. Real coral. How did she appear to him then? Could not stop crying. Why did he make her cry now?

When he sang before their marriage of a starry muggukarra. When she went to him stealthily, though her father was upset and her mother scolded her, saying it was his fault entirely. When she hid herself against his chest and spoke out the concluding lines to his song. Why did he yearn so much then? How could she throw away that yearning saying that that was all a lie? If it were a lie why would it be like that? As she approached the reddenadi mound, what did she recall? How often did his calling her by many names on the edge of the row of palm trees next to the mound, her getting wet in the rain, her running away so as not to be seen when the reddenadi called out, 'Who's there?' as he guarded the field canal—how often had these things not happened? Those were shameless days. But what good days! Those were certainly not untrue. The moonlight shining over the stream. The cold baths in that moonlight. Even when mother cursed her saying she was totally shameless, they did not appear as abuses then. Those baths were not lies. Those curses were not lies. As he looked out eagerly for her and kept away from sleep saying, 'I didn't sleep all night thinking you'd come,' looking at the red streak in his eyes, how sorry she felt. Wasn't it then, when he stood in the bazaar gazing like that, that she broke all rules, held his hand and pulled him into the house? Wasn't it then that her father saw them? Wasn't she upset and didn't she refuse to eat? Her father searched for a bridegroom from Kolla Dinni. When she was adamant, when she said she would not marry anyone but Yellanna, did he not perform the marriage grandly? How could all those be lies? He was not a lie. Her marriage with him was not a lie. Moonlight, stream, the verses, the running around—none of these was a lie. When it was not so, when nothing was a lie, why did he throw away everything and leave?

The tears were not hiding in the eyes. The heartache was not hiding in the heart. Felt like sitting down right there. Felt like crying loudly. Felt like shouting aloud, had the three not been there,. Why had the moonlight and shining stars appeared only now? Memory haunting her like a wound. She steadied herself. She wiped her tears with the edge of her saree.

Perhaps the reddenadi had been watching for a long time; he said, 'What's it, how come you're here?' Poladu said, 'To meet the migrant coolies.' They seemed to have just eaten their food. All the women were sitting together in a group. The men had spread the mats on the sand and were lying down. They got up on seeing those who had come. The women raised their heads and saw. In the moonlight, Subhadra gave them a strange feeling. They invited them cordially to sit down. Subhadra sat next to the girl who had been singing.

'I want to listen to the song you sang while harvesting,' she said.

The girl felt shy. All the women said in unison, 'Sing.' The girl raised her voice. The song began. Subhadra made her sing two or three stanzas over and over again.

'Where did you learn it?'

'Mala bairagi taught me.'

'Only this song?'

'He taught me many.'

'On the mattress of the sky . . . '

No sooner had Subhadra started on the first line, the girl caught on. Saying 'on the cotton sheet,' she sang the entire song.

What she thought turned out to be true. It was Yellanna. Her Yelladu. But the girl said mala bairagi.

'Who did you say taught you?'

'Mala bairagi.'

'Isn't it Yellanna?'

'Yellanna?'

'That's it . . . the dancing Yelladu, the singing Yelladu.'

'I don't know who Yellanna is.'

Subhadra gave a weak look. She did not understand how to tell the girl. She did not understand how to get it out of this girl. She bent her head. Drops were falling down. The father of the girl who had been looking keenly only at Subhadra till then came forward. Said his name was Sina Subbanna. Said he performed. Said he was well-known for his role of Balarama. Said proudly that he would play no role other than that role. When they were told the girl's name, it was clear why he had such craze for the role of Balarama. The girl's name was Sasirekha.

He also uttered that name just as Balarama would utter it. Naganna would call Subhadra just like that. This was a strange trait among the malas who performed Veedhi Bagotams. There was no special sect in that caste who performed Veedhi Bagotams. Anyone would learn it. But if a girl was born into that family and if the father, grandfather or uncles or someone was a dancer, they would give a name from the puranas to the girl. They would also pronounce it quite clearly. Not like saying Boodevi or Latchimdevi, but very clearly like Subhadra, Sasirekha or Prabhavati.

When they told her the girl's name, Subhadra looked at the girl.

Sasirekha! Did not know why she spoke like that. She spoke. The girl raised her head and saw. She lifted the lamp with dindiga seed oil that was at a distance and looked. Felt jealous. She was not so clearly visible in the tender moonlight earlier. But the girl's look was different. The girl was not too fair. Not too dark. Captivating looks. In that light, Boodevi too looked at the girl. She looked at her eyes. The same attraction. The captivating look. Boodevi felt like laughing. When Subhadra came searching for Yellanna, she too looked like that. Involuntarily, Subhadra took the kohl from her eye with her fingertip and placed a dot on the girl's cheek. The girl was nonplussed.

. Sina Subbanna began to narrate how they met Yellanna.

Sina Subbanna saw a man teaching songs to boys who tended the cattle. He saw Yellanna like that the first time. The voice was great. Went near. A song from the Chenchu play. The man was tired out. The beard had grown. It was grey here and there. Eyes were large. Nose was sharp. Was straight. He looked wonderful when he laughed.

'Bairagi of which village?'

He looked surprised. Sina Subbanna did not know why his words surprised him. Yellanna looked at him as if he was searching for something. He looked as if he was being addressed strangely. Did not tell the name of the village.

'What's your name?'

'Bairagi . . . mala bairagi.'

He said laughing. Did not understand why he laughed. But he felt it would be good if he laughed again. He opened the bundle of food and kept it in front of him. He ate. When Sina Subbanna said they should come home, he did not object. He came. He taught the dramatic art to malapalli. He made them perform. They gave him clothes. They gave him *gurudakshina*. He did not say where he came from. He did not say why he came. But he would always weave some song or the other. Subhadra would be in every song he wove. When asked who this Subhadra was, he did not tell them. One day Sasirekha asked him. She asked, 'Is Subhadra attha's name?' He looked at her when she asked him, 'Is Subhadra attha's name?' the same way he did when he was asked, 'Bairagi from which village?'

Sina Subbanna could not digest it. The girl called Subhadra
attha.

Sina Subbanna kept narrating.

Subhadra looked at Sasirekha once again. The girl had continued
to keep her head bent.

'Lift your head,' said Subhadra.

Sasirekha lifted her head.

'Look at me. How do you find me?'

The wind that was wafting over the stacks of crop stopped all of a
sudden. The migrant coolies, all looked at her at the same time. Sina
Subbanna could not utter a word. The songs that wafted through all
their minds at one go were Yellanna's songs.

13

Subhadra went to the reddenadi's mound to find out about Yellanna
and search for him. Though she could not find out where Yellanna
was, she found a daughter-in-law. Even ten days before Subbanna
set out for Yennela Dinni as a migrant coolie, Yellanna had left that
village. Though Yellanna was not there, she performed the marriage
of Sivaiah and Sasirekha. In the open yard next to her house she
had a hut built for both of them. Now, in the morning, Sasirekha
accompanied her to the mala's mound. Boodevi remained at home
weaving the string of the cot. As Chinnammi was a strong person,
she was not crushed.

In the villages there are pairs such as Ramudu and Ramulamma.
Sitaiah and Sitamma. If there are such pairs, they would make them
rotate the pestle to cure back pain. But it was indeed strange that
Subhadra and Sasirekha were mother-in-law and daughter-in-law.
For the washerwoman Venkayi that was something strange too. As
for Chukkireddy, some spirit kept chasing him. Atchireddy's wife
sent for the washerwoman Venkayi to her backyard, made her sit
and relate everything to her. Venkayi told her everything. Later, as
Atchireddy's wife walked past the mala's mound, she wanted, without
being noticed, to look at the mother-in-law and daughter-in-law

bending low in the mound and removing the weeds. But once she saw them, she did not feel like moving.

Time was fleeing on its own accord.

The drought that had started somewhere seemed to hit Yennela Dinni rather obliquely. It appeared as if the wind was blowing only now. Every evening there was some change in the wind blowing across the ocean. Even Atchireddy was finding it difficult. The condition of the lower reddys was deteriorating. The poor peasants were enveloped in the fear that they might not be able to tide over those days. There was therefore no need to speak about the condition of the malas and madigas. As for Sivaiah, toil remained merely that. There was no result other than the mother-in-law and daughter-in-law breaking their backs. Chukkireddy said the mother goddess's jatara had to be performed. He made children tie the frog-mother to the stick, threw neem branches at it, and had people shout, 'Frog-mother, become pregnant.' Neither did the frog-mother become pregnant nor were the pots filled with water.

As the travellers sat at the foot of the gaviti tree in Yennela Dinni, they began to relate the hunger deaths here and there in their regions. Not only did those words frighten Yennela Dinni, but hunger deaths surrounded Yennela Dinni.

The severe drought known as *Datu karuvu* took the lives of lakhs of people in southern India. No rains. No crops. No work, nothing at all on the parched earth. People ate leaves. They ate weeds . . . The *bonta* fruit did not help them survive. *Nagajemudu* began to create burning in the stomach. They drank muddy water thinking it would infuse life. Even so, hunger deaths did not stop. They died violently shaking their legs. They died straining their stomachs. They died contracting diarrhoea. They went on starving and died. Along with it cholera.

In the region where Yellanna lived, the people who had been left behind after the deaths were migrating. Knowing that the Buckingham canal[29] was being dug, hoping that they would find employment there, that they would be able to survive, holding on to their lives, they went finding their way. When they came to the outskirts of the village, they went ahead beyond it. They hoped that the cholera there would not touch them. Even so, someone or the other was dropping dead on the way. Groups of people were undertaking very long journeys. Did not know what their destination was. It definitely ought to be some place. It had to be on this earth. Mala bairagi Yellanna joined these groups.

He remembered the tomb of sampenga flowers on the way. He remembered potter Pedakoteswarudu and yanadi Ramanaiah. The hungry intestines were not willing to put up with so much toil. Even so, he moved out of the group. Astonishing. Some walked, following him. When he said, 'Where to?', they asked him 'Where to?' There is no need for any other example to show how chaotic life was. A run for livelihood. Could drop dead on the way. Could reach the destination. That was not in their hands.

He reached the tomb of sampenga flowers. There were no sampenga flowers on the tomb. Did not know when the sampenga tree that shed flowers had become half dry and begun to struggle for life. Could not find yanadi Ramanaiah. Did not see his beautiful waist and the serene smile in his eyes. There were no emaciated dogs barking in the huts of the yanadi mound either. Did not know where malapalli had migrated. Did not know which corners madigapalli was searching. He sat next to the tomb. He kept remembering Ramanaiah. He remembered the dappu stick. Ramanaiah was a great sage. He did not feel like staying there any more. His hunger disappeared. He did not die. Why was he still alive? Lightning flashing far away. That was not lightning. An illusion that was like lightning.

Yennela Dinni!

Yennela Dinni!!

The place of his birth. The place he grew up.

He came away intending to go back. He had to go back. Had to go till there. Had to go to Yennela Dinni. He again merged with the crowds. He was weaving something within himself. In that weave, he was singing for someone. His pallavi was Subhadra. That was all. Only that word remained. That one word alone was being woven, over and over again. He set out towards Yennela Dinni.

In Yennela Dinni, each day a man was turning into a corpse. Atchireddy in fact died of cholera. Chukkireddy died of hunger. Even as he died, some goddess kept tormenting him and killed him.

The same with the washerwoman Venkayi and the new daughter-in-law of the potters. Atchireddy's wife was battling for life.

There was no need to talk of the houses of the malas and madigas. Sivaiah began to dig pits for his people. In the morning, he buried Pittodu. In the evening, Chinnammi. The next day Boodevi. In the early hours of the night, Yenkatanarsu. Sivaiah kept digging pits. He was digging for his people. He was digging for the neighbours. At every pit, Subhadra was sitting like a haunted spirit. Even when so many were dying, she felt death would not touch her. She decided she would live till he returned.

'Eat *kalekayi*, my girl.'

'You eat, attha.'

'The stomach will become sore, my girl.'

Sivaiah could not listen to those words of the mother-in-law and daughter-in-law. He picked up the spade. By then he had already dug up the grain-pit of tender palmyra sprouts four times. Even so, a hope. At least one would be found. He began to loosen the soil. It was then that he found a sprouted palm seed. He planted it back in the mud again. Though the pit was growing larger, there was no sight of the tender palmyra sprout. Even so, an anxiety. Man toils to live. Toils even as he dies. People of Sivaiah's age group died even before death struck them. Mother remained. Wife remained. Did not know whether the father was dead or alive. If he was alive, it meant three were alive. His mother's name was Subhadra. Wife's name was Sasirekha. Puranic names. Royal names. Names that had been fostered with a lot of fondness. How clearly those who had kept those names had pronounced them! But his father was not Arjuna. He was not Abhimanyu. No Lord Krishna was on their side. There was no Kurukshetra that would take place because five villages were refused. All that they had was caste. The caste outside the four castes. A castaway caste. All the struggle was only to live. Whether they flee or run the only thing that does not touch them is the poisonous snake-like culture.

But had to live conquering hunger, conquering untouchability. And that too in such drought.

The malas and madigas of Yennela Dinni, saving the meat of dead cattle from the vultures, separating the bones and the flesh of those cattle, roasting and eating them. Fight over that, fight with the eagles. Fight with the vultures. Fight with fellowmen. For just a small piece of meat. For roasting and eating it. The four-caste system ate living people. The caste outside it only ate dead creatures. These were non-voilent people. That's why this hunger. That's why this untouchability. Yellanna could be a great singer. But Sivaiah could not imagine that now. That great artist, chasing the eagles to roast just a small piece of meat . . . the looks of a wolf. . . . On the trees the looks of vultures. No. No need for such thoughts.

He was digging. Hoping that he would find at least one tender palmyra sprout. Finally, when he paused to see he had dug a pretty deep pit. He felt it even without thinking about it. A pit big enough for two. He felt fear at such a thought. He threw the spade right there and came out of the palle.

There was a lot of commotion under a gaviti tree as if the number of migrants had increased. They were all coming down from atop. They were walking holding their hunger in their stomachs. For work during the drought. For digging the Buckingham canal. For work. The groups that reached there. He wanted to go near them. Did not feel like going. Went half way and returned. But he felt someone was staggering and coming that way. He was coming from the groups under the gaviti tree. The man came close. He was about to die soon or at this very moment. The one who came repeated one word many times over as if he could not utter anything else.

'Subhadra . . . Subhadra . . . Subhadra.'

Sivaiah was startled by those words. He looked deep. His father? He was calling out his mother's name. It was his father. Yes, it was his father. The man was unable to understand any of this. Only one word. As if he knew no other word.

Subhadra . . . Subhadra. . . . He was indeed his father. His father.

Sivaiah hugged his father. He was crying really loud. But only one word.

Subhadra . . . Subhadra.

Sivaiah told him his name. He said he was his one and only son. He said, 'Ayya, look at me.'

But . . .

Subhadra . . . Subhadra.

Only that word. Father and son. Mother and daughter. What was this bond? Whatever there was, was only one bond. It could be for the haves. Could also be for the have-nots. Could be for the upper castes. Could be for the untouchables. Only one eternal bond. The husband- and-wife bond. 'I and my Subhadra. She and I.' He was unable to say all these words aloud. Was able to say just one word.

Subhadra . . . Subhadra..

Was about to collapse.

Sivaiah caught hold of his father. Carried him on his shoulder. Hurried steps. Father had to live till then. Had to live till he reached his mother.

The dusky light was wearing its final smiles. It was of that light that Yellanna wove the song, 'Rabbit of dusky light Subhadra, Subhadra who passes through the field mounds.' He called it an old dusk. Awakening ray. The clenching dusky lips. The last stage of sprout-waves. The stream's heart wrench that caresses the speechless earth.

Those were all the tunes of Yellanna's songs. Sivaiah did not want any of those. Father had to live. Father had to live till he reached mother. That's all . . . The steps were heavy.

The steps stopped at the threshold.

Sivaiah raised his head.

Subhadra in front.

He took his father in both his hands.

'Ayya . . . my ayya'.

Only one sound. Subhadra. Subhadra.

Subhadra stopped just there and looked. Her man indeed. How did he go? How did he come now? In this twilight what dark light had pushed him? Having roamed all kinds of places, why was the song so tired, when it came near?

Subhadra kept looking like that. She collapsed looking like that. She stretched her hands towards Sivaiah. She kept her looks towards Yellanna.

'Lay him here, bidda.'

Sivaiah rested Yellanna's head in her hands.

Subhadra . . . Subhadra.

Subhadra could not utter a word. She covered Yellanna's head with the fringe of her saree. She hugged him close. She was caressing

Yellanna's head with her hands. Overpowering sleep. A sleep from which she did not wake up.

Silence. That was it. He was not there for him to call out. She was not there to hear him.

Only Sivaiah's sobs remained.

Sasirekha's wails kept them company.

The last shadow of the vestiges of the vanishing dusky light that had run in Yennela Dinni's fields, like a raw blood spot that had combined hunger and untouchability.

Sivaiah did not like to separate the two. He placed them as they were in the pit with great difficulty. He threw in a palmful of mud. He asked Sasirekha to push it. They went on pushing the mud. They themselves did not know why they were doing this. When they thought the pit was filled, they lay down just like that on the pit, tired.

Beneath the mud, the song and the pallavi. On top of it their echoes.

Did not know what Yennela Dinni would feel. As for the yennela pitta, it perched there but did not run away crying hoarse.

A new day dawned. Sivaiah tied the few clothes he had into a bundle. He kept the rice pot and the vegetable vessel in the basket. He tied the basket on one side and the bundle on the other of the yoke. With Sasirekha he mingled among the migrants.

As he kept going, he turned back. He remembered his mother and father beneath the mud. Yenkatanarsu, Poladu, Pittodu, Boodevi, Chinnammi, Poladu's wife . . . he remembered one by one. Both the palles were like two burial grounds. Some skeleton seemed to have risen in the ooru just then. As he crossed the mala's mound he felt terrible. All a struggle for survival. Did not know whether they would return to this village or not. He definitely wanted to come back. This was the earth into which all his blood had sunk. This was the earth that had drunk their sweat. Had to come back. Had to come back definitely.

'I remember attha.'

'Move on . . . the migrants in front have gone a long way.' Though hunger restricted her from taking a step forward, Sasirekha was running along with Sivaiah. Did not know why, but the man who was walking stopped suddenly. He looked towards Sasirekha.

'You know all of ayya's songs, don't you?'

'I know many.'

'Preserve them. We'll have them written down.' Walk once again. They reached Kavali. They stopped near Kalugolamma's temple. They thought of staying back at that temple itself for the night. The people were not stopping there. They prayed to mother goddess. Kalugolamma knew no caste. She was Parvatamma's sister. They started to walk again. A small forest came their way. When they asked the man next to them, he said they neared Rudrakota. Did not know when it had been dug. There was a really large ground well. There were *neredu* trees all around. They fell on the trees like monkeys. They tied as many raw neredu fruits as they could lay their hands on into bundles.

'Eat.'

'Stomach pain.'

'Have to live.'

She ate even as she complained of pain. They drank a palmful of water from the step-well. Sivaiah brought water in the rice pot. They slept that night there. They slept next to each other in a row. Hunger-sleep, tired-sleep.

Walk once again. In the very early hours. Some said it would take another day. Another man said not one but two more days. For five days, 'Walk? Walk on. Forever complaining.'

'Who's lagging behind?'

'Wait.'

'He fell down.'

The entire crowd reached there. The one who had fallen down, lay right there. Did not move. They pulled him to a side. Did not know to which village he belonged. They placed the leaves of the branches of the forest on him. They did not have the energy to dig a pit.

'I'm scared.'

'Walk along.'

Crowds and crowds of people. People all along the way. People walking without any energy as if they had no option. No matter whose eyes you looked into, there was no spark. A sorrow of having lost a lot. A young boy in that group spoke to Sivaiah. There was also a young girl next to him.

'Six sisters. They became one with the dust in front of my eyes. I'm a madiga from Bayyaram. I'm the only one left. The one in the middle. Father died earlier. Mother went along with him. What's your name?'

'Sivaiah. I'm a mala from Yennela Dinni. She's my wife.'

'You're the only two left?'

'Yes!'

'You're better off. I'm the only one left.'

'This young girl . . .'

'I met her on the way. She seems to be a girl from further west. She must also be the only one left behind like me. We thought we would live together if we survived till we reached the canal. We thought we'd dig a pit for whoever dies on the way. We're alive till here. My name's Jinkodu. I don't know the girl's name. Don't know her caste. The girl can't speak. Just sign language.'

He laughed uttering those words. Sivaiah did not laugh. He felt as if someone had gnawed at his heart. He kept staring at the boy.

They were walking all through the day. As they kept walking, the girl would stop. She stopped like that many times.

'Loose motions . . . yesterday too it was like this.' Surprise—he would himself take the girl behind a mound or tree. The girl would go only if he went. Sivaiah would be surprised. He did not understand how the girl had so much confidence in him.

They kept walking even as it became dark. It seemed like some village. They could hear dogs barking. Sivaiah felt scared to go into the village. But he said it did not matter and asked them to come along. There could be cholera in the village. They stopped at a mango grove a little distance from the village. There was a water hole in the grove. They did not know if the water was good or not. Even so, there was no option—they had to drink.

Hazy moonlight.

They swept the dry leaves and rested their backs on the sand. Sasirekha was tired. No sooner did she lie down than she slept. She fell into a light slumber. As for the girl, she lay down holding the boy's hand tight.

'Shall we go into the village?'

'Why?'

'If we search the houses, we're sure to find food. I searched the houses like that twice on the way. I found food. This girl and I ate.'

'I don't think so.'

'Let's see. The women are sleeping. The village is quite close by. Everyone would be asleep. Somewhere or the other, we're sure to find a morsel or so of food. From childhood, I've been adept at stealing food. If we find it, your poor wife will be able to eat something.'

Sivaiah softened at those words. He woke Sasirekha up from her sleep and said he would go to the village. She said okay.

There was no other sound in the village except the barking of dogs.

Did not know which village it was.

At some places, they could see the light of lanterns. They felt this village was better than many others. Sivaiah was doing what Jinkodu asked him to.

Houses where no people were there at all.

Perhaps they were there some days ago. They might have migrated. They might have died.

Even if there were people there, they were sleeping as if drugged. But there was no food in any pot. Even so Jinkodu was not tired. He kept searching still. He felt the last three houses still remained.

In one of the houses, next to the central pole, there was a lamp. A little distance from the lamp was a sunken cot. Next to the cot was a food plate. He took it greedily and looked at it. Someone had eaten half the food. They had kept half of it behind.

'Food!'

Jinkodu in fact said it loudly.

'They have left it half eaten.'

Sivaiah listened to Jinkodu's words in surprise.

'My husband . . . died without eating all of it.'

Sivaiah and Jinkodu looked with surprise and fear in the direction from which those words came. In the shade of the pole, there was an old woman. There was no cloth on her body except over her private parts. The darkness was horrific in the shade of the pole.

Jinkodu lifted the lamp next to the pole and looked. On the sunken cot, the dead body of the old man that had become stiff.

'Great man. He left this for us and died,' he said laughing. Sivaiah was surprised at Jinkodu's words. He looked frightened.

'A ghost's food? Is there a ghost other than hunger! Come . . . '

Saying that, he turned back. Sivaiah had not still turned this way. The old woman in the shade of the pole fell on Jinkodu in one leap. Jinkodu was startled at the unexpected turn of events.

'Keep the food there, you fellow.'

Saying those words, the old woman caught Jinkodu tight. Even the tiny tattered cloth covering her private parts fell off. She was like a strange animal. Sivaiah felt like running away from there. As for Jinkodu, he pushed the old woman with force. That old woman fell far away. Jinkodu held Sivaiah's hand and came out pulling him. The old woman got up, gathered strength and followed them. Jinkodu began to run. Sivaiah was running involuntarily. The old woman was running abusing them. When they turned around and looked, she appeared terrifying. The dogs chased the old woman. Even as she chased the dogs she abused Jinkodu. She stopped unable to run. Now only the barking of the dogs was heard. After they neared the grove and when they turned back and looked, the old woman was seen in the middle of the dogs. The barking of the dogs was heard. The old woman's voice was not heard.

'Poor old woman, the dogs must have killed her.'

'Wake her up, she'll eat the food.'

'That's the food of two ghosts.'

'It'll be enough for the four ghosts here, if we adjust . . . wake her up.'

'She won't eat even if I wake her up.'

'You?'

'No.'

'Good . . . then only two ghosts will eat.'

He woke up the girl. She opened her eyes as if she was exhausted. He mixed a morsel and put it in her mouth. The moment the morsel of food entered her mouth, the girl's eyes opened completely and she got up.

She signalled as if to ask if it was food.

'Eat.'

Another sign as if to ask from where.

'Some fellow died without eating half of it . . . eat this morsel.'

She nodded as if to indicate it was good. He gave her another morsel. She shook her head as if to indicate it was enough. He pleaded. She kept saying no. He forced her and made her eat another morsel. Sivaiah was moved. He looked in the boy's direction. He made the food into three mouthfuls and ate it. He dipped his plate in the water hole, filled it fully and drank it. He brought water and washed the girl's mouth. He made her drink water. He placed the plate under his head and lay down. The girl placed her head on his shoulder. She placed her hands on him.

Water swirled in Sivaiah's eyes. He did not know why water was swirling in his eyes. But it was happening like that.

That whole night, the girl had loose motions. Sivaiah did not know when he fell asleep. At about dawn when Sivaiah got up, he heard Jinkodu crying. Sivaiah looked at the girl.

'When did it happen?'

'It was not dawn then.'

Silence. No one knew what to say. Sasirekha got up, saw the scene and could not bear it.

'You go. I'll fulfil the word I gave and will come if I'm alive.' There was nothing other than this he could do.

He looked at the girl. She was getting over her tiredness for ever.

They left Jinkodu there and set out. The journey that started at dawn ended when the sun was right on top as they neared the place where the digging of Buckingham canal was going on.

The entire region was filled with coolies. Groups from all kinds of places seemed to have gathered here. Those who were supposed to dig were digging. Those who were supposed to fill the baskets were filling them up. Those who were supposed to carry, were carrying them. Sivaiah found everything confusing. Struggle for life. Everything was just that. A struggle just for living.

He did not know whom to approach to ask for work. Sasirekha who was tired was standing with the support of his shoulders. On reaching there, Sivaiah was no longer afraid that they may not live. It would be enough if he started working. He could save Sasirekha.

At a distance he saw a rotund man. He was wearing a palm leaf hat. The man looked strange. The way he wore his pancha was strange. Sivaiah found wearing a pancha on a shirt something new. He had a leather belt over it. On his forehead were three well-drawn vertical lines. It was not clear whether he was talking or shouting. He came to know that he was the one who employed people. He went eagerly. He stood at a little distance. Sasirekha did not let go of the support of Sivaiah's shoulders. It appeared as if she would fall down if she let go.

He bowed to him four times. He did not know if he noticed him or not. The fifth time the rotund man looked at him enquiringly. That look was like that of a vulture looking at chicken. Sasirekha looked on, frightened.

Sivaiah said he wanted work. He said he came from a great distance. He told him of Sasirekha's condition. Did not know what mood he was in, he nodded his head to indicate yes. He stood under the shade of an umbrella on a thick bamboo pole pierced in the ground. He sat on a bench there. He took out a book. He took the pen tucked over his ear. He dipped it into the inkpot on the bench and asked his name.

'Sivaiah.'

He raised his head and looked. He again dipped the pen in the ink pot and was writing.

'I'm a mala from Yennela Dinni.'

The rotund man who was writing stopped, raised his head and looked. His face indicated he had heard something evil.

'She's my wife.'

The eyes of the rotund man were reddening. He was looking at them, one after the other, as if he was looking at demons. He started screaming like an insane man. The only words that were comprehensible were mala and madiga. At his shouts, the people who were working stopped right then and there. It was not clear what was happening.

'This son of a mala wants a job here, I believe.' The rotund man was screaming as if the houses were on fire. The coolies who had stopped working started to hurl mud pellets at them. One or two of the coolies were swaying and rushing towards them with crowbars.

Sivaiah could not understand why that rotund man was screaming, why two of the coolies were attacking them with crowbars and why mud pellets were falling on them from the four directions. He could understand only one thing. That there was danger to their lives if they remained there. When this thought came to mind, he took Sasirekha's hand and sped from there. He felt a few coolies were chasing them. They picked up the strength they did not have and ran faster. After chasing them for quite a distance, the coolies turned back. Not having the energy to run any more, they slumped on the dry casuarina grove path. The sun was severe. It was all the more hot in the casuarina grove. Even so, they slumped on the burning sands. Sasirekha was looking terrified.

Everything happened in an inconceivable manner. It was like a lightning strike. Why did it happen like that? What had he done? What had he said? Sasirekha was crying. Sivaiah was frightened hearing her cry. He looked into her face and hands helplessly. Mud all over the face. Slush on her eyelids. He was wiping the mud off her face involuntarily. Her crying had intensified. He did not even have the energy to console her. They had walked miles and miles for work. When they neared the canal, there had arisen a desire to live. Even that single desire was lost. Now there was no way they could live. He dug pits in a row when hunger took his people away one after the other. She was the only one left for him. But . . . but . . . he was unable to imagine. He took her face in his hands. The crying was increasing not stopping.

'Look here.'

She stopped crying and looked. A pitiful look. The helpless look of hunger. Tears swam in his eyes. He wiped her face and the tears on her face. He wiped them again and again. He covered those pitiful looks with his lips. He was saying something to himself. He thought he was saying it so she could hear. But the words were not crossing his lips.

How many days since this crazy thing ate! All the way long she kept asking how much further. She walked till here only to be alive.

He recalled the shouts of mala and madiga by the coolies. He understood some truths now both clearly and not so clearly. Did not know why he felt so but he felt it would have been better if he had said he was a reddy from Yennela Dinni. He would have found coolie work. He not only had the company of hunger but also untouchability with him. Even those coolies who threw stones at them had walked miles for livelihood. They too were people like him who had dug pits for their relatives in their villages. Just ordinary coolies. But hunger too had untouchability. Labour too had untouchability.

His body was untouchable.

His Sasirekha's body was untouchable.

But Sasirekha's body was not untouchable for his body. For some reason, he caressed her affectionately. He rubbed his face with her hands. How did the world appear? Let it die, he thought. The struggle for life was in the final stages. It would have been good if the Buckingham canal was even further away. They would have lived with hope. They would have walked with hope. Now there was no distance. The walk came to a halt. There was no hope. It was burnt out. Life was ready to stop. There was a rumbling of hunger from her stomach that had become one with the ribs. It appeared as if the weak sound of her heartbeat too was heard. She was not crying now. She lay like one who had lost consciousness. He thought he ought not to dig her pit like those of others. When that thought struck him he was shaken. She opened her eyes on noticing his shock. She looked at him. She smiled weakly. She placed her head on his hungry stomach and snuggled. He held her tight. She snuggled up to him even further. They slept like that. In fact, it was not sleep. It was a feeling of utter helplessness.

Warm breeze was wafting across the casuarina grove that had dried up due to lack of rain. The west wind was blowing the sand now and again. In fact sand particles were hitting their bodies rather hard. Even so the sensation was dead. Let anything happen. Let there be a sand storm. Let it cover both of them. Let them be entombed alive. Everything was the same. That was a state without agitation, anxiety or fear. Philosophers call it *nischala samadhi*, a non-responsive other-worldly state. Perhaps this was it.

He was a Yennela Dinni mala.

She was his companion.

They were the inheritors of generations of untouchable lives. Their ancestors were flung to the outskirts of the village. They lived as untouchables.

Yes.

They lived like that.

They did not know why they had to live like that.

Those were the initial stages of history.

They were said to have ruled kingdoms then.

Like the kings ruled. Like the brahmins ruled. Like the reddys ruled. Like many such castes ruled.

Not as if proofs cannot be found if one searches for them. But there is no sign of having searched. Even if they searched, what is evident are the distortions by the exploiting classes. The stench of the upper caste researchers' personal mental make-up. That's it.

To say how all the sorrow was—

This history has less of the smell of this mud, of man.

Like Chandrappa said. Like Naganna said. Everything is mud heaps. Pits. Ditches. Valleys.

No one knows what reality has been thrown into which pit.

No one knows the count of people who had attained permanent samadhis under various mounds.

No one understands which civilisation has been buried in which valley.

A control over land.

The Kautilya quality that ruthlessly separated men and suppressed them.

Class.

Caste.

Castaway lives.

Entombed lives.

Beheaded civilisations.

Malas, madigas.

They did not walk on royal paths.

Really, they did not.

They did not drink water from the wells of the ooru.

A pot around the neck. Palm leaf over the buttocks.

They were human too. Two legs. Two hands. A brain. Like everyone else.

Just like the brahmins, the reddys, the kammas and the other upper castes.

Humans too. Brains too.

In Tamil country, *pariahs*.

In Kannada country, *hooleelu*.

In Maharashtra, *mangs, mahars, bhangis* and *chamars*.

Among Telugus, malas and madigas.

Like that in many places. In every corner of this country.

In this sacred India, the people who had been looked at as impure and disgusting.

Untouchables.

Malas.

Madigas.

Yellannas, Subhadras.

Sivaiahs.

Sasirekhas.

The culture of this country is shameless. All that is there is treachery. The culture of this country has no honesty. All that it has is deceit. Here Vedas, religion, Manu, patience and integration are synonyms for treachery and deception.

That's it.

Synonyms for treachery and deception.

Truly, that's it.

They plotted against Sivaiah. They deceived him.

The same with Sasirekha. Treachery. Deception.

That very treachery, that very deception.

Those very things pushed Sivaiah and Sasirekha to a state where anything could happen, where the sandstorm could cover them up and where they could attain a living samadhi in the burning heat of that casuarina grove.

Sivaiah and Sasirekha did not know how long they lay like that.

The sun was dipping into the hills.

Sivaiah felt someone was tapping him awake.

He opened his eyes. He looked impatiently.

A stranger was smiling in front of him. There was some insignia hanging from his neck.

Sivaiah did not know that that insignia was the 'Cross'.

14

Oh my lone star! Shine. Shine with a brightness that no star has shone, amidst a hundred crore stars. Shine.

On Immanuel's forehead.

Oh my lone star! Shine. Shine. Shine, Oh lone star that enveloped the earth and the cosmos, born in Bethleham. Shine.

Nehemiah! May what you wrote down come true! The ecstatic sounds born in Jerusalem would be heard far away, very far away. Like a river flooding, engulfing and drenching the wide fields.

Witness to the first rays of a thousand years!

Oh lone star!

Shine. Shine.

That is the song of the lone star that is hidden in Ruth's memories and that Ruth recollects from Reuben's old books. Whenever she reads it, she sits amidst the old books Reuben read and wrote, and reads some pages in his diary along with that song over and over again. She can see it clearly even at her age now. She reads every letter of the alphabet freely. In fact, she heard that song for the first time from Reuben's mouth.

Reuben mentioned that song while talking about Sivaiah. That song comes to the fore in the same manner that the American Baptist Mission by the name, Lone Star,[30] does in the surrounding regions of Nellore. The memory seems fresh. In that memory, the section of the untouchables who converted to Christianity. The words appear new. Christ, change of heart, protection—some words like those made their way, either because it was necessary or because it was unavoidable, into the lives of the untouchables . . .

Like many malas and madigas Sivaiah converted to Christianity. Saying those words, Reuben placed the Biblical verses in front:

'Foxes have holes, and birds of the air have nests. But the son of man hath not where to lay his head.'[31]

Why did Reuben say those words that day? Reuben would not say anything just like that. He would not open his heart out and speak unless something touched him. Every memory of Ruth has been narrated only in that manner. Those are the ones poured out to Ruth by him unable to suppress them.

In fact many scenes have not found their way into her memories of the untouchable spring. Reuben must have left out many. He must have narrated only those that touched him. That's why she has not been able to keep many to herself. Now she feels so. If only she knew that those incidents Reuben left out are such, how good it would have been! What happened to Mataiah who left Yennela Dinni? How did he survive? He only talked of his crossing the stream and going away that night. Don't know why. Thinking of it makes her feel a void. What can be more horrific in a person's memories than not knowing the last moments of a courageous man? It may in fact not be an incident Reuben left out. Could be an incident he had not known.

How many unknown situations in the lives of untouchables! How many situations that are known but those that the world refuses to see! As if all have become drenched in darkness and have remained in darkness!

Who are the sons of man who do not find place to rest? Poor people. Specifically untouchables among poor people. Sivaiahs and Sasirekhas.

What would have happened if the man with the insignia of the Cross had not seen Sivaiah and Sasirekha that day?

How did that day proceed?

He sprinkled some water on their faces. Both opened their eyes and saw. The smiling face of the man with the insignia of the Cross appeared to them. They kept looking like that. He kept smiling. He told them his name.

Martin.

The name was new. This was not a name of this region. They knew Mataiahs, Muttaiahas. Mallannas and Yellannas—they knew many such names. Martin did not appear to be a name they knew. Even so he gave them water to drink. He gave them *jowar roti* to eat. After eating that roti and drinking that water, the world around began to appear new. They sat calmly.

'Christ is merciful.'

Sivaiah did not know the Christ in his words. He repeated that word again. He sat calmly in front of them. Sasirekha was looking at the Cross around his neck, wondering whether there were such necklaces too.

'You didn't tell me your names,' Martin said. Sivaiah told him. Told him the name of their village. Told him about their struggle for life. Told him how they came to Buckingham canal. Told him what happened. When he was speaking, Martin did not question him. Was listening. But he kept repeating in between that Christ was merciful. After hearing everything he said—

In the coolie work of Buckingham canal, though what they would do too would be coolie work, the upper-caste coolies did not agree to the malas and madigas working along with them. Just like they chased away Sivaiah and Sasirekha, they chased away every mala and madiga who came for work. Beat them up. There were those who ran and lost their lives because of hunger, exhaustion and fear. So the Baptist Mission specifically took up digging a four-mile long canal for the malas and madigas at Rajupalem near Ongole. The malas and madigas started to work there. The malas and madigas from Kanigiri, Donakonda, Markapuram, Ongole and Nellore regions reached there. After giving that information, Martin asked Sivaiah and Sasirekha to set out for that place. Martin was walking in front. Behind him those two.

The journey was new. Did not know which turn life would take. No desire even to find out. Hunger in the stomach. Untouchability in the wrenching of the heart.

Why was all this happening?

Untouchable people. Untouchable labour. A specific place for that work. An expanse of four miles. No energy to laugh. Not enough strength to cry.

There was a tiny truth. That very tiny truth, man had forgotten. That was in the depths of this land. In the very depths. It would come out piercing the mud and the filth.

For the research that excavated the Mohenjodaro this very tiny truth that protruded was not apparent.

It did not strike the great intellect that searched for civilisation in the heart of Harappa to get rid of the mud around and wash the filth around this tiny truth to pronounce that such a thing happened in this country, and especially on this Telugu land. Did not find the necessity.

The expanse of the untouchable coolie space was four miles. What was the length of Buckingham canal? Its width? Its expanse? Those who knew their facts would not say. Those who wanted to say it did not know the numbers.

How many Sivaiahs in that four-mile long life! How many Sasirekhas!

Sivaiah kept walking as he looked around. Sandy path. Very close by, the ocean's roar. Sandy uncultivated land as far as the eye could see. Sandy banks swept by the wind. Here and there amidst marks of *nagajemudu* bushes, fields under cultivation. There was no trace of those who were cultivating them. The broken bushes lay scattered. Only *mogili* bushes had survived here and there. Perhaps *minnagulu* too had survived. They would certainly have been alive. They had no death. No hunger. Mogili trees knew hunger. If the minnagulu had thought that they could have survived without mogili, bushes, mogili bushes would not have survived. In fact, one could see this expansive country in these mogili bushes and in minnagulu. The malas and madigas might have survived outside the ooru like mogili bushes. They might have lived only for the needs of minnagulu. If one had thought that corn for the fields or slippers for the feet were not necessary, even while those who were killed were killed, the remaining too might not have survived.

Sivaiah felt he had indeed walked a long distance. Till then, Sivaiah had looked only at the path. He looked only at the sandy fields next to the path. He looked at the mogili bushes. He had not looked at the sky. Now he looked at the sky. Crescent moon. It looked like the birth of the new moon. He shut his eyes tight. He turned the face of Sasirekha who was walking alongside towards him with his hand. Then he opened his eyes. Looking at Sasirekha's face, he smiled and said, 'Birth of the moon.' Sasirekha looked up. She looked like that at the crescent moon. She turned her face even as she looked. She looked at Sivaiah's smiling face. Thought that was enough. She felt that smile should remain like that. But did not know why. Tears came gushing out of the heart. It was not as if Sivaiah had not noticed this. He turned back. Except for mogili bushes and for nagajemudu, everywhere sandy land, barren sandy land. A mute land that could neither speak nor even utter a word. Silent, adamant, mute, lonely. If the moonlight made them laugh, life immediately made them cry. Why was that little laughter born just like that to disappear just like that? Like clouds rushing by, becoming tired after rushing and heart breaking and pouring down as from a pot.

They came to the place where coolies were staying. Thatched palm huts. Huts hugging the ground. House fronts that could be entered with bent backs. In front of the huts, on mats children sleeping in all kinds of positions. Stove next to that. It appeared as if food was being cooked just then. The men on the mounds came forward on seeing Martin.

'These are all our people.'

Sivaiah looked at them. Sasirekha stood with bent head. Martin told them everything in a couple of sentences. It was another matter if they were people who had come for ordinary coolie work. If the people who came were chased by upper caste people, the news would reach each and every hut. That was exactly how it happened. All the men and women in the huts gathered there. That was a kind of commotion. Tales that were told over and over again. Once again there was talk about who chased whom and how they beat them.

They stayed that night at Martin's house. Martin's wife, Saramma, looked after them affectionately. All of them sat together for their meals. It was strange to Sivaiah. Sasirekha was timid. Martin was observing the two of them. He was about to say something. Saramma said, 'Let's pray.' Sivaiah looked intrigued. Sasirekha looked at Sivaiah. Martin asked them to close their eyes. Sivaiah felt that was the right thing to do. As soon as Sivaiah closed his eyes, Sasirekha shut hers. Saramma was speaking with her eyes shut. Those words appeared strange. 'Jehovah'—the two of them were hearing this word for the first time. Sivaiah's name was heard among those words. Sasirekha's name was heard. Then an unknown eagerness within them. She was saying that good should be done to them. She was asking someone to do them good. She was saying, 'Jehovah.' She was telling only this to Jehovah. Finally, saying, 'We pray to you, Our Father in the name of Your Son and our Lord, Christ,' she ended with, 'Amen.' Martin too repeated, 'Amen.' The two of them did not know what they had to say. As for their eyes, they were keeping them shut. Martin asked them to open their eyes. They opened their eyes. Martin said, 'Now, go ahead.'

They were dying of hunger. Sivaiah found the new place and the new practice rather irksome. As for Sasirekha, she found it even more irksome. Martin once again noticed their discomfort.

'Please eat. Do you find dry meat easily in your region?' Martin made conversation with them.

' . . . '

'You can't find it the way we do here. I know. It is also rare for you to add it to *gongura* and cook it. The way Saramma cooks gongura with pieces of meat no one can. Eat and see.'

Sivaiah put a morsel into his mouth.

'How's that?'

'Good.'

'Not just this, my boy. If one has to make prawn powder with chillies, only Saramma should. If she puts a handful of *sangati* in the mortar where she had made hot prawn powder, draws it out and puts it to in your hand, believe me, it'll just melt in your mouth.'

'If you add a drop of ghee, it'll be even better.'

The three of them looked surprised at Sasirekha who uttered those words.

'The parrot has spoken, Saramma.' Martin was looking eagerly at Sasirekha. Saramma looked at that girl in the same manner. Sivaiah felt it would have been better if Sasirekha had not spoken like that. Even so, he remembered mother. She would leave a bit of the hot prawn powder in the mortar and call out, 'Sasirekha.' On the sling, she would keep the ghee pot. She would pull out the hot coal and would place the ghee pot over the fire. After the drop of ghee melted, she would put the drop of ghee in the mortar. Even as Sasirekha said, 'Enough, enough,' she would put the morsel of *ragi sangati* in the mortar and stir it. She would give that morsel to the daughter-

in-law just like that. Sasirekha would eat it greedily. If only Boodevi
were to come there then, she would say, 'Everything only for you,
girl. Why don't you give her some?' Who was the small child, and
who, the mother? How were Boodevi and Subhadra born in Yennela
Dinni! Why did they die like that? As if they were born only to die,
making the dust of love! Did Sasirekha talk about the 'drop of ghee'
just like that? Did not say just like that. On this earth, there was no
greater person than her mother-in-law. That was why she said it.

'Would it be so good if you mix a drop of ghee?' asked Saramma
looking at Sasirekha. Sasirekha did not speak.

'Do you make it like that?'

'Not I.'

'Then?'

'Mother-in-law would do it. Would fry prawns, put them in the
mortar, pound chillies, mix a morsel of sangati, put a drop of ghee on
the fire . . . ' she stopped.

She was weeping copiously. Look how much this girl was crying.
Why so? In truth, what did she lose? Mother-in-law? The morsel of
sangati with a ghee drop from her mother-in-law . . . or the love that
bound the two together? How easily this girl's mother-in-law had
erased the distance between being born of one and not being born of
one. Saramma was thinking. The girl would not stop. 'I'm reminded
of my mother-in-law . . . I'm reminded of my mother-in-law.' She
kept saying and crying.

'Come here.'

She stopped and looked.

'You eat.'

She took Sasirekha and came out. The two of them did not know
what she was saying. As for Martin he gave the two their plates
and came back. Inside, the men were eating. Outside, the women
were eating. Yellanna's songs were heard in the men's conversation.
Subhadra's love was visible in the women's conversation. After their
food, they placed their beds out in the open. Countless stars in the
sky. They spread their mats under those stars and lay down. Each to
their thoughts.

Saramma was looking for the star among them that first introduced
infant Jesus to the world. With how many stars had father-in-law

drawn her mother-in-law's muggukarra? Sasirekha kept linking one star to another and was looking on.

Yennela Dinni in front of Sivaiah's eyes. These stars would be there too. They would cover Yennela Dinni. Under that cover, tombs. Sand tombs. In front of Sivaiah's eyes the sand tombs of Yennela Dinni. Dark tombs. The light of stars would not enter the sand. In the tombs, complete darkness. Sandy darkness. In that sandy darkness father, mother, grandfathers, maternal grandmothers, paternal grandmothers . . . one way they were all lucky. In that darkness there was no hunger. There was no untouchability. They would merge with the enveloping sand. The karanam would not come in the way of merging like that. Atchireddy would not come in the way. Not just they. Their caste, gods and demons would not come in the way. Once Pittodu thatha mentioned madiga Mataiah. He had chopped off the elder karanam's head horizontally. They did not bury the elder karanam in the earth. They cremated him. His body was burnt and was reduced to ashes. Then they mixed it in the Penna. Was the Penna small—it would be more than ten times as big as Buckingham canal. Was a fistful of ashes any value to the Penna? Tomorrow, the same would happen to the younger karanam. He would burn to ashes and would be of no use to the Penna. But at the time of burning it would become one with air like clever ghosts. Those flames would appear like that. In truth, clever ghosts. How they chased him! How they chased his father! His caste on the whole . . .

Sasirekha and Sivaiah stood in front of Martin's eyes.

Sasirekha started crying remembering her mother-in-law. Sivaiah mentioned her name. He said it was Subhadra. Coming to know he was Yellanna's son, Martin kept looking at Sivaiah. He had heard of Yellana. He had heard of him when he was in Nellore. He had heard his songs. Did not know the man. Did not have the opportunity to meet him.

Once he came to know Sivaiah was Yellanna's son, Martin decided to have him with him. He thought of making him go around places along with him.

As he looked at the fast-moving stars, he felt the entire life was the swift movement of stars. Every life known to him was like that. Thorns at every step. Drops of blood as you take each step.

When he was of Sivaiah's age—he remembered his appearance then. Thought better not. He thought it was better not to remember all that. He had forgotten. He had forgotten everything.

But it would not stop. The thorns and drops of blood—he kept remembering them over and over again. When he was of Sivaiah's age. No use. It would not stop even though he did not want it. Even when he shut his eyes, those very days came back.

If you were to put it in Martin's words, those were the early days when the untouchable populace was converting into a Christian populace. Martin's original name was Chinnodu. A madigapalli in a really backward place of Kanigiri province. He was born in one of the palles there. Grew up there. His father would stitch slippers. Mother would go around fields for the invisible grains. For some reason, he did not want to stitch slippers. Brother's name was Peddodu. Sister-in-law's name was Chinajali. They would toil hard at the kapu's house and come home dragging their feet. When he looked at them he felt life ought not to be so wretched. The life he saw in his house did not look like life to him. He would not be around the house except to eat. He would spend the entire time at the lake bund. Father would be angry with him. Mother would pity him. They thought he would be set right if he was married. They got him married. Polamma came to live with him. Even so, Chinnodu did not change. He would not be at home except during meal times. He did not stop sitting idle at the lake bund. Polamma would go with her mother-in-law for leftover grains in the fields. He would not like her to go for them. If she went for work to the kapu's house with her sister-in-law he would get inexplicably irritated. He would be angry with himself. He would not understand the reason for that irritation. There would be no concrete shape to his anger. He could not find an answer as to why he was so bitter with himself.

How those days went by! Why did they go by without anything happening to him? Martin was able to see clearly in front of his eyes his 'Chinnodu self.' Holding his head between his legs and looking as far as the eyes could see. How much irritation in those looks, how much anger, how much vengeance and how much of tears in the eyes when nothing was fulfilled? How he grieved hiding his eyes and the tears in them from others by shoving them into his heart! What did father say when he sat like that whiling away his days? What did he tell mother?

Father told mother in a forthright manner he could not take care of him and his wife. Mother too said in the same forthright manner, 'If you can't take care of him, I'll do so with my toil.' When he was lying down on the cot by the shade of the stone mound after food, he could hear mother's and father's words. Brother intervened. He asked her to have a separate establishment. He said father would stay with him. If he wished, he said he could take the job of stitching slippers in ten kapu houses for the grains he received in return. Father would stitch slippers for fifteen houses including those in the neighbouring villages. For having stitched, during harvest days, they would get a certain amount of leftover grains per house. Sister-in-law did not agree to this. As father-in-law would be in their house, she said the grains of all the fifteen houses should come to them. An argument began between mother and sister-in-law. For each threshing floor three baskets of paddy. If they got everything, forty-five baskets of paddy.

The baskets that were used to measure for the indentured malas and madigas were kept separately in the thatched roof of the cattleshed. They used to be half the size of the normal ones. That very practice turned into small measures for the days of distribution of grain for labour. How long could the seeds that were obtained that way in a year last? The malas and madigas never kept count of it. Had the bullock that had kept its neck under the yoke ever counted the acres that it had tilled? Did it ever count the number of hours the yoke rested on its neck? Had the cow with its udder overflowing with milk been guilty of counting the number of pots of milk it gave on a particular day? When it seemed its calf came running and touched its udder, thinking it is its child it filled the udder with milk, and when instead of the milk teeth at the udder, hands skilfully squeezed out the milk, did it ever get angry and kick? The cow and the bullock thought that a little grass and a tubful of *kuditi* was enough.

Isn't kuditi but the water that was left behind after the kapus ate and washed their hands? Isn't the grass the dried one which was left after the seeds had dropped? That very kuditi and grass became the property to be divided in their house. Became the cause for displeasure. Became the cause for abuses. Whether Chinnodu who was sleeping by the stone mound got up or Polamma who was lying on the bed opened her mouth, a big quarrel would ensue. The entire madigapalli would gather there. The caste elder's judgement would not be pronounced in one day.

Mother's voice was silenced by father's shout. As for sister-in-law, brother's beating promptly fell on her back. She started crying. As she cried, she found fault with Chinnodu and Polamma. Polamma could not control herself. She got up. Chinnodu noticed that.

'Don't go. Lie down.'

Polamma stopped at Chinnodu's words. The anger against her sister-in-law, her husband and his father burst out into tears.

'Don't cry. Sleep.'

Though he said that, Polamma did not stop crying. She kept crying without letting anyone hear her. Chinnodu could not sleep. He kept looking at a baby snake sliding into whichever hole it wished in the stone mound. Did not feel like killing it. They kept moving about in stone mounds like that. They would not know because they would be sleeping. So he kept looking to see how it played in the holes. He felt it looked quite cute then. He kept his hand on his waist as he kept looking at it like that. The horizontal fold in the pancha was empty.

'Do you have a bit of tobacco?'

Polamma took it out from the waist even as she was crying. She searched for the bit of tobacco even as she was crying. She gave a small bit to Chinnodu even as she was crying. Chinnodu broke a tiny piece out of it. Kept it in his mouth. He turned it twice over. He stuffed it under his cheek. He gave the rest to Polamma. He asked her to use it. Polama stuffed the remaining piece of tobacco in her mouth. The quarrel in front of the house seemed to have ceased. There was no commotion. Could hear father's snore. As for the baby snake, it was involved in its game in the hole in the stone mound. Now he did not feel like seeing it play. He asked Polamma to take hold of the stick under the cot. Polamma stopped crying and took hold of the stick. After she gave the stick to Chinnodu, she shut her eyes tight as Chinnodu pressed the edge of the stick carefully on the snake's head. She then fell into a sleep. Chinnodu felt sleepy.

In the morning mother and sister-in-law kept separate pots and cooked. Polamma went with mother for threshing work. Chinnodu could not prevent it. Father told his brother in mother's hearing that he was going to the elder kapu's house. So Chinnodu came to know that father's toil was for his brother and mother's toil for him. He felt bad that such a thing had happened. Everything appeared like that. He felt that all things distasteful to him were happening on this earth. So he almost stopped speaking. Now, he sat not just at the lake bund but at all places. He only replied when someone called out, heard what was told to him and spoke if he felt it necessary. What he spoke was distasteful to him. He felt as if he was speaking with great difficulty. Mother's heart would be hurt on seeing her child. Father stopped looking at him. The uncle who gave his daughter in marriage to him felt something had possessed him. He told Chinnodu's mother over and over again that the ghost would squeeze the life out of him. He did not stop at that. He brought some charm and gave it to his daughter. He asked her to tie it to his wrist when he was sleeping. He asked her not to sleep with him on the same cot after she tied it. He asked her to sleep next to her mother-in-law for a week. Polamma poured water over her hair and used incense for her hair and the charm. She tied it to the right hand of the sleeping Chinnodu. She slept next to her mother-in-law like a good girl. When Chinnodu got up at midnight, Polamma was not there. She was lying on mother's cot at a distance. Thinking she might be displeased with him, he was about to get up. He noticed something tied on his hand. A charm. He understood. Didn't like it. Irritation. Anger. He broke it with a vengeance. He flung it at Polamma. She sprang up as if a scorpion had fallen on her. When she looked, it was charm. Eyes brimmed with tears. She sat crying. Chinnodu did not like her crying like that. '*Chi*, what a wretched life,' he thought.

He set out on the road in the morning. He sat on the cot that was placed in front of Kotesu's house which was on the road. That was it. He thought of not returning home. Those listening to Yerrodu's words were those who were not pressed for work, sitting in front on separate cots. Chinnodu did not feel like listening to his words. Did not like them. He only spoke about the kapus. Throwing a piece of tobacco, he would repeat his kapu's words as if they were something great, 'For the bastard, no amount of tobacco is enough.' Not just the younger kapu's abuses but also his wife's would appear wonderful to him. Even if they caught hold of Yerrodu's wife and said, 'You alone are not enough for her' or caught hold of his mother and said, 'In whose bed did you conceive him?' those words would not affect Yerrodu. Moreover, he would boast in front of everyone that the younger kapu said such things.

Wretched life. Did not like it. Chinnodu did not like it at all. That was why as he heard Yerrodu's words, he spat on the ground. He spat not just once but repeatedly. He thought it was better to look at the spit than at Yerrodu's face.

Did not know what happened in the meanwhile. Yerrodu's boasting stopped. Laughter stopped. All got up together. He raised his head to see what happened.

The younger kapu came to the palle. People got up from wherever they were and stood up. Why should they stand up like that? Did not like it. Chinnodu did not like standing up like that. Those who got up, stood with folded hands. Stood with heads bent. The old woman with a stick got up with great difficulty, turned the cot upside down and slumped to the ground. The old man who was almost dying was shouting out to his grandson, 'Lift me up, the kapu's come.' Could not stand up. Had to make him stand and hold him.

Wretched life. Why had it come to this? Why should they stand like that? He would not get up and stand like that. Come what may. Standing up would never happen. That was it. He did not make an effort to stand up.

The younger kapu stood in front of him. He had uncouth legs. Uncouth nose. Eagle-like nose. Eyes just like those of a wolf. Not a man's eyes. What was the man like! He was like a bull. Not just a bull. A bear. A huge pot belly for that bear. Hoarse voice. His wife would not look at him properly. She would always look at the floor. Otherwise, she could not have led a married life with him for so long. She would not have had two young bears through him and let them loose on the world. They too were like that. Like bears, they would attack women cutting grass. Even so, nobody would speak. Life. Wretched life.

'Get up, you fellow!'

' . . . '

'Get up, you!'

He would not get up. There was no question of getting up. The kick that fell hard on his head. Chinnodu fell to the ground. Kick after kick. Bear. The younger kapu kept kicking. Pain. Even so, he did not scream. Even though his bones were breaking, he did not get up. He hugged the ground and moaned silently. This earth did not break to bits. At such a time, it did not split into two. Even earth will only split into two for Seetammas. It would sit cosy like a throne only for the husbands of Seetammas. Not for him.

The younger kapu became tired. He tied up Chinnodu's arms. He upturned the cot and placed it on him. He had a heavy log placed on the cot. Then he left. Everyone was watching. No one came forward. Did not untie him. Did not remove the weight. Did not turn the cot. Kept watching. That news reached the threshing floor. Chinnodu's mother and wife came running, beating their chests. The people kept looking like that even at the two women who came running. The women braved it. Pushed away the weight. Turned the cot up. Untied him. With great difficulty they took Chinnodu home.

The day went by. The entire day was spent on Chinnodu. For Chinnodu's mother, it might be a blow on her womb. For Polamma, it might be a heart-wrenching blow. But for Chinnodu, it was a confrontation. A silent revolt against something he hated.

Polamma kept looking at Chinnodu. Every day, like that. Torture. Annoyance. An unpleasant thing. Unpleasant work.

Just then, his life took an unexpected turn. There was a new tent outside the village. Everyone was talking about it as a strange thing. He went there. A white man mounted on a white horse came there. Chinnodu looked amazed at the white man and the white horse. It appeared as if the white man noticed his surprise. He signalled to him to come near. He went near him in trepidation. The white man held Chinnodu's hand. He placed his other hand on his shoulder.

Chinnodu's heart beat rapidly. Inexplicable anguish. What was happening in front of his eyes? He could not believe that such a thing happened. What was it that really happened?

The white man signalled him to come.

He went in trepidation.

The white man held his hand. He touched his hand. He placed his hand on his shoulder. He touched his shoulder.

Until now, from the time he knew things, a madiga had touched him. A mala had touched him.

A brahmin had not touched him. For him his body was untouchable. A reddy had not touched him. For him too the same. The same for the rest of the castes. Untouchable. If touched, it was so low that it could pollute.

But the white man touched him. He did not belong to this village. He was not from this region. He did not belong to this soil or to this land. He touched him. Touched a madiga born in this village. He touched his body, touched him who believed in this earth, who was born on this land and would die on this land, and who would not be touched his entire life by many who were born and grew up here. The white man touched him. He said his body was not untouchable. He did not say it in words. He said it with his touch. That was why he kept looking at the white man like that for a long time. He kept looking till the anxiety, uneasiness and anguish in his heart came under his control. He shed tears even as he looked. The white man said those tears were those of Christ. That was it. Chinnodu became one with the white man's group. Polamma too went along with him. Chinnodu's mother too thought that was good. She told her daughter-in-law, 'He's no good for work. Something has possessed him. He may be set right if he roams about like that. That alone would be good for him. You stay with him.'

A month afer this happened, the white man baptised Chinnodu and Polamma with water. As he was being baptised, Chinnodu asked, his body wet:

'Now, is this body like a brahmin's? Like a reddy's body? Can touch everything? Can touch everyone?' Question? Surprise!

He kept asking. He spoke words with inexplicable surprise. The white man understood Telugu. He heard Chinnodu's words. He heard the deep anguish of his voice. But he did not give him a straightforward reply.

'For Christ, nobody is untouchable.' He only said those words. Chinnodu heard them. The answer was not straightforward. Was not clear. He wanted to hear those words again.

'Your name is Martin from today onwards.' The words he wanted to hear again were no longer available.

'Her name is Saramma.' The words he wanted to hear again went into the background.

Martin and Saramma reached Nellore. The compound of Nellore mission gave their lives a new meaning. They learnt many things in that compound. Became educated. Martin became a preacher. Saramma became a Bible woman. That was how their new life began. On the one hand, they had the protection of the missionaries. On the other hand, they had the respect of the Christian families. They roamed about many villages. They stayed at places missionaries asked them to. They stayed where they wanted to.

The life was new. Experiences too were new. The heart that had shrivelled up till the other day, was now going about filled with confidence. But it was not easy to go about with a raised head. He had become a Christian to get away from untouchability. But Christ became untouchable here. Thinking of it, he felt like laughing. But he knew how much sorrow was there in that laughter. His new life tasted a different experience in each village.

In the village if cattle die, they call the madigas. If there are no madigas, they call malas. The madigas take the cattle outside the village. They do not bury them there. They cut them up. They surround them with vessels that they take from malapalli and madigapalli when they cut them up. They take out the good portions of the cattle and give a small portion to each. Then ensue hesitations, shouts, quarrels. They vie with each other keeping one vessel over another. By then vultures reach the surroundings and perch on trees. All around, dogs watch and wait. Abuses, shoves, vultures on the trees, people under the trees, dogs—all for the meat of the dead cattle. That's a strange scene. Finally, bundling two or three good pieces in the hide of the dead cattle, tying the dead cattle to the stick they have brought along, the madigas who had cut up the dead cattle go away. The minute the men go, the vultures from above and the dogs before all attack the remains in one go.

Martin felt this scene ought to change. He mentioned just that in his prayer. He said that they ought not to eat the meat of dead cattle. Everyone looked at him in surprise. They listened to what they felt were things they ought not to hear. They were worried as to how that could be possible. Was this something of today? When did it start? How long ago? How was it possible now? They found it strange. Martin told them. Told them many things. Finally, the caste elder said that it was the right of their caste to take the dead cattle. Martin felt like laughing. The fields by the Krishna river were the right of the *kammas*. The fields by the Penna river were the right of the reddys. But there and here too, as for the dead cattle, they were the right of the madigas. Could not stop laughing. He laughed. He said even as he laughed. Finally, that palle said okay. They firmly decided they would not eat the dead cattle.

These words reached the ooru. It came up for discussion at the munsif's porch. China Choudhary listened to the munsif. He looked at Bucchi Choudhary. Bucchi Choudhary nodded assent and kept quiet. China Choudhary did not keep quiet like that.

'I believe the madigas won't eat dead cattle.'

'They won't eat it. But they'll remove it, right?'

'They will remove it.'

'So long as they remove it, what's it to us if they eat it or don't?'

'Today he'll say he won't eat it. Tomorrow he'll say he won't remove it.'

'Oh, so you're looking at it from that angle. Then, as you wish.'

There's another strange thing about dead cattle. A madiga who has taken the cattle and its meat has to stitch slippers from the hide for the choudhary or reddy who has given him the cattle. If madigas did not eat the meat of the dead cattle, there would be no question of slippers. Bucchi Choudhary recollected all this later. 'We've got to settle this, come, China Choudhary,' he said again.

The day for solving this did arrive. The bullock of Venkayamma-garu's China Jalaiah died. Before giving the news to madigapalli, Jalaiah mentioned it to China Choudhary. China Choudhary sent word to Bucchi Choudhary. Then the news reached madigapalli. Sinenkadu and his son came. As they were taking the carcass away, Bucchi Choudhary said, 'After the work is done, come here.' Sinenkadu laid the bullock under a tree outside the ooru. Now there were only vultures above the tree and dogs away from the tree. As for people with vessels, they were not there. Sinenkadu skinned the hide off the bullock and took it. He dug a pit and buried its bones and flesh.

The Choudharies came to know that Sinenkadu had buried the bones and flesh. They also came to know he had only skinned the hide and taken it, and that the malas and madigas did not swarm around the bullock holding their vessels like in the past.

'How do you feel, you, Peda Jalamma's son-in-law?' said China Jalamma's son-in-law.

'The ooru is turning into a graveyard, Sinaiah,' said Peda Jalamma's son-in-law. More people than usual gathered at China Choudhary's porch.

Sinenkadu tied the hide of the bullock to a pole right in the middle of the house and went to Bucchi Choudhary's house. Bucchi Choudhary was not in the house. Coming to know he was in China Choudhary's house, he went there. There were many choudharies there. He stood at a distance. Bucchi Choudhary said, 'Come home at night. There's some work.' Sinenkadu was about to leave. Venkayamma's China Jalaiah looked at Sinenkadu as if he had just seen him. He said, 'Wait a bit, you fellow.' Sinenkadu waited. He asked him, as if very casually, 'When will you give the slippers?' All of them too were behaving as if nothing happened, as if everything was proceeding in a very normal manner.

'I've buried the bones and flesh.'

All of them were surprised at Sinenkadu's words.

'Didn't take the meat to eat.'

They looked at him again. It was not a small issue. An untouchable speaking like that was not as simple as sitting leisurely on the ground.

'Therefore, there's no need to stitch slippers, China Jala!' Bucchi Choudhary said in a normal tone. In fact, he never spoke in an angry manner. Having tied the upper cloth to his waist and up to the folded leg, he would speak rocking to and fro very casually, as if nothing ensued from him and he could set fire to the roof sitting calmly under it. That was what he did. He lit the fire and was smoking his *chutta*.

'He's changed his religion, right? Christians don't eat dead cattle's meat. Isn't Martin your elder? He asked you not to eat?' he said, letting off the chutta smoke, saying, 'This wretched tobacco,' and pushing it under the edge of his teeth.

The fire burnt peacefully. Burnt normally.

'The hide for removing the carcass. If you eat meat, you've got to make slippers. He didn't eat the meat. That's it, isn't it, Sinenka?' Bucchi Chaudhary was raking the fire. At one go, the flames spread skyward.

'Eat the one you buried, you wretched bastard.'

Everyone looked in the direction from where the words came. China Chaudhary was swaying. Sinenkadu looked at Chaudhary. His looking like that made the Chaudhary extremely angry. He got up. He took a long stick. He began to thrash Sinenkadu as he would cattle. The thrashings did not stop with China Chaudhary. Did not know how many blows were being received.

'Let's kick him all the way there.'

Hearing China Chaudhary's words, they chased Sinenkadu till outside the ooru where he had cut up the cattle. They asked him to dig the mud that covered the pit. Sinenkadu dug it. They asked him to take the meat covered with mud, cook and eat it. If he did not do so, they said they would bury him in that pit. They left as if they had preserved a great tradition. Martin could not forget even now the image of Sinenkadu holding the mud-smeared meat and coming into the palle. The helplessness and hopelessness on his face that day haunted him to this very day.

Not a small one. To go about with dignity was not such a small matter. Eating or not eating too was not a small matter. Actually, having one's own likes too was not an ordinary issue. Martin remembered everything. His life as Chinnodu. His mind as Martin.

A new life.

A new experience. Life was jumping about in the space between the rocks. All rocks were bloodstained. Experience too was like that. A weave of blood veins. A weave for every village.

In the early days of his new life it was Sinenkadu. In his last days, Sivaiah. Hunt. Hunting of beasts. Men were not hunting beasts. Beasts were hunting men. They were not ordinary beasts. Cruel beasts with two iron legs. One leg was religion. The other leg was caste. Like that many experiences came to mind. One after the other.

One different from the other. There was something common in all. Walking with raised head. Not a small thing.

The morning cock crowed. Martin looked startled. He came into the present. He looked at Saramma. It looked as if Saramma too had not slept. 'Didn't you sleep?' she asked. Martin said he had not.

'Sivaiah is Yellanna's son.'

'Sasirekha told me. They seemed to have buried Subhadra and Yellanna and have come here.

'He told me. Yellanna was a great songster. I've heard his name. I couldn't see him . . . When I was in Nellore, I heard that name many a time.'

' . . . '

'They'll live with us.'

'I want to keep the girl with me.'

'Christ is merciful.'

That night passed by in that manner. It was morning. Martin asked Sivaiah to come along with him. Sivaiah did not ask him where or why. He went. Sasirekha stayed back with Saramma.

Sivaiah was going around villages with Martin. Sasirekha would spend time with the children of the coolies at the canal along with Saramma. She too was learning the alphabet with them.

Though the canal work was over, many of the migrant workers wanted to stay back there itself. Some set out for their birth place. Now Yennela Dinni did not find a place in Sivaiah's heart. When he left he had wanted to get back there sometime. Now he was of the view that he could go back there sometime before his death. He said they ought to stay back here with Martin and Saramma. He dedicated himself to that region. Sand banks as far as his eyes could see. Water holes. Beyond the holes, sapling fields. The continuous oceanic roar. Did not know why, but he quite liked this region. As for Saramma, the bond that grew with Sasirekha and the affection that grew towards the children of coolies bound her to that place. Till now they had roamed about in many places. She felt it would be good if her last days were spent here. She felt that Sasirekha had come here searching for her. It was Christ who was responsible for this bond. She had not conceived a child. She thought this girl was her child. She would be content if this girl conceived. She thought she could place either her grandson or granddaughter on her chest and sleep peacefully. 'The mud for our tombs is in this sandy earth alone,' she told Martin. Valasapadu was established with thirty families. There were only two castes there—malas and madigas. There was no ooru till the malas and madigas walked half a mile. There were all castes in that ooru.

Sivaiah kept observing how Martin spoke in the palles, how he mingled in Christian houses and what terms he explained in detail during his prayers. More than anything else, Sivaiah appreciated the excitement, the roused emotion and straightforward talk that emanated from Martin. He wanted to speak like Martin. He wanted to pray like him. He felt he too should have the kind of excitement and emotion Martin had. He was able to slowly enunciate the sayings in the Bible verses. It was difficult to read. Even so, Martin would ask him to read like that. He would make him read repeatedly. What was funny was that Sivaiah had not learnt the alphabet. But he would associate the alphabet with his recognition of their sound and enunciate them slowly. Martin would say, 'Christ was an amazing person.' One day he told Sivaiah, 'Christ wants to use you for his purpose. Do you like that?' Sivaiah kept quiet.

Sivaiah became Simon.

'Pilate gave his verdict. He handed over Christ to the chief priests, the scribes and the rulers. There was only one thing left, to nail him to a cross. They were taking him for crucifixion. It was then that Simon was seen. A villager from Cyrene. They forced Simon to carry the Cross along with Christ. He would carry the Cross. You too have that Simon's name. Sivaiah, your name too is the name of that Simon who carried the Cross.'

Martin told him what the name Simon meant in the Bible.

In truth, even if the Sivaiahs did not convert into Simons, when did they not bear the Cross? They were born only to carry it. Carrying it always, tired, they were born only to be pierced by spears. If not like that, how else did things happen?

Bearing the Cross was not something new.

Climbing on to the Cross was not something new.

Giving up their lives there was not something new.

Every moment . . . in every corner . . . all over the country.

You could say so. With Martin who bore the Cross, Simon, who bore the Cross, went along talking about Christ who bore the Cross.

It is good for history to talk of each thing in its context. In this country, not just malas and madigas but brahmins too became Christians. Reddys too. Choudharies too.

Martins and Sivaiahs believed in Christ to get rid of untouchability. They believed in him to appease their hunger. More than anything else they believed in Christ to save themselves from being hunted by men. Whether Chinnodu became Martin or Sivaiah became Simon, they did so only for this reason.

Strange. John Paul Reddys, Immanuel Sastrys, Joshuah Choudharys sprung up. When Yennela Dinni's younger karanam's son-in-law appeared in religious congregations in Nellore, Simon was surprised. Simon did not know what to say when he came to know that Immanuel Sastry was no other than the younger karanam's son-in-law. The younger karanam's daughter came to those congregations. Copies of the Bible were seen in the hands of her sons. In their necks, gold chains with the Cross. They were doing higher studies.

'He's Yennela Dinni's younger karanam's son-in-law. He became a Christian when he grew older.' Martin whispered in his ear.

'Look at him. John Paul Reddy.' Simon looked in the direction Martin was pointing to. A clean-shaven face. Extremely fat body. John Paul Reddy was like a little elephant.

'Next to him is Joshuah Choudhary. Krishna region. Cotton, the white man, transformed that region. Since then the Choudhary's field has been yielding gold.'

Simon kept looking at the turbaned Choudhary. Thick moustache. Golden-edge stick. Coloured coat. Though he sat in the convention, Simon's head was filled with doubts.

They came back home after the conventions. An inexplicable fear was haunting Simon. In his province there were no such reddys, brahmins and choudharys who became Christians. But today or tomorrow reddys could become Christians. Kammas and sastrys too. If only such a thing happened. He could not sleep. He kept looking at his body over and over again. He did not know why he rubbed his stomach. He did so many times.

'Clough, the white man, did not accept this. His wife didn't accept. They mingled only with malas and madigas. They converted them to Christianity. The white man Clough's wife said it was Christ's decision to protect only the untouchables. Clough too believed that. He said he couldn't shut the gates to untouchables because of the upper-caste people. But everyone among whites is not like Clough. Not like Cotton.'

Simon was listening to Martin's words.

'I've walked along these fields many times. Hundred times, thousand times—I've walked. I don't know how much longer I'll walk. But as long as I walk, it'll be towards malapallis! Towards madigapallis!'

Simon did not say anything. He was listening.

'Yennela Dinni's younger karanam's son-in-law has a good reputation in the court. He is the one who looks after all the land disputes in Nellore region. For this, he needs the white man's patronage. That's why he became a Christian. He spends three fourths of the day in the houses of the whites.'

Simon was unable to imagine both the crucifier and the crucified under the same roof. But Christ is merciful. It is not as if he did not know how to separate things. Only after this thought occurred did Simon sleep somewhat peacefully after a long time. Man's mind is always like that. As if it was searching for something somewhere, it would feel content that it had finally discovered a meaning. Till then only anxiety.

Time was on the march casting doubts and raising hopes in equal measure in Simon. Sasirekha conceived. Happiness was not so much Simon's. It was Saramma's. Sasirekha's internal worry too disappeared. Though she never spoke out, she was worried that she had not conceived after so many years of marriage. That worry ceased. When Sasirekha kept saying she would clean rice and ragi all morning, Saramma became suspicious and noticed one day. Sasirekha while cleaning the rice was eating mud pellets. The same when she was cleaning ragi. Her suspicion was confirmed. It was clear Sasirekha was pregnant. She shared this initially only with Martin. Martin jumped with joy. He started to shout out that Saramma had become a grandmother. It was true—Saramma was indeed a grandmother.

She considered Sasirekha her only child. She ensured that Sasirekha stopped thinking of Subhadra. The child—male or female, it did not matter. It was enough if a child was born. Like that, Saramma sat counting days, weeks and months.

A child was born. A boy. She kept him only on her lap. Sasirekha's job ended with feeding him. All the rest, Saramma. Martin kept seeing a light in her that he had never seen before.

'This child's not your child. It's Saramma's child. He was born for Saramma.' Sasirekha did not say no to Martin's words. The child would sleep only with Saramma. He would bathe only if Saramma bathed him. When she bathed him, Saramma would look at his toes and fingers over and over again.

'His grandfather's toes. His fingers are long and thin. His toes too,' Sivaiah would say. 'His face is like mother-in-law's,' Sasirekha would add immediately. She would not agree if she was told that there was nothing in his face similar to her mother-in-law's. That was why Saramma liked Sasirekha so much. She saw many kids close to their mothers. Sasirekha was close to her mother-in-law. There were only a few like that. Subhadras too were like that. Only a few have their nests built in their daughters-in-law's hearts.

'Let it be, my child . . . These fingers are Yellanna's. These toes too are Yellanna's. This nose, this face . . . '

'All like my mother-in-law's.'

At that point, Saramma kept the child on her lap and Sasirekha in her eyes. She thought repeatedly she should keep them like that till she lived.

Time was speeding by. Along with time, change too. The conversion of malas and madigas to Christianity was happening like a movement. Incidents of thousands of people being baptised on a single day too were making news. On the other hand, there also began attacks on Christians. It is better to say attacks on mala and madiga Christians rather than on Christians. There was no news of attacks on choudhary Christians of the Krishna district. No news of attacks on reddy Christians of Nellore district. There were no instances of attacks on brahmin Christians who had squatted in government offices. All that happened affected only the malas and madigas, the untouchable Christians.

Fresh news each day. In every village a story. They kept sixteen mala and madiga Christians in jail in Markapuram. Tortured them. They asked them to forget Christ and pray to Krishna. They sang only Christian songs. In Kanigiri, in mid-bazaar, they paraded a madiga Christian half-naked. They burnt the Bible in his hand. There was a midnight attack on Bandlamoodi Christians. The details of the attack spread to each village, each in a different manner. In Kuchapudi, the munsif of the village sent for ten Christians who had been baptised. He asked them to dip themselves in the lake of the village and get rid of their Christian touch. They refused to take a dip in the lake. The munsif had men push them into the lake. There, they sacrificed a buffalo to Poleramma. They cut up a goat. They forced them to prostrate before the idol. They smeared the blood of the buffalo on their faces. They made them dance. They themselves danced. In the vicinity of Cheemakurthi, they hounded and caught hold of a madiga youth. He had committed two crimes. He had a Bible in his hand. He had slippers on his feet. Besides, he was walking in the ooru. An untouchable ought not to walk in the village. If an occasion arose to walk, he ought not to wear slippers. He ought not to have a head cloth. He ought not to hold an umbrella in his hand. He ought not to raise his lowered head. He ought not to look sideways, even accidentally. If, at such an instance, an upper caste woman came out and looked at him, that was the end of him. That was why in some oorus they had to walk making a strange sound. If they made such a sound, upper caste women would not come out. When they make a sound, it should be such that it would heard in all the streets. If an upper caste woman working somewhere in the backyard did not hear the sound and came out, the fault was not hers. Even though he had made the sound, the fault would still be his. Such things had to happen. But that youth happened to hold a Bible in his hand. Had converted. He had slippers on. He had slighted that tradition. That was all that happened. They hounded him. They chased him till the outskirts of the ooru. They stabbed him with spears. They hung his corpse from a tree in the little forest next to the hill. It was through that little forest that malas-and madigas would go to the neighbouring villages. That news spread to every village. Fear at every place. A state of anxiety not knowing what would happen in any ooru. Some malas and madigas wore clean clothes. There was an attack on those clothes. They said they would not come to work on Sundays. There was an attack on that holiday. They asked them to eat the meat of dead cattle. They were attacked for expressing their views on 'eating' such things. They started to study a little bit in Missionary schools. There was an attack on that education. Here and there, the untouchables raised their heads and looked. There was an attack on their heads.

If they said, the hands were theirs, attack on the hands.

If they said, the feet were theirs, attack on the feet.

If they said, the eyes were theirs, attack on the eyes.

If they said, the fingers were theirs, attack on the fingers.

Attack. On the mala people. On the madiga people. Attack. On the mala Christ. Attack. On the madiga Christ. It would be enough if Christ were an untouchable. There would certainly be an attack. Martin did not sit silent. He began to speak condemning the attack.

'We didn't join the religion to keep silent. We didn't get baptised to squirm in our bodies.' At such times Martin's voice would become hoarse. His voice would become hoarse repeating over and over again all that he said during prayers. He kept going to each and every place that was being attacked. He was informing the authorities about the matter. Martin appeared very great to Simon. He was running along with Martin. In the direction of any hear-rending cry. Along with that tireless old man.

'Here . . . I'm proclaiming clearly. I am proclaiming loud enough for the veins in my throat to burst. I'm reminding you of my Jehovah's words once again. I'm placing before you Isaiah's words, the same words Christ spoke on the Sabbath to his people in the Community's shrine in Nazareth.'

That was how Martin would begin to preach.

'I've the Lord's grace on me. He has anointed me to spread good word to the people. He chose me to get the people out of imprisonment. He sent me to release the crushed people. If that were not so, why should I speak? If that were not so, why should I become close to Christ?'

Simon did not find them as mere words. They appeared to him as the real embodiments of truth.

'They are those who attack. Their hands will become impure with blood. Their fingers will become impure with flaws. Their lips are untruths. Their tongues speak of evil. Their evidence is not according to morality. Their judgement will not be according to truth. They conceive evil in their womb. They give birth to sin.'

Sharp words like deadly arrows. On karanams, kapus, sastrys as if Christ had spoken, as if he had spoken on the mount, as if he had spoken amidst groups of people. Martin spoke as if he had full authority to speak in that manner.

'Look, I dipped into the water proclaiming my body is not untouchable. When that proclamation has become useless, I think this body itself is useless to me. I say this as Christ is my witness. If raising the head is a crime, I'll commit that crime. If the cost of it is to lose the head, I'll lose my head. That's why Christ had turned his body into bread and gave it. That's why he distributed his blood as drink. We ate that bread for the sake of labouring for truth. We drank that drink.'

Martin's words were like that. They were like resolutions. They were like field knives ready to harvest. Living in the deep earnestness of those words, Simon would sit in front of Martin. Disturbance in the heart. Each atom of the veins was enlarging.

'Here . . . I'm keeping my Father in front of you. Crown of thorns. Violet coloured dress. My Father stood in front of Pilate. The screams of the chief priests. They are asking for my Father to be crucified.'

Movement among people. A scene in front of their eyes. Christ carrying the Cross. Christ on the Cross. Flowing blood. All in Martin's words. All in Martin's anguish. He was saying all this to make 'suffering' significant. He said finally, 'We won't run away like cowards. Christ is merciful. Let's march forward courageously. Victory to the blood of Lord Jesus. End to the deeds of the wrong-doer.'

When Martin would utter the last words, Simon would join him.

Victory to the blood of Lord Jesus.

End to the deeds of the wrong-doer.

These words reverberated over and over again in the prayer hall.

It was right against this background that the issue of Valasapadu came to the fore where Martin lived. As that palle had only Christians, the ooru people half a mile away said they would not call them for work. They made fun of the Sundays. In that village, there were only five mala and madiga houses. They said, 'They'll get spoilt looking at you.' They had to go a long distance to find work. There too the same problem. Added to this, attack on Christians. Once, they had migrated here in search of livelihood. Now it appeared as if they would have to go to another place. Only, they might have to take the road back to the places they came from. It was then that they noticed the barren land west of the canal. There were more than twenty-five acres. They thought of occupying the land. Martin met the authorities. He explained the matter. They said they would definitely do it. They asked them to meet them ten days later. When they went after ten days, they resolved it was not a barren land. When they met the karanam, he said it belonged to two farmers. Thinking it was of no use, he met the white man. The white man sent word to the karanam. The munsif went along with the karanam. The two of them said they had no objections if they could convince the two farmers. Martin argued that it did not in fact belong to the two farmers. The white ruler believed it. There were rumours that Christians were swallowing the properties of farmers. They incited the upper-caste people in the ooru. They filed a case in the court. The person arguing for the upper-caste people was the son-in-law of the younger karanam from Yennela Dinni, Immanuel Sastry. Martin met him.

'I am placing two things before you. First, it doesn't belong to any farmer. Second, you're a Christian. You must stand for the Christians,' Martin said. Sastry gave Martin a long look and said:

'Those two farmers too are Christians.'

Martin was surprised to hear his words. When did they become Christians? Who baptised them? Everything was confusing.

'When did they become Christians? Where did it happen?'

'They became Christians before the case came up before me. They were baptised in Nellore.'

Martin looked at him in a suspicious manner.

'I'm a Christian. I couldn't say no after the Christians came to me.'

'But there are poor Christians. Malas and madigas.'

'But after he says he's a Christian, he's a Christian. Here they may be reddy, kamma, brahmin, mala, madiga or anyone else. All are Christians. You too won't deny that.'

Martin understood. He turned back.

'Once one says he's a Christian, he's a Christian.' He kept remembering these words that the karanam's son-in-law told him. He had spoken very cleverly. There was deception in that cleverness. It was only to deceive that they would make cleverness their own. They would increase it like wealth. His mind was not in his control till he met Simon. He told Simon all that had happened.

'Nothing happened without his knowledge,' Simon said. They met the white man. They told him everything. Martin said he would not live any more on this earth if the poor did not get the land. He met the white man time and again. He met him alone. He met him along with Simon. He took thirty families along with small children and sat in the white man's bungalow. That news spread from village to village. There was a big discussion on the platforms of the upper castes.

Finally, Martin achieved what he wanted. It was proved that the land was a barren land. The right to cultivate that land was given to the poor Christians of that village. The incident was not a small one. The upper castes could not swallow it. They considered it nothing but a defeat. They were not willing to accept this defeat. The choudharys and reddys got together.

Christmas days.

Martin and Simon wanted to go round all villages till the 24th December evening and stay at home on the 25th. The people of the village were also happy about getting the land. They wanted to celebrate the festival in a grand manner. They wanted to put up tents in the new land and wanted to have prayers and meals there. They kept aside some food grains from each house. Martin appointed two youngsters to look after that work. All the women gathered near Saramma. They put the grains in the mortar and pounded them. They pounded chillies. There was a kind of gaiety everywhere. As

Saramma looked after everything, while keeping the child on her lap, an ineffable happiness filled her heart. Sasirekha sang songs to enthuse those who were pounding the grains. All were Yellanna's songs. Listening to those songs, she hugged the child to her heart and said over and over again, 'Those are your grandfather's songs.' He laughed a toothless laugh. In between, he got up from the lap and, taking tiny steps, walked all around. 'How many mortars must sound for your grandson's wedding, Saramma?' When Subbaratnam said this, Saramma became somewhat preoccupied. She wanted to be alive till then. She wanted to be alive till his wedding.

On December 24th, Martin and Simon went around important villages. By the time the last village was covered, it was late at night. There would be approximately three hours of journey. There were villages on the way. Even so, there was no need to stop there. Both set out.

'Did you notice, Simon? After prayer, during our conversation, our people asking us to look out for a little bit of land!'

'Yes, there is a need.'

'It's necessary to have land to raise your head and walk about.'

'Yes.'

'If you think of one, there'll be another one ahead. I thought it'd be enough if the body was not untouchable. It brings along the need to have a little bit of food for that body. There's need for both. Reddy has both. Choudhary has both.'

'A big incident occurred in Yennela Dinni.'

'I heard. I also heard the names of Naraiah, Mataiah and Naganna.'

'Father wove songs about them.'

'I heard the song too . . . the son-in-law of the younger karanam of Yennela Dinni . . . Immanuel Sastry . . . though he became a Christian, he hasn't lost his tail. The 'Sastry' remains. John Paul Reddy. Joshua Choudhary . . . Though the religion has changed, the caste hasn't worn off . . .'

The sound of dogs barking was heard at a distance. Simon looked around and picked up a stick.

'Come quickly. We've to reach home before Christ is born.'

The sound of dogs barking drew nearer.

'We've to name the child tomorrow. What shall we name him?'

'You name him.'

'Let's ask Saramma . . . How's this name?'

'Which name?'

About to say the name, he stopped. Men in front of him. They were surrounding them. The barking of dogs was awesome. Those men fell on them at one go.

The knives pierced through Martin's stomach, back and the ribs. Martin slumped to the ground. Before he could know what was happening, they began to attack Simon. They did not stab him with knives. They beat him up till blood flowed. They beat him so severely that he felt it was better to be dead. They lifted Simon who was stuck to the ground. Simon was unable to stand up. They beat him asking him to stand up. He stood up with great difficulty. They asked him to lift Martin who was in a pool of blood. They kept beating him till he lifted Martin up. With great difficulty, he lifted Martin on to his shoulders. They asked him to carry him along. He was unable to take a step forward. They beat him till he was able to take a step. Simon was walking with great difficulty. Martin on his shoulders. In all this pain, he recalled Martin's words.

'Yours is the name of Simon who bore the Cross.'

That Simon bore Christ's Cross. This Simon was carrying the corpse of a Christian preacher.

Simon managed to get hold of the strength he did not possess. He wanted to reach there before it dawned. He placed step after step. He started to walk with some strength and with more speed.

Martin's blood flowing over his shoulders.

Blood that ought not to have flowed.

Blood that ought to have drenched this earth as sweat for some more time.

Blood of those who hunger and thirst for righteousness.

Blood of those who are persecuted for the sake of righteousness.

Blood that contained mercy, love and kindness in this world.

Blood that splattered on the Cross. Blood that flowed like rivulets.

Blood. Untouchable blood.

Blood-memory.

Blood-memory that remains in Ruth's memory.

The deadly massacre that appears in front of Ruth's eyes.

The Simon who reached Valasapadu.

Holding the bloody body on his shoulders, the ghastly dance Simon saw. The scene of the graveyard of Valasapadu.

The upper castes chasing the malas and madigas with spears and crowbars. The helpless running away in frenzy and in fear. Their cries of agony. The constellation of ghosts that surrounded the palle.

Did not know how many they killed. Did not know how many fled and in what direction. The thatched huts burning. The smoke from flames that touched the sky . . .

Saramma turned into a corpse. Sasirekha turned into a corpse. Simon gazing wide-eyed at those corpses and the flames surrounding them. Memory is crying.

Memory is wrenching the heart.

Memory is bringing that child's frenzied cry of agony to the fore. The cry of agony, the shriek, the screams of the child amidst the flames and the amputated bodies. Simon who saw that child. Simon who took the child and ran thinking at least his child should live, that his lineage should survive at least with this child.

That child is her Reuben.

That frenzied scream, that cry of agony are her Reuben's.

A scene.

A scene that can never be erased.

A scene drawn with blood.

When she thinks of the scene, she cannot bear it even now. When Reuben captured the scene in front of her eyes, she cried copiously that day. Then Reuben pacified her. Now there is no Reuben to pacify her. That is why whenever she thinks of that scene, she keeps the diary, that Reuben kept for many years after the incident, in front of her. She looks in it for the pages she needs. She reads those pages over and over again.

Reuben became a preacher in a hospital at a very young age. It was part of the hospital preachers' routine to keep a diary. Like that, Reuben preserved not just the diaries but many other things. In the things preserved, she reads avidly, the Lone Star song and the few pages he wrote in the first days of his preaching. She does not reply when she is asked why she looks at them over and over again. It may be because she does not like to reply. Otherwise, it may be because she thinks the reply applies only to her.

Some pages of Reuben's diary of those days that Ruth reads with affection, without any changes—

17 November 1920: It's more than a month since becoming the hospital preacher. I heard a patient tell the patient next to him, 'Such a young preacher?' I looked at the man who said it. Was very old. I have been hearing patients say this on and off. They praise me. Those praises haunt me. But I have no one close to me to share those praises. I remained an orphan in the orphanage in the Mission compound. I also hear some people say, 'Who's this handsome boy?' The beautiful mother and father who bore this beautiful youth must be alive on this earth. At least, on the day she delivered me, she must have kept me on her lap. He must have looked at my tiny body again and again. How would they have looked? What would have happened to them? Questions that have no answers even now. When alone, occasions when I cried my heart out.

18 November 1920: There are a few miracles that happen on earth. Such a miracle occurred today. Francis who worked in the early days of the orphanage came here today. He was quite old. He came to see in his last days the orphanage he had worked in. He also came with the eagerness to see the Mission hospital that was beginning to grow then. He had worked till now at the Mission hospital in Hanumakonda and retired. Even at that age he went around all the rooms of the hospital. I kept him company. When we were going about like that, he came near the same old man who said yesterday, 'Such a young preacher,' who now repeated the words, 'You're Francis, aren't you?' two or three times. Saying, 'Yes,' Francis was trying to remember him. He seems to have remembered. Even before the word, 'Jacob' came out of Francis's mouth, the old man got off the bed repeating, 'Yes, Yes' many times. The two of them came out of the room. Francis didn't look back for me. Both of them sat in the veranda of the *ashram*. Didn't know what they

were speaking. I was immersed in my work. When I was going back to my room after finishing my work, I had a message that Francis wanted to see me. I went to him. The old man too was there. In front of them was a bundle of old registers. One of the registers was open. The old man kept looking at me.

'Your name's Reuben, isn't it?' Francis said. I said, 'Yes.' He looked at the register again. 'December 24, at 11.45 at night when Christmas celebrations were going on.' He read as if he was reading to himself.

'Yes . . . ' Saying that word again and again, the old man hugged me. Doing that, he uttered the word, 'Simon' again and again. One mystery became clear. This old man was Jacob. He was the one who admitted me here. My father's name was Simon. Mother Sasirekha.

19 November 1920: I gathered more details from Jacob. On Christmas day, my father brought me from Valasapadu to Jacob's village. The man was drenched in blood. He kept me in Jacob's arms. Muttering Martin's name, he went again to Valasapadu. Jacob told me about the teacher-preacher Martin. Father told Jacob how the upper caste elite killed Martin. A horrible scene appeared in front of them. After that Jacob went to Valasapadu. Valasapadu had been burnt to ashes. Jacob did not know much about the details of the migrant coolies who settled down in Valasapadu. He said he did not know for sure from which village father had migrated. He only knew of father and Martin. He said migrants came from the surrounding areas of Kanigiri, Darsi, Markapuram, Donakonda and Ongole. He said that Nellore too was a migrant place. An inexpressible uneasiness in the heart. Wanted to know something. I had to know myself.

25 November 1920: I didn't get the explanation I needed in Markapuram. Some of the migrant coolies at that time had stayed back in Valasapadu. Those who remained like that did not come back here. Those who returned without staying back in Valasapadu went to Nizam's state in search of their livelihood.

The same in Kanigiri too. Except that the people in Kanigiri went to Patnam (Madras). There they got the job of cleaning toilets.

27 November 1920: I went to Donakonda with hesitation. Though I went with hesitation, I found an invaluable truth. My mother and father came as migrant coolies from Yennela Dinni. Mother and father stayed in Martin and Saramma's house. Saramma looked after my mother as her daughter. She brought me up on her lap. Father's real name was Sivaiah. Yenkatesu, who held on to his life on that Christmas day and escaped from that village described that scene of massacre before my eyes. Mother, Saramma and Martin kept coming back to mind time and again. Didn't know what happened to father. All that Yenkatesu saw was his carrying me and running like a crazy man. I met another elderly man there. Said his name was Jinkodu. Said many things.

1 December 1920: Yennela Dinni. Didn't know how it was then. Don't know who's there who's related to father. It'd be good if there were people who'd show affection to me once they know who I am. All doubts. I stepped into Yennela Dinni with doubts. Once I came to know that Yennela Dinni was one of those badly hit by drought, my doubts increased all the more. But pushing aside my doubts, they first looked at me with wonder and then treated me affectionately. More than father's name and mother's name, much more, I heard grandfather's and grandmother's names. I felt it strange that everyone considered me Yellanna and Subhadra's grandson. They showed me a house saying, 'This was the house your father and grandfather lived in.' There were only broken walls there. They said father buried grandfather and grandmother next to those broken walls. There was only a palm tree growing there. Father's close relative didn't let me go. I stayed the night in that house. As if all the palle had got together and sat at one place, a number of people sat in front of that house till dawn. They began to tell me and talk about our people. Then I came to know. That my grandfather, Yellanna used to weave songs, sing them. He knew

the Urumula dance. Knew Veedhi Bagotam. My grandmother, Subhadra, was hidden in his songs. Then a feeling overcame me. That I was far away from such a great lineage. Couldn't stop the tears.

2 December 1920: I heard grandfather's songs. They narrated his life in stories after stories. When they talked about grandmother I was amazed. Not just that, I felt that Yennela Dinni where my people were born had a great and long history.

3 December 1920: I saw the mala's mound. I came to know about Mataiah, Narigadu and Naganna. I came to know that grandfather had written a song about the entire history of mala's mound. That's a heroic tale. They sing all night. Couldn't find anyone who could sing it fully. But must definitely hear the heroic tale of mala's mound. The journey that began in search of myself pierced into the depths of Yennela Dinni's heart. In fact, my search has just begun . . .

His search that began in the end of 1920 stretched till December 1924.

He wrote down in his diaries his endless search during those four years. He travelled a great distance. Met a number of people. It is surprising to even think of it. In the last days of 1924, he came to know that there was a man in Hanumakonda who could sing the heroic tale of mala's mound fully. He went to Hanumakonda for his grandfather's song.

There, life did take an unexpected turn. Not just listening to the heroic tale grandfather wrote but he was able to find his life partner Ruth too there. Ruth was Francis's daughter. He went to Francis's house for the song. He heard the entire song in that house when Sambaiah sang it. Sambaiah's father had gone around with Yellanna. Sambaiah's father Dibbaiah had the reputation of singing and dancing like Yellanna. Sambaiah learnt that song only from his father. Reuben asked Sambaiah, 'Did you see my grandfather?' He felt it would be good not to say he had not seen him. If he had seen him, he felt he may tell him more about him. But Sambaiah had not seen Yellanna. Reuben was not disappointed. His search had ended. His life came up before his eyes. Now he knew who he was. Now he had an identity. He was the son of Sivaiah, the son of Yellanna, a resident of Yennela Dinni.

His mother, Sasirekha; grandmother Subhadra. There was a great life behind them. There were tears that had surged like the Ganga. There was happiness that showered like moonshine. Not just that. There was hunger. It did not stop there. There was untouchability. If Reuben thought of it, there was such a past. That past made him laugh. That past made him cry. That past raised a number of questions in front of him. It had a number of answers written down for him. Now there would be that laughter in every step he took. That cry too would be there. Those questions and the answers, one after the other. A life that would be like that, always. Yesterday, today and tomorrow—like that, with laughter, with tears, with questions, with answers.

Francis said, 'Your grandfather wrote songs well.' Reuben said, 'He didn't write, he wove them.' Ruth imagined the difference between writing and weaving. She thought weaving was greater than writing. She wrote stories. Her grandmother wove stories. Was she great or was her grandmother great? She thought of asking someone to clear those doubts. If she asked her grandmother, she would say those who wrote were great. She did not know how to write. She thought all those who wrote were great people. After listening to Yellanna's song, she remembered grandmother's story once again. Weaving alone was great. Just like that, effortlessly, as if nothing had happened. It was not a small thing to say something that touched the heart. Ruth sat thinking like that.

As for Francis's wife, Mary, she did not like all this. After seeing Reuben, she placed Ruth next to him and started thinking. She said those words to her mother first. Mother could not say no. The boy was good. No close relatives. Right match for Ruth. 'Why don't you sound him, my girl!' she said. Mary found courage she never thought she had. She told Francis. Francis looked at Mary. He called his mother-in-law. He asked her, 'Did you hear your daughter's words?' She said she heard them. She said her daugher's wish was hers.

That evening Francis told Reuben, 'Why don't you stay on till Christmas?' Reuben did not have the opportunity. He had to go back. He said the same thing. Francis thought of asking him the real question. But for some reason he stopped. He thought it would be good to tell it to Ruth first. Educated girl. Wouldn't she have her likes and dislikes! Moreover, she wrote stories. That was why he could not ask him at that moment.

After the meal at night, Mary asked, 'Did you ask?' Francis said he had not. Ruth, lying down in her grandmother's cot out in the open asked her grandmother, 'Why don't you weave a story, *ammamma?*' The grandmother said, 'I'll weave one, but will you give me a straight answer without saying this or that?' Ruth said, 'Ask.' She said, 'Your mother told me it'd be nice if Reuben became the son-in-law.' She jumped out of bed and sat down. Sitting down, she pulled her grandmother's cheeks. She said, if she spoke such things, she would dig a pit and place her there. She said she would plant a tree over her. She said, if the tree grew and bore a fruit, she would cut the fruit into four and throw one portion to the east, one portion to the north, one portion to the west and one portion to the south. Those were words in the story grandmother wove. That tree and that fruit were in fact grandmother's. The weave she had listened to with interest. All that she spoke as if it was an abuse, it was anger. Grandmother had not read books. She read life. In the morning she told Francis that the girl was agreeable.

In reality, Ruth had no likes or dislikes. If father said something, she never said no. She wrote stories. They were in fact grandmother's stories. She liked them. But recently she wrote about people who had been bad and who had reformed. One of them was a drunkard and finally turned to Christ. In another story, a man was a gambler. He lost everything in gambling. In the end, a pastor drew him close. He was reformed. All the stories proceeded like that. Only that she knew English well. She had read quite a few of those novels well. For a while, she studied in Madras. No matter how much she read and where she went, she liked to lie down next to her grandmother and listen to the stories of eagles and such birds narrated. But when she heard the heroic tale of the mala's mound the previous night, she knew there was a lot of the world she had not seen. Even now she had not read such language. The language Yellanna used was not there in books. She was born into an educated family. She wanted to listen to that song over and over again. She thought in that manner but she had not observed Reuben in a special way since his arrival. Except that when grandmother asked her that question, she wanted to see him. She saw. She thought he was good. Father seemed to have liked him. Mother seemed to have raised the matter. Grandmother too liked it. Those were the three dear to her. Even if one among them liked something, she liked it too. When all three liked him, how would she not like him?

Francis told Reuben what he wanted to. His looks implied, 'I've asked you. What's your reply?' He was always like that. He would ask what he had to and would keep quiet. As it was the other person who had to reply, he was ready to listen without any worry as to what he had to say. This habit was not a recent one. He had it even before his marriage. The same habit made him brush Jacob aside easily saying, 'What is important is that the child is admitted. It doesn't matter who admitted him,' when Jacob brought the three-year old Reuben to the orphanage and said, 'If you need the name of the person who admitted him, write my name down. My name is Jacob.' He did the same now. He remained as if to say, 'Say whatever you want to.' Reuben did not know what to say. He did not know how to say it.

He only said, 'Do you like it?' Francis was nonplussed by those words. He looked as if to say, 'Rather than answering me, why that question?' Mary too looked. She thought Francis might say all kinds of things and scare the child. She entered the scene. She told him. She said everyone including Ruth liked the proposal. She said, 'We'll have the wedding performed if you too like it.' She said, 'I have only one daughter. If you feel like staying, you can stay on in Hanumakonda. Otherwise you can stay in Ongole. Do as you wish. If you stay here, all three of us will stay with you. If you stay there, mother'll stay with you.' As Mary spoke, Francis sat calmly. That man was quite content when someone else spoke what he had to. Mary realised that special nature in him soon after their marriage. That was why she was telling him all that she wanted to. 'There's no dearth of money. God has blessed us quite well. After you become our son-in-law you can't think you have no one to call your own. I can say that wholeheartedly. I earn what I do as a teacher. He has retired. I too will retire in another five years. The girl was born late to us. As she's the only child, she must have thought—"What does it matter when I'm born!" Took her own time.' When Mary said that, Reuben could not stop laughing. He laughed out. He choked. 'Water,' cried Mary. Ruth came there with a glass of water. She kept the glass there and went away. Reuben drank the water and looked at both of them. That night, Reuben remembered his father. He did not know what happened to him. Did not know whether he was dead or alive. That would remain a question eluding an answer all his life.

Francis celebrated the wedding reasonably grandly in the Church. Reuben went to Yennela Dinni before the wedding. He asked his people to come. He went to his mother's place. He asked them also to come. All came. The wedding appeared strange to them. Sitting in the Church itself was strange to them. The wedding the pastor performed remained something they did not understand. But they felt happy looking at Reuben. Reuben wanted to eat along with them. When he went towards them to sit down and went near them, he was surprised. Ruth was sitting amidst them. She had mingled with them as if she was one of them and was laughing. They were taking liberty with her that they did not take with him. He went near them. They stopped laughing and looked at him. It felt strange. It appeared as if Ruth was closer to them than he was. 'Go on.' Saying this, he came away. Heart filled with happiness. This Ruth was enough for this life, he thought.

15

True.

Just as Ruth said, Reuben came quietly into her life. He went away just as quietly. As she said, he did not just go away. Saying, 'Here, this memory, you hide this in your heart,' he went away.

What kind of memory is that . . . ?

A scene.

Memory, like the heart of an artist that sees the moon and the moonlight. How is the heart that sees only the moon and the moonlight like that? Ruth says, ask the colour pictures that are stuck in the snowy mountains.

Colours. In the entire scene. Summer colours. Winter colours. The union of colours that can display the moonlight merging with the moon and the melted flowing snow and the sun. How they have woven densely in every turn! A smile that will not be erased even if erased. A cry that will not dry.

A life's scene.

An untouchable spring.

True. Reuben talked only of the spring. He talked only of the shower of moonshine. He talked only of the movement of the stream. The witness to all this is the yennela pitta.

Did she see the yennela pitta? Did not see it. After their marriage, on the moonlit path, she heard its cry. She experienced its swiftness. By the time he said, 'Look there's the yennela pitta,' it went a great distance away.

How many people would know Yennela Dinni the way Yellanna knew it? How many had the capacity to become like Yellanna to see this? How many times did Ruth draw the picture of the chukkala muggukarra in her heart? But was she able to capture the image of Subhadra in front of her eyes? No. Yellanna hid it like that and went away. Folk culture has such maleness. Has such femaleness. There was such beauty that it would make one touch and get excited all over the body like that. That's why it became the folk. Beauty, expression, and weaving are the adornments that have stuck on to the folk so very naturally.

Ruth is slipping into her memories searching in that manner. Into the tent of her memories. Everything's a new beauty. Everything's a vicious circle. The entire memory drenched in tears, vengeance, anger. A suddenly erupting volcano. Flowing lava. Needs solace. Some water is needed to cool the burning old throat. Who'll give it?

Reuben isn't there.

Immanuel isn't there.

Jessie won't come.

The only one there is Mary Suvarta. Her daughter-in-law. Her only support. She keeps looking like that into her deep eyes, into her broken heart, into her wrinkled body. Attempt to pacify. Who's to pacify whom? Her daughter-in-law her, or she her daughter-in-law? Who's to do it to whom? If you swim across and sit on the shore, each time there is a flood, it keeps cutting up the shore. No one knows when the flow will engulf it.

Look above, the lone star.

Look below, the ruins of the mission compound. The half-broken wall with the oil painting of Christ bearing the Cross perpetually trying hard not to collapse amidst the ruins. She thought that it would collapse in the recent stormy wind. But it did not fall. It is competing with her. Would this millennium go away before her or would she go before it? She does not know. As for this wall with the painting, it looks as if it will collapse only after she does. It has remained like that only for her.

Yellanna lay on his aunt's lap and listened to stories. She lay on her grandmother's lap and listened to stories. Her liking for stories was born that way. Her desire to write stories began that way. She wrote. She wrote several moral stories. She thought that they alone were stories. But when she heard Yellanna's heroic tale of the mala's mound, there was a big difference in her way of thinking. There was the life that was lost in the stories, which was out there, naturally, in real life. It was very direct. Its mode was different. The words it spoke were different. Those words were full of honesty. They were very ordinary. She felt that honesty being so ordinary was indeed surprising. Reuben told her. He told her of that honesty, of that ordinariness, of that directness. Talking of his ancestors, he revealed his life. She really felt that there was more of a mutineer than a preacher in Reuben. Perhaps the depths of the lives of his ancestors might have converted him like that. He toiled hard to find himself. He read life. Read society. Read literature and art. He hid all that in Ruth's memories.

Ruth underwent nurse's training only after marriage. She joined the mission hospital itself as a nurse. Reuben as a preacher in the mission hospital and she as a nurse cultivated a great bonding with that region. Now Ruth is searching for that bond in those ruins. Reuben left as if he was tired after the search. She seems to have remained as if only to search.

They were provided quarters in the hospital. Tiled house. A hall, two rooms. Grandmother stayed with them. Reuben planted a sampenga flower creeper in front of the house. The creeper began to breathe life quite quickly. It did not waste its time just like that, to survive, grow and flower. When they had just started living in the house, a pigeon peeped into the house. Ruth dropped broken rice in a line from the front yard to the middle of the hall. It came into the hall eating the broken rice. Another day, when the door was closed, it peeped in through the window. When the broken rice was poured next to the window, it ate the broken rice and roamed about the hall. The third day, it came right into the middle of the hall. It began to search for the broken rice. It searched the entire house. It searched for it, found it and started eating it. From that day on, the pigeon became a member of the household. When it was not seen, Reuben would ask, 'Where's your sister-in-law, Ruth?' Yes, it would behave like half a husband. What a tough sister-in-law it was!

Once Ruth told Reuben, 'Let's raise the walls of Yennela Dinni that have collapsed. Let's build a house.' She did not know why she spoke like that. But she felt Yennela Dinni was her own. She thought it would be good to spend at least the summer there. At first Reuben was surprised. Later he said, 'Okay, let's do as you like.' In summer, they built a house in Yennela Dinni.

There itself.

At the very place where Subhadra's life had been entwined.

At the very place where Yellanna as a child wove songs about his aunt.

At the very place where Sivaiah dug a pit big enough for two people for just one tender palmyra sprout.

They built a house. Ruth would look forward to the coming of summer. They would spend the entire season there. In summer *ponnangi* birds would come into the house. They would make space for themselves on the roof. Didn't know what it thought or what happened one summer. A ponnangi bird fell in between the two of them. Ruth caught hold of it. It sat snugly in Ruth's hands. Its beauty was out of the ordinary.

The ponnangi bird in the village. In truth, how beautiful it was! As beautiful as life.

In the city only a pigeon. Is it an insignificant thing? It was wonderful. As wonderful as living. Life, living. Beauty. Wonderful.

She did not think that that beauty, that wonder would come searching for her. She did not know tiredness in the midst of the patients in the hospital. Did not know fatigue. She felt like touching them always. She felt like rubbing courage on their hearts. When they came to Yennela Dinni, a search. For the songs, for the scenes. When the moon shone, walking on the edge of the fields with Reuben, listening to the chorus of the ducks singing—now and again searching for Subhadra in the songs of Yellanna that Reuben sang . . .

She had really felt that life seemed to be galloping. That it was an endless flow.

That flow united the time beyond time into it. It touched a generation beyond generation. Any moment passed would not be like the previous day. Every generation would not be like the previous one.

But there was a uniqueness here.

That uniqueness was all the more unique in the lives of the malas and madigas of this country.

Untouchability. That was always the same. Was there at all times. Was there in all generations. They had no life without its touching them, without its meeting them. No family.

After Sinasubbadu, Yellanna. After Yellanna, Yerrenkadu. After Yerrenkadu, Yellanna. After Yellanna, Sivaiah. After Sivaiah, Reuben. After Reuben, Immanuel. After Immanuel, Jessie.

Just like that.

After Sinasubbi, Latchimi. After Latchimi, Lingalu. After Lingalu, Subhadra. After Subhadra, Sasirekha. After Sasirekha, Ruth. After Ruth, Mary. After Mary, Ruby.

It could be any generation. Life could be anyone's. It did not go without touching. It did not go without untouchability stinging it.

Family. Did not know when it began before Sinasubbadu. Did not know how Sinasubbi's mother-in-law was. But, as for their life, it swam in the everflowing current far away from the ooru. This is the truth. Even if history goes back further, we can recognise this truth. Beginning from Sinasubbadu to Reuben and Sinasubbi to Ruth that we know . . . they may be ordinary people. May be poets. May be artists. Can convert to another religion. Can be the owner of a little bit of land. But . . .

Untouchability, it will not but stick on.

Ruth thinks like that. Thinking like that is not her mistake. She thinks she should not think in that manner. But she cannot avoid it. When all memories revolve around that reality, she can only think like that. The family she was born into, the family she was married into, on the whole the caste she was born into and brought up in—reveal that reality.

That's why she used to repeatedly call her Reuben, 'My beautiful, untouchable man.' Saying that she would drown his body with kisses. Saying, 'A girl called Ruth is crazy, a perfectly crazy girl,' Reuben would laugh. Ruth would love to hear that laughter. Beautiful laughter is always like that. It will be like Reuben's laughter. If it is not like that, it is no laughter. She said the same to Reuben.

'Your selfishness.'

'Perhaps. I want my child to have this laughter. If I have the opportunity, I want my child's child to have it too. The old people in Yennela Dinni said. That your laughter was not yours, it is your grandfather's Yellanna's. Christ is merciful. He will not let that laughter be erased.'

She would feel like that. It felt like that. Crazy. To think like that is a crazy illusion. How much happiness does that craziness give? It might be the reflection of the imprint on the mind. Immanuel was born with that very smile. After that only Jessie. Immanuel's son. Ruth and Reuben's adorable grandson. Just like that he was born smiling that smile.

Immanuel . . .

Jessie . . .

Memories . . .

Memories related to experience.

Like Yellanna's memories, like Subhadra's memories, not heard ones. Not ones that made her wonder if they were indeed like that.

Her son's.

His son's.

The scenes that happened in front of her eyes. Memories that were born breaking the umbilical cord.

They said, 'You're pregnant. Don't go to Yennela Dinni now.' But she was adamant. She said she would go, look and come back immediately. Reuben said okay. Grandmother said she too would go. She said no. She pulled a long face. For some reason she thought that no one other than Reuben and herself ought to be in that house. She felt like that. That was why she said no. Just when they were to leave the following day, mother came. 'Father asked me to bring you home,' she said. She made a fuss. She said it was tradition to deliver the first child in the parents' place. It was Yennela Dinni that remained in her eyes. Yellanna was born there. Subhadra had her delivery there. Reuben alone was born during migration. Her child ought to be born only there. It must be born only at the place his forefathers were born. Why was she feeling so? 'Your craziness,' said mother. Perhaps so. Even so this child had to be born only there.

In Yennela Dinni. That night when everyone was sleeping and the morning star had just come out from behind the clouds and was looking wide-eyed at the earth. It appeared as if the child had started becoming restless to touch the earth, to see how the mother who had carried it safely all these months in her womb looked like. The pains began. Reuben was anxious. He was about to step out to call aunt Lakshmi. In all that pain, Ruth was amused at Reuben's anxiety. She signalled to indicate, 'No'. Reuben stopped and looked.

'I'll call aunt Lakshmi.'

'Wait a bit. The child's restlessness has just begun.'

Reuben looked perplexed.

'Sit here.'

Reuben sat on the cot. She placed her head on his lap and lay down.

'Let me lie down like this for a while and then call your aunt.'

She had hardly lain down like that tired for two minutes when she began to have unbearable pain.

'Call . . . Call your aunt.'

Ruth said in pain. Reuben went out screaming. Lakshmi came running. By then the child was making its own effort. His effort was strong. He came into Lakshmi's hands in a relaxed manner. With the child crying, Reuben who was outside came in. Ruth who seemed to be tired. The child who was screaming and making a fuss.

Immanuel.

Sweet memory.

After Immanuel, Rosy. Time raced past in front of the eyes. The children grew up.

Rosy got married and went to her in-laws' place. Vandanam was an employee in the Revenue department. Reuben asked him to stay back here. He said they would do so later.

Immanuel wanted to undergo teacher training. They asked him to go ahead. When he had a job in a village, he said he wanted to go. They said okay. One summer he said he liked Mary Suvarta. Mary Suvarta was Ruth's uncle's son's daughter. They said there was nothing they would like better. They had never said no to Immanuel's wishes. They got him married to Mary Suvarta.

Something amazing happened on the wedding day. Ramanujam came. Came on the wedding day. Did not expect it. Did not expect he would come. All those who worked with Immanuel came for the wedding. Did not think that Ramanujam would be among those who came. Immanuel said, 'He works with us in the school.' Since when was he working?

Ramanujam!

Ramanujam who got introduced in Yennela Dinni.

Ramanujam who introduced Avalapadu . . . memories . . .

As for Reuben, he looked at Ramanujam in a surprised manner. Ramanujam too did the same. He was thrilled saying, 'Is Immanuel your son?'

'It's many years.'

'Yes. Many years.'

Talked all night. Putting forth a lot of the past.

Yennela Dinni. The Harijana Seva Sangham workers.

Venkatadri . . . Lingareddy . . . where should that past begin? The one who got separated then, how did he meet him now? That too how did he come to meet Immanuel and come searching for Reuben? The one who got separated as Reuben's friend, how did he meet him again as Immanuel's colleague?

'When did we get separated?'

Ramanujam searching . . . going way back to search for the day they got separated . . .

He began to remember. How was it possible? To forget . . .

We can't forget anything.

Everything haunts us.

Ramanujam! Immanuel!!

Memory . . . Pushing each other, standing in front . . .

For some reason, when she thinks of Immanuel, Ramanujam comes to the fore. In fact, Ruth wants to look at Immanuel only from thereon.

Ramanujam did not come to Yennela Dinni only to teach. He came primarily to live. They asked him to teach children because he was educated. They erected a shed in between the mala and madiga palles. It was there that he used to teach children. In the first few days of his coming to Yennela Dinni he met Reuben. The two of them used to talk about many things. Sometimes, Ruth would enter their conversation.

Once Reuben asked him, 'What do you think of Gandhi's word, "Harijan"?' Ramanujam remained silent for a while. Then he only said, 'In what way is that word better than mala and madiga?' He did not stop with that. He said he did not like that word at all. This brahminical society had made the malas and madigas untouchables. With the word Harijan, Gandhiji was making them orphans as well. Ruth felt that was true.

Such were the conversations with Ramanujam. Ramanujam was not married. He did not even have the desire to get married. But his eyes always appeared as if they were dreaming. Though there was no beloved in his eyes. Neither did he have his own image imagining great things for himself. It was true up to that point. That was because he never talked about himself. One day he came saying, 'Did you hear this?' 'What's it?' said Reuben. Those were Christmas days. After Christmas they went to Yennela Dinni.

'Tomorrow the Harijana Seva Sangham workers are coming here.'

'Harijan . . . !'

'That's Gandhiji's Harijana Seva Sangham workers.' That night the discussion was about the Seva Sangham.

Next day the Harijana Seva Sangham workers did arrive. Among those who came was Lingareddy from that village. Lingareddy was the grandson of Munnareddy Sivareddy. In Yennela Dinni after Atchireddy, Sivareddy became successful pushing aside Atchireddy's dominance. Atchireddy's son, Mallareddy, was not all that capable. Mallareddy's son was studying. They said that the younger karanam who went to the city was the unseen force behind all this. It was not clear how far that was true.

Lingareddy became Gandhi's disciple. When Gandhi came to Andhra, he roamed about with him. Lingareddy had another specialty. He kept good relations with the British authorities of the region who praised Gandhi's qualities. His relationship with British authorities increased his land. Thanks to his relationship with Gandhiji, he was included in the list of patriots. At present, it could be assumed that he had taken the responsibility of the Nellore District Harijana Seva Sangham on his shoulders. At the same time, he did not lose his association with Justice Party's Hanumappa Choudhary either. In Ramanujam's opinion Lingareddy was a very clever Congress leader. That was why when Lingareddy spoke to the former before the Seva Sangham workers were to come, Ramanujam pretended not to hear him. But Lingareddy did not let it go. He kept telling Ramanujam about his programme. As soon as he came to the palle, he asked for Ramanujam. He came to know that Ramanujam had left saying he would be back.

The Harijana Seva Sangham workers gathered at one place. They said *jai* to Gandhi. After that they took up the broomsticks. They tied up the khadi panchas. If they had pyjamas on, they folded them up. They started sweeping the bazaars of the mala and madiga palles. The malas and madigas looked at them surprised. When they looked at their faces it appeared as if they were proud to be doing it. They also sang while they swept. The people did not understand those songs. Even so, they sang as they swept. Lingareddy was among those who swept. This was all the more surprising to the malas and the madigas.

After that, drinking water in the houses of the untouchables. That took place in a highly theatrical manner. It appeared like great amusement. They kept the big cauldron used for mixing *panakam**

---

* *Panakam*, a drink chiefly made of jaggery and spices is offered to Lord Rama on his birthday, Rama Navami, and distributed among the devotees.

during Rama Navami in the middle of the village. They asked each house to pour a pot of water in that cauldron. The householders thought they would be found fault with and poured a pot per house. There too they sang songs. They spoke out. They said untouchability was a crime. They said they were doing all this to eradicate it. There were lectures for nearly an hour near the cauldron. After that each one drank a glass of water from that cauldron. As they drank, they felt proud. As for one worker, he swayed as if he was possessed. He said, 'My life has become all the more sanctified after drinking a glass of water from your hands.' Going further, he said, 'Pour a little more. I'll wash myself. Spit there. I'll lick it with my tongue. For having considered all of you untouchables till now, I'll purify myself. I'll become one of you.' Saying so, he was swaying. He was speaking with heightened emotion. One of the workers said with the same intensity, 'Jai to Gandhiji.' Everyone caught on to that slogan. With that the programme for that day was over. Then came Ramanujam. Lingareddy embraced Ramanujam so everyone could see. He said, 'You should have been here.' He asked him to come the next day for the entry into the temple.[32] The workers, who announced that the entry to the Siva temple was fixed for the next day, went away.

That night Ramanujam came home. He told them all that had happened. He also told them about the announcement of the temple entry.

'In Machilipatnam the orthodox people, I believe, wrote to Gandhiji.'

'On what?'

'Harijans entering the temple.'

'What did Gandhiji say?'

'I heard that as a compromise, the plan of Kasi Rama-krishnamacharyulu came out in the open between the orthodox ones and the Association to Eradicate Untouchability. According to this they'll give Saiva and Vaishnava faith to the malas and madigas and make them eligible to enter temples.'

'My grandfather was a devotee of Siva. My father's name was Sivaiah. A lot of people in Yennela Dinni are in fact devotees of Siva. Parvatamma is the caste deity. Why then did not they allow these people to enter the temple all this while?'

Ramanujam was stunned at Reuben's words.

'I too have the same question. Actually, I don't like the term, Harijan. Gandhiji hasn't opposed the caste system. Moreover, he has justified the caste system. He says there's nothing sinful in it. If you retain it and want to get rid of untouchability, how's it possible?'

Reuben nodded his head to indicate agreement with Ramanujam's words.

'He accepts the Vedas as sacrosanct. He mentioned this very clearly in Durga Kalamandiram in Vijayawada. He said that Harijans would have the right to enter temples only when they also followed principles of Agama Sastram.'

'There's nothing more comical than this.'

Ramanujam looked surprised.

'Let's for a moment think that malas and madigas are lowly people. But those lowly people have an art. Have a literature. Have a culture. All of this happened outside the temple till now. Happened naturally. My grandfather brought Ganga down from the sky outside the temple, amidst people in his song, in his dance. There's lifeless struggle in the temple. To ask them to give up that which has life for that which is lifeless is to look down on the culture of the people that combined in it their art and their literature.'

Ramanujam caught on immediately.

'They are talking of a purificatory ritual. Purification for whom? For us? For them? They say that both the casteless and the upper castes must realise the importance of the cleanliness of the soul. That's what they call a purificatory ritual. It's strange. They say that Harijans must be physically and mentally clean. For cleanliness, they project the principles of Agama Sastra. For inner cleanliness, "the chant of Rama" and for external cleanliness, "a bath." Must not eat meat of cattle. Must not eat beef. Those who are habituated to it aren't Hindus. They've no right to enter temples. Tell me, how does all this sound? What do you think?'

'Strange. When malas and madigas converted to Christianity and said they wouldn't eat the meat of dead cattle, it was they who forced them to eat. There are many such incidents in villages.'

'This isn't in fact the the upliftment of Harijans. This is protecting Hindu religion. It's to ensure that powerful castes and classes don't move away from it. There too there are restrictions on malas and madigas. In the name of purification, to cage them in a frame.'

'That's hundred per cent true.'

'Who's Birla?'

'A fanatical Hindu.'

'He's the President of the Committee against Untouchability. How's this great wonder!'

'Dr Ambedkar has talked clearly about their deceit. So long as malas and madigas remain lambs, they'll be slaughtered on the altar. It's necessary for them to live like tigers.'

'Beware, Gandhi's there!'[33]

The two of them laughed at those words. Ruth too felt like laughing. Beware, Gandhi's there! She said those words to herself.

'No. No need for purificatory rituals for us. No need for them to drink water in our houses and put on a pose that they are working for our upliftment. Each one knows the greatness of his caste. If I'm an untouchable to him, he's an untouchable to me too. They're becoming great killing us. They're becoming great reformers saying they'll uplift us. No need. No need for their sympathy. It's better to die than live with sympathy. Don't drink. Don't drink water like that. Don't renovate the ruined temples for our sake. If they've a little bit of sincerity in their reform, ask them to do something small. There's a lot of land adjacent to the mala's mound. The malas and madigas will occupy it. Ask them to watch and keep quiet. That's enough. Gandhiji won't talk about this. These Harijana Seva Sangham workers too won't say a word about this.'

The discussion stopped at the last expression. Ramanujam kept reminding of this and left.

After he left, Reuben wrote in this manner in his diary. All the while he wrote, Ruth kept quiet. She asked him to read it out to her after he wrote.

'I'm searching for that which my ancestors have lost. Grandmother told me that grandfather too searched like that. Mother said father passed away searching. Then grandmother too searched. Mother too searched.

Now, I'm searching. I'm searching for that which my ancestors have lost. Along with me, all my people started searching. As we searched and searched, searched the whole world and came from that corner to this, the account of the lost land became clear. The account of life became clear.'

That was not like a pastor's diary.

It was filled with self-respect related words. Search related to land.

'Did you hear the last words of Ramanujam? Those are asking us to see another person in him. For some reason Ramanujam appears a man of substance.'

Ruth remembers even today those words Reuben said as he fell asleep.

Those words are true to the core.

For the purpose of temple entry, they renovated the Siva temple outside the ooru. The Seva Sangham workers came with a lot of pomp. They started the temple entry procession. The elders of the ooru were calling out to everyone, 'Come on, fellows.' As for the workers, they sang songs about the temple entry of Harijans. They gave speeches. The procession began. Ramanujam too was in the procession. Lingareddy expressed happiness that Ramanujam came. The procession went near the ooru. But it was not going into the ooru. It was going by the ooru. The Siva temple was at a little distance away from the ooru. It was dilapidated. Now they renovated it. The entry was in fact into that temple.

'Stop.'

The procession stopped suddenly. Ramanujam who spoke that word came to the front of the procession.

'The procession must go into the ooru.'

Everyone looked stunned. The malas and madigas were looking at Ramanujam. An inexplicable excitement. Lingareddy did not say a thing.

'Siva's temple isn't in the ooru!' One among the village elders said.

'There's a Vishnu temple. There's a Rama temple next to it,' said Ramanujam.

'The entry is into the Siva temple,' said one of the Seva Sangham workers. Even now Lingareddy did not speak.

'We're thinking of entering the Vishnu temple,' said Ramanujam in a loud enough voice.

'Siva's temple is in our programme.' Those were not Lingareddy's words.

'Vishnu's temple is where we want to enter. Otherwise to Rama's temple.'

Argument commenced. The workers tried to convince Ramanujam. Ramanujam did not listen. Even the people thought Ramanujam's idea was good. As for the youngsters among them, they stood next to Ramanujam. That night Ramanujam spoke to them. There were two or three intelligent people among the youngsters. They felt uneasy with all the work of the Seva Sangham workers. At first, they were the ones who talked to Ramanujam and asked, 'Is this all true?' After that Ramanujam went further. They decided that if the procession could not go into the ooru, they would turn back. The elders of the mala and madiga palles did not know any of this. As for Lingareddy, he did not underestimate Ramanujam. But he did not speak.

'Say one way or the other, we wish the temple entry to take place in the temple in the ooru. If that's not possible we'll turn back.'

Now Lingareddy spoke. He said the procession ought to go into the ooru. The workers were surprised. In the programme of the workers, there was no entry to the temple in the ooru. But now Lingareddy was saying the procession must go there. Their wish. He was speaking to the people that if they wished to go into the Vishnu temple it would be the Vishnu temple entry and if they wished to go into the Rama temple it would be the Rama temple entry. As for the villagers, wanting to know why Lingareddy was speaking in that manner, they tried to pull him aside. But he said, 'Ramanujam, let the procession go into the ooru.'

The procession did go into the ooru. As Lingareddy was walking into it, the malas and madigas entered the compound of the Vishnu temple. The compound of the temple was very large. Lingareddy stopped near the first step of the temple. There was the cool shade of the trees in the compound. The malas and madigas who entered the compound found the environment strange. Lingareddy kept noticing that. Not just that, he noticed Ramanujam who was looking at him.

Lingareddy said, 'All of you please sit down.' He said, 'Now say jai to Gandhiji.' They did so.

He began saying, 'My dear Harijans!' He began to say how great the word Harijan was. Saying so, he looked at Ramanujam. He knew Ramanujam did not like the word. That was why he was praising it so much. He was trying to bind Ramanujam's thought process to that very word. In one way, Lingareddy was achieving what he wanted. Lingareddy was a clever intellectual. Making the people get caught in words by erecting a stage, he could keep the people away from the real subject. The actual issue was the temple entry. The place they were sitting in was the compound. The discussion that began was on the word, Harijan. Lingareddy praising the word Harijan like that was making Ramanujam angry. He was in a hurry to say how deceitful that word was.

'In fact, Ramanujam doesn't like this word. I know this. I believe in non-violence. Truth is the prime principle of non-violence. In order to get at the truth, I want to know in your presence why Ramanujam doesn't like that word.'

Ramanujam had not guessed that Lingareddy would say such a thing. But he was able to understand how he was dragging him into it and why he was dragging him.

'Tell me Ramanujam . . . Otherwise accept Gandhiji's term . . .'

Lingareddy threw a challenge. No escape. Ramanujam began speaking.

In the meanwhile, the priest came out with the *harati* from the sanctum sanctorum of the temple. There was commotion. Ramanujam looked impatiently. Pretending that he could not control his excitement, saying, 'The harati has come to us. Touch the harati to the eyes. Distribute the *prasadam*,' Lingareddy began shouting in excitement. Pushing and shoving among the people for the harati. The distribution of the prasadam began. Everything was happening in a frenzy. The workers kept saying, 'Jai to Gandhiji.' In a strange manner, the temple entry happened only with the entry into the temple compound. Everyone came out. The village elders praised Lingareddy saying, 'After all an educated man is indeed an educated man.' That night Lingareddy got the temple compound and steps cleaned with cow dung and cow's urine as the priests recited mantras.

It was not as if the Harijana Seva Sangham workers were not there. As idealistically as they performed the societal service called temple entry of Harijans, they also did the purificatory task of the temple in a similarly pious manner. In fact, there was such a flexibility in Gandhiji's mode. If that were not so Gandhiji would not have appeared so great to people like Lingareddy.

But Lingareddy did not know something. He did not know a youngster called Vankatadri from Krishna district was among the workers. He did not know he was a Harijan. He did not know he was close to the Harijan doctor of Guntur district. He did not know he was one of those admirers of the Rajamahendravaram Harijan poet. The Krishna district workers knew this information. There was Siva temple in their programme. If there was entry into the Siva temple, there would not have been any trouble. But everything went haywire. Venkatadri could not swallow the purificatory work of the temple. He felt that everything was deceitful. He did not feel like staying there. He came to the palle. He met Ramanujam there. He met the youngsters who were with Ramanujam. He told them everything. He said how much Lingareddy had deceived them. Ramanujam was not surprised: 'I know. This programme of upliftment of Harijans is being done to bind the malas and madigas in the Hindu frame. Do you remember 1924?'

Venkatadri searched for an answer to Ramanujam's question. In 1924, there was the Vaikom satyagraha for the temple entry of the untouchable castes. Periyar took part in it.[34] Gandhiji spoke about it as the internal matter of the Hindus. Periyar exposed the hyprocrisy of the Congress orthodoxy. But Venkatadri did not understand why Ramanujam was referring to it now.

'You're surprised that Lingareddy acted in that manner. I am not surprised at Gandhiji's purificatory ritual.'

'That means . . .?'

'I don't have the illusions about Gandhiji that you have.'

Venkatadri stayed back there that night. Reuben met them in the morning. He asked them to come to his house. Then Venkatadri said that Gandhiji would travel past Bitragunta in two days. Reuben wanted to see Gandhiji. Ruth too wanted it.

They set out from Yennela Dinni early in the morning. Venkatadri told them he would meet Gandhiji and tell him everything. Ramanujam said, 'You have too many illusions.' They were talking during the entire journey. Ruth was listening silently.

'It appears as if the British rule is breathing new life into the institution of caste.'

Saying that, Ramanujam looked at Reuben.

'Tell me. Don't stop saying things you want to because I'm a Christian. First and foremost, I'm an untouchable.'

'They have embedded the caste system in the judicial system.'

'As for me, I'll also say, they have also given the caste system an autonomous status and respected it.'

'You've said it very directly. Brahmin pundits are the advisors of these English judges. What would they naturally desire? I don't know whether you've noticed it or not, along with English, the study of Sanskrit is increasing. The translation of Sanskrit texts is on the rise.'

'Venkatadri isn't speaking.'

'His mind hasn't got away from Gandhiji.'

Venkatadri was indeed walking silently. The night's incident had not gone out of his mind. So long he had felt that the Harijana Seva Sangham would do something good for the Harijans. It was this thinking that had distanced him from his family. But everything was unclear. It appeared as if honesty had taken a back seat. He thought it would be good to go immediately and meet the Guntur district doctor and the Rajamahendravaram poet. If it was not going to be possible to meet Gandhiji, this was what he had to do. But the mind was not going to remain calm till then. As for Ramanujam and Reuben, they were involved in their talk.

'You know about the Satya Sodhak Samaj 'tamasha' groups?'

'Phule's revolt against Sethjis and Bhatjis was very powerful.'[35]

'You've heard of the Self Respect Movement in Tamil Nadu. It justifies Socialism. That's a new development.'

'Perhaps it's the result of Periyar's Russian trip.'

'It appears as if the influence of Soviet Russia is rubbing off very well on the intellectuals of this country.'

In their talk, the word Communism was heard.

They kept walking as they were talking in that manner. There was a lot of discussion on movements against brahminism.

Reuben appeared strange to Ruth. She was able to comprehend what he was thinking deeply when he said, 'I'm first and foremost an untouchable.' He went about mostly among the white men. White men in the Church he was in. White men in the hospital he went around. But his views on the British rule were entirely different. He did not have a good opinion of white men other than the white man, Clough. Reuben was unable to tolerate the brahmin domination in government offices, courts, and hospitals. It seemed as if his father, Simon's, fears were also haunting Reuben. He hated the uppercaste converts all the more. 'He didn't come for Christ. He came to dominate,' he would say. When a reddy was appointed the headmaster of a mission school, he was enraged and said, 'Couldn't they find a mala Christian? Couldn't they locate a madiga Christian? They needed a reddy Christian!' He mentioned this at many places. For saying this, the elders in the mission met Reuben and asked him not to speak in that manner. Reuben did not agree. He said he would say so.

'He's a Christian.'

'No, a reddy.'

The elders of the mission felt it was unnecessary to speak further. Sometimes Reuben was even willing to give up being a pastor for the sake of caste. It was morning by the time they reached Bitragunta station. People were awaiting Gandhiji's train. They said he would come by Calcutta mail. Important people were in front to welcome him. Venkatadri noticed Lingareddy among them. He swelled with anger.

'I'll show his real form to the Nellore reddys.' Venkatadri was about to go in front.

'They too are reddys. Don't forget that.' Ramanujam said those words sharply. Venkatadri stopped. In the meanwhile, with the Calcutta mail coming into the station, the people pushing each other saying, '*Jai* to Gandhiji'—all these happened. Ruth saw all this from a distance. Venkatadri stopped at Ramanujam's words. They said that Gandhiji was leaving for Kavali by car.

That day was December 30th. The new year round the corner. Reuben said they had to reach Ongole. Without going to Yennela Dinni they set out for Ongole. Venkatadri accompanied them till Ongole. He did not stay back even though they asked him to. He went saying he wanted to meet the Guntur district doctor. Saying he would meet them again, Ramanujam set out towards Yennela Dinni. When they went to Yennela Dinni again in summer Ramanujam was not there. They met him now, someone who had got separated like that then. They met him in this manner.

'After that I didn't feel like staying there. I joined the training school. After the training, I joined as a teacher in an aided school. Not one school. I changed almost ten schools.'

'Why?'

'I can't find an answer but I'm not able to be alone. Like not being able to stay in Yennela Dinni. Some situation, some circumstance . . .'

Ramanujam kept speaking.

'15 August 1947—where were you?'

'In Ongole.'

'But I thought of you. I do not know whether you came to know or not. But I thought I would tell you if I met you. I thought of saying it to you and asking you, did you hear such a thing?'

Reuben kept looking at him. The same heated emotion. Except that it was the emotion of a slightly older person.

'How come you don't ask what it is?'

'Tell me.'

'Periyar gave a call asking people to observe August 15th as a day of mourning. As for me, I felt happy. He wanted freedom from brahmin rule. I'm telling the truth. I felt like hoisting a black flag. As there was a sooty cloth next to the pot in the house I lived, I picked it up with a stick and stood in the bazaar. That's it. There was trouble with the Congress people of that place. That place didn't change. Now I'm in the tenth school. This is now tied to my life. Life has become hard with experience.'

Yes. As Ramanujam said, life had become hard. What kind of a life was that? Why did it become hard? How did it become hard? The same question all day long. What did Ramanujam say? Why again and again like that? Just for two palmfuls of water. Just for a stomachful. What a long journey this was!

The period when a structure of a community had been ruined—

In the first dawn of the excessive output becoming agricultural,—

When the toil had changed into something to be divided,—

When land was turning into private property.

Reuben!

How did your ancestor scream?

Ramanujam, how would you recognise that scream? Where to search for that scream? Among priests, among merchants, among rulers, among slaves, among sudras, among even meaner people, among even the meanest.

Where to search for that scream!

When kingdoms were born. When kingdoms were destroyed. When kingdoms had expanded. When kingdoms were shattered.

When civilisation danced in the middle of the house.

When the ruins were ruined and turned into the excavations of historians.

Iron plough. Ritual sacrifice. Manu. Mayas, Kushans, Sakhyas, Mauryas, Guptas, the dark ages. Golden ages . . .

How much of history on the land of this country . . .

In which turn to search for that scream. That hardened scream.

The dirty jobs distributed in cruel kindness among the malas and madigas under the shade of the four-caste hood—in which Veda, in which sastra, in which darkness that swallowed the light . . .

The Mohammedan invasions, the Mughal empire, the British merchant intruders. The British empire established. 15 August 1947 . . .

After that the village life that was subject to change . . . the weakening brahmin authority on the land . . . the ancestral history of kings that were remaining merely as names . . . the reddys who have placed a firm foot on the land . . . kammas, patidars, lingayats, vellatulus . . . change in power . . . brahmins in key government positions . . . brahmins, kshatriyas, reddys and kammas in higher judiciary and bureaucracy. Politics arising out of their quarrels. How does it sound? The scream that began then. Why is it still heard like that?

How many stages has the country witnessed?

How the country has changed . . .

Here, now, how is it heard? Why is it still heard like that . . . all only in the form of questions for Ruth. Everything is a search for answers.

Just for a mouthful of water. What does the Avalapadu story say . . . the malapalli story of that village that united Ramanujam and Immanuel . . . .the story of malas.

Ramanujam narrated the scene in such a manner that it was before their eyes, when the stars were shining in the front yard. Reuben was listening. Ruth was listening. Did not know when the newly-wed couple Immanuel and Mary Suvarta came, they too were listening. In between, Mary Suvarta brought tea. The bride was not someone new. The girl knew where things were in this house.

'Have you put less sugar for *mamayya*?' Ruth asked. Mary Suvarta laughed and kept quiet. The meaning of that laughter was that she ought to keep her mouth shut.

She knew everything. What she was, what Reuben was, what Immanuel was—she knew everything . . .

She came to this house knowing everything.

Knowing everything.

No need for memory up to that point. My lover! My God! Let my memory stop with Ramanujam.

There, with Ramanujam, let it stop, right there . . .

Ruth thinks in that manner. She cannot stand the memory of her child. She wants the memory to stop with Ramanujam. She does not know if it will stop like that or not. But as for Avalapadu, it stands right in front of her.

16

There was a hundred-house malapalli in Avalapadu. The ooru had three hundred houses. Hundred houses of reddys. Hundred houses of kammas. The rest, the remaining castes.

Strange. There, the malapalli was not at a distance. There was only a long path between malapalli and the ooru. On that path, a cart carrying maize stacks could go easily. In the middle of the ooru, there was a lake. Houses surrounding the lake. On the bund of the lake, Siva's temple, Vishnu's temple, Jalamma's temple, and many Shakti-type temples.

The lake full of water. The lake was adjoining the palle. But the malas could not step down and take water from the lake. They would stand away from the lake holding pots. When the upper castes stepped into the lake, they would have them pour water. No one pours water on their own accord to malas and madigas. It was like that even before 1947. It was like that after 1947 too. Like in all villages. There too. What was worse was that even if a well was dug there, it would not have any drinking water in it. Therefore, there was no other source for water. They could get water from the stream on all three sides for all other purposes. The stream was far away.

A development that the village landlords did not imagine took place in that village. Even before '47, Communists set foot in that village. Do not know how things happened. Leaders at the district level and state level would visit the malapalli. When the party was banned that palle gave asylum to the main leaders. The party was not just in the malapalli but also in the *chakalipalem* (the area where washermen lived). It used be there among the poorer reddys too. Ramireddy was one of the important members of the party.

The term Communist had never been far away from Ruth. It was a term close to her. She saw Communists. Spoke to them.

Knew about Russia. Heard about China. From Ramanujam's words it was clear that not only did she hear that word but the malapalli of Avalapadu too had heard of it. With what hope was the malapalli of Avalapadu giving asylum to Communists! She did not need to think specially to understand this. She was born in Hanumakonda. She knew the situation in Telangana. She knew the story of Chakali Ailamma's leased land.[36] It was not as if she did not know of Visunooru Deshmukh with his goondas shooting at the people's procession, Doddi Komaraiah's[37] death and thousands of people performing his last rites. Though she was not an eyewitness to that incident she had known of it from close quarters. It was not as if she did not know that in many villages people were revolting against the landlords. Though Ruth was not in that region then, mother would tell her all of this whenever she came. Because she knew how atrocious the landlords' rule was, she would feel in her heart of hearts that such a rebellion was good. That rebellion did not seem surprising to her.

What was surprising was a meeting being organised in Avalapadu in the coastal region in memory of Komaraiah's death. That was what appeared astonishing. When Ramanujam was narrating this incident, she was filled with intense emotion.

The meeting took place right in the middle of the malapalli. Ramireddy spoke in the meeting. There were men and women from malapalli in that meeting. People from chakalipalem too came to attend. As long as the meeting was on, ten to fifteen youngsters sat on the bund of the lake. The ooru had more of the Congress people. There was a ban on the Communists. Even so, there were two main leaders in malapalli. It could be said that the meeting took place in the most secretive manner. People from chakalipalem came one by one even before the lamps were lit. After that it would be a problem. If malapalli was on that side, chakalipalem was on the other side. In between, the houses of kammas, the houses of reddys.

'Did the reddys from Ramireddy's side come to the meeting?'

'They came. The important people had dinner right there. They sat where the meeting took place.'

'Did all sit together?'

'They sat together. After dinner, the malas taking the water from the tank of the ooru came up for discussion.'

The part that Reuben liked very much. He said, 'Ruth, we want tea again.' Ruth was about to get up to make tea. Immanuel said he would make it. Mary Suvarta went along with Immanuel.

A canopy of stars in the sky. Reuben held hands with Ramanujam.

'You're giving new hope, Ramanujam. Now, the midnight water thieves of Yennela Dinni stand before my eyes.' Saying those words, Reuben was becoming very excited. As everyone was looking on, as reddys were looking on, as kammas were looking on, as brahmins were looking on, as Siva was looking on and Mother Jalamma was looking on, the malas of Avalapadu were going to step into the lake of the ooru. That very scene unfolded in front of Reuben's eyes as if it was happening in his imagination. In fact, they had heard what happened in Avalapudu even before Ramanujam told them. It was very interesting as Ramanujam who had been a party to it had said it. It appeared as if they were seeing it right in front of their eyes.

The canopy of stars was being dispersed. There was the smell of the wind before the rain. That was why it felt extremely hot during the day.

The morning cock crowed. Immanuel and Mary brought tea. After drinking tea, Ramanujam began to narrate again.

They had to wait many months for the day to get water from the lake. Rather than say months, it is better to say a year. But the year did not go by just like that. Many isolated incidents. Even though there were isolated incidents, they continued to increase self-confidence in malapalli. The youngsters in the village began to learn new things. They learnt to read and write. After coming back from work each day, they would eat food at night and go to the centre of the palle. As for moonlit days, there used to be a lot of fun and frolic. They would play *kolatam*. They learnt new songs.

> Tamarind tree flared, tamarind tree flared
> What happened to the beams, it's deceit, Raja
> I am young for sport
> I am young, I'm deceived, Raja
> I'm young for sport.

The words of that song changed. Meanings changed.*

> Why worries for us, why worries for us—the hammer and sickle
> have come, move along, coolie!

It would go on like this. They would form into pairs and dance. Every occasion had a new song. The planting songs changed. The harvesting songs changed. Everything was new. It was all strange to the landlords of the ooru. There was some change in the palle.

---

* The word *chinta* for instance changes from being 'tamarind' in the first version to 'worry' in the second.

There were new people coming to the palle. Things that had never happened began to take place.

Pedanarisimma went towards Naidu's granary for maize stacks. Naidu stared at Narisimma from top to toe. 'Who're the new people coming to the village?' he asked him sternly. An unexpected question. Narisimma did not speak. 'Committoo people?' Naidu asked. Narisimma did not speak. 'Why don't you speak, you son of an ass?' Saying, 'Will you speak out or shall I kick you?' Naidu untied the rope. He was about to twirl the rope strongly and whip Narisimma's back. Narisimma caught hold of the rope. Due to the power of the grip, Naidu who was older, fell forward. Rosaiah Naidu of the neighbouring granary saw this. With a terrible scream, he pulled out the wooden pole to which cattle are tied and ran towards Narisimma. Unexpected turn. Narisimma started to run. Granaries on all four sides. The Choudharys of the granaries surrounded him. No one asked what happened. They only saw Naidu chase Narisimma. The entire fault was Narisimma's. Narisimma was caught in the middle. He just about survived. Even the Choudharys did not realise how they hit him. How he escaped even Narisimma did not know.

That night the palle did not sleep. The blood of youngsters was boiling. Worry in the hearts of the older people. An urge to do something. A situation where they did not know what to do. In the past, no matter what happened they would tremble in fear. They would take the blame on themselves and plead with the choudharys and reddys. Now they were not thinking in that manner. The elder mala said he would go into the ooru. The youngsters asked him not to. If such incidents happened in the past, the elder mala would meet the elders of the ooru. He would plead saying, 'You beat them up because our people made a mistake. Let go and pardon their mistake.' There were also instances when the elder who had gone to plead was abused and kicked. The situation was not like that now. They had to do something. What to do? That was what was not clear to them.

The party people who came from outside went to the next village that same day. Ramanujam too went along with them. They finished their work and started from there at midnight. The journey would take half an hour. The maize fields were an elbow's length taller than a man. A path amidst the fields. Dew had just started forming.

As the maize stalks touched the body, the entire body was getting wet. Ramanujam and the two party members were walking even as they were getting wet like that. As they were walking, they heard commotion in the field on the left. They stopped there. They heard the sound of maize stalks being pulled out. Ramanujam was about to go ahead. The party man stopped him. They stood examining everything closely. Sound of the maize stalks being pulled out swiftly. The field was full of cobs. Did not know why but the party man had a sudden thought. The second man asked Ramanujam to stay right there. Pulling the maize stalks aside noiselessly, he went forward. It was more than ten minutes since he left. He was taking a long time. An anxiety in Ramanujam. The second man was thinking and looking in the direction the first man went. The man who went returned in a relaxed manner. After coming back, he asked them to come with him. When he was asked what happened, he did not tell them. He asked them to come along and see. They had hardly taken ten steps when they saw a circular ground in the midst of the field. Ten or fifteen people had charged on to it and were pulling out the maize. The field was looking good from outside. They were pulling it out in the middle as if a circle was drawn. About half an acre of land. The entire field had been pulled out. Seeing them, they stopped pulling them out and came near.

Men from malapalli. Malas. All young men. Among them, Sinasubarayudu said, 'They didn't beat him just like that. Tough guy. He survived. Didn't know what to do. We thought we'd let the older people sleep and decided on rooting out Naidu's field.'

He said so calmly. After that, together all of them pulled out everything leaving ten arm-lengths around. If one looked at it from outside, it appeared as if nothing had happened. Only if one came in, would the real thing become clear.

'Was it wrong?' Sinasubarayudu said on the way.

'No,' said the party man.

'In the morning, that bastard's heart will stop beating on seeing it,' said Sinasubarayudu.

'Should make sure there's no sound when we are pulling them out,' said the party man. Ramanujam seemed surprised at those words.

'Let's think after going to the palle. Pulling out quickly, not making a sound. We've got to think.'

Sinasubarayudu was listening to those words as he walked. Behind him, fourteen youngsters.

Sinasubarayudu did not have a father. Had a mother. Whenever she saw anyone, she would say, 'We should get the boy married, pantulu.' Saying, 'I'll give this nose ring to the woman who comes, pantulu,' she would start the history of the nose ring. It was a brass nose ring. Soon after her marriage, her mother-in-law had taken out her own nose ring and put it on her nose. She also said, 'Before I die, I'll make you stone ear studs, dear daughter-in-law.' Mother-in-law died. She did not make stone ear studs. 'But I must say the right thing, pantulu.' When she was about to die, mother-in-law took five bedas from her waist, tied it to the edge of the daughter-in-law's saree and said, 'Don't tell him.' Saying that, she shed tears. That sobbing would not stop. Such a great person would not be born. The issue of marriage would be side-stepped. It would stop with the talk of the mother-in-law. Only that, whenever she saw anyone. What was surprising was that her mother-in-law had never treated her well. She would always create some problem or the other. She would openly say that she could not feel happy unless she died. But the woman spoke of her mother-in-law as a great person after her death. This seems a wonder in these lives.

That wonder touched the hearts.

Ruth looked towards Mary Suvarta.

Mary's eyelids were fluttering.

It appeared as if the cloud had sat tight in one place and had become cold. It started to drizzle. Immanuel brought the things from outside and arranged them inside. Then he sat looking at the red crotons that were getting wet in the rain.

'This is not a rain that'll last, tell us, Ramanujam. Of Sinasubarayudu. Tell us. Without omitting anything,' said Reuben looking impatiently at the rain. Ramanujam kept narrating.

Sinasubarayudu had no one. He was working with Naidu for a salary when he was young. After growing up a bit, he left the job. If he could find a mud job, he would do that job. He would go for threshing, at the threshing time. He had a good reputation of putting up the hay stacks. If there was a need to turn over the granary pit, they would only call Sinasubarayudu. He would keep doing something or the other. He did not smoke a chutta. Did not smoke a *beedi*. If he did not have work he would play *billakodu*. No matter how big the *billa*, he would hit it just like that. He could throw a top in the air, put it on his palm and spin it effortlessly. It would be amazing to see how the top spun speedily on the palm. At dusk, he would have his food and come to the bund. He would sleep on some bullock cart or the other. If there were no carts, any place was the same. Sleep would not but come.

If you think Sinasubarayudu was just that, you are mistaken. Yenkayi was Suttillu Kotesu's daughter. If you asked her to take a stick from this side to the other side, you had to push her sixteen times to do it. She was such a girl. She would not do any work. As for speech, she had a bad tongue. If she said something, the other person had to twist and turn. Her mother would say it was her father's trait. Suttillu Kotesu had a foul mouth. If he opened his mouth, only obscenities. That daughter had the same foul mouth. Her mother would moan, 'The third day after you send her, she'd burn up that house and will come back home. How do I cope with her, pantulu?' Such a Yenkayi, as her mother forced her, went with her mother to the stream to wash clothes and was walking in the middle of the maize field. Her mother went a little ahead. There was a short distance between her and her mother. Who was that man who came pushing aside her mother, she wondered. Sinasubarayudu. He was the right one. Talkative. Did not stop. Sinasubarayudu did in fact come near. She stopped and looked. He lifted his foot from this ridge and placed it on the other. With another jump he came back to this ridge and was about to go away without turning to look behind.

'Stupid brute. Is it enough to drink a little bit of kuditi for the stomach?' The mouth was such. It would not but speak out.

Sinasubarayudu stopped. When Yenkayi's mother who had stopped having come to the end of the maize field, turned around, she did not find her daughter. She shouted out a couple of times. No response. She came back. She came back to the middle of the field and screamed. No response. She screamed again. She remembered Sinasubarayudu who walked past her. She went right up to the bund of the stream. When she stood there and saw, there was no trace of anyone. She turned back. She came back home that same path. Yenkayi came half an hour after she returned.

Nothing is unnaturally hidden in mala and madiga palles. What you see there is spewing out things as they are. They do not have the crooked brain of holding on to someone's pigtail and tying it to other people's pigtails, make them kick each other and watch the fun. They do not hide anything. Their faces too are like that. Their hearts too are like that. They do not have the great culture of covering their anger with a smile on their face. They have the ordinary culture of showing anger as anger. They are not karanams. They are people with starving stomachs. If the stomach is empty then it will be filled. If it seems to be stirred, it will throw up. Human relationships too are like that. To quarrel when angry. To deny oneself and feed others when in difficulty. That is a culture they have inherited quite naturally. To get upset inwardly and, unable to express it openly, to cry in a closed room are not the done thing there. There, love is not artificial. Hatred is not artificial. There are no two-faced people there. That is why the upper castes call them the riff-raff. Among the riff-raff lives, there is no artifice. Its culture is natural.

Yenkayi's mother did not hide her anger. She pounced on Sinasubarayudu's mother. She said, 'Is your son such a man that he pulled my daughter into the maize field? Has he become so manly! Let him come, I'll bury him.' At first, Sinasubarayudu's mother did not understand. Then she understood. She started to answer word for word. The fight between the women did not stop till the men came home. Yenkayi's brothers came with sticks to attack Sinasubarayudu. Sinasubarayudu said, 'If I died I'd be the only one. If I lived, I'd be the only one. Come on, you fellows,' and drew a line in the bazaar.

Ramanujam stood looking on. He was about to say something. In the meanwhile, Yenkayi's brother's stick fell on Sinasubarayudu's head. Sinasubarayudu's mother let out a scream saying, 'My child's dead!' The fight stopped.

That night Ramanujam sat right next to Sinasubarayudu. He tied a bandage on his head. As someone was standing near the bamboo screen, he went there to find out who it was. At first he thought it was Yenkayi. Yenkayi's mother. Yenkayi's father was at a short distance. Yenkayi's mother held on to Ramanujam's hands. 'How's he, pantulu?' She asked. 'Just a case of shock. He'll be better in a couple of days,' he said. He asked them to come in. 'She has a foul mouth. I was pained. I abused her. If she hadn't abused me, there wouldn't have been a fight. He wouldn't have suffered such an injury. He's fatherless.' Ramanujam was surprised. She was still speaking. He had not noticed till then. Yenkayi's six brothers were sitting next to the screen.

If by chance Sinasubarayudu were to ask the six of them, 'Come in, fellows,' it appeared as if they would come running in. They went away because they did not have the face to come in. Yenkayi came an hour later. Ramanujam was not surprised. He only asked her, 'Your people let you come?' She said, 'They were all sleeping.' She said, 'I let them sleep and came.' That girl did not know that they were not asleep but pretended to sleep as Yenkayi left. On seeing the girl, Sinasubarayudu's mother sat turning her face the other way. 'Did you eat?' Yenkayi asked her. She did not speak. Then she took out the dinner plate that was in her arm pit behind the saree edge. Saying, 'Eat,' she put it in front of her. Did not know what she thought, she started to mix her food. 'Bloody bitch, what would her mother-in-law lose if she kept her mouth shut?' With these words of Yenkayi, Sinasubarayudu's mother felt anger boil up inside her. 'You get your mother to shut up. Ask her to kick the woman who pulled him into the field. What did my child do?' She was shouting twice as loud. 'Yes, I did pull him. What's it, if I pulled him? Why had he come like a dancing bull? Why didn't you hold him so he wouldn't come?' Yenkayi asked her straight. Ramanujam felt like laughing. There was no faltering in their words. They had not a thought of what others would think if they spoke like that. Sinasubarayudu's mother too ate even as the fight continued. Yenkayi washed the plate and put it on one side. She placed the ramshackle cot outside and said, 'Now, lie down, I'll be here.' Without saying a word, she went and lay down. 'If you had four others along with him, would he have suffered such blows,' Yenkayi said. Ramanujam looked, surprised.

The night went by. Another month went by with silent signals. It was summer. He became the brother-in-law to the six brothers in summer. Sinasubarayudu's mother gave the nose ring to Yenkayi. She also said, 'I'll make you stone-studded ear studs, daughter-in-law.'

Among those who were walking with Sinasubarayudu, who pulled out Naidu's half-acre field, in front were the six brothers of Yenkayi. Sinasubarayudu's brothers-in-law. In that palle, Suttillu Kotesu's gang was not small. Kotesu's brothers were themselves ten in number. Sinasubarayudu became one with such a gang. It was Sinasubarayudu who in fact called the party men home for the first time. That could be one of the reasons why the party men could so quickly mingle with the palle.

After coming into the palle, Sinasubarayudu and two others stayed on with the party men. The rest headed back home and went to bed. They sat down in Ramanujam's house. Sinasubarayudu narrated in detail all that had happened. In the morning, the situation came up for discussion.

In the morning, Naidu saw the field. Along with Naidu, the important people among the other Choudharys too saw it. Venkata Choudhary conducted a panchayati. Did not know how the panchayati happened. As for the Choudharys, they pretended as if nothing had happened. The party man said that it was better for the youth to learn to fight with sticks in the palle. They took out the sticks from the loft. They called for Narsigadu the expert in the fight with sticks. He had a reputation that he could twist and twirl the stick in the rain without a drop touching it. After food they levelled the Bengal gram field that had been harvested in the palle. Till the middle of the night, the sound of the sticks was being heard. That too became the topic of debate among the elders of the ooru.

Exactly three months after the maize field incident, another one took place. Sinasubarayudu would say it was a lucky occurrence. As for Ramanujam, he could not think of it as unexpected. Bala Kotadu was not such a courageous person. As he was coming by the mango grove, he stood transfixed looking at the fruits of the cashew tree. He looked this way and that. No one was there. He dared it. No one would imagine he would do something so daring. He took out his loin cloth. He plucked the fruits and tied them with the cloth. He got down from the tree and looked around. No one was there. He was about to cross the fence. Did not know how he was kicked on his back. When Choudhary Kotaiah pushed him into the thorny brambles and beat him twirling his guard stick, he became a lump of blood. He came like a lump of blood to the palle. That day went by. A week too went by like that. On the eighth day Choudhary Kotaiah's young buffalo vanished. Pisodu had the brains to untie the animal without a whisper. Sinasubarayudu would say that Sinnodu and Nallodu showed the same acumen as Pisodu. Venkata Choudhary had a panchayati to discuss the disappearance of Choudhary Kotaiah's buffalo. In the panchayati, he made it clear that he suspected the palle. Ramireddy wanted him to clarify how he had the suspicion. Venkata Choudhary did not think Ramireddy would support the palle like that. He stopped the discussion at that. He was waiting for an opportunity.

As women in the palle were stealthily cutting grass, they were caught. The news that they had tied up the women near the Choudhary's granary spread like wildfire in the palle. Ramanujam did not imagine this. The entire palle moved. They went past the kapu's fields and came near the Choudhary's granary. The reddys and choudharys at the fields looked in surprise at the malas walking across the fields. At some other time, if someone walked across fields like that, his lifeline would have gone haywire. The first surprising thing was to see so many people together. The second was their not taking heed of who was near the field. What was more surprising was that among those who were walking across the field like that, there were not just men but women. Even more surprising was that washermen came from the chakalipalem. Venkata Choudhary did not imagine that they would come so openly. Ramireddy's followers coming too was irksome to Venkata Choudhary. The matter was confined only to an argument. The people from the palle returned bringing back the women with them. Venkata Choudhary took some more people and went to the town. There, he went to the police station. The life of Avalapadu was taking another turn. Ramanujam said that their going to the station was their first defeat. The ooru was heating up.

The palle assembled in the centre to discuss the malas taking water from the Avalapadu lake. Ramanujam was one among those assembled. Ramireddy was there. The important people of chakalipalem and malapalli were there.

'They'll attack.'

'We'll counter attack.'

They discussed at length who should be where, who should do what, and how to enter the lake. There was a separate gathering with people of Sinasubarayudu's age group. It was decided that the women of Yenkayi's age would get into the lake first with pots. That was a wonder. The shore in front of the cart path. It was pointing to a historic scene.

The malas who used to stand for hours together at the lake bund for a potful of water came near the shore with their pots. On one side, Ramireddy. On the other side, Ramanujam. Yenkayi standing in front holding a pot. Behind her, the rest of the women, . . . in hundreds, . . . malas.

They got down into the lake . . .

For the first time. Malas, . . . women carrying pots. Got into the lake. How was the earth under the feet when they were placing their feet in the lake for the first time! A strange experience. Excitement. The water in the lake that was encircling the feet. A fantastic, tickling sensation. How to think of this scene! In which songs to hide it!

As the water in the lake was filling up Yenkayi's pot, the tears welling up in her eyes were falling into the lake.

Peda Yenkatirangayi. A sixty-year old man. Did not know what happened. Did not know why he sat on the edge and was crying. Ramanujam was looking at Peda Yenkatirangayi. In front of Rangayi, on the other side of lake, there was a temple on a mound. It appeared to the trustee Chinareddy, who hid behind the temple, that the temple top had tilted a bit. But for another trustee of the temple, Choudhary, the temple that had tilted seemed to have broken down.

The women who got into the lake had crossed the shore and were proceeding further up. They felt like going like that. Those on the shore were shouting out not to go forward as there would be pits. But they were not stopping. They felt like going round the entire lake. They felt like splashing the water with their feet. How many hundreds of years of desire was that! How many such lakes were born in this country? How many had dried up without the feet of untouchables touching them! How many years! Hundreds of years. How many centuries . . . What would the last century of this millennium see! How would it like to proceed?

The mala children jumped into the water. They stretched out their arms and began to swim. Chinareddy could not stop near the temple top. He signalled. The sticks and axes in the temple ran towards the palle shore. This was not an unimagined development. The mala, Munaiah, who was hiding in the tamarind branches right in front of the temple top, whistled. It was not just Sinasubarayudu, Sinnodu and Pisodu who were waiting for the right moment, but half the youngsters of the palle who went towards the elders of the ooru with sticks and axes. The first blow by Sinasubarayudu as he ran fell on Choudhary Malyadri's back. He fell to the ground with a terrible shriek. That warning blow had a huge effect on the elders of the ooru. They took to their heels. It was now the turn of the elders of the ooru to flee. It was now the turn of the dispossessed to chase. That was how that day dawned in the lives of Avalapadu. This news created a sensation in the surrounding areas. This news gave a new force to the mala and madiga palles. A discussion began among the upper castes as to why such a thing happened. A strange chain of events began. One or two people from the neighbouring mala and madiga palles began to visit Avalapadu. Though it is strange to think that the kapus of that ooru enquired of the mala and madiga who came there whether they had been to Avalapadu, it is not a surprising thing. Not just that, the names of Ramanujam and Sinasubarayudu were being heard in the neighbouring villages. Avalapadu was dreaming. It was not stopping at being just dreams. It was translating them into reality.

But these upper castes see a lot of villainy in the dreams of untouchable people. This government suppresses them very cruelly. The government after 1947. The government that proclaims ours is a free country.

Venkata Choudhary set up home in the police station itself. Chettodu[38] entered the scene. Chettodu was a police officer. Sympathy, pity, compassion—these words were not in his constitution.

The news reached Avalapadu that the police were coming. Youngsters like Sinasubarayudu left the palle. They crossed the stream. They searched for a safe place in the fields. Only women were left in the palle. Children remained. Old people remained. About five middle-aged persons stayed back to guard the palle. At night, they would sit behind the thatched gates in darkness. They would have a mound of stones where they sat. For the present, these were the weapons in their hands. The tamarind tree from a long time ago. Did not know when it was born. A man on the branches of that tree. Without blinking his eyes, being alert to any movement. A stream in the middle of the palle. Dense bamboo bushes on the mound next to the stream. Amidst the bushes, they tied up a plank and made a watching post out of it. If you sat there, the entire palle would be visible. Three people would always go around the palle. The palle was not sleeping. Those who were going about would talk to each and every householder in the palle. In the granaries of the eastern field, there were rumours that police had descended. Those granaries were in ruins. They were on the shore of the stream. From there, the stream would turn into the shape of a sickle. The entire wet land where it had meandered in that manner was filled with tall Bengal gram stalks. A path in between the Bengal gram field. If one proceeded on that path, one would meet the turn of the stream. They would not be able to cross the Gundala shore. The stream turned into a whirlpool there. In fact, it was not the police who were there. Sinasubarayudu and the youngsters with him. There were five among them who could cross the Gundala shore. Though the people who were walking around the village knew that, they were merely listening to rumour, but did not say it was so and so.

Just then an incident no one had imagined took place. At midnight a constable came to Sinasubarayudu's house to take him away. The police did not know that the palle had taken precautions knowing the police would attack all of them together. In fact, it was the elders of the ooru who had started the rumours that they would attack. They did so to frighten the palle. It was not that the attack was fiction but it was not going to take place today or tomorrow. It was then felt that they ought to capture Sinasubarayudu. The constable came with that very purpose. The other constable who had come to keep him company stayed back in the ooru.

The constable stepped into the palle. Holding the branches of the tamarind tree, the man on the tree shook them hard. The storks and other birds screeched loudly and flew away in a rush. That was the signal. One among the three patrolling the palle ran towards the eastern granary. The other two sped off to some other place. The constable was coming in without making a sound. The bamboo screens and doors of the houses were being shut. The constable came near the bamboo screen at the turn of the lane. If he turned right there and proceeded, he would come to Sinasubarayudu's house. Behind that screen a mound of stones. The man who hid there was watching the constable. No sooner had the constable turned the corner, than he pounced on him. The constable was nonplussed at the unexpected charge. He fell at that push. The gun fell at a distance. He screamed out aloud. The sound of the shaking of the bamboo doors of the houses in the palle was heard. The constable thought that a number of people were attacking him. He picked up strength and began running. Penchili who had jumped on the constable picked up some stones. He started pelting the fleeing constable with stones. The stones hit the constable hard. As he ran he crossed the ooru. The distance between Avalapadu and the village with the police station was three miles. It was only after reaching there that he realised he had forgotten his gun.

Penchili looked at the gun that was lying there left behind by the policeman. He took it in his hand. A wonderful experience. A strange fear. He did not know what to do with it. He knew there would be bullets in it. He knew they could kill people on the other side. He knew it would be in the hands of the police. He had heard that ten miles away from the ooru in Chintalapalem, Naidu's Butchaiah Choudhary went about holding it in his hand. But he had not imagined that it would lie at the entrance of the mala palle like this. How did they fire this? It would be good to know that. He felt very sad. He lifted his head even as he felt sad. Half the palle was around him. All of them were looking at him and at the gun in his hand. Perhaps the first mala to hold a gun was Penchili. That was why, in the days after that, they called him Tupakodu (the gunman). There was no trace at all of the name, Penchili. He looked at the people who observed him. Three or four elders came near him. They touched him.

'It's only with this that Naidugaru's Butchaiah killed his wife,' the oldest among the three said.

'It's because he's a wretched bastard that he killed his wife. Give it to me. Ask him to come here. I'll shoot him,' another old man said.

The third old man told him worriedly, 'It's dangerous if the police comes. Hide it, Penchili.' Penchili felt it was right. He crossed the palle to hide it. Among the hay stacks, he identified one, hid it underneath and covered it with hay leaving it just as it was. For some reason, he did not want to move from there. He thought of staying there all night. When he got up at dawn and was coming towards the palle, he saw the police coming into the ooru. He crossed the field. He crossed the stream. He walked along the dust track amidst the fields. If he walked a mile he would come to his maternal uncle's village.

That night the constable went to the station running. He told them about forgetting the gun and the way they attacked him. Immediately, the news reached the town. Chettodu was at Ongole. The malapalli of Avalapadu did not appear normal. The police started making up stories. The people of the palle had stepped into the water of the lake. There was a fight when they dipped into the water. They chased the farmers and beat them up. They attacked the peasant women. The police kept weaving the story. The dark night would not give testimony. That was how the malas committed a crime. They did not inform the police when they stepped into the water. That was how they disregarded the law. The police came to know about the situation only through the farmers. Venkata Choudhary was a respectable person. The entire ooru respected him. Such a person said that the malas attacked the houses of the farmers and misbehaved with the women. The big man would not lie. He had self-respect. He was a choudhary. Not an ordinary choudhary. A choudhary with hundred acres. Though his father was with the Justice Party before Independence, he said no to his father and joined the Congress Party. When Gandhi came to Andhra, he attended almost all his meetings. He was such a man. Such people had a lot of self-respect. But if he put his self-respect aside and complained that their women were insulted by the malas, the authorities could understand how horribly, how cruelly, how barbarically the riff-raff had behaved. The complaint of the Congress supporter Venkata Choudhary who had self-esteem, self-respect, power and money moved the hearts of the authorities. There was no need to be surprised that it moved them in that manner. Only if it did not should one be surprised. Not just this, Venkata Choudhary gave invaluable information too in his complaint. That information was not a small one. It was about the Communists. Great information. It was information that only a big man like Venkata Choudhary could give. Venkata Choudhary did not stop at that. He said, 'If you come, I'll go around each house and get the Communists caught.' Such a great man was willing to offer such a great help. The police departmet spent five minutes of priceless time that night congratulating him.

More than anything else, those malas, those Communists, snatched the gun of the police. Therefore, there was no alternative. Even if the palle was totally destroyed, there was no way they could tolerate this atrocity.

They began to write the names in the first investigation reports.

Sinasubarayudu. Age 30 years. Caste mala. Communist.

Pisodu. Age 30 years. Caste mala. Communist.

They kept on writing like that. Venkata Choudhary gave them about twenty names. The most important name was Ramanujam's. Same caste. Teacher. Communist leader. Along with those names, there were three names from the upper castes. There were three names from chakalipalem. Chettodu picked up the necessary papers. The police force entered Avalapadu. In the early hours of the day, they ate thirty hens as tiffin. They emptied thirty bottles.

It was dawn. The attack on the palle began. The people of the palle were aghast. Women, old people, children—no one knew what was happening. Next to Chettodu, Venkata Choudhary. As their first move, they went towards the school. Ramanujam was in a class. Only a few children had come.

'That fellow is Ramanujam.'

Pointing out to Ramanujam, Venkata Choudhary said this quite loudly. They arrested Ramanujam then and there. When Sinasubarayudu had left the palle, he had asked Ramanujam also to come along. But he was under the impression that they might not touch him because he was a teacher. His belief came to nothing. The children were shocked to see their teacher being taken away by the police right in front of their eyes. The school's headmaster, Yelamanda, asked them why they were doing such a thing. Chettodu's lathi fell on the teacher's back. The old man's heart beat quickly. They arrested him along with Ramanujam. In fact, Yelamanda was a very timid person. He too was a mala. But he never even peeped to see what was happening in that palle, even though a lot was happening. Poor man, how far he was from all that! He did not realise that the first blow of Chettodu's lathi would be on him. Two young teachers who were watching all this from the next classroom, jumped over the wall and scooted. The police chased them. Those who chased them like that entered the palle. Chettodu and Venkata Choudhary entered following them.

They started searching the houses. They were asking people to tell them who had taken the gun. They were asking them to say where they had kept it. They were indiscriminate. Did not care whether they were women, they were children. Did not care whether they were old people. They were beating them up. They were enquiring about the names in their list. Venkata Choudhary was pointing out and saying he was so-and-so's father, she was so-and-so's mother and she was so-and-so's wife. Chettodu was torturing those who were pointed out in this manner even more. The assault that began at eight in the morning continued non-stop till eleven. Chettodu said that they would come back in the evening and they would ask them again. He wanted them to inform in the meanwhile where the gun was hidden and who hid it. Saying this, he went towards the path that separated the ooru and the palle. He sat down on the chair Venkata Choudhary got for him under the shade of the tamarind tree. Did not know what he thought but he asked them to get ten children from the palle. They dragged the children even though they were crying. He counted the children who came. There were twenty of them. He told the children to get two hens each within an hour. The children were shaken up. He said if they did not bring them, he would cut and eat them up.

The children ran to the palle. Did not know how they ran behind the hens. They brought back two hens each. They tied the feet of the hens and laid them in a row. The children were watching. Their tender hearts were beating rapidly. Their eyes were closing unable to see that horrible scene. Their entire bodies were shivering. Chettodu took a long knife. The children screamed out loud. The hens had their heads cut off and their torsos were flying and falling down. The chopped-off heads were falling at a distance. The children hugged each other. They saw such a ghastly scene for the first time in their lives. That scene did not disappear from their minds for many years. A year after that incident, when the school inspector came and asked them what police did, they could not remember what they had read in books. They said they kill hens and eat them. That inspector was surprised. After the teacher explained in detail, his heart melted. He related that to the teachers in the central room and shed tears. That was such a scene. Chettodu laughed looking at the frightened children. But it did not appear like laughter to the children. Then he asked them to skin two hens each. Children with tear-filled eyes.

The lake of Avalapudu was witness to this.

The tamarind tree was witness to this.

The cart pathway that began there, proceeded through the fields and went up to the lake was witness to this.

The children crying and pulling out the feathers of the hen. Untouchables.

Chettodu's men pulled down a hut. They lit a bonfire with the palm leaves. It was the children themselves who held the hens by their legs and roasted them over the fire. They felt they themselves were burning when they were roasting those hens. They kept the roasted hens in a tray-basket and sent them to Venkata Choudhary's house. Venkata Choudhary went along with them. Chettodu looked at the names again. There was Ramireddy's name. He wondered what the relationship between this Ramireddy and the malas was. Communist. That alone was the relationship. After that, there was Jala Ramaiah's name. His caste was mentioned as washerman. Singaraju's caste was mentioned as *raju*. All these people were Communists. Among them, Ramireddy and Jala Ramaiah were very dangerous people.

After food, Chettodu asked Venkata Choudhary about Ramireddy. Choudhary was not willing to go with him there. He gave him directions. Chettodu went to Ramireddy's house. Ramireddy was not there. Ramireddy's wife was there. Though Venkata Choudhary said he would not come there, he said he should frighten Ramireddy in such a manner that he would not support the malas again. He hinted that the house was filled with grains. Chettodu thought that it meant that he ought to burn down the house. That's it. The large tiled house of Ramireddy was set on fire. Under the tiles they had laid very good bamboos. As the bamboos were burning with a cracking sound, the tiles were flying far away. All around fumes of the flames. Now even the reddys were running helter-skelter. The malapalli trembled looking at the burning house of Ramireddy.

They arrested Jala Ramaiah of chakalipalem. They dragged the elder sister who tried to prevent them right into the centre of the bazaar. They hurled choicest abuses on her. They sent Ramanujam, Yalamanda pantulu and Jala Ramaiah straightaway in the police van to Ongole.

There was another raid against the palle at six in the evening. The same words. 'Where have you hidden the gun? Who snatched it? Where's Sinasubarayudu?' A blow for each word.

Scenes.

In front of Ruth's eyes.

The scenes Ramanujam placed in front.

Children crying. The burning house of Ramireddy. The palle people beating their chests. Separate scenes. For just a mouthful of water. After '47 . . . In the first stage of still recollecting the '47 memories.

Scene after scene.

How ghastly, each scene! Subbaiah's wife, Sendri, was having pains. How did the scene end? The pains started on the day the gun incident took place. All that night, she fought a battle with those pains. They thought she would deliver that day. The mid-wife sat waiting for the delivery. The pains stopped at dawn. They started again in the heat of the morning. The police assault was continuing. In the house, the mid-wife kept waiting like that. Sendri who was suffering like that received a blow of the lathi. The midwife who was waiting for the delivery too suffered at their hands. By evening the pains increased. Seven in the evening. A time when darkness descended. Severe pain. Chettodu asked them to drive the people of the palle to the tree. They were bringing them, kicking. The people were reaching the tree, crying. There was no other light than that of the petromax lamp under the tree. They chased Sendri too. They kicked her as they chased her. The midwife did not let go of Sendri. They caught hold of their hair and brought them. They kept all the women in one place. They placed the men in front of them. The children were looking in some other direction. The scene of the hens was etched in their minds. Those very questions. A blow for each question. Did not care if they were women or men. All the whim of the police.

Sendri's pains increased. She was screaming. She had slumped to the ground. The midwife was looking only at Sendri silently. She did not remember the blows of the police. She did not take note of what they were asking. From the previous night an untouchable was struggling to fall on to this earth and to set his first sight at this violence. She was eagerly waiting for him. Definitely a male child. All the movements seemed to indicate it. Sendri was screaming sporadically. The midwife asked everyone to stand around Sendri. That was it. All the women surrounded Sendri like a screen. Chettodu came there holding the petromax lamp. He was about to peep inside saying, 'Is she delivering?' The women saying, 'Chi!' swarmed around Sendri like a hut. Chettodu's lathi blows were falling on them. The police were hitting them on their hands and legs. But that human hut formed around her did not crumble. Did not disperse. All their attention was on Sendri. The lathi blows that were falling on them did not trouble them. They did not hear the swear words by the police. In all that ghastliness, an earsplitting cry . . . a baby boy's shriek. The first scream of an untouchable.

Silence.

The midwife was doing her work. She picked up the child in her arms and showed it around. The wailing child. Black colour. Black hair. What beauty! Black was so beautiful. In all that atrocity, in all that sorrow, a happiness bloomed and was peeping out.

Life was a big struggle.

The first message the child learnt. Chettodu retreated. Four women tied a *doli*. They kept the child and mother in the doli. Carrying it, they took Sendri to her house. Chettodu kept looking. Venkata Choudhary kept looking. The police kept looking. The mid-wife silently walked next to the doli looking at the mother and child. Chettodu continued to look till they went into the palle. In one swoop he vent his entire anger on the men. Blow after blow. Wound next to a wound. Blood all over the body. Even in all that darkness, the blood was visible.

In this country, the air that one breathes has caste.

The water one drinks has caste.

The field canal that flows and the land that yields harvest have caste.

The school, the temple and the village square have caste.

The food one eats, the house one lives in and the clothes one wears have caste.

The word one speaks has caste.

Literature and culture have caste.

The State has caste, its laws have caste.

Justice and the courts have caste.

The corpse and the cemetery have caste.

God has caste. Devil has caste.

That's why that blood flowed like that. The blood that flowed like that too has caste. But there was a uniqueness to the blood that flowed in Avalapadu. That was the blood of the malas of Avalapadu. The blood of the Communists of the malapalli of Avalapadu.

Memory of blood.

Scene of blood.

That scene continued in that manner for two days. Coming to know of the presence of the police, Sinasubarayudu and his friends split up. They crossed the stream and went to the next village. It was only on the third day that Sinasubarayudu came to know about the gun business. He got to know the details. He thought Penchili must have taken it. Penchili was not in the palle. So he sent a man to Penchili's maternal uncle's village. He met him and found out where he had placed the gun. Penchili did not know that so much was happening because of the gun. That very night the two of them met friends who were in other villages. They discussed. They thought that the information about the gun ought to reach Chettodu. They came to the conclusion that if this was not done, the assault on the palle would worsen. Sinasubarayudu met washerman, Mangaiah. He asked them to see to it that that information reached Venkata Choudhary. Mangaiah saw to it that the information was in the air and it reached Venkata Choudhary's ears.

The attack stopped.

That scene ended like that. But fifty people were arrested in the palle. They arrested Sinasubarayudu and Ramireddy a week after this happened. The police thought of shooting them. But no idea why such a thought was stalled. For about a year almost sixty people from malapalli went round the court.

They would not have enough money to go often to the court. They had to do it once a month. Sometimes Ramanujam, Sinasubarayudu and Penchili had to go to the court three times a month. Ramanujam thought he would lose his job. That was a Christian-aided school. That was why he retained his job.

Though they went through such difficulties, they did not find it a problem. There was a single reason. The desire of generations was fulfilled. They were getting into the lake. They were drawing water. The landlords did not have the courage to stop them.

Just for a mouthful of water, a battle did take place there. But that did not mean they loved wars. If they could get water by peaceful means, there would not be anyone more peace-loving than them. But their lives taught them that they could get anything only if they fought for it. That was why they fought for it. Perhaps historians would not call it a war. They could call it thus. They could say they quarrelled about it. They could say they fought. They could say anything. But one thing is true. When their lives told them that they could gain self-respect only by giving up their lives, they were ready to give up their lives.

When Ramanujam was talking about Avalapudu, not just the coastal Avalapadu but the entire Telangana region stood in front of Ruth's eyes. Nehru was right in front of her eyes. Along with him, his army. Sardar Vallabhai Patel and Captain Nanjappa[39] stood before her eyes. She recalled their inhumanity. She remembered their cruelty. She remembered the devilish methods they discovered to strike terror into the hearts of the people.

In Telangana, every palle was a military camp. Palle filled with police. Armed Madras Police. Armed Malabar Police. Armed Maharashtra

Police. Each one was an Avalapadu 'Chettodu'. Licensed authority to kill people. It was then that killing people in 'encounters' began.

Nehru.

Patel.

Nanjappa.

It was not sunrise in the east still. The attack began. Police in lorries. Aiding them, Congress workers. Butt of the rifle, tamarind barks, booted feet, bayonets—into the chests of men, into the chastity of women. Food grains that were set on fire. Paddy fields that were set on fire. Houses that were set on fire. Women who had been violated, pregnant women and infants. Young men and women who were becoming corpses. Arrests.

The bloody sight of Telangana. The cruel reality mother had related.

Mother cried as she narrated it.

Mother made her cry as she narrated it.

Why so?

For many things, life itself is the answer. Ruth feels that it is so true.

Ramanujam was a school teacher. Why did he become a Communist? Why did he go to jail? Why did he go round the court? Life itself would have to give the answer. All that night he spoke about Avalapadu. After that Ramanujam said many things. Ruth does not remember all of them now. Nehru's army landing in Telangana. Nizam's surrender. Suppressing the Communists. The ending of the Telangana Armed Struggle. The 1952 general elections. He kept talking of such things. At every place, he kept bringing in Avalapadu.

But there was one thing that surprised Ruth and Reuben. When Ramanujam was struggling to remember in between, Immanuel was helping him out. He was reminding him along with the dates.

17

Not just reminding those parts Ramanujam had forgotten, but as time went by they came to know many sides of Immanuel that were interesting. Some of them even caused a little anxiety to Ruth. But Reuben was not surprised. He went way back and spoke. He said it was swimming against the stream. He said swimming like that was in his blood. He said it was also in the friendships his ancestors had embraced. He reminded them of Subhadra who had picked up the spade and stood over the dike. He placed Narigadu and Mataiah in front of them. He reminded them of Yellanna's songs, one by one.

He said it was Yennela Dinni's inheritance.

He said it was the life Avalapadu gave to a Christian.

He said his body was questioning him every moment. Like it questioned Martin. Like it frightened Simon.

He said repeatedly that that question and that fear were haunting him. He would say that that fear and that question were not of today. That it was coming from before Yerrenkadu.

'But . . . '

Ruth looked as if she was asking him to speak out. He looked at her very calmly. The eyes were filled with a brightness that was to be studied.

'Immanuel was Reuben not haunted by fear.'

How would Reuben who was not haunted by fear be? He would be like Immanuel. Who was Immanuel? Her son. The one born before Rosy. Was that all? Was there nothing more to think of when she thought of her son? There was. There was a lot. Sinasubarayudu said many things about Immanuel.

What did Sinasubarayudu say about her child? How he said it! The day they went to Avalapadu. Joining him on the way. What he said of her child!

'A very good man. "*Naxite*."'

She then looked at him as if she did not understand. After she understood, she was anxious. She made a great effort to control the heart that had become totally disturbed. The same word all along the way. Very good man. 'Naxite'. She looked at Reuben. He kept walking. He took a couple of steps forward. She could not hear what Sinasubarayudu and Reuben were speaking to each other. It was only Immanuel who stood before her.

Immanuel who would sit very docilely at the family prayers. Immanuel who would be deeply involved whether he sang a song, read a verse or prayed. How did he become that? What was he running in search of?

'Don't you know? Ramanujam teacher isn't in Avalapadu now. He went to Seekakulam.'

She heard those words Sinasubarayudu spoke. She had been hearing of youths, intellectuals and students from the coastal regions going to Sreekakulam.

Ramanujam was not in Avalapadu.

He had gone to Sreekakulam.

Ramanujam was a Naxalite. In Sinasubarayudu's words, a 'Naxite'. Her child! Immanuel!

Avalapadu was way behind. At that distance Immanuel. He may not hear even if she asked him to turn back.

She decided to listen to Sinasubarayudu's words. She was walking next to the two of them. She asked them to slow down. Reuben was not saying anything. Was listening. Sinasubarayudu asked at the pond, 'Do you want to drink water?' Rather than drink water, they felt like sitting on the boulders. Carts with green leaves of tobacco were coming from the fields.

The carts came on to the road. Behind the carts the tobacco coolies. They appeared odd in muddy pants and muddy shirts. They sent off the carts and took the short cut. Sinasubarayudu said that by the time the carts took the route around the eastern field and reached the tobacco pandal, they would go by the short cut, reach the palle, give milk to their children, ensure that there were enough sticks under the stove, cross the stream and reach the tobacco pandal, and that they would come sometime in the night and cook their food. He said he would do the 'rise' duty in the tobacco barn. He said there were three stokers under him.

'I'm some crude kind of a fellow. I speak in a crude manner. I became a "comnist" in forty eight. Till fifty two, talk only of revolt. But things have changed. Everything changed after the elections. Our village got into the malapalli lake even before fifty two. It could not have happened after that.

Ruth was listening.

'Mine are all crude words. Crude thoughts.'

Perhaps they were. But Sinasubarayudu had studied life. Even if Sinasubarayudu was called 'Naxite,' or 'Comnist,' or 'Ceepem,' or 'Ceepai' or 'Seekakulam,' they did not appear to Ruth as printing errors. They appeared natural. Mistakes in print were for the educated. There were no printing mistakes in coarse lives. The way they spoke, that was the right speech. When they say, 'After they tied two Ceylon budlu the fever came down, *mava*,' the term used is not saline bottle, it is Ceylon budlu. It is not an English term at all. Even if it were a Sanskrit word, the same with it. 'Koodu' did not become proper Telugu only in Potana's verses. It is being used in the houses of malas and madigas every day in a wonderful and beautiful manner.

'Want to go to Seekakulam. Ramanujam pantulu went without telling us. If I ask Immanuel to tell me how to get there, he doesn't tell me. But have to go.'

Those were the last words Sinasubarayudu said as he set out towards his house.

Did not know what Reuben was thinking.

The house drew near. Jessie came running. He jumped and put his arms round his grandfather's neck. Mary Suvarta's eyes were filled with laughter. Immanuel came back from school and seemed to have gone somewhere else again. Mary Suvarta said it might be late.

They waited for Immanuel hoping to eat together. The coolies who had brought down the leaves in the green tobacco leaf pandal were returning home. They tied up dirty clothes and were running towards the lake for water. Everything appeared like a war. Children with sleepy eyes were crying and following their mother who was running for water. Some mothers were carrying their baskets and going to the market. To get rice, to get a little bit of *dal*. That too was a run. Behind them little children. For a tiny piece of jaggery . . . commotion. Commotion for appeasing hunger. Commotion of weeping for a piece of jaggery.

After bringing it, after cooking it as if someone was chasing them, as they had to eat to live, after stuffing a hot morsel into their mouths, sleep.

A short nap taken due to tiredness. Sleep after leaving the breast to the child.

In the early hours of the morning, the supervisor's screams.

Again dirty pants. Dirty shirts. Rushing towards the green tobacco · leaf pandal.

Sinasubarayudu came. He said he was going to the 'rise' duty. When he came back, he brought Yenkayi along. As Yenkayi was not feeling well, she did not go to work. It appeared as if Immanuel had not come. Telling Yenkayi, 'Keep them company,' Sinasubarayudu left. Yenkayi stayed back there. She started her complaints. Said she had three daughters. They had given the eldest one in marriage outside. They gave away two others in the village itself. Ruth asked her to show the nose ring that her mother-in-law gave her. She smiled and showed it to her. It appeared as if she had not made stone studs for her. Saying, 'I couldn't have them made for you, daughter-in-law' she closed her eyes. 'The bitch who had no sense of cleanliness or anything. She got along somehow. Even the day before she died, she had quarrelled with the neighbours. She had a foul mouth. But to put things right, she would not open her mouth to me. She would be at home like a crushed louse. If she wanted to get rid of the itch in her mouth, she would quarrel with the neighbours. Silly woman, how many times she raised the matter about the stone studs! Though I told her, forget about it, she continued to talk about it. That was the last word.' Yenkayi kept talking in that manner. She placed the betel nut and leaf on the rock. She took the chutney pestle and squashed them. She said her teeth had become loose. She said her teeth would tingle, if she did not chew betel nut and leaf. In fact, she was not all that old. Hunger changes the entire shape.

Immanuel had not yet come. It looked as if he would not come in the near future. Mary Suvarta said, 'You eat.' Jessie sat between his grandparents. He said both of them should feed him a morsel each. As they were competing with each other to mix the food and feed him, his happiness knew no bounds. Mary placed the cots outside the verandah. Did not know when Yenkayi slept. She spread the edge of her saree on the platform and lay down. Mary said, 'That's her. You lie down.'

Jessie squeezed in between his grandparents. Ruth remembered the ponnangi pitta of Yennela Dinni. That bird had snuggled into her hand. This bird placed its head on her stomach and placed its feet on the grandfather's chest. That was the only difference. Felt like laughing. She said, 'ponnangi pitta' as she sweetly caressed Jessie's cheeks. Jessie asked her to say what it was. She talked of Yennela Dinni houses and the ponnangi pitta's arrival. He did not stop there. He asked her why they were in Yennela Dinni. She said, 'It is my mother-in-law's house.' He said, 'What is your mother-in-law's name?' She said, 'Sasirekha.' He said, 'The name, Sasirekha is so wonderful.' She said, 'Her mother-in-law's name was Subhadra.' He said, 'Do you only have mothers-in-law. Don't you have mothers?' Ruth felt like laughing. Reuben too felt like laughing. He asked Mary, 'What's your mother-in-law's name?' Mary said laughing, 'Shut up.' Reuben said, 'Come, Chinna. I'll tell you.' Saying, 'Tell me,' he turned around quickly, putting his head on his grandfather's stomach and his feet on his grandmother.

'Yennela pitta,' Reuben said laughing.

'Yennela pitta . . . ponnangi pitta . . . yennela pitta . . . ponnangi pitta.' Repeating this over and over again Jessie got up and jumped up and down. With that the song of the bird did not stop. 'What sorts of birds?' asked Reuben. 'Yennela pitta,' said Jessie. 'What kind of a bird?' Reuben asked again. 'Ponnangi pitta,' Ruth followed. Laughter . . . Laughter that could touch the outskirts of Avalapadu . . .

Laughter that Ruth can hear clearly even now.

Jessie's laughter.

Ponnangi pitta's laughter . . .

The tear drops falling from Ruth's eyes. The turmoil of memories that cannot be hidden in the heart . . .

Jessie slept that night laughing like that. Ponnangi pitta. Between the two of them. Hugging them tight imagining that they might run away without telling him. Reuben slept. To indicate it he began to snore lightly. Jessie was dreaming about yennela pitta and ponnangi pitta. Ruth too fell asleep. At some late hour when she got up, she saw Mary still sitting.

'Is this the case every day?'

Startled, Mary looked at her mother-in-law who spoke those words.

'Did you eat?'

She kept looking at her mother-in-law. Did not speak.

'Waiting has become the norm for the daughters-in-law of this house.'

Mary did not understand what her mother-in-law was saying.

'Subhadra too looked out. Sasirekha too looked out. The same with Mary Suvarta. I'm the only exception. Until now Reuben hasn't made me wait for him. I can't say of tomorrow. Come and eat.'

Saying those words, Ruth walked in. Mary went in along with her mother-in-law. It was Ruth who put the rice on her plate. She served the curries and sat in front.

'Eat.'

Mary Suvarta was looking out into the frontyard.

'You can look after you eat.'

'Eating together . . . '

'I know you ate with him after marriage. But the daughter-in-law of this house, the one before me. My mother-in-law's mother-in-law. She ate stealthily with the man she wanted to marry even before marriage. She cooked *bommadayi* fish *pulusu* secretly for her man. After marriage, she cooked the same pulusu openly and ate it with relish sitting along with him. Subhadra ate like that. She wanted to eat like that all her life. Did it happen? It didn't. The man who went, came back during his last moments. He came as the last breath after the drought ate him up. What did she do, the one before us? Not just bommadayi pulusu but not even a single grain of rice in the pot to eat together. She kept looking at her husband. Her husband was not saying anything else except her name as he lay in their son's arms. Who did Subhadra see in her man then? The Subhadra who ate together. The Subhadra who mixed and fed him. Whom did she see? She saw a child. She asked her son, "Here, give me that child." She kept her man's head behind the fringe of her saree. She hugged him to her bosom. Why did she do that?'

Ruth stopped. She was unable to proceed. Some inexplicable anxiety. Mary Suvarta was listening, looking at her mother-in-law.

'Why did she do that? A son as large as a tree. A married son. If Subhadra were alive, a son who would have placed the baby Reuben in her hands. Did she think of all that? Caressing her husband's head, she felt it would be good if a drop of milk could fall again and again in this child's throat after so many years. It can't happen. It can't happen like that. But an illusion as if it was happening. She closed her eyes with that illusion. Didn't open them again. Subhadra who ate together. Subhadra who mixed and fed him. She became one like that.'

Ruth stopped again. This time she took a long time to speak again. Mary Suvarta could not bear that silence.

'Eat . . . do you mix like this . . . hold this morsel.'

'I'll eat.'

'I fed you like this when you were a child. You're not yet old. Days are ahead when you'll have to mix and feed me like this. Then, if you recall this day, you won't feel irritated.'

'Enough. I'll eat.'

'Eat.'

She gave the plate to Mary and looked towards Immanuel's table. Several books. Some pages were turned and kept just like that. She moved forward and reached out to two books. She flipped through them. In the middle of the books, there were notes written down. They seem to have been written down to remember them. Reuben would write down like this before his speech. She sat looking at those pages. Everything seemed to be in the present. She stopped looking and started reading. The points written down to remember the present history.

A struggle.

A violent struggle.

A wounded struggle.

A heart-wrenching struggle.

Naxalbari struggle.

That was a spark of fire.

The gust of a stormy struggle.

Ruth was reading a new world. In big letters, the word Sreekakulam was written down. It was underlined.

The notes ended there. She knew Immanuel's handwriting quite well. It was her child who wrote. She shut her eyes tight.

In front of her eyes . . .

Some world.

It was very strange.

It was worrisome.

There was a wonderful thing happening on the earth.

Amidst that wonder, Immanuel.

Why did Immanuel become one with the wonderful? Talk to the earth. It will give you knowledge. It was a sentence she had read many times. Why did she remember it now?

Her child. Immanuel. He must have spoken to the earth. In fact, he did just that. He spoke to the earth. What would the earth have told him? It would have told him innumerable secrets. It would have told him about its children who had trusted it but could not own it. It would have told him about the lives of the threshing grains. Was that all? It would have also told him about the deception of landlords who kept the earth imprisoned and did not let its children get hold of it.

What else did the earth say?

How would it have said it?

All these years . . .

After looting so much . . . These looters who did not allow anything to remain on its chest and kept it imprisoned. After sucking in the entire resources, look what they leave behind for this poor race—the earth would have asked him to look into this.

It would have shown him such a deep bloody streak on the ground. It would have introduced him to the sweat of the poor that had sunk into the layers of its heart.

No matter how much they twisted and turned, they could not get hold of even a bit of mud. Though they had lived entwining it day and night, even a bit of mud did not touch them. It would have said, 'Did you see all this, bidda?'

The paddy ripened for harvesting. Maize, *sajjalu, ragi, korralu, arigalu*—all food grains ripened.

But none turned into even a small granary in their houses.

Hunger, a day-to-day truth. It was born just like that along with them and grew up like this along with them. Thinking it is well-liked, it squats right there against the central pole.

Earth must have spoken in that manner.

It would have asked for one more season other than the ones already there in nature for children.

It must have stirred the furnace of history and raised the coals of fire.

In the light of the coals of fire.

Malas and madigas.

No hut. No land. No work. No food.

Domination. Everything, domination from above. The domination of the upper castes. The domination of the landlords.

The season changed. Its name changed.

Winter. Spring. Summer. Not like that. Season of exploitation. Season of thieves. Season of atrocities. Season of hunger. Season of the smell of blood—

A life.

An exploitation.

A death . . .

That was it. Earth must have spoken in that manner.

It would have asked him to read it like a book as it turned its own pages.

It would have touched the heart like love.

It would have talked like the courageous man who died many deaths, like one disgusted with death and like one that stood proclaiming that he would not for the life of him die.

What sort of a man was her child? Very soft. Kind hearted. Eyes that shed tears. Heart that responded. Blood that boiled. On the whole, a great lover. A beautiful, wonderful lover.

He would have cried.

The child would have cried.

Hugging Mother Earth, just as he hugged her and cried for milk when he was young. He would have spent tearful nights.

That was how her child's steps would have been taken towards Sreekakulam. Perhaps all lovers were like this. Perhaps they walked only towards a struggle. Perhaps all those capable of love were like that. Perhaps it was always like that.

Thinking in that manner, she opened her eyes. Mary Suvarta was looking out into the front yard. She was looking out only for Immanuel.

Yenkayi was swearing in her sleep. She was abusing to her heart's content. Mary said it was always so. She would do so at least twice before the morning.

'Who's she abusing like that?'

'Chettodu.'

Yenkayi's swear words did not stop. Ruth thought it would be good if it did not end. That world seemed to be moving very close to her. If it did not happen like that, she herself wanted it to move close.

Ruth did not go near the cot the grandfather and grandson were lying on. She lay down on Mary's cot itself. She took Mary's hand in hers. She wanted to tell her about the wonderful quality of the chillied prawns that Sasirekha had talked about. She told her. After telling her that, she said, 'Sleep, he'll wake you up when he comes back.' Mary slept. Yenkayi's swearing seemed to have stopped. The breeze was bringing in the songs the coolies were singing in the tobacco leaf pandal, weaving all night long.

Could not sleep.

Thought she should not sleep till her son came back.

Without her being conscious, Rosy came to mind. She was born after Immanuel. Vandanam was Rosy's husband. He was a devotee who learnt how to live. Actually Reuben was of the view that for someone in the revenue department to become a devotee was a wonder. He used to be very close to the white men. He stuck to the white men when they were leaving for their country. Rosy too was with him. One of the white men gifted his house to Vandanam. He told Reuben, 'Your son-in-law is a great devotee.' He said, 'For such a devotee this house is only a small token.' Reuben looked at Ruth as if he did not know when Vandanam became such a great devotee. Ruth too did not understand. When they looked at Rosy, she was laughing happily at the white man's words.

After that the most surprising thing happened. Vandanam became a member of the Mission Field's governing body. There would be letters from foreign countries addressed to Rosy. Rosy would send letters to the white people along with photos saying that prayer meetings were taking place at various places. Once a year, meetings would take place in a grand scale known as religious congregations.

White people would attend those meetings. Rosy and Vandanam would appear as amazing people to Reuben. The governing body of the Mission began the task of dividing the Mission's properties. Reddys and Choudharys who had political clout fell on the Mission's properties like vultures. Not just at Nellore, Kurnool, Kanigiri and Ongole but at all places where the Mission had properties, such a scenario took place. Reuben said that was atrocious. He bemoaned that his Christian heart could not bear such atrocities. Ruth could not tolerate the fact that her daughter and son-in-law were a party to those atrocities. They bought a car too. They admitted their two children in a convent in Madras. The older one was Victor. The younger one was Ruby.

Reuben severed his relationship with his daughter and son-in-law. There was no difference between them and Judas Iscariot. Even if Rosy came home, Reuben would not speak to her. Though Ruth spoke, she would be ashamed to speak freely to a girl with such a mentality.

As for Ruby, she would come to her grandfather. Reuben liked speaking to the girl. Someone in Yennela Dinni said Sasirekha had been like that. Perhaps it was because of that. He would say, 'Mother's come, Ruth' when Ruby came. If they had any contact with the daughter's house, it was Ruby alone. Not clear why, but Ruby would spend her entire vacations with her grandparents rather than with her mother.

It appeared as if the song in the tobacco leaf pandal reached a high pitch. The song gave Ruth comfort in the cool night breeze. She looked at Jessie. He had snuggled into his grandfather's stomach. Ponnangi pitta.

Dawn was breaking right before their eyes. She looked in that direction as the wooden compound gate made a creaking noise.

Immanuel.

He opened the gate and came in. He came in asking, 'When did you come?' Even before the child came in, his smile touched her heart. They stayed two days there. Both the days, except when he spoke to his father, Immanuel was not at home at most times.

During those two days ponnangi pitta kept company with yennela pitta. He was a chatterbox. Not just words. He used to sing songs too. His voice used to be wonderful. Ruth thought that that kind of voice was their family heritage. He would dance to the song. Saying Yellanna might have done so, Reuben would feel thrilled. The second night he sang. He sang watching the stars.

Reuben looked surprised. He was surprised even as he sang the first charanam.

'Listen Subhadra.

The little mouse drank the water under the roof.

Listen Subhadra.'

Reuben had not got over the surprise. The song was continuing. Quite normally. Heart filled with pity. Anxiety of aeons. It proceeded like that and stopped at the first charanam. Reuben's eyes were filled with tears.

'Who taught you?'

'Mother.'

'Immanuel sings it every day. That's how I learnt the complete song. Immanuel is very fond of that song. He asked me to teach him a song. I sang it for him. He learnt it.'

Crazy Reuben. What a young child he really was! He had him sing it over and over again and listened to it. Man from the past. Truly, a man from the past.

On the third day, as they left, Reuben said, 'We'll take him with us.' Immanuel could not say no. Ruth said she would also have Mary with them for a week and send her back. Mary said she would not come. When she pleaded, she could not say no. Though she came to Ongole, her mind was only on Avalapadu. When they came, Sinasubarayudu was not there. She told Yenkayi. Immanuel wrote a letter, saying Sinasubarayudu enquired about them.

There was another letter from Immanuel. That he was going somewhere on work, asking Mary Suvarta to stay there till he returned and that he would bring her back after he returned.

Where could he have gone? Mary Suvarta said she did not know.

It was more than a month. There was no news from Immanuel. Then they came to know. That Immanuel had been arrested.

Immanuel!

'Why so? Why, my dear? Just like that, without saving anything for yourself . . . ' Ruth kept thinking that.

Everyone started talking about it in puzzlement. The same talk in the church.

What did she say?

What did Rosy say? What did Rosy's husband say?

'Just the same wherever you heard. What's it about the pastor's son getting arrested? It's so shameful.'

Jews.

Judas Iscariots.

They were the ones who got Christ arrested.

They perhaps could not walk with heads held high. But Reuben walked with his head held high.

What did he say to him? What did he say to the C. I.? That fellow. That Charles. C. I., Charles. He said, 'Aren't you feeling ashamed, Reuben, as a Christian for having given birth to a son like him?' What did Reuben say, what did he say to that?

'I'm proud. For having given birth to a son like him, I'm prouder than Joseph. Ruth is luckier than Mary . . . ,' he said.

To his face. To that C. I.'s face. There was not a spot of blood on that Charles's face. Like Pilate sprinkling his entire face with the water with which he had washed his hand, his face was filled with perspiration. Khaki perspiration. Not the smell of man. Not the smell of earth. Deceit had such a dung-like smell. Finally, unwilling to accept defeat, he brought forth the issue of religion. He raised the issue of faith. What did Reuben say to that?

'Christ is my faith. Struggle is my necessity. My child is the representation of centuries of struggle. My child is a struggle. It's not a decoration to a mala or a madiga. It's not an ideal. A necessity. I was born an untouchable. I was born without a cent of land. I was cast away. I was ostracised. My child searched for answers for everything and placed them before me . . . Take the Cross off your neck. You're not on the side of those bearing the Cross. You're one among those protecting those who crucify. I've come to meet my child. Not to listen to your speech.' He said just those things. Reddened eyes. Lifted shoulders. What rejection in those eyes! What dignity in those eyes that looked at Charles as an insect given to Reuben! Only if looks are like that, they are good. Only looks capable of love have such dignity.

They vacated the house in Avalapadu after Immanuel was arrested. The books there. They were not just books. Bloody letters of the alphabet. She read them. Reuben said laughing, 'The Communist devil has possessed you.'

The child was not a devil.

She kept reading, searching for Immanuel.

She kept waiting as she read like that. For her child. Counting days along with Mary, along with Reuben, along with Jessie. How to hide that memory? How to write down that heart-rending blow?

She thought the child would return.

But.

She did not think the child's martyrdom would touch her heart.

The child she thought would return did not return alone. He brought along hundreds of men. He did not speak. He used hundreds of voices to make him speak. She could not believe her child was dead.

'I know only to send God's children. I don't know how to send people's children.'

Reuben said so when Vandanam talked about the arrangements. Looking like that. Why were there no tears in the eyes? Why did they remain vacant, plain as if nothing had happened?

Reuben remained silent. Vandanam went away. He was speaking to Rosy.

Did not have the strength to pacify Mary Suvarta. In fact, Ruth could not pacify herself. She looked out for Jessie. He was looking only at his father. Ruby next to him.

People. So many people that sand would not slip through. Did not think a death could move people so much. Sorrow in everyone's eyes. Why such sorrow in those faces? What bond was it? What was Immanuel to them? Son, older brother, younger brother, friend . . . What was he? Comrade. What meaning did that word convey?

How the thousands of people swarming around Immanuel looked at him! At Sreekakulam Immanuel. At Comrade Immanuel. At her child.

They loved her child.

They understood her child.

They felt the experience of life with her child.

Her child was an example. Her son was a struggle. How different are to love, to understand, to experience and to follow!

Her child was indeed an example. Otherwise, among thousands of people they would not love her child. They would not be able to understand her child or experience with him.

What did Immanuel do? All that he did was just one thing. He did what every revolutionary did on this earth. He searched only for that which was necessary. He strung the bow and aimed it at the shameful torture, horrible exploitation and cut-throat culture. A tribal did that. He turned what he did into a weapon. He looked with a compassionate heart into the path of the Nagavali, the swift flow of the Vamsadhara and the rippling sound of the Swarnamukhi.

True. With tenderness alone.

How many can see with a heart? Her son saw like that. Only because he saw like that did he see a future in Sreekakulam.

That future came forward quite naturally.

The Vempatapu Satyams, Kailasams, Bhaskaras, Ganapatis, Panigrahi Subbaraos, Chinababus, Krishnamurthys, Nirmalas and Ankammas[40] that she came to know, as she studied her son, also fought quite spontaneously. There was no scheming in any of their struggles.

The people were praising him while bidding him goodbye. Sinasubarayudu was saying, Immanuel. Entire Avalapadu was there. Yenkayi was right next to Mary Suvarta. Mary Suvarta was amidst the people of Avalapadu. A tractor that was decorated in red. Flags. Red flags.

Immanuel was going ahead.

Praise be to Comrade Immanuel.

Praise be to him.

Thousands of voices, thousands of hands, fluttering flags—

A flag in Jessie's hand.

A flag in Ruby's hand.

Only her hand did not have a flag. Only Reuben's hand did not have a flag. Only her daughter's and her son-in-law's hands did not have flags. Only a few did not have flags in their hands. There were many in the church who had flags in their hands.

Immanuel was moving ahead.

Reuben was walking silently. She looked at him.

She looked into his eyes. Why were tears welling up in his eyes now? Why had they stopped till now? Which vent of the heart had breached that it was flowing like that?

'Tell me, Reuben. You're saying with a heart-rending cry, "Praise be, Comrade Immanuel." Within yourself. To yourself. Very forcefully. That's why those tears. Isn't that so?

'You won't lie. Tell me the truth, tell me.'

She was asking Reuben within herself. Struggling in that manner, she pushed her silence aside and said, 'Praise be!' Reuben looked at her. She said it. She said, 'Praise be!' to her child. Reuben's old heart. The heart that had sacrificed a tree-sized child to this devilish State. He pressed her hand hard.

Immanuel was moving forward.

The procession was going ahead.

Both stopped.

Then Reuben screamed. The first cry of the untouchable of centuries past. As he shouted for the yennela pitta. In such a weak voice so Ruth alone could hear for his blood that revolted against this social structure that sketched so cruelly his birth, his life and his future. He cried shouting like that. Suddenly, he looked towards the procession as if he remembered something. That was not a walk. A run. They joined the procession . . .

18

They say one scene fades away and another comes in front. Ruth says that is not true. None of the scenes that she had experienced has faded away. Scene after scene, each one stands very clearly in front of her eyes. Time flows by like that. Flows by like a scene. Flows by like memory.

The fading clouds of dawn. Stars that sprout at midnight. Breeze from a distance, a great distance, that wafted by after touching forest flowers. The season seemed to have changed. Spring seemed to have arrived. Mornings that went away. Evenings that went away. Nights that passed by lethargically. It appeared as if Spring was over. Winter seemed to have squatted in front of the house.

Reuben could not sleep. He would get up at an unearthly hour. He would simply roam about outside. He would sit in front of the table. He would open some book. His mind would not be still. Irritation. Void. A search for something. Did not have the courage of the past.

'Will you drink some water?'

'Don't want it.'

'Shall I make tea?'

'No.'

'Then, sleep.'

'Can't . . . '

Not just for Reuben. For Ruth too. Could not sleep. Did not feel hungry. Immanuel was the incident that flowed with time. He proceeded like a revolutionary movement. He went like a procession. The child did not die. His clear voice was still being heard from this earth. His face appeared like the full moonlight in front of sleepless eyes. Did not feel like wiping the tears at that time.

But she would wipe the tears for the sake of her daughter-in-law. She would make sure the tears in her eyes were not visible for the sake of her grandson. Her heart had turned into stone. It had hardened. Eyes stopped getting wet. The body that had aged did not have the strength to carry the burden. Had to live. For the daughter-in-law. For the grandson. Had definitely to live.

Jessie grew up playing with that old heart. Like his father, he would also look at the red crotons getting wet in the rain. When it rained heavily, the house would leak. Did not have the capacity to do up the roof. Rosy said she would have the roof done. Reuben said that was devil's money. Reuben would keep plates, dishes and pots below the spots where it leaked. Jessie would hand them over. The dishes would fill up. Jessie would place paper boats on that water. They would twist and twirl. He would point to the boats that twisted and twirled to his grandfather. That was a game for the two of them. There was no worry that the house was leaking. Rainy season would pass by for the two of them playing that game.

It is here that Ruth does not know how to keep her memory in front of her. This may not be a memory. May be an experience. She cannot write down this memory, this experience. She has tried to write down Immanuel completely several times. But that memory, that experience itself drains her heart. Shatters her heart. Cannot write that. Cannot think in that manner. Wants to evade that. Wants to forget immediately.

She recalls every word Reuben told her. She keeps it in front of her as if she has read a masterpiece. All that is experience that moves her. That is perhaps why she is able to detail every little part. Even if she goes, the memories Reuben provided will remain.

Immanuel is not like that. He comes in the way of memory. He comes in the way of writing. Mother's womb twists and turns. Then mother's heart becomes very weak.

In fact, she forgot the pain, seeing Immanuel in Jessie. The same with Reuben. He did every work possible with Jessie and was forgetting his child.

Time does not stop just like that. It does not go on just like that. It has its own whims. Its turn is its own. It may be the smile that does not disappear from the lips. May be the pain that tears the heart. Time is a deep breath. It will surely not stop. On this green earth, full moonlight will shine. Dense darkness will envelop it. Time will be like that. Life will be like that. Life is memory. Life is experience. Life is reality. The problem for Ruth is when all of them have to do with Immanuel, when it has to do with Jessie, when it has to do with Ruby.

She cannot see Immanuel as she sees Mataiah, Narigadu, Yellanna or Simon. Cannot see Jessie. Close ties. A tie that grew up on that lap. Whenever she remembers the child, she cannot bear it. Whenever she thinks of the grandson, she wants to meet him immediately. At that point that memory fails. That experience ends. Here too man's life alone is the answer. Time is not something else, it is the non-stop walk of a man. A final journey . . . In that journey, Mataiahs, Narigadus, Yellannas, Martins and Sivaiahs, all contributed their own bit. They did so in their own way. Immanuel turned those steps into his weapon. Jessie too. He is walking to push that armed struggle further, a little further.

That walk is proceeding in that manner. That walk appears in front of Ruth.

Rainy season in front of Ruth's eyes. Memory of interminable rain.

Jessie . . . Ruby . . .

Jessie is no longer a boy. He can see the world with his own eyes. He can read it with his heart. Being responsive is not new. It is a word known in his house for a long time. The embodiment of sacrifice on this score was Jessie's father. That responsiveness may be familiar. That sacrifice may be their nature. That is not letting Jessie sit still. Thoughts. Tiny little decisions. Search. A little bit is clear. A little bit is not clear. Just one thing is true. In front of him, his forefathers' determination stands. His father's sacrifice moves. That has had a rebirth on this earth. Not just what he reads in the classrooms. It appears as if there is a lot to read as a man.

Hunger.

Untouchability.

Exploitation.

Atrocity.

From Yellanna to Immanuel. From Subhadra to Mary Suvarta. Words that need to be seen. Words for which reasons have to be searched. His father used to teach. He may have thought he would not be able to explain those words in the lessons he taught. He may have felt those words fell beyond the scope of the lessons. That is why perhaps he left the school. He left those four walls. He went into life. He went among the people who were victims. He mingled with them. He searched for the meanings of the words, hunger, untouchability, exploitation, atrocity in the large expansive school of life. He searched for their solutions. He stood like that. He walked like that. His walk should not stop . . .

Those very thoughts in Jessie. Those very turmoils. He would not come home until the early hours. Not known where he would roam about. Once in a while, he would come up to the gate and stand outside and go on talking under the shade of a tree along with two or three friends.

Words. Thoughts. Meetings. Everything a thirst. Everything a desire. Everything a movement. Everything a turmoil. Everything a struggle. Ready to revolt. Jessie would appear like that.

Now and then his friends would come home. Their words would be direct. Would look like arrows taking aim. There would be a lot of arguments between them. They would stop at some point as if they came to an understanding. Reuben would listen to them with interest. He would roam around the entire room when they were speaking as if he remembered something, as if he was searching for something. It appeared as if he remembered Immanuel. But it would seem as if that was not true. He would speak as if he was sharing a secret with Ruth about the youngsters' words. He would listen very intently.

When Ruth saw them, the world in motion would remain in front of her eyes. Once in a while, they would sit up at night. Along with them, Ruby too. Looking at them, it felt as if the night's darkness slipped to the corners of the room. They appeared like new shapes. They appeared as new companions.

'These governments are completely deteriorating. The leaders' brains have been bought by imperialist governments. In this country every step is targeted to be mortgaged. Our state has gone way ahead on this score. Our government is the pet child of the World Bank. It does not have faith in people. It has no trust in their future. All that is left for them is the police. All that is left is the army. To hunt people. To attack people's movements. To kill the children of the people in the name of encounters. They use people's money only for that. They use the media only for that.'

That is how their discussions went . . . When Reuben would hear those words, he would look at Ruth. He would ask her, 'Will you make tea? Want to drink tea.' Ruth would make tea enough for everyone. When they drank tea, they would sit amidst the young people. They would mingle with them. After drinking tea, he would leave them to their conversation and go back to his room.

'There'll be computers here. There'll be statements of income and expenditure. There'll be groups of multinational companies. These governments say that is in fact progress. They are preparing plans only for them. That's not what we have in front of us. The most wretched of lives of poverty. They do not have even a loin-cloth size of land. They don't have jobs worth even an old cloth. There's no safety of life in the village. There's no work for the city poor. They don't have their own field, own house or own job. Everything is a life in a dark cave. Hundred years of life was born yesterday and dies today.'

Using such small words, they were speaking of the state and the country! Not yet crossed twenty. If at all, two of them may have. Who taught them?

After everyone left, Jessie would go near his grandfather and grandmother. He would lie down between them like a small boy. The two of them did not know the dreams he would dream. In between he would speak in his sleep. Whenever he spoke in his sleep, Ruth would get up. She would pat Jessie awake. She would say, 'What are you talking in your sleep?' He would laugh and sleep. Ruth would not be able to sleep. Her eyes would go searching somewhere. An emotion she could not lay her finger on would come in front of them. Once she closes her eyes, an ocean in front. Surging waves, brushing the shore, cleaning the sand on the shore. Why did she feel like that? That scene would remain like that. It would be like that till dawn.

Ruth did not imagine that those conversations, those meetings, those dreams, those words in sleep, those moments of getting up in the middle of the night, that ocean with waves would not remain like that with her for long.

But.

Learning was prohibited. Speaking was prohibited.

Prohibited.

On knowledge, on speech, on movement, on breath, on the political struggle . . . the State turned into a dark dungeon.

A rainy night—a night of incessant rain.

Jessie told them his decision.

'I'm thinking of going only after informing you'.

He sat in front of the three of them and spoke out. No one else spoke. Ruby came, getting wet in the rain. Did not know why the girl came then. Felt it was good she came.

'Father has gone away from you. I know that you're trying to look at me and forget him.'

Ruby kept looking at Jessie.

'I'm speaking to you with the confidence you won't say no. It's necessary to fulfil that which Yellanna yearned for, that which frightened Sivaiah, that which Reuben searched for and that for which Immanuel gave up his life. Immanuel hasn't become one with the earth. He has sprouted like a plant. That too, he has sprouted in your backyard.'

He spoke like that. Reuben did not know what to say. Ruth too. Mary Suvarta sat listening. He spoke a lot. Did not think the youngster would speak such big things. He spoke. In that pouring rain he left, slinging a cloth bag over his shoulder.

That was how he went away. Bundling up the dreams. To fight. To free his people. He went like that. Ruby kept looking in the direction he went. In fact, rain was not wetting Jessie's body but Ruby's heart.

Nallamala mountains were very far from here. No energy to go and meet him. No chance of his coming whatsoever.

Christmas came and was going away. The Christmas tree was being left alone. Only three shared the candlelight in that house. Ruth, Reuben and Mary Suvarta. That was it. Ruby would come to keep company. Reuben's voice was no longer heard in the church. Every Christmas day they would think. It would be so nice if Jessie came. Good if he came. Felt worried thinking like that. The night would pass by in worry and despair. But why this worry? Why these nights of despair? What did he do after all? Did he leave saying no to grandfather's love, grandmother's love, mother's love or the love of one who loved him, no to anything? Did he go away renouncing everything saying such love is an illusion? He did not go like that. He went with eyes, in fact, full of love. He went with the idea of retaining love permanently on this earth. He went for several crores of Reubens, Ruths and mothers. He went with the intention that their bodies ought not to remain permanently untouchable. He went so as to create a bit of right over the land they lived in. That was how Jessie went. A hero's son. He went like a hero. He had not distanced himself by leaving. He became closer. Why worry about someone who had not become distanced? Why this looking forward to in anticipation of his return? It felt like that. The three of them felt like that. Then the pride that was hidden somewhere, hidden in a corner behind some affection, hidden behind affection for the child would surface. Funny. It appeared in that pride too, to share that pride with him. It felt at that time, that it would be good if he came. Felt like saying a lot to him. Felt like listening to a lot of things.

One day . . .

She told her daughter-in-law, 'It'd be good if he came tonight.' Just then Ruby came. 'Who's to come?' she asked.

'My ponnangi pitta.'

'Did he send word like that?'

'It'd be good if he came.'

Ruby stayed back that night with her. It would be good if he came. If not for her. For Ruby. At least for Ruby . . .

Knew he would not come. Even so, like that . . .

Ruby was studying in a college. Her father was getting marriage proposals for her only from America. Said she would not get married. Said if she married, she would only marry Jessie. Vandanam said, 'Which hill in the Nallamala range did he say he'd give you?' He said it sarcastically. America taught him quite a bit of such sarcasm. Then he abused her. He abused Rosy saying, 'Does your family know how to live?' Surprisingly, Rosy did not get angry. She heard those words with a smile. Reuben did not know how to live. Ruth did not know how to live. Immanuel and Mary Suvarta too. Jessie did not know. But Rosy knew how to live. If she did not know, she would not have lived with Vandanam.

Unable to sit idle that night, Ruby wrote a poem. She titled it, 'I'm awaiting my lover.' After writing the poem, she said, 'I'll read it. Listen.' She asked Reuben too to listen.

He'll come

at the time the stars blossom.

He'll come

knocking at the heart-doors.

He'll come

when the dew slides down.

He'll come

wiping the wetness of eyes.

He'll come

on the pitch dark heart-ways.

He'll come

like a composite sorrow

searching heart depths.

He'll come

the people's war soldier, my beloved will come.

He'll come

in the early hours of a long night

enclosing laughter and sorrow in his lips.

He'll come, coming he'll proceed straight into my heart.

He'll come

like the seed embedded deep within the earth

the one who doesn't care for death for the sake of life, my beloved, he'll come.

He'll come

though he didn't say he'll come.

He'll come, he, my man, he'll come, my friend, my lover

will come, he'll come

the sound of his footsteps motivating my heart.

Though I don't have such information, he'll come still.

He'll come getting wet

he'll come without the rain drops wetting the red crotons.

He'll come, he'll really come

the one who is larger than life, deeper than love.

A dream as the eye closes

all of the dream, olive green

he'll come with a rifle over his shoulder.

He'll come though he didn't say he'll come.

He'll come, he who is as expansive as the sky

as pure as a waterfall, as free as the birds.

He'll come though he didn't say he'll come.

He's always like that, he'll come like that, without telling, knocking at the door.

Ruth could not speak after listening to the poem. Silence seemed cruel. Did not know what to say. Reuben's eyes, full of tears.

She looked at Mary. Immanuel stood before Mary's eyes. Jessie too. One she was married to. One who was born tearing her womb. One went away to infinite distances. One went searching the path he took. One became red. One was going about carrying that redness. Why did they become like that? She knew. Her daughter-in-law knew. The granddaughter too knew. Even though they knew, once in a while the scene would be like this. These words. These heartwrenchings. Disappointment about someone. Eagerly looking forward, full of hope.

Felt like making both of them lie down on her lap. Felt like kissing those breasts. 'If you feel like sleeping, sleep. If you dream, dream on. The ones you desired are such people.' They dreamt. They say it isn't life if there are no dreams.

Immanuel dreamt like that.

Jessie too was dreaming like that.

Perhaps Jessie and Ruby might be the last generation of the family she set foot into. Her looking out might end with them. She also desired its stopping like that.

Jessie would sleep with his head snuggled into her stomach. Ruby would watch with jealousy. When she pulled her close, she would move far away. For some reason the girl too wanted to lie snugly there. They grew up. They grew up right in front of her eyes. They abused each other any number of times. They hit each other the same number of times. Reuben was Ruby's support. Jessie would seek her support. That was also how they tried to forget Immanuel. They forgot, playing with the two of them.

Sometimes the two of them would sit together properly at one place. They liked the moonlight. They liked to sit there in that manner. There was a lot of attachment between the stars and this family. As for Jessie, an explicable love. He would keep looking. Into the sky. Into the shining and fleeting stars. Then he would recite poetry. Would tell stories. Once in a while song would drip from his throat like dew. How crazy was the girl! She would sit listening to his words. She would sit listening to his songs. Listening like that she would look into his eyes. Swaying her head like that she would rest on his shoulders.

Those were the days when Jessie would visit home. One day she said, 'Ruth, your grandson's so wicked!' If she was angry she would not say ammamma. She would only say Ruth. She would not say atthaiah. She would only say Mary Suvarta. Otherwise, she would say, 'You know what your daughter-in-law said?' If she said so, it meant she was angry. If she oozed with love, then too it was like that. She would say, 'Hey, you Reuben.' She was a peculiar girl. Ruth asked Ruby to tell her what happened. She was telling her in a casual manner. Ruth felt like laughing. That girl told her in a manner that made her laugh. It was a week since he left. He left singing songs. He had not yet returned. That was the complaint. But there was affection in that complaint. That girl loved him. The day Ruby said so, it was a moonlit night. The full moon was going away without narrating a story, without reciting a poem, without singing a song. Ruby did not like it going away like that. That's why she said those words.

Jessie went away. Carrying the song with him. A week went by. He had not returned. He would keep singing on the full moon night that Ruby was looking forward to.

Now there is no full moonlight in front of Ruth's eyes. There are no wonderful experiences of Jessie and Ruby in that night's frontyard. There are no searchings.

Seventeenth July stands before her. 17 July 1985 appears before her. An incident that made Jessie walk in another direction stands before her. Karamchedu madigapalli, the attack with deadly weapons of the landlords float before her eyes. That's what Jessie will be singing now. Aryala too. Belchy too. Padirikuppam too. Keelavenmani too. He will be singing the story of the Karamchedu struggle. Kanchikacherla will appear in his song. It will begin in that manner and stop at Karamchedu. The attack of brutes on the humans on 17 July will begin in that song. The cruel hacking with axes of Muttaiah, Moshe, Joshua, Jacob, Ramesh and Vandanam of madigapalli will be heard sorrowfully from his throat. The cry of anguish will appear right in front. He will be singing about the houses destroyed, the women raped and the children becoming targets of the flying swords.

Jessie went away singing like that. As Yellanna did not get an
answer, he left Yennela Dinni and went away. Jessie did not do that.
He went away with an answer. He is in the tent of the victims of
Karamchedu. One day Rosy said he had joined the radicals. After
coming from the tent of Karamchedu there was a lot of change in
Jessie. He was behaving as if he had identified his life's goal at such
a young age. Singing songs he is going about places. Not alone, like
Yellanna. Going about with some who sing like him. Those who
came to the church from villages said so. That there were programmes
in their village by Jana Natya Mandali, that Jessie was the most
important member in them. He had made his life. Like Immanuel
did. Immanuel became one with the earth and sprouted.

Reuben was becoming lonely. He was not coming out of his room.
He would appear smiling on the day Jessie returned after going
about the places he had wanted to. He was anxious to spend every
moment with his grandson. He was unable to distance himself from
Immanuel.

Jessie kept returning home. Whenever he came, Ruby was always
with him. She would write down the songs he had penned in good
note books. She would make him sing the songs she had written down
and listen to them. This did not last long. Jessie spoke his intention
on that rainy night and left. He completely stopped coming back
home. Ruby too appeared different. Did not live by herself. Two or
three girls would come and go. Time was going by in its own way.

'You've seen to it that my child isn't close to me.' Vandanam
berated Reuben one day. It was not initially clear why Vandanam was
speaking like that.

'He too became like his father. You've let her into that bog so that
you could get her married to him.'

It was becoming clear. It was becoming clear why he was speaking
like that. Reuben sat listening.

'What are all these Women's Organisations? Have to bow my head
in shame. Did you ever scold her not to go about like that?'

Though Vandanam was saying such things, Rosy did not ask him
not to speak like that. She was behaving as if she too liked what
he was saying. Ruby was arranging some papers all along. She was
behaving as if all that was unrelated to her.

'I'm telling you. Whatever you do, her marriage to Jessie won't take place. Remember that.' Saying those words, he was about to go away. Rosy too, who was sitting, got up, about to leave.

'Just one word.'

It was Ruby who spoke. Vandanam stopped. Rosy looked in surprise at her child.

'The marriage between Ruth and Reuben's son's child, Jessie, and Ruby, their daughter's child, has already taken place.'

Vandanam appeared shocked. Rosy looked confused. An unclear emotion in Reuben. What did all of them hear? What did she hear that day?

'Don't be surprised. Don't be confused. If you want to hear, listen calmly. Reuben didn't conspire for our marriage. Ruth didn't play any part. Even if you look for it, you won't find selfishness in Mary Suvarta. We got married on our own. On our own we promised each other that we'd be together all our lives. It's up to you whether you'll accept it or reject it. We don't care what you desire.'

Ruby said all this in a very casual manner. Vandanam forgot himself. That great devotee abused in the choicest of words. He kept abusing and then left. Rosy did not go. She sat as if she had slumped right there. Did not know why she was crying. She was crying.

'Why do you cry like that? I don't like people crying like that in my house. If you want to cry, do so in your house.'

What was Ruby saying . . . in my house . . . in my house. It was only then that it struck Ruth. Yes, isn't this Jessie's house? These children were not young. How directly and clearly they enunciated their rights! Reuben kept looking at Ruby. His mother would appear. His mother would speak such words. A very young boy. Reuben, a boy of bygone days. Knew only relationships, bonds. Looking at his granddaughter like that, he searched for his mother. An old-timer. A true old-timer.

It appeared as if Mary Suvarta did not like Ruby saying such things to her mother. Immanuel never said anything like that to Rosy. She went near Rosy. She said, 'Don't pay heed to the girl's words.' Rosy knew what kind of a person Mary Suvarta was. That was why she remained silent. When did this marriage take place? How did this happen? That was what Ruth was thinking.

That night Rosy stayed back there. For some reason she did not want to go leaving her daughter. She felt her daughter had moved too far away from her. Ruby told them the real thing. Jessie and Ruby met in Yennela Dinni. They got married in that very house. There were only five friends at that marriage.

'Ruth, I stole the keys to your house. Your grandson has also made me steal.'

'Yours is the stealthy mind. What can he do?'

Ruby laughed at those words. It appeared as if a wonderful world stood in front of the girl's eyes. Though it appeared to be floating away, she talked of it quite naturally.

'The two of us met like that. We have a goal in front of us. We thought of walking together to reach it. That's all. We spent a week together after we got married. Telling each other that we'd look forward to the day we'll meet again, we separated. At Yennela Dinni's outskirts, he went that way. I came this way.'

Ruth thought it was not a small thought. She did not envisage this change. When girls came for Ruby, she thought they were ordinary college girls. But she realised now that they were workers of the Women's Organisation.

Jessie inside.

Ruby outside.

They turned out to be like that. They changed their lives quite ruthlessly. Every step they took would make Ruth quake with fear and anxiety. At another time she would feel proud like a courageous woman.

Their words and method would seem to suggest, 'We're taking the steps. It's enough if you know that.'

There was depth in their words.

There was clarity in their method.

They were waging a war.

At this moment they were alive. Whether they would be alive the next moment was not in their hands. But a lot of future was in every step they took. It was in every moment of their lives. They said, 'It's okay for us to die so that the poor of this country can live freely.' Their selfishness was like that. They felt that it was more important for those alive to see a great life than for those who were dead.

'It seems your grandson's in the "party"!'

Such comments. She would say yes where she could say yes. Where she did not want to, she would be silent.

'It seems your granddaughter is in mass organisations!'

Why did they have to ask like that throughout the day? She was going about villages. She would get on to the dais and speak. They would get letters from Jessie now and then. When she received a letter Ruth would think, 'How the tiny heart of my ponnangi pitta has come with so many folds!' After reading the letter, Reuben would say, 'He knows very well how to open the doors of the heart and go in.'

Such would be Jessie's letters, like the light breeze touching the spread-out fields. As if being thrilled by the touch. Every letter of the alphabet filled with love. Those were love letters that came flying from the battlefield. They would begin with, 'Dear Yennela Pitta.' They would begin with, 'Dear Thatha.' Grandfather was not given a name of any bird. He would say he would lie down on high hills and keep looking at the sky. He would look lovingly at the stars just like Yellanna. Yellanna saw Subhadra in the stars. Jessie saw in those very stars martyrs and immortality.

'When you lie on high hills and keep looking at the sky, how many stars! We give our martyrs' names to those stars. Even if we sleep soundly, the brightness of those stars keeps illuminating us.'

Those letters. Ruth would read them over and over again. Reuben too. He would read them with a lot of interest.

Mary Suvarta told Ruth, 'Isn't it a fact that those letters were keeping you alive?' The truth could be just that. If it were not for that, Reuben could have been very different. As if searching for something. As if he had not found something he had lost. He would go about as if it was not near him. Though Ruth thought Reuben was like that, her condition too was the same.

But how far? How much longer like that?

Reuben said he had no energy. Said he had no energy to travel. Said he had no energy to search. He spoke one day. Said he would go and see Jessie and come back. She looked at him in surprise. Ruth said, 'I too will come.' She said that controlling her laughter. He said, 'You won't be able to walk.' Ruth could not stop laughing. She picked up all her strength and laughed. He asked her, 'Why are you laughing like that?' He called out to Mary Suvarta. He said, 'When I say I'll go to see him this girl says she'll come. Tell me, will she be able to walk?' Tears in Mary's eyes. It was not clear if those tears were from laughter or crying.

There was a change in the wind.

It appeared as if there was no time at all for the rays to hide in the mountains.

Reuben.

Beautiful Reuben. Wonderful Reuben. How much she kissed that body! Over and over again till she was tired.

Memories.

Silent memories. The sound of falling leaves. The memories of the rustle of dry leaves before being swept away somewhere.

That day. When the dusky darkness glimmered.

He asked for Ruby. He asked for Jessie. Asked for them over and over again. He asked her to get his letters. Asked her to keep them next to him. He said it would be good if he came.

That night.

He asked her to sit right next to him. She sat next to him.

He said, 'Sleep, Ruth.'

She said she did not feel sleepy.

'I feel sleepy. Lie down, my Ruth,' he said.

Those words made her cry.

'I'll lie down, Ruth,' he said again.

She kept looking at him. She kissed him all over his body. A slight smile on the lips. A weak streak of tears in the eyes.

A man of the past. Completely, a man of the past. A man of the past who could not break the ties of love, affection, bond, emotional bond so quickly. Completely, a man of the past.

He came to Hanumakonda. Then, he did not come for her. He came for his grandfather's song. He did not stop with the song.

How quietly he had entered her life!

How quietly he was going away!

No fuss. He left even as she looked. He left saying he was feeling sleepy.

Ruth sat looking just like hat. Till daybreak. Just like that. Mary Suvarta who was at home too did not know that Reuben passed away that night.

A slight drizzle.

After that.

Sunset.

A flame.

What a terrible struggle life is!

Life is indeed a battlefield. That was what Reuben said and went away. Jessie said the same thing and was fighting.

Memories . . . truths . . .

Memories about the wars her people fought. The reality of the war her children are waging today. Memories born at every corner. Memories that flowered and drooped. Realities that faded and sprouted.

Memories that stories shaped.

Memories that poems wove.

Realities that have created turbulence.

Everything is war.

This body, house, hunger, tree, field . . . everything . . . everything . . .

Everything . . . everything is war.

From Yellanna who fled holding his life in his fist and ran to Jessie who is fighting an armed struggle for the people.

From Subhadra who placed her foot on the dike and lifted her spade to Ruby who has become one with the people like fish in water.

Everything is a war. A long struggle.

What is happening here? What will surface here and in what form?

What meaning have these people and so many years of bonding placed in front to the word life?

War. Only war. Reuben talked of Chandrappa's words that there was much to dig and bury. If you dig, war. If you bury too, war. From the moment of sunrise to sunset on this earth. Everything is war.

Ruth thinks in that manner.

After Reuben has gone away. When she sits all by herself.

When she looks into the lone star. When she looks into the eyes of Mary Suvarta. Sitting at the end of the millennium. Keeping this century in mind.

That is what she is thinking.

Reuben is not there for her to share her thoughts. She thinks of sharing it with Mary Suvarta. Can share with her. She will hear. She will listen carefully to whatever she says. But she would not speak. That is so from the time Immanuel had gone away from her. Can share with Ruby. But it appears as if Ruby does not have the time to speak to her. She finally comes to a decision. She wants to tell it to Jessie. She wants to write what is on her mind only to her grandson. She thinks that it might be the last letter she will write.

She takes paper and pen and sits down. She sits down at the table Reuben used to write on. When she looks out of the window, a star-filled sky. She writes, 'To my sweet grandson.' Does not like it. She writes—Ruth and Reuben's beloved grandson. When she writes these words she recalls the Jessie who placed his head on her stomach and his feet on Reuben's chest in Avalapadu. Ponnangi pitta. The ponnangi pitta that fell between the two of them in Yennela Dinni. A bird with sweet little beautiful wings. Laughter bursts out. Heart full of laughter. Eyes full of love. She begins saying, 'To my dear Ponnangi Pitta.'

To my dear Ponnangi Pitta,

As I write this letter to you, your mother is right next to me. She says she enquires after you. But I don't know where your beloved pigeon is flying. It is many days since we met.

In the garden of graves, your grandfather sleeps on that side of your father. I too feel like that. There's enough space on this side.

In fact, my journey isn't short. It's your grandfather who got a little tired before me. I said, why don't you wait a little, I too will come along. I said I'll write you a letter and then come. Didn't listen to me.

When your father left home and went away, our lives were overwhelmed with sorrow. But when we saw his life leaving his body and becoming one with the people, pride peeped out of us in all that sorrow.

Even before we decided what inheritance to give him, he himself gave us an inheritance. The struggle he believed in made children give inheritance to their parents. He gave an inheritance to those who gave birth to him. He also gave an inheritance to the ones he gave birth to.

You have made the struggle your life. You have set out to increase the faith in the future in the hearts of men on this earth. You have felt it your responsibility to imbibe this faith. You announced it as your duty.

For that you'll endure all the hurdles you encounter. You'll put up with them. You'll overcome them. If necessary, you'll give up your life. In that manner, you'll keep winning. The one who fights will not fight to lose. It's not even possible to finish him off. It's not possible for anyone to see he's no more. Your life is like a sprouting plant. Like a ripening field. Like the brightness that the wonderful starry sky spreads. It's permanent.

You're dreaming of the new man. You're dreaming of a new world. All those who are fighting in all countries at all times will be dreaming for that historic truth. All those dreams make up the book of revolution. Love, struggle, sacrifice—all these will be like songs in that volume. You taste victory. My confidence is not a small thing. You'll conquer the world. My faith will not go waste.

At one point, I used to think there would be no one to take notice if I'm born or not born, if I live or I don't live, if I die or if I'm dying in this country. But I'm not disappointed now. You're there to take note of me. You're there to take note of this body, this hunger. Love, sympathy and compassion are there in your words. They emanate from your heart. That's love for the community of human beings. That love is your struggle. It's filled with courage. It is a historic responsibility that will firmly stand by man's side.

After my long journey, I'm gaining inspiration from the endless work you're doing for the societal values of those who toil hard. I believe cent per cent that it will produce heroes of war and new-generation men. I've seen many incidents in society in my life. I've seen historic changes. My life went along inspired by all of them. That inspiration made me one with you.

Sitting at the end of this millennium, I'm trying to remember the first days of this century that I heard about. I'm keeping in front of me the middle of this century that I was a part of. I still keep seeing the sacrifices of heroes and the atrocities of the wicked in the last days of this century. In this context, I visualise the portrayal of the successive stages of the people's movement.

I'm dedicating this to sacrifices you made to the century that is ending and to the victories you'll achieve in the next century.

I remain, my dear ponnangi pitta. I remain.

Your grandfather went away though I asked him to stay. The one who went away won't keep quiet. He'll be looking forward with hope thinking why hasn't this girl come. I know that boy very well. He'll really be looking forward to it. I'll remain for now.

Your loving,
Yennela Pitta

Note: I don't know whether this letter will reach you or not. Even if it reaches you, I don't know when. I don't know if I'll have the opportunity of reading your tiny heart that'll come hidden in the folds. That's why, I have a small wish. Beneath my grave, the words below, just these few words are enough. Make sure they're written.

'Her memory rested in the on-going war.'

Final Word

One can write life in any number of pages. 'Untouchable Spring' is not a life that will be completed in these few pages. In fact, it has not been completed. There is more to say of Immanuel, Jessie and Ruby. Ruth was unable to narrate the complete lives of those three. Immanuel is her son. If she remembers him, it hinders her memory. Jessie is her grandson. If she remembers him, she wants to rush and hug her grandson. That's why she could not talk of them fully. There is Mary Suvarta who remained almost silent in the novel. Not a small person. She dedicated her husband and child to the movement. It is enough to rid her of her silence—Immanuel, Jessie and Ruby will stand fully in front of us.

What has rested is only Ruth's memory. It is necessary to shake Mary Suvarta. If she is moved, another part of 'Untouchable Spring' will commence. Then we cannot say life is embedded only in these pages.

Notes

1. The story of Kamadhenu: This story has been told in many ways. No matter how many ways the story has been told there is Kamadhenu in it. There is Jambavanta. There is Chennadu. *Chennapuranam* is of the malas. *Jambapuranam* is of the madigas. The final twist in this story is Siva's curse.

   They say the mala and madiga castes are descendants of the nagas. The nagas are adivasis. The first people on this earth are malas, madigas and girijans. The civilisation, culture, sculpture and literature of these castes appear unique. We see folk literature and culture only in these castes. Even today the madigas proclaim themselves as belonging to the jambu caste. Guruswami has written in detail about the Matanga kingdom. He says that there are inscriptions in Kannada country that Matanga kings ruled Jambu island.

   'Madigas were the oldest inhabitants of the land and they were at one time rulers of the country. Invaded and defeated by some neighbours, they were forced to accept the position in which they find themselves today.' This is what T.R. Singh says in his *'The Madiga—study in social structure and change.'*

   There's a theory that the Kakatiya kings belonged to the mala caste. Acharya Ranga wrote a big book to say that the Kakatiyas were in fact kammas. Bonigala Ramarao has explained that Kakatiyas are malas. *Recharla gotram* was put forward as an argument. The gotram is that of the malas. There is also an argument that it came from them to reddys and velamas. Malas in all of Prakasam district and in certain parts of Nellore district belong to this gotram. Gusta Voppert talked of all the mala rulers of this country. All this has become material for research now. It will be good if the historians who have kept silent all along about malas and madigas speak out now.

2. Urumula Nrityam: This thunder dance is the grand dance that is performed during Ganga Jatara. This is the indigenous art form of the Telugus. It still exists in the Dharmaram region of Antantapuram district. This is the dance of the malas. During the period of the

Vijayanagaram empire, they were given lands. 'Perini' dance is artificial. Urumula dance is natural. Here is an instance of making the natural artificial and imprisoning it in the temple. For the ordinary masses there are no 'palm leaf manuscripts' as proof. That's the greatest tragedy.

3. Yenki-Nayudu *bava*: The Yenki songs written by Nanduri Venkata Subbarao (1895–1957) have been widely publicised. In them he wrote about the beauty of the love affair between Yenki and Nayudu bava. What is surprising is that they have been praised for their pastoral language and for 'Teluguness'. Yenki- Nayudu bava have demonstrated how to make pure pastoral language and 'Teluguness' wonderfully artificial!

4. Selling cattle: It was not only prevalent in those days to drive cattle from Rayalaseema region to coastal region during drought and sell them, it is so even now.

5. Sweet potato carts: Sweet potato carts would come from Kanigiri region to the villages of Ongole and Kavali. Once in a while, entire families would come along with those carts. Occasionally, those carts would roam about in that area for almost a month. If they came to a village, they would be there at least for a week. The Prakasam Bhavan in Ongole today used to be like a forest area in those days. There used to be a huge well and really big trees. First the carts would stop there and then go to the villages of Ongole and the places around Kavali.

6. *Nalla*: Cattle, goat or pig would not be sliced and weighed those days like they do now. They would place them in heaps. They would then sell those very heaps. They would place the blood separately in pots, put some good pieces of meat in them and cook that blood separately. That which comes out of such cooking is 'nalla'. In those days they would send some portion of the 'nalla' to the pedda madiga and pedda mala. That was a mark of respect. Those who sliced and distributed would take the rest. They would give it to those whom they wanted to. Just as everything is being marketed, this too is being sold at a high price in the market.

7. Ravi Varma: Has the reputation of being a great artist. Was born in a royal family. Painted gods and kings. In fact they are beautiful, wonderful calendar portraits that do not reflect Indianness. But Ravi Varma has been praised to the skies.

8. Rajamannar: Pakala Venkata Rajamannar. Playwright. Critic. They say in his 'Tappevaridi' ('Whose Fault is It?') of 1930, that he continued the modern dramatic tradition started by Gurazada. He is one of those praised to the skies.

9. Viswanatha: Viswanatha Satyanarayanagaru (1895–1976). Poet, scholar, writer, critic, novelist, playwright and traditonalist.

10. *Yendorikalu*: Dried pieces of meat. They also call these *yavaralu*.

11. Flying through the slits in the rocks: 'O my dove, that art in the clefts of the rock . . . .' A line from the Bible. *The Song of Songs*, Book 2 Verse 14.

12. Bitragunta *tirunala*: Venkateswarapalem is near Kavali in Nellore district. Close to it is Konda Bitragunta. That is also called old Bitragunta. In those days a grand tirunala (fair) would take place on that hill. The people in the neighbouring places would flock there.

13. Chenchulakshmi: This is also called *Garudachala Natakam*. The most famous *veedhi natakam* of the malas. The yanadis have performed this play. Yerra gollalu have performed it. Madigas have performed it. This is one of the first Telugu plays created by folklore. Mostly malas performed plays like *Subhadra Kalyanam*, *Prahlada*, *Brahmamgaru* along with the *Garudachala Natakam* called *Chenchulakshmi* in the coastal districts. Chenchus giving their girl, Chenchita, in marriage to Ahobila Narasimha and becoming his in-laws is narrated in this play in a very theatrical manner. Chenchita is a girl belonging to the yanadis. It is said that one stream of yanadis are chenchus who came down the hill. There are names like Chenchamma, Chenchita and Chenchulakshmi among yanadis. They are there even today. The character, 'Chenchulakshmi' does not compromise anywhere. She does not compromise with Narasimhaswami. She says she will marry him only if he agrees to her conditions. She does not compromise even with Adilakshmi. She argues that her own culture is no less than that of Adilakshmi. She also wins. She says she does not need the greatness of Narasimhaswami. She asks him if he knows 'how to climb trees, how to climb hills' like an ordinary chenchu youth. What is amazing is that those of our Telugu critics on drama, our researchers and our PhDs who pay attention to 'Vasantasena' in the Sanskrit play, *Mrichakatika*, and 'Madhuravani' in the modern Telugu play, *Kanyasulkam*, do not perceive the 'Chenchita' in *Chenchulakshmi*.

14. *Veedhi Bagotam*: Scholars have not been able to see the beginnings of Telugu drama in Veedhi Bagotam. There are many critical works on Telugu drama. There are very few good ones among them. Even among them, there will not be any mention of *veedhi natakams*, street plays. Kandukuri Veeresalingam Pantulugaru alone raised the issue of *Yakshaganam*. Our critics did not pay heed to even his words. The untouchable castes put on Veedhi Bagotams. They performed dances

like the Urumula dance. They hid their toil in songs. They passed on their great inheritance to the world of literature and the arena of art. In those plays, gods behaved like ordinary mortals. You can see traces and examples of what we in fact consider the great Greek tradition, the postmodern theatre, Brecht's plays and Bol plays in the Veedhi Bagotams. But scholars and critics did not notice that. Rather than say 'did not notice', it may be truer to say 'did not have the inclination to'.

15. Bangarakka, Ketugadu: Wonderful comic characters in puppet shows.

16. *Vissurrayi pata* (Song sung while grinding in the grinding stone): What's left after death? No matter in which manner the question is posed, the folklorist's answer is only one, 'good.'
    'The sticks alone the relatives, the wood alone, the kith and kin
    The Fire god has remained our relative
    The logs of the pyre our brother-in-law and sister-in-law
    When Yama takes away no one follows
    Kith and kin sitting all around
    Shed tears and finally leave.'

17. *Manishadam*: It is said that this is the basis of Valmiki's work, the *Ramayana*. When two birds are together, a hunter shoots an arrow and kills the male bird. The female bird cries. They say that Valmiki's *slokam* (verse) was born from her *sokam* (sorrow).

18. *Mahaprasthanam*: Sri Sri's poetry collection. A great work that was instrumental in making Telugu literature come down to earth.

19. Brown: Charles Phillip Brown was born in Calcutta in 1798. He loved the Telugu language. He worked hard for its upliftment. He wrote of himself: 'In 1825 I found Telugu literature dead. In thirty years I raised it to life.'

20. Vemana: A true Telugu poet to be proud of. A protest writer. Pundits said his poems were not poetry. He responded to religion, to rotten traditions, to caste, and to contemporary politics. One can call him a movement. Not just pointing to false values, he criticised them. By 1834, Brown had collected about three thousand verses of Vemana. He felt that Vemana's verses were of immense help in learning Telugu. It appears as if the research works that are coming out now are not doing justice to Vemana.

21. *Pundits*, Copywriters: On Brown's request these people went around villages and collected works. The scribes corrected the imperfections in prosody, cut the papers into equal parts, drew lines so that the sequence would not be lost and would hand them over to the copywriters. Brown

paid the scribes a rupee a day for two hundred poems, that is eight hundred lines.

22. The poet Chowdappa: The poet from Kundavaram wrote a hundred verses (*satakam*) under the pseudonym, Chowdappa. The 17th century poet was strong in *kanda padyam*. He had borne the burden of being called an abusive poet, swear word poet and moral poet. He used swear words openly in his poems. Brown edited and published poet Chowdappa's *Satakam* in 1832.

23. *Sumatisatakam*: *Satakam* of morals. It too was edited and published by Brown in 1832. *Bhaskara Satakam, Krishna Satakam and Kalahasti Satakam* were also published then. *Sumatisatakam* was a *Satakam* that used very simple words to reveal great truths.

24. Potana: Bammera Potanamatyudu (15th century), author of *Bhagavatam*. Ancient Telugu poet who became famous as Potana. The poem '*Bala rasala sala navapallava . . .*' is enough to reveal his integrity. He says that dedicating a work to the kings is like eating rotten food. He used pure Telugu words.

25. *Dvipadas*: The Kannada people have *tripadas* (three-lined verses). The Telugus have dvipadas (couplets). The dvipada has woven itself into the fabric of the lives of the Telugus. In fact, in Telugu, dvipadas existed even before poetry was written. It has remained in folk literature from very ancient times to the present. Laughter, sorrow, anger, pity, compassion, toil, sweat—not just these, there is no aspect of Telugu lives that is untouched by the dvipada. Such a natural literary work was proscribed by the Sanskrit pundits for a while. In a way they were dark days for the dvipada. Pundits imposed sanctions and ban on the dvipada and its naturalness. Palkuriki Somanatha Kavi's *Basavapuranam* and *Panditaradhya Charitra* came as a response to reject these views. Basavapuranam is the first poetic work in the dvipada in Telugu. The writing proceeded in pure Telugu rejecting grammar and rules of prosody. A major part of *Veerasaiva* literature remained in the dvipada. We can see almost sixty famous dvipada poets in *Veerasaiva* literature. There are many versions of *Palnativeeracharitra*. Sreenatha's *Palnaticharitha* is well-known. There is also a view that like the *Mahabharata*, Palnativeeracharitra may have also been written either as separate parts by Sreenatha, Mallaiahkavi and Kondanakavi or that they may have been three independent works by the poets. The dvipada is not subservient to language. It keeps language in its hold. That's the special feature of the dvipada. The words used by Palkuriki in *Basavapuranam* and *Panditaradhya Charitra* are far removed from

scholarly language. That is the special feature of folklore. That is why folklore and the dvipada have mingled together. Pundits criticise the dvipadas calling them '*mudivitulu* (an inferior form of verse), whores, prose poems.' Dvipadas are to a large extent written by people other than brahmins. Brown was of the opinion that *Basavapuranam* was a wonderful collection of stories. He also edited Banala Sambhudas's dvipada poem, 'Sarangadhara.'

26. Potuloori Veerabrahmam: He led the *Kalagnana* (Knowledge of Time) movement. Veeerabrahmam, Nasaraiah and Ramanujam condemned caste restrictions. In the beginning, a number of malas and madigas joined those religions. Before the advent of Christianity that was a very strong trend.

27. Basavadu: There were many revolts when brahminism was spreading in the South. These had a lot of Saivite features. They say that is where Basaveswara's Veerasaivism came to the fore. Basavadu (Basava) is a religious revolutionary who revolted against brahminism. It seems Basavadu prayed to Sivanagumaiah, a low-born devotee. Seeing that, brahmins went to the King and complained that the Kalyana Katakam had gone into the hands of the malas. This incident is seen in *Basavapuranam*. It is necessary to know in detail about Basavadu who revolted against the caste system. It is important to do much research on Basavadu who had a lot of influence on Vemana. In the novel, Pedakoteswarudu searches for Basavadu. Yellanna wonders who this Basavadu is.

28. 'Listen Subhadra. The mouse drank the water under the roof': This song is sung differently in different regions. The verses too change. It is a folklore-type 'weave.' The weave changed according to the situation. It also varied depending on the nature of the utterance. It changed according to the conditions of life of that place. These two lines have been added by me. In the same way, I added a few lines to suit the situation. Some that I had heard, I retained them just like that.

29. Buckingham canal: That even coolie-work in the digging of the Buckingham canal became 'untouchable' is found in the old records of the missionaries. We can also look for evidence of attacks on Christians in those records.

30. 'Lone Star' or LONE STAR MISSION: In Nellore region, the American Baptist Mission began under the name, Lone Star Mission. We can know in detail how Clough, the white man, met Talakondapadu Yerraguntla Peraiah and how malas and madigas converted to Christianity. It is necessary to read Christian records to find out about the lives of malas

and madigas in the 1840s. 'Buckingham canal's incident', not found in any work of history, was found only there. Though Bishop Neill's work, *A History of Christian Missions (History of the Church)* has brought to the fore a lot of information, the lives of untouchables in Telugu society can be found only in the Church records.

31. 'Foxes have holes . . . .': A verse from the Bible. Luke, Book 9 Verse 58. The Telugu translation of the Gospel of St. Luke was published in 1838.

32. The temple entry of Harijans: The letter of the orthodox people in Machilipatnam. The plot of Kasi Ramakrishnamachari and others—can be located in Gandhiji's travel to Andhra Pradesh.

33. 'Beware of Gandhi': — In the work '*Gandhi and his fast*', there is a detailed discussion by Dr Ambedkar on issues such as *Poona Pact, Harijan Sevak Sangh, Temples and Untouchability,* and *The Gandhian Way.* In this context Gandhi's call for the temple entry of Harijans was '*not spiritual but it is positively mischievous*' and Ambedkar says, '*It would be the duty of all honest people to warn the untouchables "Beware of Gandhi".*'

The workers of the Harijana Seva Sangham conducted the entry into the ruined Siva temple according to a plan.

34. Periyar: He led the self-respect movement in Tamil Nadu against brahminical domination. He desired independence from brahmin rule.

35. Phule: Jyotirao Pule (1827–1890). He is the father of the struggle to abolish casteism in Maharashtra by fighting against brahminical domination. He led the Satya Sodhak Movement. He was the ideal for Dr Ambedkar. His most well-known work is *Gulamgiri* (State of Slavery).

36. Chakali Ailamma: In Palakurti, Chakali Ailamma had a small piece of land. She was a worker of the Sangham. Visunooru Ramachandrareddy wanted to occupy her land. Sent *goondas.* With the help of the Sangham, she was able to counter the attack. Under those circumstances, the police arrested six of the Sangham workers. Ailamma was able to retain the harvest of her land. The landlord was defeated.

37. Doddi Komaraiah: The people celebrated the defeat of the landlord in a big way. They had a big procession. The procession was going in front of the landlord's mansion. The bullets from the guns of the landlord's goondas got lodged in the stomach of Doddi Komaraiah who was walking in front of the procession. Komaraiah became a martyr. People

did not run away. They surrounded the mansion. 'A life for a life — we'll take the landlord's life.' They shouted such slogans.

38. Chettodu: An extremely cruel police officer who attacked the villages of the coastal regions in the present Prakasam district during the days of the Telangana armed struggle.

39. Nanjappa: The first police officer who gave orders to kill Communists in the name of 'encounters'.

40. Vempatapu Satyam: Vempatapu Satyanarayana (1935–1970). He was born in Booravalasa in Bobbili taluk. He worked as a school teacher in Kondabaridi near Mondekhal. Everyone would call him Kondabaridi Master. He was the leader of Sreekakulam Girijan Struggle. He became a martyr in the police shoot-out in Borikonda on 10 July 1970.

Kailasam: Adibhatla Kailasam (1933–1970). He too was a school teacher. He laid the foundation of the Sreekakulam Peasant Coolie Movement. He became a martyr along with Vempatapu in the police shoot-out on 10 July 1970.

Bhaskar: Dr Chaganti Bhaskararao (1940–1969). He belonged to Paruchur in Prakasam district. In 1968 in Ongole he ran a public dispensary. He took part in the Sreekakulam struggle and became a martyr on 22 November 1969 in a police shoot-out.

Ganapati: Tamada Ganapati (1934–1969). He belonged to Boddapoduku of Sreekakulam district. He laid the foundation to the peasant struggle. He became a martyr on 22 November 1969 along with Bhaskar in the police shoot-out.

Panigrahi (1933–1969). People's poet. Artist. Hero in the struggle. One of the Communist leaders of Sreekakulam district. Revolutionary worker. Took part in the Girijan Peasant Movement and became a martyr in the above police shoot-out.

Chinababu: People's artist. He would narrate and sing in Panigrahi's *jamukula katha*. Sri Sri's song 'Oogara' ('Swing!') celebrates Chinababu's martyrdom.

Krishnamurthy: Panchadi Krishnamurty (1937–1969). Studied M.A. One of the Communist leaders of Sreekakulam. He took a lead role in the Sreekakulam struggle. He became a martyr in the police shoot-out.

Nirmala: Panchadi Nirmala. She played an important role in the Sreekakulam struggle. She became a martyr in the police shoot-out.

Many poor children were given this name. Today there is a Nirmala in every village.

Sri Sri sang in the song titled 'Swing':

'You think of Manchala
You pray to Mallamma
You frame the picture
of Jhansilakshmi and praise her
Thinking of Panchadi Nirmala
You tremble in fear.'

Translators' Note

Touch the Spring: An 'Intro'spection

What happens when a narrative circumscribes several other narratives within it, each of them presented in an oral mode? What happens when a text, which contests written histories wherein the entire life and cultural heritage of a people have been neglected, derives its authenticity from, besides neglected written church records, intergenerational memory? What happens when, in such a narrative, the narrators are informed, not so much by what happens to them in actual fact, but by what they experientially feel about actual facts? What happens when a Dalit community, pushed into the crevices of mainstream history, surfaces to tell its stories, by inventing an in-between genre that simultaneously interrogates 'objective' histories and 'self'-driven autobiographies? Such an attempt would perhaps result in something like Kalyana Rao's *Antarani Vasantam* (Untouchable Spring) (2000).

The 1970s in Telugu writing are characterised by their revolutionary fervour. The 1980s saw the emergence of women's writing. Part of this women's writing was also the output of women who had felt sidelined and neglected in the 'Left' movements. The Dalit literary movement that came up in a big way in the 1990s too is considered an offshoot of the experience of the Dalits who had felt oppressed by the domination of the upper-caste leadership within the movement. The decade saw the appearance of two influential anthologies of Dalit-Bahujan writing—*Chikkanautunna Pata* (1995), edited by G. Lakshmi Narasaiah and Tripuraneni Srinivas, and *Padunekkina Pata* (1996), edited by G. Lakshmi Narasaiah—which brought together poets that included minority voices from backward communities who empathised with the Dalit cause. The Dalit reaction to the 'left' movement is a significant aspect of these two anthologies. The other anthology, *Dalit Manfesto* (1995), edited by Keshava Kumar and K. Satyanarayana, is different in that it combines both Left and Dalit consciousness. Noteworthy among individual autobiographical prose writings by male Dalit writers that came during this period are Spartacus (G. Mohan Rao)'s *Khaki Batukulu* (1996), which is about the caste problem among the police force, Chilukuri Devaputra's *Panchamam* (1998), which deals with the caste discrimination experienced by even one who has moved up the social ladder and holds an important position of a Deputy Collector, Yendluri Sudhakar's *Mallemoggala Godugu: Madigakathulu* (1999), which was serialised earlier with the title *Antaranolla Atmakathalu*, dealing with the 'self-stories' of 'untouchables', and Vemula Yellaiah's *Kakka* (2000), which deals with the plight of the Madiga labourers in the Telangana region of Andhra Pradesh. Dalit women felt the need to establish their voice, yet retaining their solidarity with the larger Dalit cause, in a sense to establish 'a tradition within a tradition' (to borrow the African American critic, Joanne Braxton's term). *Nalla Poddu: Dalita Streela Sahityam: 1921–2002* (2003), a compilation of 'self-stories', short stories, prose pieces, poems etc., edited by Gogu Syamala, is a significant contribution in this regard. A few years later she joined Jupaka Subhadra to bring out *Madiga Upakulala Streela Kathala Samputi* (2006), which reveals the lives and the culture of the women of the Madiga and related castes.

We must view Kalyana Rao, a writer, a Dalit, and a Dalit convert to Christianity at that, and one who continues to believe in the revolutionary ideology and an important functionary of Virasam, Viplava Rachayitala Sangham (Revolutionary Writers' Movement) and his work, *Antarani Vasantam*, in terms of the growing body of Dalit writing.

On more than one occasion, Kalyana Rao has claimed that he has 'written out his life.' in this book and that many of those who have read it have found their lives in it. In this sense, it is clearly autobiographical. It is a testimony of a Dalit experience, a Dalit Christian experience. It has also been written by a writer belonging to the Revolutionary Writers' Association, a group that believes in the armed struggle. The novel needs to be viewed in the context of the time in which it was written.

Kalyana Rao himself makes some of these aspects clear in an essay which talks about 'The Story behind the Story' of *Antarani Vasantam*, from which we quote the following extract:

> That's true—my ancestors lived really outside the village. But they were inheritors of a magnificent culture. Great artists. Litterateurs, too. They did not know how to write. They'd weave songs. Weave poetry. Weave *padams*. Same with plays—they'd weave them. Perform them. Mine is that weaving heritage. That's magnificent. All that magnificence has become untouchable. Has been suppressed. Why so? This brahminical dominance couldn't tolerate its naturalness. In this country, more than art and literature, caste has become important. Art and literature have been assessed from the perspective of caste. The dominant upper caste culture does not feel ashamed of this. That's the great tragedy here. That's truly tragic. Why? Why is that so? *Antarani Vasantam* is an exploration of this. (114) ('Gnapakala Vasantam', *Chatura*, December 2008: 114–117).

Responding to those who asked him why he had sent Jessie, one of the characters in the book, into the armed struggle, he says:

> I haven't sent him. Jessie went there himself. His father Immanuel too went willingly in the direction of Srikakulam. I liked their going there. That speaks for my belief in the armed struggle. As Ruth says, everything is a struggle—from Yellanna who flees with his life in his fist to Jessie who takes to arms for the sake of the people. From Subhadra who keeps her foot on the dike and holds up the spade to Ruby who becomes one with the people like fish in the waters, everything is a battle. The entire life of those characters is but a prolonged struggle ('Gnapakala Vasantam', 116).

Antarani Vasantam is significant for its critique of literary historiography. It contests several prevailing tendencies of literature such as the privileging of the written modes versus the oral modes, the prosodic poetry over the song, the textual and bookish language over the ordinary, everyday language. This is done not only by the actual use of non-standard forms like the oral re-telling of stories, weaving of songs etc., but by critiquing the 'accepted' standards. Kalyana Rao claims that he wrote the novel in the style of his illiterate grandmother who used to tell him numerous stories. Boodevi's narratives in the text could be viewed as an extension of this. Most of Kalyana Rao's characters, especially the non-urbanised ones, speak directly, in plain and simple language. He himself admits: 'Listen when ordinary people speak. Those sentences are short. There's rhythm in them. My people came out of that ordinariness. . . . When it comes to people's style, there's nothing like one's teaching and one's being taught. There's nothing like being keenly interested [in learning]. It's as natural as the wind, water and light' (26) ('Nadi Allika Varasatvam', interview in *Prasthanam* [Literary Special] [2002]: 24–27). The novel however uses a combination of the 'standard' language as well as the 'ordinary' language (to use Kalyana Rao's description). We must hasten to say that there is a definite ease with language in the way in which Kalyana Rao uses it that makes the text extremely readable. It is for the readers to judge how far this has been carried across in the English text.

The novel also questions the so-called authenticity of 'written' histories. Mainstream histories, he complains, do not represent the truths regarding the way certain communities have been treated. He says that the 'untouchables' were being kept out from even coolie work during the digging of the Buckingham canal—a historical event that the text tries to re-present, kept out of standard histories. He claims to have excavated this from Church records, even as they too have been 'written' records. Thus the book seeks to provide an alternate history. Another way in which the text tries to interrogate the 'written' forms of history is by relying on the experiential knowledge of a people who have been denied access to the basic need of drinking water, access into society, access into temples and access into the portals of learning. When such a people cultivate their own art forms, of music, theatre and dance, the same have been dubbed coarse, crude and uncultured. These art forms help them preserve their own accumulated knowledge. Denial of these forms therefore amounts to denial of their knowledge systems. Intergenerational memory is an important medium they use for the preservation of their knowledge. Hence, the novel thrives on narrativising memories of many generations of Dalits to authenticate the experience of their suffering over centuries.

Do the sufferings of the Dalits over centuries, their everyday fight for survival, their struggle against caste oppression and the final war through armed struggle for equality comprise enough matter for an epic? Kalyana Rao seems to say yes emphatically. The result—*Antarani Vasantam*. If Arthur Miller subverted the meaning of tragedy in his *Death of a Salesman* and insisted that the failure of an ordinary man is fit enough material for tragedy, Kalyana Rao does this with reference to the epic. Using eighteen chapters for his text, which cannot but remind us of the eighteen *parvas* of the *Mahabharata,* he is obviously re-envisaging the heroic. How can we miss the resemblance of the names of the likes of Subhadra and Sasirekha in *Antarani Vasantam*? Who is to decide what is grandiose? Who is to decide whether only the travel of the Pandavas in the *Mahabharata* is an epic journey? Who can say that their request for a minimal five villages alone is honourable? Who can say that the Kurukshetra war alone is a just war? Why is war justified in one context and not in another? These and many such questions can be asked to show how Kalyana Rao succeeds in writing a 'Dalit epic'.

In spite of its heavy autobiographical content, Kalyana Rao still terms it a novel. Why isn't it termed an autobiography? The obvious explanation would be that such texts deal with the lives of more than a single individual self. The term for autobiography in Telegu and some other Indian languages is *atmakatha*, literally a 'self-story'. Whether in Telugu or in the culture of their origin, these have been self-driven (*atmasraya*) stories. The 'self-stories' of the marginalised on the other hand are community-based. The more plausible explanation with reference to *Antarani Vasantam* would be that it posits a possible solution to the problem of the Dalit community through their joining the armed struggle. This solution seems to have so far eluded them. Calling it an autobiography may have forced the writer to have represented this fact as well as made him focus on the problems of caste dominance within revolutionary movements.

It is in this context that we can think of a text like Narendra Jadhav's *Outcaste—A Memoir: Life and Triumphs of an Untouchable Family in India* (2003) which brings together the voices of the father and the mother by editing the father's notes and recording the mother's stories, the writer's own voice and then the voice of his daughter. It is also the voice of the community, and the text cannot be read without an understanding of the socio-political scenario of India and the role of Ambedkar in the lives of the Dalits. If Kalyana Rao places importance on Christianity, the impact of Buddhism cannot be missed in Jadhav's works. Jadhav's too is a story of generations— of the Jadhav family, of the community, of urbanisation and of education. We have just touched on one other text to show how a term like 'autobiography' is not sufficient to understand this complex web of life-stories.

Early Dalit writers, especially Marathi Dalit writers, were influenced by movements like the Black Panther movement and writings of African Americans. Maybe it is pertinent here to see how the word 'autobiography' operates in the African American context. When African Americans started writing slave narratives, the slaves, writing under the aegis of abolitionists, had to use available forms like the autobiography but had to subvert them to retain their self-dignity and power. Take for instance, the acclaimed narrative by Frederick Douglass written in 1845. It was titled *Narrative of the life of Frederick Douglass, An American Slave, Written By Himself*. It is clear that many things are happening simultaneously. Douglass asserts his power to transcribe his life, to sift through his memories to decide what he wants to say to describe what happens to him, while yet talking about the abhorrent system of slavery which dehumanises the man. So how do we judge this text? As autobiography? As autobiography of the community? As a subversion of the genre of autobiography? As a history of the American South during slavery? Or take another example, W. E. B. Dubois's *Dusk of Dawn: An Essay Toward an Autobiography of a Race Concept* (1940). What Dubois is attempting here seems to be almost impossible—to concretise a 'concept'. Writing after the War of Emancipation, a period that was to be the 'dawn' for the African Americans, he weaves a part of his life into the narrative while bringing out ways in which race operates in the American context. So what is the text, autobiography—of the 'self' or of the 'community'—, biography, history, a tract on the study of race or something more? What happens when a writer decides to 'fictionalise' a self-narrative as a strategy to conceal an identity, yet reveal it in many ways as in Harriet Jacobs's *Incidents in the Life of a Slave Girl—Written by Herself* (1861; published in the name of Linda Brent), and to use the existing genre of the sentimental novel (read especially by many women), yet subverting it?

This brings to mind the widely talked about work by Bama, a Tamil Dalit woman writer—*Karukku* (1992). While Bama recreates her own life with sensitivity, she also lays bare the caste hierarchy prevalent in the village. Though she critiques the Catholic Church from within, she is conscious of the gains made by Dalits through education, a boon of modernity and Christianity. Hers is once again a work that fails to fit into either genre—novel or autobiography. Though one may feel that Bama is more concerned with caste than gender, she subtly draws out the gender concerns within the community while at the same time applauding the ability of women like her grandmother to outwit the hegemony of those in power. That she transcribes her own life is testimony to her determination and strength.

It is through the voice of Ruth that Kalyana Rao depicts the saga of generations. In *Antarani Vasantam* too there may be women like Boodevi who fill Yellanna with the desire to knit songs by narrating stories and exposing him to the theatre. Maybe it is she who is vitriolic in her anger towards those who beat Yellanna and chase him away. Subhadra may take the courageous step of diverting the water so that it reaches the fields of the Dalits. It may be Ruby who decides to join her husband in his armed struggle. There may be many other such women characters. But does this make *Antarani Vasantam* a story about women by a woman (albeit as the main narrator)? Certainly not. It is here that we can see *Antarani Vasantam* diverging from Bama's *Karukku*. The generations that Ruth is so fascinated to talk about are of a male lineage. The text is Ruth's memory of Reuben's memory. It is his father Sivaiah/Simon's story. It is his grandfather Yellanna's, story. It is his son Immanuel's story. It is his grandson Jessie's story. Yes, women do come into the picture. But they do so as daughters-in-law. Their husbands' families become their own. We feel that this is true though it does not take away from the fact that these women portray strength. That Kalyana Rao has moved many steps forward in depicting women needs to be appreciated.

Telugu has had a rich tradition of translation, in that many significant texts have been brought into Telugu from Indian and foreign languages. Bur relatively fewer texts have gone from Telugu to other languages. There is obviously an imbalance here. We have been very conscious of this unequal power relationship and our endeavour has been to contribute our little bit in setting this right. Let us take this text, *Antarani Vasantam,* as an example. Alex Haley's *Roots* has been translated into Telugu. So in an attempt to valorise the Telugu text, critics, both *savarna* and Dalit, have compared the search for roots, the family saga, the plight of the Dalits to *Roots.* But it would be unfair to both Kalyana Rao and to *Antarani Vasantam* to consider this text significant because of its obvious parallels to *Roots.* Its complexity, its context, its uniqueness, its special flavour and its very own rhythmic quality, to name just a few facets, will all be missed out. How are we to understand Kalyana Rao's re-writing of myths, especially of the myth surrounding the origin of the Malas and Madigas, his bringing to the fore the rhythmic quality of the Urumula dance of the Malas, the sonority of Yellanna's songs, the impact of urbanisation, of modernity in the form of Christianity and education, of the specific socio-political context/s in the text, and of Kalyana Rao's own political and cultural affiliations, if we were merely to read the text through a comparison with *Roots?* The Telugu text had to reach a wider audience. Therefore, our decision to translate *Antarani Vasantam* into English.

Antarani Vasantam was first serialised in 1999 in the Virasam run journal, *Arunatara,* and published as a book in Telugu in 2000. The Tamil translation, *Theendada Vasantam,* published by South Vision came out in August 2004. Another edition known as People's edition was published soon thereafter in October 2004. This was reprinted in January 2009. A book containing all the reviews on the Tamil translation appeared in February 2005. The book is being serialised in *Lankesh* in Kannada under the title 'Asprusya Vasantam'. The translation into Hindi as 'Achuta Vasant' is to be published soon. We gather that it is being translated into Marathi and Bengali too. We give this information to indicate the impact of such a work.

We are told it is fashionable to be interested in translation. We are also told that when we translate Dalit texts, we do so because it is politically correct to do so. But then we are also attacked for attempting to translate a Dalit text as we are told that our own identity and location as '*savarnas*' can never really allow us to enter the text and negotiate it 'authentically'. What then are we to do? Not attempt any translation, no matter that we find a text powerful enough that should be read by all? Kalyana Rao's *Antarani Vasantam* put us in such a dilemma. We decided to be brave and with the encouragement of the author, the publishers, friends and others like us who wanted to take such texts to the English-reading public, we ventured to translate. We were conscious of who we were, where we were placed; we were also conscious that the text grew out of the author's involvement with his community and with the Naxalite movement; we did not even for a moment forget the kind of language that the Telugu text contained—with its mixture of the 'standard', the dialect and the rich texture of an oral text; nor did we forget that we did not have within our reach many dialects in English that we could manage and even if we could we knew the artificiality of using them. We did not want to lose out on the natural, inherently rhythmical nature of the narrative, that is, we wanted to approximate the orality provided in a 'memory' text.

Kalyana Rao himself has felt it necessary to provide footnotes to contextualise, to explain and to critique certain references. That too for a Telugu audience. While retaining these, we also felt non-Telugu readers may need a little more help. We added some notes, always conscious of the need for added information, and of the notes affecting readability and of pre-empting the readers from forming their own opinions. It is for the readers to judge our efforts.

So here it goes—our 'intro'spection of the text is open to your 'spec'ulations!

Note: All the translations of the critical texts used are our own.

Alladi Uma and M. Sridhar
Hyderabad, April 2009

Glossary

1.	*ana*	An old coin, equal to one-sixteenth of a rupee
2.	*beda*	Two anas make a beda
3.	*Dammiddee*	One-twelfth of an ana; term also used for anything/anyone that can be dispensed with
4.	*jamu*	A period of three hours

Translators' Acknowledgements

We cannot but begin by thanking Kalyana Rao for having trust in our ability to translate a text which is not only complex but also very specific to a culture of which we are not a part. He has patiently sat with us and helped us with parts which were culturally loaded. Thank you, Kalyana Raogaru for allowing us to take such an important text to an English audience. Many people have helped us in this project but we must specially thank our friend Suneetha who read the first draft very keenly and offered very insightful suggestions. There were biblical passages and allusions in Telugu and but for the help of Reverends Prabhu Prasad and B. Vijaya Ratnam, pastors, we could not have found the English equivalents. Ramabrahmamgaru as usual helped us with some difficult terms and concepts. We benefited from our conversations on the text with Swathy Margaret and Muralikrishna. Our friend Nagarajangaru with his usual enthusiasm was there to help us get the manuscript ready. Finally, we thank Orient Blackswan for offering to publish our translation. We thank Sivapriya who was with Orient Blackswan when she initiated this project, Hemlata Shankar and Suranjan Roy who understood the problems of translating such a text and offered valuable suggestions.